THE SHELTERING

STORY RIVER BOOKS

Pat Conroy, Editor at Large

THE
SHELTERING

A Novel

MARK POWELL

The University of South Carolina Press

© 2014 Mark Powell

Published by the University of South Carolina Press
Columbia, South Carolina 29208

www.sc.edu/uscpress

Manufactured in the United States of America

23 22 21 20 19 18 17 16 15 14   10 9 8 7 6 5 4 3 2 1

Library of Congress Cataloging-in-Publication Data

Powell, Mark, 1976– author.
  The sheltering : a novel / Mark Powell.
      pages cm. — (Story River Books)
    ISBN 978-1-61117-434-2 (hardbound : alk. paper) — ISBN 978-1-61117-435-9 (ebook)
  1. Families of military personnel—Fiction. 2. War on Terrorism, 2001–2009—Moral and
  ethical aspects—Fiction. 3. Loss (Psychology)—Fiction. 4. Psychological fiction. I. Title.
    PS3616.O88S53 2014
    813'.6—dc23

                                                                                2014004292

This book was printed on recycled paper with 30 percent postconsumer waste content.

For Silas, my only son

You come to us once each day and never a day rises into brightness but you stand behind it; you are upon us, you overwhelm us, all of each night. It is you who release from work, who bring parted families and friends together, and people for a little while are calm and free, and all at ease together; but before long, before long, all are brought down silent and motionless.

JAMES AGEE, *A Death in the Family*

It occurred to me with some amusement that a student in the future might have his grade dropped on an exam from a B to C because he misguessed the exact number of My Lai dead.

JIM HARRISON, *A Good Day to Die*

FOREWORD

The Sheltering is at once haunting and an act of pure grace. What you notice first when you come to Mark Powell's fourth novel is his remarkable gift for language, the bleeding edges around his dialogue, the starch and vigor of his sense of place, the sharp delineation of his characters, and a stylishness all his own. He is that rarity among male writers of fiction in that his female characters are as strongly presented as any of his troubled, endangered males. In these spiritually exhausted times, *The Sheltering* is a philosophical novel with a belief system that collapses in on itself because the membranes of our storm-tossed faith always seem so gossamer and imperiled. Powell's dexterous novel is deeply spiritual and deeply religious, but in ways that might scare you to death. You find yourself wanting to believe in Powell's characters because he turns them into townspeople of your unconscious by the power of his art. They capture and take possession of you even as these unreliable pilgrims can no longer hold on to a firefly's belief in themselves.

Powell's narrative voice is surefooted from his first sentence to the last. This book is a study of concision by a writer who can make you hurt as he takes you through hard lives and bad choices and who can assuage you with the pleasure he takes in the juice and bite of our delicious language. In his stories of two families, Powell juxtaposes the modern South with the old South. He seems as comfortable in a Florida country club or Miami Beach hotel as he does in a honkytonk in Waycross or a Victorian house in the Garden District in New Orleans. He possesses as well a poet's eye for the fuzziness and fragility of a besieged vision of the American dream.

On a U.S. Air Force base near Tampa, Predator drone pilot Luther Redding sits at a control panel, staring at a small house and a Chevy Bronco parked next to it. This watched building in southern Afghanistan houses several families and a terrorist, Kareem Samaan. There is no escape from the eye of the drone, no act of absolution, no purging that will alter time's verdict on Kareem's life. Luther is about to kill a man six thousand miles away in an all-consuming fountain of light. The image of light is used to great effect in this book as Powell reminds us that it can wield destruction, creation, or those moments of epiphany when we long for tongues of fire to light our way. The all-seeing eye of the Predator drone is an overarching vantage that sets its faraway gaze on the lives and destinies of our major players; it can watch in untroubled composure at the scrimmage of troubled souls who will flounder in helpless bondage to their fates.

While Luther Redding is launching the hellfire missile that will kill Kareem Samaan in Afghanistan, Bobby Rosen is meeting his brother Donny, who has just been released from prison in a ghastly Florida town. The brothers come from a far more traditional geography of the southern experience, as seen in the works of Erskine Caldwell and Harry Crews. It's an unsentimental, hardscrabble background that produces two sons of loving, hard-working parents, sons who both go bad for different reasons.

Bobby is an Iraq war veteran burdened with the disabling knowledge of a young life he took under direct orders, a wound that traps him in an everlasting nightmare of regret. He has lost his wife, who still loves him, and has little contact with a son who adores him. When he takes his son to a lake on the last night in our lifetime that Venus will align with Mercury, it is a moment of emotional grandeur in the novel, a beacon in the darkness far removed from the explosive burst that ended Kareem. Like his former sister-in-law says, "You are a good man, Bobby," and it's true—but it's already too late to make a difference.

Bobby's brother Donny walks out of prison a far more dangerous man than when he entered it. Donny is one of the most authentic psychopaths to surface in American fiction in a long while. He carries the scorpion's sting and the conjurer's charm. Everything he touches turns leprous and dangerous. His love of death is the moral pivot that turns into an unforgettable flight toward madness and beyond.

From a different social order entirely come the Redding women. There is the mother, Pamela, the Ivy League–educated real estate agent and yoga student who has found her salvation in the gym. She and Luther had gained and lost a fortune during the real estate boom and bust of the Bush era, falling prey to the age of greed when the American economy imploded and the country began to consume its own entrails after easy money and floating mortgages evaporated almost overnight. With their livelihoods threatened, their property devalued, and their dreams of themselves now wingless and floating, Luther and Pamela turn briefly to each other, each desperate to cling to something precious in their tenuous love of each other. They are in a free fall from each other when we meet them, and their tragedy is one of the cohering forces of this novel.

In his descriptions of the two Redding children, sisters Lucy and Katie, Powell achieves masterful portraits of late teenage angst. When we meet Lucy, she is attending a fundamentalist Christian college in Jacksonville and wears her faith heavily in a family that does not. Her commitment to Christ is Bible-haunted, ferocious, and enough to include her well-thumbed copy of Thomas à Kempis's *Imitation of Christ*. She has read à Kempis deeply and can quote him with accuracy, as she tries to live up to the selfless directives of his visionary Christian life. The committed Christian has been thrown overboard in the modern fictional world, but Lucy's fiery spirituality is delightful to encounter, and her lack of confidence and constant warfare with her beautiful yet harrowed sister lend both comedy and pathos to their story. When Lucy, with her sister tagging along, helps lead a group of summer students to a Bible theme park, Powell produces a comic tour de force that is itself worth the price of the book. Yet it contains a conversion scene of the cynical Katie Redding that brims with a power that is as surprising as it is transcendent.

In that fearful world of American girlhood, Katie harms herself in secret, thinking that her own pain is the only knowable reality in a life dulled by drugs and alcohol. Still, in her lostness, it is Katie who has the most transfiguring spiritual moments in the book. Her despair leads her on a journey that seems conceived in a nightmare by Dante as she seeks out enlightenment in a dreadful flight away from her own best instincts.

Like all good novelists, Mark Powell is a precise and all-knowing weatherman of his locale of choice, and he understands the despair and loss to be found in the futile orchards and starving lawns of the suburban southern coast. The American suburb has become one of the most demonized landscapes in American fiction—the Yoknapatawpha County of the modern young writer—and so it is again in Powell's novel. The old southern whir of cicadas and the rustle of wind through palms are usurped by the sound of sprinkler systems on endless acres of green lawns, the hum of air conditioners, the noisy labor of icemakers, and the murmur of surrounding pool cleaners. The manicured neighborhood of suburban mansions begins to rot around the lives of the Redding family like some incurable germ disease. Houses foreclosed by banks suffer in the chilling silence of abandonment. The fruit of orange, lemon, and grapefruit trees drops off by the thousands and decays in the brutal Florida sunshine.

This crumbling modern American dreamscape is juxtaposed in the second half of the novel with an older landscape of the American dream, that of the vast, unknowable West. Powell lets us ride shotgun on one of the most nihilistic road trips into the wounded heart of Americana I've ever encountered. He can race along with Kerouac any time he desires, but he could teach Kerouac things about a shared darkness that Jack never dreamed of in his nomadic life. The Rosen boys take wing across the remnants of the western frontier as loyal Bobby comes to realize too late that Donny has fallen in love with chaos and death. Powell crafts an outlaws' journey where going to seed would seem like an act of mercy. Donny is so psychotic that he makes Las Vegas look like a rest stop for pilgrims on the way to Fatima. Their flight across the American underbelly is fascinating—yet it ends as it must, with horror.

In first reading *The Sheltering* I could not fathom a connection between the Redding family and the Rosen brothers. It seemed to me that Mark Powell had written two well-conceived parallel novels, but without conjoining them in any overt way. Mathematicians far smarter than Citadel graduates such as Powell and myself assure us even parallel lines converge at infinity, and Powell's vision here points us to the convergence of all human lives in unexpected ways. In a moment of extraordinary power and artistry saved for late in the novel, Powell lands a hellfire missile of a revelation squarely on target. It is not a trick or an artifice or a cheat, and it caught me in my Chevy Bronco unaware. His drone had circled back to ambush me with a realization that transforms the meaning and experience of the novel, leaving me with a yearning to traverse the book once more, emboldened by this uncloaked discovery.

The Sheltering is a book of the spirit and a deeply spiritual book. It is a hallucinatory work of visions for our visionless world, and I think a work of magic realism. I would not want to visit Mark Powell's eerie illusion of Florida or New Orleans or the American West, but I'm grateful he brought me along with him for this illuminating ride through the darkness and let me witness the alignment of Venus and Mercury, one that we shall never see again.

Pat Conroy

PART ONE

HE LISTENED AS THE REAPER CIRCLED nine thousand feet above the valley floor, green eye fixed on what appeared first as a rectangle of white light but looking closer—and Luther Redding had been looking closer for three days now—revealed itself as a squat aluminum-sided building, a worn Chevy Bronco parked against it. That he had come to hear the sound of the drone's engine, even here, six thousand miles away, a planet between them—he understood this as perfectly normal. A form of projection, he had been told by a psychiatrist at Holloman out in New Mexico, a coarse-handed woman who wore a flight suit and stuck pencils in her hair. A form of alignment, she said, the bodies need not to be separate, evolution having not prepared the soul for this form of disjunction, stick-and-rudder, fiber-optic line.

"Motherfucker has to have ants in his pants," the man beside him said and Redding did not bother to look. To look would be a deep violation of the intimacy he had come to feel with the man hiding inside the building. Kareem Saman was holed up with his wives and bodyguards, perhaps a few trusted lieutenants in what composed a small cell of the Haqquani network. Redding had been twelve hours on, twelve hours off since Tuesday but actually it was more like eighteen hours on, coffee and Red Bull taken like sacrament, followed by four Tylenol PM and six hours of sleep on a break-room couch. It was the world he knew, had come to know. Outside the control room it was all unreal: glittery sand and surf, mermaids and the Fountain of Youth. And somewhere beyond it Mickey Mouse and his crew of trademarked goons. But Luther was staring at the mountains of Southern Afghanistan, Luther was *in* Southern Afghanistan, and he didn't know when he would come back.

The Reaper banked slowly and the building made its lazy pirouette. The landscape was green on green, the darker demarcations as fluid as the sea, while the metal of the Bronco seemed to radiate white light. Somewhere to the north four thousand marines were moving south from Khost toward Tani, only a few miles away now, Redding suspected. But they would come no closer until the target was invalidated.

"Gotta be squirming," the man beside him said. Tanner his name. Maybe Chris, possibly with a K, Redding thought. Twenty-four, twenty-five. Twelve hours over the mountains and off to some club in Ybor City, techno music and an all-night Twitter feed, a tattoo of a winged Grim Reaper mapping one shoulder. Redding had nothing in common with the boy, old and married as he was, forty-four with two teenage daughters and a house in Orange City he couldn't afford to refinance.

"Gotta be moving."

Pattern of life, they called it, hanging for days above a target, one bird going up as another came down. Given time, you saw things, came to believe things, read the future in the past. Watched men and women for days on end, pissing at night in the gardens they'd spent the day hoeing, eating under trees with their children, and just once: burying an IED along a trace of road eleven or so miles out of Kandahar. That had been Redding's sole engagement. A Hellfire missile that looped its graceful arc and erased the man in a flush of incandescence. That had also been the squadron's only engagement and from it Redding had come to be seen as some sort of sage, the silent prophet wired into a headset and flying nap-of-the-earth, one hand on the joystick, the other instant messaging with the customers on the ground. It was fine with him, really, to be seen like that. He had come to understand his work as holy, the complete immersion a form of self-emptying so that it became pure duality: Redding and the Reaper, as omniscient and whirling as God.

He leaned toward the screen. They had been over target for almost seventy-four hours now and he knew the end was near. He knew too what would happen: at some point the door would fly open and a figure would scurry from the building toward the truck, his body the green of a fir tree but around him and ahead of him a halo of phosphorescence, as if in running for the Bronco he had made certain to carry with him his soul. The truck would swerve wildly—there was the illusion of safety through speed—and he would get the fire call from a JAG officer in some basement office. Redding would align the sites and dip the drone's nose. Firing the missile would amount to little more than a slight bending of his index finger. And then the marines would march forward. His only concern was whether or not Saman would prove worthy.

He let the Reaper drift up to ten-thousand feet, checked the radar for air traffic, and thought of his girls. At first he had made certain to ward off such thoughts, to stay fully in the green slur of the moment, but now he understood that distraction only heightened his concentration. Thinking his way through their days was what allowed him to sit with complete focus for hours on end. A Zen renouncement of the present, and thus there was only the present. He had no real notion of what time it was—his watch and cell phone were checked and waiting at the entry desk—but sensed late afternoon, four, four-thirty. Just after midnight in Khost. Kareem Saman sleeping. Redding's own daughters doing he didn't know what. Lucy was home for the summer, her first year of Bible college in Jacksonville behind her. Katie would be a high school senior in a few weeks' time.

It was July but he had yet to divine how they spent their days. Arguing—there were the arguments. Katie's goading of her sister, bad skin, bad hair, though in truth she had grown into herself in a way Redding had never expected, taller and less baggy, her face pocked from childhood but now almost as clear as her sister's. She spent her evenings at the church helping with the youth group, Katie tagging along, Redding suspected, out of two parts boredom and one part spite. There had been issues with both girls—how could there not be issues?—Lucy with her fundamentalism and fanaticism and Katie with, first the boys and now, Redding feared, some form of cutting. *Self-mutilation* the word, though that seemed unbearably direct. The cuts rowed symmetrically along her inner wrist, not deep but long and sinuous. The only time he'd seen them was that night in the kitchen when his wife Pamela reached for Katie's arm and what had followed was screaming. Pamela—

The Reaper rose to 10,200, 10,225 and he edged back the throttle, allowed it to float back to the ten-thousand foot hard deck. Kris or Chris spitting sunflower seeds and sweating, his chin water-bright, lips chapped.

Pamela was probably leaving the office, or had already left. She sold real estate, but the work had withered over the last few years and now she spent as much time at the gym as she did at her desk. They had drifted but he suspected that was as it should be, the creeping desiccation of their love neither better nor worse than that of the couples around them.

"Dance, dance motherfucker," Kris—Redding remembered the K now—said, and turned to Redding. "You know he's in there, don't you?"

"He's in there," Redding said.

"I mean actual visual confirmation. I keep disbelieving and having to run the tape back." He shook his head. "Dude can hear our orbit. Either he's lost it or the man has balls of like gigantic steel." He kept shaking his head. "What do you think he's doing? I'm betting on an orgy. There must be ten women in there."

"More like three."

Kris wiped his chin. "One wild send off before the Reaper comes knocking. That's the way you do it."

They made another slow pirouette. Seventy-five hours over target. Chatter of marines on the ground. The room smelled like foot spray and day-old pizza.

"I gotta life, man," Kris suddenly said. "I gotta a fiancée and a new boat, a two-fifty Evinrude on the sucker, and I am just about to lose my patience here. That motherfucker better cha-cha on out here in a minute."

"Just wait."

"I ain't done a thing but wait, cap."

Redding instant-messaged a pointless flight-status update to the squadron commander. Pointless because there was nothing to report, and pointless because they were all watching, how many he had no idea. All you needed was a laptop and security clearance. *Predator Porn* they called it. He thought of them sitting in the D-ring of the Pentagon, debating lunch. Thai, Ethiopian. No, no, let's order in and watch shit blow up. Redding felt it a grievous violation but one he had learned to live with, and it wasn't the voyeurism that upset him so much as the intentionality: your intentions had to be pure. Lucy had taught him that. He and Pamela were never church people, not in any conventional sense, but suddenly their thirteen year old girl was busy giving away her tennis shoes and quoting the Gospel of Matthew. It had seemed to happen overnight, a few C.S. Lewis books and a silver cross around her neck and suddenly she wants the family to hold hands before dinner, daddy to bless the meal. Are we saved by works or grace? And Katie looking at her big sister like she's about to vomit, like she can barely contain what wants to pour forth.

Redding thought it had something to do with her skin. He'd never known how much bad skin could matter to a thirteen year old until he had a thirteen year old with bad skin. Nothing debilitating. Childhood acne, light purple splotches when she was hot. Somewhere three or four generations back Pamela had a relative who must have been part Seminole as Pamela's skin was the lightest shade of olive imaginable, smooth and unblemished. It had taken Redding years to realize how Lucy must have seen this as a reproach. The trips to the dermatologist, buying Proactiv in bulk, all the while Lucy going dumpier by the day, pear-shaped, doughy arms. Redding never noticed until the day he suddenly did.

Lucy must have been fifteen—Pamela had just taken her to get her driver's permit—and she came home buoyant, laminated card in hand as she stood in the foyer and bounced. Redding came from the kitchen and spotted his daughter, how happy she was, he knew now he should have fixated on how happy she was. But all he could see—and he saw it for the first time—was this strange heavy girl, so similar to his beloved daughter and yet not, an older, uglier version, and what had shamed him hadn't so much been that revelation—that shame would come later—but his too late understanding of how hard the last few years must have been for her, the teasing, the parties she didn't attend, going alone to whatever dance the school sponsored. Those nights when Redding dropped her off outside the middle school gym while around them boys and girls poured laughing from minivans and the occasional rented limo—how could he have missed the tired implications? No friends. No enemies. No one, not even her father, to mourn her living. How could he have missed that?

Because she had smiled, he realized later, because she had always continued to smile. It was Pamela who took her to the dermatologist—for a while there were weekly trips, pills, scrubs, liquid oxygen sprayed against her bleating cheeks—and Katie always rode along, bored, earbuds plugged into her head, Katie who, though two years younger, was already two inches taller than her sister. Blonde, lithe with deep-set green eyes. At some point Pamela had allowed her to get a series of piercings in her upper ears, which followed the black mascara and black tights, which followed the black knee-boots. Goth Barbie, the other kids called her, with a sort of wonderment, it should be said. And it was easy to get carried away: she was smart and sarcastic and saw the world with the sort of caustic amusement usually reserved for cosmopolitan exiles, rich plutocrats fleeing revolution. She could do whatever she wanted, and because of this, though only here, deep in the bowels of MacDill Air Force Base and high above the southern mountains of Afghanistan, would Redding admit that he loved his youngest daughter a little less for it.

When Katie was twelve she had convinced Pamela to let her enter a beauty pageant in Orlando and for the month leading up to the event she had pranced around the house balancing a book on her head. It was the great ironic statement of her life—Katie as beauty queen (though she was certainly beautiful)—and she had treated it with such mock-seriousness that even Lucy had come to enjoy the running joke. *Look at us,* Katie would say, her body in slow stately motion around the living room, Algebra II text riding perfectly, *Look at this perfectly lovely family, father and good mother and two agreeable daughters who intend to marry young and pass through their loins a brood of brooding grandchildren for the newly minted grandparents to dandle on their knees.* Or primping before a mirror: *Scholarship money! I want scholarship money. Oh, and world peace, world peace and a year-long supply of Ben & Jerry's. But mostly the peace stuff, and for the little babies not to die in Africa.* But the night of the pageant Katie had become deadly serious, face set, eyes alive. She walked on stage and it had been an embarrassment, Katie looking as if she had sprung fully-realized from a fashion magazine while the other girls slumped and stiffened and smiled too bright. She had won the trophy and on the way home, when they stopped to eat at a Pizza Hut, tossed it in the bathroom trash. Over and done. Just like that, and just to show how easy it was, Redding suspected.

He remembered—

Then Kris was screaming *shit, we got a squirter, oh shit* a gush of profanity that flecked white against the display screen. Kareem Saman was out. Chatter filled Redding's ears but he heard none of it, his eyes fixed on the figure who ran from the building toward the Bronco exactly as Redding had known he would. *Roger, he's out* a voice said, and he was, the Bronco in wild motion and he heard Kris, perfectly and radiantly clear, request the fire call. And the response: *clear to fire, I say again: you are clear to fire . . .*

He was disappointed in Saman and thought it okay to admit as much. Almost seventy-six hours over target—he had thought the man capable of so much more. But such were the risks, you study a man, fall in love with the possibilities, but ultimately there was free will, one's inability to endure.

He put his finger to the trigger.

You set yourself up as judge, jury, and executioner, Pamela had said, but that was wrong: you set yourself up as angel, and await the word of God. Seventy-six hours. How much would've been enough? He found he could not answer. He knew only that the man's name would not be scripted in the book of life, and knowing as much, Redding allowed him a last breath before he touched the trigger, and Kareem Saman became brightness.

When his shift ended Redding logged out and walked to the locker room where he changed into his civvies, got his phone and keys back from the flight sergeant. The shuttle was running but he decided to walk. When the shuttle trundled past he regretted it. The early evening was muggy and overcast and he was sweating by the time he made it to the parking garage. There had been a lot of whooping and naked cheering, a soft roar of chatter, and then everyone had stood around as if winded. The heavy dump of adrenalin. The missile-induced hangover. A review board would examine the shot but about that he had no concern. He had done his job, and even now marines were proceeding out of the mountains and through the ravines, some probably approaching the charred remains of the Bronco. Saman was reputed to have beheaded several farmers who refused to assist in the movement of bomb parts. Now the man was dead, and deservedly so. What remained for Redding was sheer emptiness.

When he sat behind the wheel of his Acura he realized he was just a man again, his clothes soaked through and his car rank with the vanilla air freshener Lucy had hung from the rear view mirror. He was hungry and felt hollowed by the caffeine, a blistering absence beneath the fat mounded around his waist. He started the car and pulled from the garage and over the speed tables and along the base's access road. It was twenty minutes after six. Pamela was at the gym. Lucy at youth group. Kareem Saman was in hell. He didn't know where Katie might be, though he felt a grinding sameness to the world. Seventy-six hours over target, and still the Lee Roy Selmon would be bumper to bumper.

He drove to the Extended Stay America and climbed the exterior stairs to his room. He wasn't back on shift for the next four days. It was time to go home but he couldn't, not yet, and instead stood on the balcony and drank a Bud Light while he stared down at the pool. The problem, he had once believed, was that he was in charge all the time. He'd even believed it enough to tell Pamela. I walk in at work—flight leader—and people ask me what to do. I go home, same thing. I need to not be the authority for just once. But if it wasn't true then—and it wasn't—it was even less true now. Pamela did what she needed to do and the same was true for the girls. He finished the beer and walked back inside, popped another, sat for a moment and dug his toes into the carpet, shirt untucked, belt loosened.

When he walked back out a woman sat by the pool in cut-off shorts and an orange tank-top, long-legged, skinnier than appeared healthy. He didn't recognize her. Not that he necessarily should. But over the two years since he started flying drones he'd come to feel he knew everyone who passed through the hotel, not names but a head-nodding familiarity, passing each other at breakfast by the waffle iron or juice fountain that offered apple and orange and—just once—pineapple. A circle of mid-grade business travelers reading complimentary copies of *USA Today* while navigating America's mid-major cities. Tampa to Memphis to Dallas to Phoenix. Dinner at chain restaurants and the occasional airline upgrade. A great circus of mediocrity. But he didn't recognize the woman. And no one ever used the pool.

He put on a pair of sandals and a nice guayabera Lucy had bought for him on a mission trip to the Caribbean, took a fifth of rum from the mini-fridge, stuck a Bud in each of his pants pockets and headed downstairs. When he reached the landing she was still there, head back and eyes shut, bare feet spiny and tan and propped on the chaise longue. He had his cars keys out when she asked what was the rush. He looked at her: eyes still shut, head still back.

"Didn't you just get here?" she asked.

"Like twenty minutes ago."

She nodded and he waited for something else.

"Nice night," he said finally.

"Could be."

He took 275 back through the city, across the Old Bay, and into St. Pete, where he hit a Burger King drive-thru in Pinellas Park. Three Whoppers and thirty-two ounces of Coke he sipped all the way out Seminole, not removing the plastic top until he made Reddington Shores. The cup was down three fingers and he filled it with rum, refitted the top and stirred with his straw all the way south to the causeway from Madiera Beach to Treasure Island. He'd discovered the place over a decade ago with Pamela and the girls. They'd spend the day at the zoo and drive to one of the high-rises that overlooked the Gulf, let the girls play in the white sand while they sat on the beach and drank. The land here was impossibly narrow, on his left a slim bay, on his right hotels, the ocean visible between them. There was the road and a lane for parking, the occasional seafood joint when the spit widened, but not much else, and it wasn't difficult to imagine the water turning against the string of islands. The geography as fragile as the moment. Erasure, he felt, never that distant.

He waited for the light, crossed the bridge, caught another red by a 7–11, the windows boarded with plywood. The sense of fatality seemed to have crept and blown into every possible crevice—or maybe it was just the failing economy—but whatever it was, a seediness prevailed. Stripes of peeling paint. Rutted parking lots. Empty fields strewn with plastic bags and the remains of crushed shell. He parked in the near-empty public lot and walked along the boardwalk carrying his burgers and Coke. The Buds he left in the car for the ride back. Decompression. Warm beer and the salt air blowing through the open window. He would wake in the morning from his stupor, head clouded and stomach churning, empty his bowels, shower, and go home.

Almost no one was out despite the warm breeze, a few joggers and leathery women power-walking, a man prowling the sand with a metal detector. He sat beneath a cabana and faced the darkening water. The giant umbrellas and chairs were meant for rental but he saw no one else and sat quietly eating the sandwiches and periodically topping off the Coke. His scalp began to sweat and his mouth filled with saliva and by the third Whopper it became a matter of breath, chewing, swallowing, remaining perfectly still to make sure the hamburger didn't come bubbling up. When the nausea subsided he filled his mouth with rum and Coke and swallowed slowly.

Finally, the food was gone and he collapsed back into the sandy fabric of the chair. He'd gained twenty, maybe twenty-five pounds in the last two years, all fat and all situated loosely around his waist. He thought of it as a statement of sorts, a response to an indifferent universe. The need to explain and self-justify was relatively recent. Retroactively ordering the past. His dead parents with their genteel poverty and archaic lives. Behind his childhood house, deep in the cypress and black gum, stood a calcified tomb that had served as one of the southern-most stations of the Underground Railroad. Now it felt freighted with a different meaning, a private history, that he had played there, that he had taken girls there. Or that Thanksgiving morning with his dad, the Macy's parade on TV. Surely the night he ferried the dead home to Dover AFB. It wasn't nostalgia, he thought: such accounting was instructional. He was learning something.

He had flown MD-11s for United for seventeen years and learned nothing but now, in just thirty-six months of downward spiral, he knew about all sorts of subjects, a few of which—things like toxic assets and credit-default swaps—he could have done without. Arrogance—that was Pamela's diagnosis. We got arrogant and we started grabbing. Which was true. As soon as the real estate market started to boom, they had tried to grab everything in sight, a series of condos on Cinnamon Beach, a few strip malls around Daytona, and, finally, a thirty acre housing development just as everything evaporated, first the economy and then his job. But for a while it had been magic, every day their net worth growing, appearing in their accounts as if out of nowhere, a string of ones and zeros transmitted over fiber optic lines.

It was gone before they could count it.

But they had survived, banded together after the crash to save both house and marriage. Counseling. Date nights. Three trips to a psychiatrist in Winter Haven they couldn't afford. It had proved to be enough, and eventually Redding had wrung himself clean of the Welbutrin and Paxil, while Pamela had joined a gym and hired a personal trainer. They had salvaged enough, he thought, and for months he dreamed in ocean metaphors: withstanding battering waves, swallowing seawater but still afloat. They weren't in love, but neither were they going anywhere.

The compromise was clear to the girls, even if it wasn't to Redding, and around the time he turned his part-time commission in the Florida Air National Guard into a job flying UAVs he belatedly noticed an uptick in his daughters' collective powers of sarcasm. Which surely was natural, he thought, and could probably have been dealt with by talking to them had he not been sick to tears of talking.

By that point he was sick of everything, to be perfectly honest, and traced the failing arc of his life back to two moments, if only because, he believed, what was true was always discernible, the catalytic moments, the very *instants* life chambered and split. He attended the Citadel because he assumed his father wanted him to. *Assumed* because his father had never actually said. Luther, using the logic he already sensed he would never outgrow, based everything on a stray remark when he was ten and watching the Macy's Thanksgiving Day parade on TV with his father. They were both on the couch—a dreary morning of gray rain and wet leaves washed against the patio door, his father mournfully smoking a Winston, his mother in the kitchen, cheerily burning their dinner—when a drum and pipe band quick-stepped up Fifth Avenue.

"They're cadets," his father said, "they're from a college."

"Like UF?"

"No, not like UF." His father smiled, amused yet serious. "You go to UF to get a job, son. You go to the Citadel to be a man."

His father had been to neither, but the statement felt definite enough that this idea of *being a man* took on the quality of a safari, a lifetime's quest to view manhood in its natural habitat, to catch a glimpse of elusive and endangered man. Luther thought of that parade when it was his turn to *be a man*—every boy he knew had heard it every day of his life: *be a man, why don't you*—which happened to fall on a Tuesday in early August of 1985, three months after his high school graduation. They drove up I-95 in near silence, arriving in Charleston, South Carolina, as the sun began to sink over James Island. Luther's mother had reserved a room at the Holiday Inn and from the balcony Luther could see up the Ashley River to the Citadel's white battlements, gone pink and then purple in the evening gloam.

They ate a very silent dinner in a seafood place Luther knew they couldn't afford—salmon, squares of fried Brie on a bed of mixed greens—and it occurred to him as they walked to the car that he had spent his entire life preparing for an unhappy goodbye, the tense meal, the sleepless night. When they got back to the room his mother climbed into one of the double beds, swallowed a Valium, and disappeared into the luxury of dreamless sleep. Luther sat on the balcony. When his father turned in, he walked to the lobby where several other boys were talking about the next day. One's brother had graduated and that boy—Anderson, Luther would come to know him, though never to like him—had any number of Knob Year horror stories, the beatings, scaldings with hot water, marching naked in the swamps. A few guys were joking but soon enough the bullshitting stopped and what followed was a reverential quiet Luther identified, but could not make himself feel, as dread. When he walked upstairs he considered how the stories had failed to move him. He felt somehow past it all, and slept beautifully, up and alert before six.

They were outside the white-castled barracks by seven. Cars lined the sidewalks and young men in shorts and t-shirts carried in boxes and duffel bags while men barely older stood with their clipboards and shaved heads, duty uniforms—the uniform Luther would come to imagine a second, more pliable skin—starched and tucked. From inside he could hear yelling, a whistle, a drum and pipe band that may or may not have been marching around the red-and-white checkerboard quad, as crisp and interminable as a wind-up toy. Luther had everything he was supposed to bring—undershirts, handkerchiefs, socks: all white, all new—in his father's old seabag, packed and folded in the Florida heat by his mother who, Luther noticed, was crying, very quietly, into a single ragged tissue she kept crumpled and hidden in her palm. He hugged her on the sidewalk outside the sallyport—she had no words for him, only her wet face—and hefted the bag over one shoulder.

"I'll walk in with you," his father said.

"That's all right."

"Just see you to your room."

They crossed the sidewalk and apron of grass past boys saying goodbye and the morning felt unbearably mournful to Luther, the mothers crying—it wasn't just his own—the fathers offering handshakes and square jaws, all of it beneath the silent gaze of the cadet cadre, eyes narrowed by the sun, half gentleman, half bird of prey. Past the sallyport, the high walls of the barracks came into sudden relief: boys lined the galleries, standing at attention while cadets screamed and slapped, spilling bags of clothes so that the squares of the quad were littered with new socks and handkerchiefs that skated and caught in the far storm drain. The band played what sounded like a funeral procession, a slow dirge as they crawled toward the main gate. Two steps inside and Luther watched a mattress fly off the fourth floor—fourth division, he remembered from the *Guidon* he'd spent the summer studying—as airy as a sail. Three steps inside and someone was screaming in his ear. He turned to look and the voice hollered *Don't look at me. Don't you ever look at me, smack.* He looked at his father instead, and there on his father's face was a sort of sad shrug, monumental in its equivocation, a look that dated, perhaps, to his own time in the Navy, a look that said: I'm sorry I couldn't better prepare you for this, but there was always your mother to think about. Then the voice again: *What is your name? Do you have a name, smack?* And Luther realized this was an actual question, this man and his clipboard wanted an actual response.

"Luther—"

"I don't want to know your first name," the man screamed. Something flecked against Luther's newly shaved cheeks, warm and wet, but he knew now not to look. "You have no first name. You are trash to me, you are below trash, I hate you and I hate everything about your pathetic self. Last name, smack." He thumped his clipboard against the side of Luther's head. "Last-fucking-name."

"Redding."

"Cadet Recruit Redding."

"Cadet Recruit Redding," Luther repeated.

"You will sound off with 'sir.' 'Sir, Cadet Recruit Redding, sir.' You will bracket your life with 'sir,' and you will sound off like you have a pair."

"Sir, Cadet Recruit Redding, sir."

"Room four-twelve, smack," the man said. "Fourth division. Put your shit in your room and get online."

Luther and his father made it up the stairs unmolested. Room 412 was dingy and spare, a sink and mirror, metal bunk beds, two metal desks, chest of drawers, and full presses—man-sized closets with a thin rod Luther would learn to hang from. Another duffel bag, olive drab with the trace of a name, sat against the far wall beneath the window.

"Your roommate," his father said.

The door was shut and the noise below registered as a dull roar, a blunt disorder slightly muffled by the thick wood. His father sat down on the bottom bunk's bare mattress and exhaled

"I need to get back down there," Luther said.

"Let's just sit a minute."

"He said for me to get right back down."

"You're going to be 'right back down' for a long time, son. You're going to be down there the rest of your life." He patted the mattress beside him and Luther saw that his father's hand was trembling. He realized his hands were trembling too. "Sit beside me a minute," he said.

Luther sat and when his father put his hand on his shoulder Luther realized the hand was still, calm now. They sat for a moment and listened to the noise from below, the screaming, the pipe band, an air horn that erupted periodically.

"You're sure about this?" his father asked.

Luther looked at him, panicked.

"I'm not trying to tempt you," his father said and smiled. "There's no other way, is there?"

"I don't know."

"There isn't," his father said with a great deal of resignation, "not that I know of, at least. Not to find what you're after." He took his hand from Luther's shoulder. "Do me a favor though, when the time comes, don't tell your mother about any of this."

Before they could stand the door flew open and another cadet was screaming. *Get online, knob. What the hell are you doing up here? Get your PTs on, didn't you get your PTs?* Turning to his father: *I'm afraid you'll need to go, sir.* And then back to Luther: *Where are your PTs? Wait right here. Strip down to your skivvies and wait right here.* He bounded out of the door and Luther's father gave him his hand.

"It's all right," he said, and before Luther could respond his father was out the door and gone.

Three weeks later classes started and Luther began wrestling practice. His days were more ordered then. There was still the yelling and marching and the assholes who occasionally came in at night to make them hang from their full presses or drive t-pins into the soft flesh at the base of their throats, but mostly his days were composed of classes, practice, studying and sleep. By Thanksgiving the forty knobs in November Company had been reduced to twenty-three. They had entered the grind, short days, uniform depression, one day bleeding into the next. The upperclassmen seemed to have lost interest in torture. There was the sense of having weathered things.

Luther took a particular pleasure in the sense of shared suffering. What were his old high school buddies outside the gates doing? Playing cards and beer pong. Getting fucked up and oversleeping. Not that that didn't hold a certain appeal. But if he couldn't have it, he could at least revile it. Four days a week the wrestling team met at five-thirty to push through an hour-long weight circuit of box hops and power cleans and pushups and dead lifts, and it was slipping out of the barracks and along the sidewalk by the mess hall, campus just beginning to stir—lights coming on, the steam of reconstituted food rising from grates—that Luther sensed he was part of something special, that he might have to rise early and study late but that was a small price to pay for such belonging.

He raised his cup. It was as much rum as Coke now, more rum, perhaps, the ice melted. The beach remained empty, but he knew that somewhere behind him lurked the mass that was Tampa: he could feel it press against him, light and noise, Kris and his fiancée and new boat.

He took a drink.

Here is how to save your life, Luther: one: go see your mother. Wrong, too late. He tried again. One: consider your wife and daughters. Two—but there was no two, and he wondered to what extent there was even a one. He studied the sky for stars, points of orientation. But no stars were out. Only the drones, somewhere the drones circled. Otherwise, the sky was a wash of darkness, the light drifting out to this nebulous place where the only difference between God and science was the word you used. One night he'd taken Lucy to the IMAX in Kissimmee, and what they saw on the giant screen was the Orion Nebula, a star nursery where entire galaxies spun up from the dust, some of them swallowed and gone, some of them spiraling into space, unhinged and unfurled. Alive and joyous —you could sense the joy in the way they spread. It was no different than the turtles he'd seen run for the ocean, the baby loggerheads picked off by seabirds. The circle of life, Katie said, except she was making fun of it. Which, Luther thought now, was maybe the proper response: laughter.

He took another drink. He didn't believe in anything, but had sense enough to know that whatever truth there was picked up where grammar left off.

It was truth he had sought, that something past the noise, and in the spring of his freshman year he vowed he would never yell at a knob, never raise his voice, never perpetuate the stupid and the mean, but by his junior year he found himself incapable of viewing knobs—a new class, there was always a new class—as anything but irritants, spiteful children always underfoot. For the most part he had kept his vow but more from indifference than virtue. He wrestled at 197 and spent most of his energy either reading books or lifting weights. He had come to love the Citadel and in his love was able to disdain its customs and mores. Evenings he would cross the parade deck and one night, as the lights came on in the barracks, he suddenly realized how beautiful it was. It had taken him until his senior year to realize as much, grasping it just as it was taken from him. It was always that way. Years later, at Pamela's first ultrasound he had stared at the screen, at this shivering mass humming with white noise. It was uterine lining, but it was like peering inside the universe, the kind of place where a star might be born. And then something he couldn't really articulate had hit him, how the physical boundlessness of outer space was no different than the boundlessness of interior space. It was the first time he had understood what was meant by the world of the spirit.

The second time had been the night ferrying home the dead.

But that too was in the future.

The summer before his senior year, he worked at the City Marina and rented an apartment with four other wrestlers in West Ashley—West Trashley, some of the Chi Omega girls he knew at the College called it—across the bridge from the city. His job was easy enough: he worked Sundays to Fridays from one to five washing and gassing the sport-fishing charters that ran half-day outings. If he finished with that there was always busy work, spraying down the sidewalks or cutting the narrow apron of grass that ran between the Bait & Tackle shop and Lockwood Drive, but it was easy, mindless work and he was left alone and he never minded.

He made just enough money to pay his fifth of the rent, eat, and drink beer; it was all he needed and all he wanted. He lifted weights in the mornings, showered and went back to sleep until around noon, ate, pedaled his bike across the bridge. After work they grilled hamburgers and drank beer and he would sit up in bed until one or two in morning and read—because a professor said he might find there the truth he was after—*The Norton Anthology of the American Short Story.*

The book ran chronologically from Hawthorne to Amy Tan, and he was somewhere around Crane the day he saw Pamela. The last time he had seen her had been the summer after his knob year. Now she had completed a year of college—a year at Yale, his mother would occasionally remind him. She was still narrow, though lightly muscled now, looking elastic and powerful, the long tendons of her neck clearly articulated when she turned her head. She had cut her hair to just above her shoulders and was wearing flip-flops and a sun visor, a gauzy white tank-top over the darker shape of her bikini.

Luther was hosing down the wood butcher's block used for cleaning fish when he felt the feathery tip of excitement. Nostalgia, maybe. An old acquaintance. But whatever it was, he made no move. He was shirtless, wearing wet boat shoes and a baseball cap that read CAPT. DICK'S GULF STREAM ADVENTURES. Fish scales shimmering on his shins and ankles, a glimmer like chainmail.

Pamela was on the deck of a fifty-four foot yacht he had seen docked all summer but never out, an expensive boat with teak railing and a forest of masts and communication gear, two aft fighting chairs, a deck big enough for sunbathing at the bow. She was with a family—father, mother, girl about Pamela's age, boy maybe fourteen or fifteen—and Luther knew right away the man owned the boat; he had seen the type before, and recognized in the expensive Ray-Bans and knit shirt a very wealthy man who had fallen in love with the idea of owning a boat only to find that he hated the reality. The certainty of sunburn, the film that gathers along the upper lip. So now he had gathered the family for their yearly outing, the one for which he had bought a new wardrobe—his boat shoes gleamed white as marshmallows—the one that justified the several thousand dollars in maintenance and dock expenses he paid every year.

There were lots of old salts running shrimp boats or, if they could stomach the tourists, sport charters, crusty men who had swallowed their sea water with the Navy or the Merchant Marine, men with swirls of jailhouse tattoos, fading green parabolas from Okinawa or Bangkok or Oran, and Luther knew there was no one they hated as much as men like this, the dermatologists and trial lawyers, the bankers with First Federal, and Luther had come to affect the same distaste. Later, he would discover the father to be a remarkably patient and decent man, and that would be one more thing to regret, but that discovery was still months away.

He stared long enough for Pamela to spot him. She turned and said something to the girl and the girl's mother. None of this registered, and he couldn't hear a thing over the sound of the ice machine, but a moment later she hopped onto the dock and strode toward him, her mouth forming his name.

"Luther?" she was saying, smiling. "Luther Redding? My God, is that you?"

She slapped his arm and leaned in giving him a sort of quick half-hug.

"I guess I knew you were down here," she said, "but I didn't think I'd see you. It's been so long."

"Two years."

"Oh my God." She put her hands on her hips and he saw how pretty she was, her aqueous eyes and dark eye lashes, the long ellipse of her almost oval face. There was something too about her enthusiasm, about seeing her as a just-made adult there in the bright May heat. "Oh my God," she said.

They talked about their moms and home before canting like satellite dishes toward the yacht.

"Who's the guy?"

"Don Laird. He's like this huge maritime lawyer or something. I met his daughter—we're both in Trumbull College together—but I met Charlotte and she asked if I wanted to spend the summer together and I thought she meant here, like Charleston, but she meant Amalfi—I had never even heard of it, the Amalfi coast, which is like Italy—but then who's going to say no to that, so?" She stopped, caught her breath. "I think they're waiting on me."

"I think they are."

"Look," she said. "I'll be here another week or so. We should get together, catch up." Her visor lay a little triangle of shadow over her face like a mask. "They have this fantastic place on Prioleau Street and I know you'd love Charlotte."

"I already do."

"Give me something to write with." She spotted the marker on the dry erase board where someone had written IVAN: 7AM MIDDLE GROUND TO FOLLY CHAN-NEL. "All right. Paper?"

He offered her his left arm and down the sandy underside she wrote the number.

"Call, all right? We'll catch up."

She winked at him beneath her visor, turned and bounded down the dock where two workers were throwing off the bow lines.

I should call her, he thought.

A week later she called him.

"How embarrassing," she said, "the lengths I go to, having my mom call your mom just to get your number." He could sense her smiling. "But you probably thought I was eating calamari in Sambuco by now, right?"

They had gone without her, something about a visa, or maybe it was an issue with the house they were renting in Amalfi, or maybe it was just that they needed, absolutely couldn't do without, someone they trusted—*really truly trusted, I mean trusting like you trust family*—to watch the condo while they were gone. A different answer every day, she said. It was fine. She had caught the drift and was planning on heading home to Florida until they offered her the house for the summer, offered it in the form of her doing them a favor, desperate to have someone water the plants, bring in the paper, keep an eye on things.

"The Consolation Prize," she said. "And here it is. I'm sitting on the balcony right now. It's fantastic, actually. I can see the bridge, the Yorktown. Which is like this huge aircraft carrier, but I'm sure you know that. Down in the park there's—let's see—people on benches, people on blankets, dogs, leashed—I can see the leashes."

"People doing park things."

"From dawn to dusk. You'd have to see it to believe it."

Somehow, Luther couldn't imagine traveling there on his bike, so he borrowed one of his roommate's car, picked up a bottle of cheap red wine at the Publix, and drove that evening past the Marina and Coast Guard Station. It was almost eight when he parked the Camry on the street and looked at the new brick covered with holly hock and trumpet vines and climbing toward the roof. The Lairds condo was one of six overlooking Waterfront Park—a sliver of grass and palms centered on a large pulsing fountain—the only new construction to have taken place in the area in the last hundred years. All of this he would consider years later as he cut the lawns of his foreclosed neighbors, and all of this he would lament.

Pamela let him in the foyer and led him up to the kitchen. The house—he could no longer think of three stories and four bedrooms as a condo—was sleek and modern, the floors parquet, the kitchen spare and expensive with a copper hood mushroomed above the stove and a series of burnished pots and pans hanging from a ring above the island.

"This is really nothing," Pamela said, "*This* is the kicker."

She led him through a glass door that opened with a hush into a wine cellar the size of a bedroom; what appeared to be thousands of bottles lay in ranks, tilted forward in their wooden slots.

"Every three months," she said, "every bottle gets a quarter turn. One complete rotation a year."

"Do you get to do that? Turn the bottles."

A look traveled across her face: amusement. He could see it relax the corners of her mouth, lips sliding out toward a smile, and it took him a moment to realize she was laughing at him, had been laughing at him since that day at the marina.

"June eleventh," she said. "I'm the bottle-turner."

She took him through rest of the house, up the stairs where a skylight spread a rhombus of buttery late day sun, into an oak-paneled room with dentil molding and prints of waterfowl. Along the halls were black-and-white photographs of the ships docked in Boyces and Adgers Wharf, steeples of masts cluttered against the gray sea. On the top floor was the master bedroom where, she told him, she had begun to sleep in the massive bed, and beyond that the wrought-iron balcony that looked out over the park and bay. They leaned against the railing. Grains of pollen dusted a fine golden patina atop the black paint.

"Behold," she said, "the sea."

Every moment that evening had about it a sense of the ridiculous, as if Luther had not yet caught onto a joke that was being told and retold, and it took him weeks to realize how utterly serious she was in all things. Pamela was a woman who made plans and worked systematically to achieve them. It was years before he discovered he was no different, just another middle-class striver writing lists and goals in a notebook, fantasizing about the future before sitting down to concoct a way to bring it about.

But that night all this was lost on him, and he was surprised to find Pamela not at all like he remembered her. Then he realized he'd never actually known her. The girl turning handsprings until her palms bled and her mother forced her to stop, the high school athlete who ran in the mornings so she could spend the hours after school doing homework, the incessant need to be the best at everything—had he conjured these? He thought he had, because that night she was all distraction. They drank the wine he had brought and some Chardonnay she took from the silver refrigerator downstairs.

It was a warm night, heady with smell, and a container ship sat at anchor off Sullivan's Island, its gray shape balanced like a cloud along the horizon. The sun went down and the Cooper River Bridge became a necklace of light. They finished the second bottle and she went inside and returned wearing a sweatshirt and carrying a third bottle and they no longer bothered with the glasses, passing the wine between them until Luther could no longer distinguish the shape of the bridge from that of the aircraft carrier. He looked at Pamela and saw her long legs propped on the railing, the sleeves of her sweatshirt down to her fingertips.

"Why did you go there?" she asked. "The Citadel. It seems an awful place to me, cruel. When I saw you on the dock I was excited. Old friend, you know. Then I thought: what if he's mean. What if he's turned mean down here, all the yelling and marching. I never saw you as a soldier."

"I won't be one."

"You'll be too busy seeking the truth."

That seemed cheap, and he looked at her. He had said something earlier, he supposed, maybe something a little grandiloquent, but they were both drinking and it was a night by the ocean with all the accompanying sensations, and to throw such a line back seemed a little unfair. But when he looked closer he saw she was being serious. It was an affirmation, and it reached him in a way that nothing else had. He realized that above all other things Pamela was loyal.

He slept that night on a leather couch on the second floor beside a glass liquor cabinet and woke to find a note taped to the coffee table: *Gone running. Had a good time. P.* Below that: *PS—eat something.* The next day Pamela called and invited him back, there was a meteor shower that night and she thought they might be able to see it from the balcony. She would pick him up after work and at five o'clock he saw a brown Volvo wagon pull through the parking lot. She honked once and Luther loaded his bicycle in the back.

"I'm so yoga mom in this," she said. "Like the trophy wife who spends her morning at the gym and the rest of day complaining about the gardener or the pool boy."

"Pilates," he said, "not yoga, I think. It's maybe cyclical."

"Pilates," she repeated. "Of course. I love it."

He showered and changed clothes and in the kitchen sautéed mushrooms and spinach while Pamela drank a glass of wine and cooked rice. She asked if he had lifted weights today and he said no. He hadn't lifted or ran, in fact, for the last three days. It was the longest stretch he could remember and it felt liberating. He didn't much care for wrestling, to be honest. Never had, and getting fat seemed a luxury too long denied. Over dinner they talked about running—she was faster than Luther had thought, running fourth on her cross-country team as a freshman—but it felt perfunctory and stilted, and he realized they had exhausted every meaningful connection the night before.

Still, they kept drinking, and eventually wound up in the giant soft bed, naked between eight-hundred thread count sheets, both drunk enough to be forgiven, Luther supposed, though neither desirous of it. The next morning he woke alone, still naked and with only a vague sense of what had happened the night before. Pamela was running, he guessed, and he listened to a clock tick somewhere beyond sight. The French doors had been left open and he turned his head just enough to see the floor-to-ceiling curtains move gracefully, listened to the house settle around him, voices from the park, cars trundling along the cobblestones, the sunlight spreading in long tines, dissolving across his eyelids. When he woke again Pamela was in the bathroom.

What happened after was to become their routine. She came naked and pink from the shower to the bed, skin still damp and glimmering with baby oil, hair a wet rope twisted onto her neck. Her eyes stayed shut and when she twisted her neck he saw the same long tendon he had seen days before on the dock, still perfectly articulated. He moved his hands down her body and his lips along the inside of one thigh and Pamela tilted her pelvis forward, the slightest of movements, though in hindsight Luther imagined it the most daring thing she'd ever done. Little stillborn sounds escaped her throat, and when she came it was in a small, perfectly controlled fit. He moved up her body then, slid inside her, moving slowly, and then faster, and then faster still atop the oil-slick of her body. It felt reckless in so many ways, like driving a car on black ice, in control but only just, always a moment from losing everything. The sex was unprotected—as it would be all summer; she didn't have enough body fat to ovulate, though this never occurred to Luther at the time—and he began to apprehend not just the possibility but the probability of wrecking his life.

He didn't care.

After, they lay in sweat and oil, bodies cleaved, fingers tangled in the rods of the headboard, and Luther saw that her eyes were still shut—if she opened them all summer he was never aware of it. He walked to the shower and when he came out she was asleep. Within a matter of days Luther moved out of the West Ashley apartment and into the house on Prioleau Street. He still paid his share of the rent but no longer lifted weights or ran, and in a matter of weeks had very little to say to his old roommates.

He had even less to say to Pamela, despite the time spent in bed.

She would run the pre-dawn streets—ten, twelve, fourteen miles a day; she looked like an arrow—shower and return to bed. Sitting on the balcony reading, Luther would hear her rise a second time. When he came in around noon to eat she was gone. He biked to work and would come home to find she had bought groceries. In the kitchen they would speak for the first time all day; she would tell him of her run; he would tell her about anything at the marina. Nights they sat on the balcony and drank wine—they had started taking it from the cellar by this point, two, sometimes three bottles a night—and watched the harbor lights glimmer like sunken stars.

Around this time she started buying records, used LPs from a record store on George Street—Lutoslawki's Third Symphony, Mahler's Ninth—and at some point during the darkness she would take Luther's hand and lead him inside to the armchair where she would sit him down and begin to kiss him, her mouth warm and viscous with wine. He would lower her body onto his, legs curled around his back, rocking against him so that he saw her abdominal wall flex beneath her copper skin. She was louder at night, clothes hanging from them like torn flags, finished in a spent fury, sweating, glazed and drunk, sleeping on opposite sides of the bed and never touching until the next morning when things began again.

That was their routine, their idyll, the wine and mushrooms, the Shostakovich and Katherine Mansfield, Pamela racing through the waking streets in her training flats, and on June eleventh they rotated the wine bottles a quarter turn. They should have noticed then how many they had gone through in the three weeks Luther had spent there, the gaps in the shelves evident as missing teeth, but they didn't, and it was that evening Luther began to explore the second floor liquor cabinet he had noticed the first night.

Inside it, were four 750 ml bottles of Johnnie Walker Blue Label, and thereafter he would drink one small glass each evening on the balcony, sun-drunk from work, word-drunk from the five or six short stories he would have read, veering toward simply drunk. He was gaining weight, the newly puffy skin above his groin tender from friction, and had almost convinced himself he was in love with Pamela though he could never truly believe it. She was reading Hannah Arendt's *Eichmann in Jerusalem,* sometimes reading passages aloud while he cooked, and at night he began to dream of gas chambers. He would be cutting grass at the marina or checking bilge pumps and suddenly find himself considering the great well of guilt he felt like a pool of lukewarm standing water.

One Saturday at the end of July—the last time they would be together for two years—they drove the Volvo out to see Angel Oak, the sprawling octopus-like live oak that is believed to be the oldest living organism east of the Mississippi. The end of summer was near and in last week they had fallen into so dense a silence the air felt stacked with what wasn't said. In another two weeks Luther would be back at the Citadel; the Lairds would return and Pamela would go home to spend some time with her family before returning to school. Later, Luther thought that what he wanted from her was some sort of declaration. This summer was everything. This summer was nothing. Any skeleton he could hang meaning on would do.

But instead of speaking they rode in silence. The summer had spun itself out, the momentum was lost, and standing beneath the arms of Angel Oak— branches four or five feet in diameter, twirling into the ground to emerge twenty feet away, branches so heavy they were supported by steel cables—standing there he decided he would leave the next day. He was still paying rent on the apartment in West Ashley and there might just be enough time left to get into a semblance of shape before wrestling began. He decided all of this while he waved away clots of gnats and watched Pamela move around the tree, face turned skyward, bright as a sunflower.

"It's amazing," she said, "It's endured, you know. Nothing endures, but it has. It's stood through everything."

They were halfway back to the car before he realized she was crying.

When they got back to Prioleau Street he told her that he was leaving, and without saying anything they agreed to one more night: mushrooms, wine, his single glass of Johnnie Walker Blue—he was well into the fourth and final bottle now—sitting on the balcony, sex in the armchair. In the morning, Luther thought, he would touch her a final time and then walk away and see what came of things. He knew he wasn't in love, and even had come to feel a strange ambivalence about what had transpired. They seemed to suffer from too much gravity, too little air. They were wrong for each other.

It took three glasses, but that night Luther finished the last of the scotch, listening to Stravinsky's *Rite of Spring* while the streets filled. When she led him inside to the armchair they were both drunk. Their clothes were off by the time they moved to the bed. And that is where they found them, Bonnie Laird screaming a half second before her husband entered behind her, a suitcase in each hand. A moment later Charlotte and her brother were in the room and Luther was suddenly sober, or sober enough. Pamela began to weep and Luther remembered his father: *Do me a favor though, don't tell your mother about any of this.*

Somehow he wound up sitting barefoot in jeans and t-shirt in an oak-paneled room with waterfowl prints, drinking a tumbler of tap water across from Don Laird. Four empty scotch bottles sat by his feet. Earlier Luther had sat on a barstool in the kitchen while Charlotte and her mother counted missing wine bottles. There were one-hundred and three empty slots.

"You two have had quite the summer," Laird said.

Luther tried to raise his water glass in a little salute but the gesture fell apart.

"You're at the Citadel," Laird said.

"Yes, sir."

"I could probably call someone in the Commandant's Office and make life miserable for you, I suppose." He looked at Luther. "They're capable of that, aren't they, making life difficult?"

"They are. Yes, sir."

"I won't do that." He said it as if he had just settled the matter. "No," he said, "I won't do that." He seemed to study Luther. "Pamela is a wreck," he said. "I don't know her—I don't presume to know her—but she acts like she's had some sort of breakdown."

Luther slouched deeper into the chair. "That's your professional opinion, as a maritime lawyer?"

"That's my professional opinion as a human being. You took something easy this summer, son."

"I'll pay for what we drank."

"I'm not talking about that." He made a little motion of dismissal and for a moment he was silent, holding his head as if calculating a sum too great to be named. Luther looked past him to a print of a fox hunt, another of a hound dog. "It was easy. That's how you should have known it wasn't right."

"Sometimes it's just easy."

"No." He shook his head. "It's never easy. You've confused ease with a lot of other stuff and I think you probably realize it, and I think you're probably ashamed of yourself. Professional opinion," he said.

Luther returned to school out of shape and overweight, and within two weeks had torn his right quadriceps. Which was fine. He had no desire to wrestle, and in October told his coach he felt he no longer had anything left to give to wrestling. More to the truth was that he no longer felt wrestling had anything to give to him. A few weeks later, he sent a check for three hundred dollars to Don Laird—hardly enough to cover all that they drank, but at least enough to replace the four bottles of scotch—and applied for a pilot's commission with the Air Force. He wasn't going to be a seeker of truth. He knew nothing of the truth.

Surprisingly, or perhaps not, he thought very little about Pamela. At times he wondered about her, but more often than not he recalled the summer on Prioleau

Street as a fever dream. He heard nothing about her from his mother and dared not ask. Then in mid-November, just before Thanksgiving break, a letter arrived.

Her handwriting was a small tight script, very neat and very focused, spread evenly across the front and back of both pages.

> *I'm sorry,* she wrote, *to have been so long out of touch. I doubt it will surprise you when I say that I needed some time and space to sort things out and try to make sense of the summer. But before I say all that let me say this first: in no way do I hold you responsible for anything—good or bad—and I want you to know that I have nothing but good thoughts about you. That's a way of saying: please don't let it be awkward and weird when we meet again, which I know we will, I just don't know when.*

She had heard through her mom that Luther had injured his leg and couldn't wrestle—*Your quad-string, my mom said. I told her she had to have misheard. I told her there was no such thing as a quad-string but you know my mom. Anyway, I imagine it was your quadriceps, and I do hope it wasn't too serious*—She went on like this for a while, relaying meets and times and training schedules, the kind of thing they had discussed with great specificity in the Prioleau kitchen. But Luther found his eyes wandering down the page, skimming ahead to what he knew must be a return to the real subject, half-anticipating it, wholly dreading it when it came.

On the back of the first page she wrote:

> *OK. So that's not what this is about, I know. It's not what you want to know and not what I'm trying to tell you, but oh God, how to get around to it, right? Here's the thing: everything that happened last summer I intended. I sort of planned it you might say, somewhere between the moment I saw you and the time the Lairds asked if I'd housesit—Charlotte has avoided me all semester, by the way; I've given up trying to apologize to her. But anyway: I planned it. I wanted it to happen, Luther. Understand that. I know you probably feel responsible for things and oh God, what a last night, a crazy awful night for you, I know, and I was ashamed, for a long time I was so completely and utterly ashamed and didn't know what would happen next. I knew I wouldn't die, of course, but I couldn't really imagine how life would go on, either. But I'm past that. That's the purpose of this letter, I suppose, to tell you that I'm past lots of things.*
>
> *So, like I say, I was ashamed for a while. Even when I got home I just sort of moped around the house, sleeping a lot during the day and running at night, until my parents thought I must just be miserable and asked if everything was all right. (The Lairds were too decent to tell my parents anything, which of course just made me feel worse.) But my shame, my towering overweening shame. I know now that eventually you just have to let things go, to forgive yourself, and if you've*

25

come out unscathed—and I have, so relax, you're the one with the bum knee (kidding)—but if you come out clean then forgiving yourself is the hardest part. I had planned to seduce you, Luther—God, that word is ridiculous but it's too late and I'm too far into this to think of another—but I planned it because, and this is going to sound so arrogant but, again, let me just say it: I did it because I felt very powerful, very alive, if you know what I mean, and I think I wanted to sort of find out just how powerful I really was. It was that sense that the whole world was constructed just for me, everything aligned for my pleasure or waiting for my approval. I'd never done anything like what we did before or since. I want you to know that and not think whatever thoughts you might think of me (and God knows are entitled to).

(There was never any meteor shower—do you remember that?)

All semester I've thought of these things and this is probably the fifth or sixth time I've sat down to write this letter. I think I'm only writing it now b/c I'm scared to death of the thought of running into you at home at Christmas and just . . . well. I'm writing it. It's very late—or early, I guess, almost four in morning now—and I'm writing it to say that at some point this fall I realized the whole shame thing was an illusion, a façade. I've been praying a lot this fall, Luther, and I think maybe I'm gaining some sort of clarity for the first time in my life. It's bad form to say that, I know, but it's part of the change I'm making, part of testing the limits of my power and finding myself not nearly so powerful and impervious as I thought. My big regret is that I dragged you into it, you, sweet decent you. So I'm sorry about that. Please don't worry about me—God, what arrogance, you must be thinking, she's worrying about me worrying about her?—but I know you, Luther, and I know—and Mr. Laird even intimated this to me later—that you hold yourself somehow to blame. Only don't. This summer allowed me to see the world as it is, not as I wished or deluded myself into believing it might be. So everything worked out fine. Except for the wine—another joke, a bad one, I suppose—but seriously, I hope you think about this almost never, and when you do I hope you just think good thoughts. I have a picture of Angel Oak taped to my desk. I look at it all the time.

Love,

Pamela

PS—he found tacked into the margin—I've been listening to Stravinsky all night. I think I love it more than anything else now. It took a while, though.

Luther never wrote her back, and she didn't write again until he was a First Lieutenant flying supplies to the Gulf, Tinker to Ramstein to Prince Saud. They'd had their second fling by then, their short-lived Labor Day weekend reunion. It was done and over, he assumed, and now the war was coming, Saddam Hussein with his poison gas and old Soviet tanks versus Luther air-lifting humvees and heavy trucks. Her letters started in November and continued into the spring when she surprised him in Oklahoma. Just weeks later he would ferry home the dead, twenty-seven soldiers from the Pennsylvania National Guard, killed when a stray Scud missile struck their tent.

That was the other moment, the second. There was the Thanksgiving morning with his father—*You go to UF to get a job, son. You go to the Citadel to be a man*—and years later there was flying the dead back across the Atlantic, one leading to the next. That night it was the isolation, the perception of keeping solitary watch. He was somewhere over Newfoundland when he realized he alone was awake. The twenty-seven dead in their flag-draped coffins. Their sleeping Honor Guard. His crew had drifted into the shining blackness, the silvered sea below, the leaded clouds above, how they floated, how they slipped through the dark. Luther's face gauzy with the green of the panel lights as he flew them home. It struck like a blow. For the last hour, he had distracted himself with sexual fantasies of Pamela which weren't so much fantasies as memories of the five days of her visit. They had barely stopped touching, making love constantly, flesh to flesh, but talking too, a torrent of words and whispers and hints, telling each other every buried moment while they crawled across the damp mattress or the couch or the passenger seat of Pamela's car

He was running his mind over the contours of her body when he felt someone watching him. He swung around but the cabin door was closed. His co-pilot slept deeply. Luther was alone but was certain he was not, and at that moment thought, briefly, yet definitively, that he sensed heat from the green dials. It was a great comfort, this warmth, but when he put his hands to the panel he felt nothing. What was left was an awareness of his task: he was ferrying the dead. He was ferrying the dead yet he was alive. He thought again of Pamela's body, every curve, every valley and rise, touched the nape of her neck, the hollow of her throat. Every square of flesh as holy as his task. He was at one with it, and there seemed nothing more beautiful. There seemed, in fact, nothing else at all.

The rest—the wedding, Lucy and Katie, the job with United, the house in Orange City—the rest followed naturally, logically, as if in the green light of crossing what he had gathered and stored wasn't comfort so much as direction. But he had failed to learn, wasted the night's guidance, and could sense now how much of his life had been a drone-like tracing of these points, a series of constricting circles that winnowed the green brilliance to a nub of light.

He thought of Lucy, maybe fifteen and soggy with late adolescence, the two of them driving through middle Georgia to meet Katie and Pamela in Atlanta, the country a series of rolling hills gone brown in the chill of early November and suddenly they were passing a white fence, behind it cows bedded in the muck. Hay bales shrink-wrapped in plastic. Empty feeding rings. The fence kept going, paralleling the road until Luther felt he had to say something.

"This fence," he said. "How long has this thing been going? A mile? Two miles?"

Lucy shrugged.

"I want to say," Luther said, "something in me wants to say that six hundred acres is a square mile. This is one serious spread."

A moment later the house came into view, a compound really, seven- or eight-thousand square feet of prefab material perched on an easy rise, an RV in the driveway. A wrought iron gate read B & M CATTLE, the letters curlicued and brass-tipped.

"The main house," Luther said, "the big house. Lot of money there."

He looked at his daughter where she sat watching beads of rain blow off the windshield. Sullen, he thought, she looks sullen and he wanted a response.

"Lot of money," he repeated, and again she shrugged.

"Does that impress you?"

"The house?" He considered it. "Not really. Or maybe it does. Just the sheer size of it all. The ambition."

She snorted. "They still die," she said.

"What? You mean the people in the house?"

"As surely as the poorest villager in Africa." She was staring out the side window, her face—he felt certain—deliberately turned from him as she fingered the silver crucifix around her neck. "You can't fence it out," she said. "You can't make it not real."

"That's seems incredibly morbid, honey. Pretty uncharitable, too."

"It's the truth." That snort, that shrug, those fingers massaging that nineteen dollar cross. "If you don't want to hear the truth just say so and I'll shut up."

They were quiet all the way to Atlanta where he was relieved to find Pamela and Katie had spent several hundred dollars on Dorado riding boots. It was ridiculous and wonderfully distracting. Something to consider besides death. *You can't fence it out.* Something to engage besides the balled anger of his oldest daughter: the frivolity of his wife and youngest daughter.

A man and woman came down the beach, holding hands and laughing. They were a little older than Luther and Pamela but there was something childlike in the way their hands met. It was a private affair, nothing about it intended for public consumption, and Luther realized that in the shadow of the beach chair they couldn't see him. He watched them with the green-eyed objectivity of a drone, lifted his rum and Burger King Coke, and tried to remember where it was Pamela had gone for the weekend. She'd told him, of course, he knew she told him. But wherever it was, it was wrong. She was meant to be here with Luther, here watching their girls play in the sand the way they had ten, no, fifteen years ago.

Most of the Coke was gone but he topped it off anyway. *What are you doing to yourself, dad?* Lucy's question. You could go days and forget Lucy. He blamed himself, but blamed Lucy too. When Katie was born Lucy was given a microscope and Luther stuck his finger so that she could smear his blood across the glass slide. It had made her immediate, that simple droplet of demand welling below the nail, but it faded, receded, Lucy drifted off and, except for sleep, never asked for anything else again.

Like his father. Thoughts of his parents came unbidden. His father dead for over a decade. His mother put away in an assisted living facility in Green Cove Springs, a yellow brick monolith with an angle of river-view if you pressed your face to the welded-shut pane. Window AC units like square tongues: the walls panted with them. Inside a chemical cold. He never visited her, not really, until one day she was dead too. Was he ever a good son? Did it even matter?

His father's late life conversion to a Pentecostal Christ was not at all unlike Lucy's teenage conversion. His church in an abandoned dry cleaners so that you entered beneath the awning and past the curbside drop-off. His Jesus as much fire as light. God is never so much God as when he is absent. He'd said that to Luther just before the cancer was made official. Luther visiting and he and his father going out on the black water in the aluminum john boat just as they always had. This in the quiet hum of months between the end of the Gulf War and Luther's wedding. God in the silence, in the slow winding of the trolling motor, the ebb of the tide as it slinked back through the cypress trees and into the estuary where they would sometimes hook a tarpon blown in by the shifting current. *If it didn't bother you,* he told Luther, *then I'd be worried. If you felt all right with it, that's when I'd get upset.* He was talking about the war. His father had watched it on CNN, the green gun sights, the Patriots and wire-guided smart bombs. Which was to say his experience was as real as that of anyone else, all it lacked was the sand. The sand everywhere: fine-grained in the carpet of the motel-like room they'd given Luther at Prince Saud Air Base.

The maze of barracks hallways there not unlike the maze they had navigated the night Lucy was born. Pushing Pamela in that wheelchair. One forty-four in the morning—the exact moment they stepped from the car outside the emergency room. He would forever see the readout on the dashboard. The rain-blown night. Water steaming off the pavement. Hours from the light and the temperature hovering in the low eighties. They'd never made it out of the triage room, Lucy born at two-eleven in the morning. She appeared a bloody angel. The antiseptic had about it the stink of truth and he went weak before it, bowed beneath what felt like the absolute.

It was similar when his father died. Except now it wasn't the weight he registered but its absence, the lifting of a burden, though his skinny Vitalis-headed father had never been anything approaching a burden. But it was no less a freeing. An unmooring, he thought. As in a ship, as in cast adrift. There was freedom, a terrible bounty of freedom, the certainty of his father's death seeming to erase the possibility of his own. The world cracked open. And, because he felt certain he couldn't make the right move, he made every move: wife, house, kids, job. He ran manically from the night he ferried home the dead to the days he sat under his umbrella in San Diego. *Wake up! Wake up!* Except he didn't believe it. He was playing a part he'd spent thirty odd years waiting on.

Kareem Saman as dying star: all that collapsing light.

Kris with a K.

He poured the last of the rum and thought of Pamela.

What to make of her absence? Twenty years of marriage and what to make of her? He knew she married him because she had used him to test the limits of self, and afterward felt guilty and more than a little silly. Hadn't she always made too much of things—the meditation, the prayer and fasting?—and here was this perfectly acceptable man, this *stable* man, whom she thought probably loved her. So she married him and in binding her life to his left behind her old self and took forward only the body. The body, she told him once, climbing out of bed for a six AM Bikram class, because everything else failed to *obtain*. But Luther had obtained once, Luther had shone. Luther the brightest star in all the starry sky (she had honest-to-God written this).

He was in San Diego when the Towers came down, driving out to Mission Beach when NPR reported a plane had crashed into WTC 1. Five-forty-six in the morning and Luther unable to sleep and instead headed up I-5. By the time the second plane hit he was in a beach chair, watching coppery morning light gather dutifully behind him while figures jogged and power-walked and ran metal detectors over the sand. He liked the wrongness of facing west, everything inverted and bad-eyed in the way it becomes after a lifetime of watching the sun rise over the Atlantic. He was thirty-five and—he remembered from college—quite possibly lost in a dark wood. But for the moment he was sitting in the soft sand, eyes glazed across the Pacific, barely registering the flurried movements around him, everyone running back to cars or jogging in place before suddenly standing perfectly still, ears bent to headphones.

A man came toward him, Hawaiian shirt open to a V of coarse silver hair. "We're under attack," he said. "They're are all up and down the east coast. New York. The Pentagon."

It seemed not to register. Luther immune, Luther in starlight. The dimming of a certain phase of his life, though he only began to register as much when he realized another woman walking toward him—what was it that drew them to him?—was herself crying. People rushed past him while behind him cars started and he realized with some disappointment he was sitting in front of a parking lot; they weren't seeking him out because of his calm demeanor. (Calm in the face of ignorance, Pamela would tell him later when he tried to explain the morning.)

By the time Luther reluctantly dusted his shorts and walked back to his car the North Tower had collapsed. He sat with the door open and radio turned up. The parking lot had emptied and he thought of driving back to the hotel and using their internet but somehow it felt too flimsy, as if by flying jets into buildings all technology had betrayed them. He listened through the collapse of the South Tower and found a phone to call Pamela.

"The girl's want you home," she said.

"I know."

"I want you home."

"I'm not sure how possible that is."

"Rent a car, Luther. Buy a train ticket." The constrained hysteria was something he'd never heard in her voice. "However you have to do it. Just find a way."

But he didn't. The FAA grounded all flights and instead of reporting to the Amtrak or the Alamo car rental, Luther drove back to the beach. He had the shore mostly to himself and spent the days scanning the sky, wondering at the emptiness, a sort of virgin wilderness above him while below people cried by the light of CNN. When he returned that night to his hotel—September 13th now, flights rumored to resume in the morning—he found the rest of his United crew in front of the lobby TV with several other guests. A green-on-green nightscape of Kabul—where the hell was Kabul?—lit by the flash of incoming rounds. One of the flight attendants cried softly while another sat stoically, leaned toward the screen, knee-to-knee with Luther's copilot.

"Are those ours?" she asked as another rocket exploded.

"Not ours," the copilot said, "not yet."

Luther stood at the edge of the scene, just beyond sight, strangely touched by the intimacy of it all, the domesticity. His copilot the grim father, teeth set, one flight attendant the stoic mother, the other a weeping child abandoned to her fears. Luther was meant to be the wise grandfather, older, quiet with resolve. He was meant to take his place in the armchair, to comfort. Instead, he walked out before they could see him, back to the beach, dark now, overtaken with guilt and a sense of his own truancy, being neither with his real nor his adopted family. Things felt badly disproportional, his orientation damaged, and he realized it had sneaked up on him, the world, life. He found his chair and sat there thinking and thinking until the burden felt almost impossible, so long was the night, and so dark.

But by the time they flew out the following afternoon Luther had seen clearly his life, an objective view that felt not unlike death. After the waves of sadness—now the tide coming in, now the tide going out—he had entered into a reckoning, weighed its parts, measured and considered the sum, and come finally to the conclusion that his time on earth amounted to very little. It wasn't until daybreak that it occurred to him that he was still alive. Then he started really thinking. Somewhere above the southwest he thought of the dormant garden of his marriage. Over the Mississippi he considered Lucy and Katie, daughters whom he loved dearly but daughters who felt more like kind strangers than children. He thought of money, he thought of flying, he thought of every day he could remember since leaving the Citadel, and what it felt like was a slow numbing of whatever richness he had once imagined. It *did* feel like death.

But he was still alive.

Pamela was not prepared for the man who came home that evening. He took her to the trattoria in Winter Park where they celebrated anniversaries. Nina Simone and French posters of old train lines, lithographs in heavy frames. A slow aquatic feel to the restaurant, the dim corners and ovals of white light that lay scattered like coins across the floor. They sank into the leather banquette, forearms on the table amid half-circles of condensation and the rinds of squeezed limes—it felt like some sort of arrival: the place from which they would dive into some new incarnation.

"Look at our life," he told her, "think of all that's wrong with it."

"I don't think anything's wrong with it."

"Pamela—"

"I mean besides the normal things."

"Pamela. Look at us, baby." He was speaking louder than he intended. "We're sleepwalking. We're numb."

She lifted her wine and he saw the glitter of tears. "Oh, God, Luther. Everybody's scared and upset but this is such a cliché."

"I don't care. I honestly don't care if this is the most clichéd boring-ass thing in the world. Like that's the worst thing to be, a cliché."

"Please lower your voice."

"Please listen to what I'm saying."

She was almost whispering. "All right," she said. "We're sleepwalking."

And then they weren't. Pamela got her real estate license and started accompanying Luther on trips. For a few sacred months he flew the Orlando-Buenos Aires route and they spent their evenings eating grass-fed beef in Palermo and San Telmo. Their children were growing and, if Luther and Pamela squinted just enough, appeared happy. Things, as they are wont to do, fell into place, and while the world burned, Luther began to lose weight, following Pamela to the gym and after to her office where they began to divine what undervalued properties might appreciate violently in the coming months. Homes, lots, office buildings. They cleared thirty-two thousand on a house in Kissimmee after only seven months. Then a villa near Rollins College: forty-one grand in a little over five months. The trades came with more rapidity, selling after a week, a day. Pamela became fierce, a knight errant seeking bungalows around Thornton Lake, or pre-fabs in stucco ghettos hugging the Beachline Expressway, Luther her squire, hunched at her shoulder while she scrolled through the MLS database. That Lucy had become a religious fundamentalist seemed a footnote next to their account balance. That Katie might be cutting herself and, if rumors could be trusted, sleeping with a sophomore at UCF, an unfortunate circumstance that should be viewed in light of current market fluctuations. It wasn't that they were malicious, mom and dad, so much as busy. They weren't bad parents. They weren't really parents at all. They were in investors, riding an American tide that refused to ebb, watching their bank account swell, in love again with each other as much as possibility.

They were in Miami the November weekend it happened—the girls fourteen and twelve and riding horses in Ocala with Pamela's parents—Pamela sitting on their bed at the Gansevoort in South Beach, laptop logged into the hotel Wi-Fi. They were going practically every weekend; it seemed appropriate. A room overlooking the ocean, twenty-five dollar mojitos along Lincoln Drive. Luther had shaved his beard and lost weight and had the haggard good looks of an explorer back from some polar region, a man who had spent months living off the land now returned to find civilization oddly frivolous. It was an easy three hour drive they would make Friday morning, slightly drunk and back in bed by twelve-thirty. Sex with the balcony doors open and the gauzy curtains blowzy with sea breeze. Pamela weighed 107 pounds, could see the veins in her biceps and abdominal wall, and thought herself as sheer as the curtains. Again and again, she found herself in Luther's lap, sex having returned, rediscovered as if it had slept hidden in the fat that ringed his waist.

That day she sat cross-legged in her underwear while Luther showered. It was a little after three; they had made love, drank a bottle of complimentary pinot-noir, and fallen into careless sleep. Pamela checked her email and logged into their Bank of America account. The concern was Katie. The concern was

Katie using the credit card they had foolishly given her for emergencies to buy two hundred dollar corsets. Pamela scanned the transactions line, satisfied all was well, and was about to log off when 'Account Balance' caught her attention. She leaned forward and back, her mouth suddenly dry.

"Oh my God," she said. "Luther, come look at this."

He was toweling his head and pranced into the room, pink and flaccid and smiling, more giraffe than bear.

"Look at this," she said.

He bent his head close enough that droplets splashed on the keyboard but neither were concerned, neither could take their eyes off the line that read:

ACCOUNT BALANCE ENDING XXXXXXXXXXXXX0567 $1,026,560.00

"One million twenty-six thousand five hundred sixty dollars," Luther read slowly.

They were millionaires.

She said it, "We're millionaires."

"Holy shit." Luther squinted his eyes, leaned back and laughed. "We are, aren't we?"

That night they ate duck leg confit and tobiko cavier at Nemo. Luther smoked a cigar, and after dinner they strolled along the ocean with a boozy grace. The money: there was something in it about having arrived, of having survived those lean years when Luther was flying C-17s out of Tinker, of moving past the early days in Orange City, the moldy bathroom carpet and decrepit garage too narrow for even their used Honda. Neither had ever been particularly acquisitive but what spread before them was the possibility of a new way of being. That they hadn't cared about expensive clothes or cars didn't mean they couldn't learn. They would acquire the taste for good wine, take another trip to Europe, maybe buy the girls horses. What had been a game became a world-view, a philosophy of life, and what it felt like, Luther thought, was adulthood. *I hadn't know it until now* (though he would think the same thing years later when the money was gone: *so this is what it means to be an adult, I'd never known it before.*)

"I think maybe it changes something," Pamela said, "on a chemical level. I think maybe we live longer because of it."

The tide slid a gray wash over the sand and out on the horizon cruise ships lumbered in and out of the harbor.

"The money," she said. "One million twenty-six thousand five hundred sixty dollars."

They made it back to their room and onto the bed, sloppy and drunk, Luther on his back while Pamela pulled the waistband of his boxers down around his thighs, the act sweaty and inefficient. When she went down on him he was soft and only began to rise just before a hot spasm jerked his hips forward, hard enough to bounce his wife's head against his pelvic bone. She coughed, wiped her mouth, and was still. He felt her breath against his shriveling groin, the mossy smell of himself, the messy selfishness of it all, and, looking back, realized he should have seen it as a sign of what was to come: their mutual groping, the pathetic climax, but instead only looked down and said the one thing he could think to say. "One million twenty-six thousand five hundred sixty dollars," he told the swirled crown of her dipped head. Then slower, as if invoking something still unseen: "One million twenty-six thousand five hundred sixty goddamn dollars."

She was asleep.

He slipped his arm from beneath her and lay on his back, tried to calm his heart for he realized now it was beating wildly. He both knew and didn't know the reason. He looked over at his wife, her hair fanned across the pillow. Her nose appeared raw, sunburned. He thought it might be the most human thing he'd ever seen. He put his dead parents against hers. Their health against how he was suffering. The heartburn. A headache. It wasn't the drinking so much as the cigars, burning them down like he was a twenty year old cadet. Fourteen floors beneath him Miami went to sleep. Or didn't, as it were. Just went on with its sparkle and flash and the noise of traffic that carried even through the double-paned windows and the hush of the air conditioning. The thump and pack of engines along Collins Avenue, the smug air. Because it was all smugness, Luther thought. The city that belonged not in Florida but on another planet. It reminded him too much that at heart he was a country boy, a swamp thing, coarse and rough-hewed. But secretly dainty, privately effete. Only his size had served to mask it, his bearlike lumber a pose: he had the gliding feet of a dancer. It was Pamela who was refined, all that money. But then she would claw at him and that always undid him. Her nose flushed red: yes, without question the most human thing he'd ever seen, the sexiest. He got hard at the thought of it, even here, even now, with his mouth raw and his throat packed with acid.

They had spent part of the afternoon by the pool, Luther on his back, submerged but for his toes and hands and the oval of his face. The feel of the sun, the crossing jets and parallelograms of light. Around him was language, and he loved knowing he understood not a word, that he would never understand. It implied the largeness of the world. To find himself utterly senseless was to validate his very being: he had transcended the swamp. All of it a measuring stick against how far he had come—those mornings on the water in the john boat, he and his father running crab traps; ringworm from an unwashed wrestling mat; feeling the lift of Globemaster, the little bump when the landing gear retracted.

God, he regretted the cigars. His groin a hot mess. Pamela a hot mess, breathing on the pillow beside him. His desire for her had never waned. *God is never so much God as when he is absent.* As if in death his father had bequeathed what was unnamable: certain ways of seeing, the gravity of speculation. Except it wasn't speculation. It was that night ferrying home the dead, the solemnity. He would never feel it again.

He had never again—

Jesus, the drinks he could live with, the heartburn, the headache, it was the cigar that was killing him. He hadn't a choice though. In my defense, he thought, the night demanded it. The string of numbers in his bank account. He looked again at Pamela. He felt like he'd abused her, somehow broken trust. He touched her hair, finer now than when they first met. She had aged better than him, beautifully, in fact, but he felt the years in the thin strands that curled from her scalp, saw it in the bend of her neck and the backs of her hands. Too much sun. Children. He'd hardly thought of his children since morning. The relief that Katie hadn't used the credit card—it seemed too simple an emotion, somehow not worthy of a child.

He wished the city to sleep. The absence that is a presence. His father again. The Pennsylvanian National Guardsmen wrapped in flags. His father had died the summer after the war, the summer after Luther's wedding. The summer after Luther's mother had driven to Oklahoma—just as Pamela's mother would later do—to persuade him not to deploy to Kuwait, to MOAB: the Mother of All Battles. He pitied her: his poor mom and her antiquated ideas. She saw blood and baby killers, marches on the ROTC department. It was a newsreel dead a generation ago, Kent State, crowds outside the Pentagon—there would be none of that. But how was she to know? She didn't yet understand that it was a video game, that none of it was real. Not even the dying.

That lazy summer on Prioleau Street: short stories and Johnnie Walker and sex in the cushy armchair. He knew his mouth would hurt in the morning, the palate ribbed and bumped, the dry rasp of smoke in his lungs. He would feel it. If he ever slept. If morning ever came. Which, of course, it did. And with it came the hurt. And then the salve, the number that quantified the rising star of their lives:

One million twenty-six thousand five hundred sixty dollars.

But it never went higher, and by that fall they were back down to six figures. Not that it mattered. They made purchases, investments. When you're money works, a financial planner they met at a New Smyrna party told them, you don't have to. They read stock prospectuses and attended showings for new condos. While the girls existed on a separate plane, a realm to which they periodically threw cash, Pamela and Luther found themselves moon-eyed and money-drunk, making love in the mornings and slipping away to some spa or resort on the weekends, barely attentive to anything beyond the black and white account digits they had come to check several times a day, as certain and dutiful as any religious office.

It spread throughout the neighborhood, wealth. Guys with roofing businesses flipping townhomes, wives getting real estate licenses while their husbands fished the Gulf Stream. The parties began, a round of Friday and Saturday soirees where everyone walked over to get shit-faced while the kids disappeared upstairs or into the basement. The talk was money, property, a story that grew throughout the holidays and on the through the New Year: *this cat in Tampa, I think it was, buys a house in the morning, flips it, then it gets flipped again, and then again, on and on until by the time the lawyer draws up closing papers for the* first *sale—and I'm talking like late afternoon, let's say fourish—that motherfucker has been flipped seven times.* By February it's was ten times. By March it was twenty. It was like flying blind to another planet, you couldn't see it, but you came to feel its gravitational pull; it had its own rules, a series of dislocations that promised only to upset any inherited sense of balance; a string of numbers that became more theoretical, and thus more mystical, until it had about it the scent of God, a wispy corona of immortality. A title agreement a form of sacrament, borrowing money the influx of Spirit. They imagined themselves saints newly uncloistered, the pursuit of money no different from the pursuit of truth.

"It's factoring into my dreams," Pamela told him one night after another party, the kids drowning in the pool while the adults slouched in wicker and discussed vacation plans in St. Bart's. "Like it's this breathing thing, almost like a totem, almost like I'm supposed to respond somehow."

They were on their backs, Luther's left foot dangled off the bed and onto the floor so that the room would stop spinning.

"Except it's not even money," she said. "It's more like this entity. It's just waiting except I don't know for what."

In April they decided to borrow enough to buy into a thirty-acre development on Cinnamon Beach. They drove up to watch the ground-breaking—a Cat D6 tearing through palm fronds and tangled vegetation—drove back periodically to watch the home-sites cleared and excavated. When buyers failed to materialize it seemed more a puzzle for their amusement than a concern. They were well-hedged, diversified, their money was working so they didn't have to. When the Cinnamon Beach consortium filed for Chapter eleven life seemed to spark with chance. Pamela cut her hair to the length of her thumbnail and flew with Luther on the Orlando-San Fransico route. They had lost the better part of a quarter million dollars but it felt exhilarating, the chance to unhinge things, to self-destruct in a matter of hours. And what did it matter, really? It was play money. It was pretend. The flame out would be spectacular.

But then it wasn't spectacular.

"Not with a bang," Luther grew fond of quoting. This was the summer he perfected that sad shake of his head. "Not with a bang."

They roller-coastered through another year and by late 2007 found themselves somewhat chastened, their girls almost grown and the Florida real estate market in steady decline. When Bear Sterns collapsed, Luther was on a layover in Denver. When AIG fell he was in Cincinnati. He watched the president's speech from gate D-19 at LAX and it occurred to him he was ordering early middle-age around financial ruin much as his father had ordered his twenties around Kennedy's assassination.

He flew out of Los Angeles for Orlando, somehow sensing he was racing his own life, trying to outrun the account digits in sudden free fall, the plummeting numbers that had come to define his place in the world. When he called Pamela from the airport tram he realized he had lost, and came home to find her unloading the dishwasher, bent to the task as if she had only now remembered it, two years after the rinse cycle was complete. Watching her, it occurred to him that the only reason they been able to buy their way in was that people in the know—people far smarter than the Reddings—were already selling their way out, and he filled with a profound tenderness, a tremendous pity for both he and his wife, good-hearted if greedy, more stupid than wrong.

"It was always theoretical," he told her in consolation.

"Apparently," she said, "so is our future."

They weren't alone. The entire neighborhood seemed bent under the weight of ruin, the grim anticipation that the next call might well be the bank. It felt like a time to acquaint oneself with laws about repossession, to use the last of the petty cash to invest in a firearm and water-purification system. It was like being at a loud lively party, Luther thought, and suddenly the music stops, silence, a single voice out on the patio until it realizes it's alone. People go starry-eyed and quiet, awkward in their stillness, yet unable to flee, the jolt too sudden, the structures too firmly entrenched. They were all poor and they were all staring at each other. Overnight they turned stoic, too proud to rage, or maybe too self-aware, having known all along, at least on some level, that they were playing a game far beyond their level of skill. The mortgage-backed securities. Credit-default swaps. The end was bound to come. The only wonder was they that they had lasted this long.

For the last year—two, maybe three, if someone was particularly attentive—the smell of decay had gathered, rot, strings of meat between the teeth, you touch something and watch it crumble, not at all surprised to find it windy with termites. But what could be done? Everyone they knew had houses and kids and cars. They were too far along certain paths, too far along in their lives to turn back. They would ride it out, go down with the ship. There were any number of clichés meant to convey catastrophe though in the end it came down to nothing more than men and women sitting at night in their dim kitchens, drinking Maalox and plugging numbers into Excel spreadsheets, their lives round pegs in the square holes of the future. A nation of dumb bastards with their pontoon boats and home equity loans, but American dreamers, every last one of them, right down to their busted cores.

Meanwhile, they watered their lawns and took the kids to soccer.

When they disappeared—the neighborhood cleared in what seemed a single weekend of yard sales and U-Haul trucks, as sudden as spring rain—Pamela and Luther woke to find themselves among a handful of survivors. They also woke to find they had daughters, and that Luther was meant to pilot a load of Disney tourists back to Atlanta. There were no more weekend parties, no more hangovers, and it seemed they had woken from a long delirium, a manic state not unpleasant, but not wholly real either. He traced it back to the trance he had entered that morning on the beach in San Diego—was that the third moment? Could there be a third moment? Only now, alone on the beach, did this seem a possibility—all that death, all that carnage, and all of it necessary to wake Luther up. The Buddha beneath the bodhi tree beneath the beach umbrella.

It was only when he lost his job during a third round of layoffs that the panic set in, the rabid scrambling, the clawing and counseling, half the day for wounds financial, half for wounds psychic. That they survived seemed more miracle than event. They were going to lose the house then didn't. They were going to file for trial separation then didn't. And then it was over, and, having been awake the better part of a decade, all Luther could think about was getting a good night's sleep.

When he felt somewhat rested, he began to look around for signs. He started watching the President again (he had ignored him for years, weary of the bluster, the flight-suited speech from the carrier deck, the cowboy threats from the Rose Garden) and felt a genuine sympathy for the man. He was just like the rest of them, the President. The silver spoon that was Andover, Yale, the Texas Rangers—ultimately it didn't matter. He was no different, as spoiled, lazy, and, ultimately, as in over his head as everyone else Luther knew. The moral rightness with which he moved, as if the world owed him more than just material comfort, it owed him its collective gratitude—Luther understood it completely. They raised their children on hand sanitizer and tee-ball trophies, buddies and best friends trading texts; there wasn't a competent adult under sixty-five to be found anywhere. They were a nation of eternal adolescents. The bantering, the wavering calls to violence or patriotism or shopping: they were arrogant and vague where they should have been humble and precise. But who could suffer the focus, the discipline required? It wasn't their fault. The wars, the economic crash, they were many things, but they were most certainly not their fault.

The drones—the job of flying the drones, the job of killing Kareem Samman—came through a friend of a friend, an old Citadel buddy now an Air Force Colonel holed up in the basement of Central Command in Tampa. Luther had six years active and six years reserve and it wasn't difficult to reactivate his commission. The future was unmanned warfare. The future was unmanned, systematized and free of the chaos that infected living. Luther sought this. He wanted order and the drones provided it, a top-down schematic that defined a clear hierarchy, a great chain of being on which he might locate himself. He felt himself growing fearful, and the more frightened he became the more important it was that institutions validated his existence. Bank accounts. Political primaries. He took his name off the national Do-Not-Call Registry. The girls thought he was crazy, but he needed to know that he was a part, a contributor whose opinions were being weighed and sifted, helping to reinforce the stolid core of civil society. That a man's fingernails might need to be removed in the basement of some Eastern European black site to preserve this ordination of the daily came to feel acceptable, reasonable even, given the volatility tracked on CNN. He developed routines, cultivated habits of thought, came to love the TSA, the FBI, the Florida Highway Patrol, grateful for all forms of authority that stood as bulwarks against the dissipation of the real. He became lost in the pleasure of belonging, the narcotic lure of assurance, and by the time he packed his toiletries and headed for New Mexico Luther dreamed in flow charts and organizational tables.

He trained at Holloman AFB for five months, fast-tracked because of his prior service, fast-tracked because of need. Twelve hours a day on the simulator and then, weeks later, twelve hours a day operating a Predator over the Granite Mountains of the China Lake Naval Weapons Center in California or over the Cactus Range north of Vegas. There were fabricated villages and columns of humvees and heavy trucks, paper targets to silently erase. Operation Provide Shelter, it was officially known, though they called it 'the sheltering' in deference to the God-like omniscience of their drones. At night he drove into town for buffet barbecue. The weight he'd lost in the previous years now felt like an unaffordable vanity, a swelling of the ego he had come to disavow, and he drifted back toward his bear-like state. By the time he was back in Florida he had gained forty pounds and felt something in common with Lucy, their shared doughiness, while Katie looked more and more like her mother, an elastic bird of prey, gray-eyed and heartless.

He tried now to order things.

Yes, he'd been poor growing up—relatively, he told himself—and wanted money all his life. But when he'd lost it, all one million twenty-six thousand five hundred sixty dollars of it, he lost the desire as well. Which had proved to be a wonderful thing. The death of his ambition bringing with it a great peace. If only he had lost everything sooner, made it and lost it and understood it, for what he wanted now were the toy tracks in the carpet, the square mail trucks and circus trains pushed from the knees, the abandoned half-dressed baby dolls.

The moments he most wanted returned were those evenings when the girls were still small, Lucy a toddler, Katie a baby, that slender interregnum after they were down for the night and the doors were locked and even Pamela had drifted into the lightest of sleep. The dog tucked on his rug. Outside, perhaps, rain. A scrim of rain, tide-like, that mists through the screens while Luther checks the locks, and switches off the lights, a last walk through the kitchen and living room, the house settling and then set. Night. Sleep. How complete it felt, how safe. And how squandered. It was all darkness.

The night he ferried home the dead he had walked back into the cargo bay to tell them to expect some turbulence over the Shetland Islands. The turbulence never came, but he remembered how he had steeled himself before stepping back to speak to those few living among the dead, and the surprise at how many there had been, all in their neat rows, flagged and somnolent, and Luther's awareness, too, of how many would follow, and how, when he turned his back to return to the flight deck, he had encountered such darkness.

In a way, it all felt like too much. But it was his life. So what could he do but carry it?

Except, it occurred to him sitting on the beach, it wasn't his now—and had it ever been?—it belonged to someone else, it belonged to the air.

He crumpled the empty waxed paper cup and buried it in the paper bag, left the bag under the beach chair and stood a little unsteadily, allowing his big feet to dig into the sand before he began to lumber back to the car.

The first time he'd taken a drone up over Afghanistan he had been overwhelmed with the presumed simplicity of lives, the herds of barnyard animals and the neat garden plots. Waking in the morning and tending to the body's needs: food, shelter, water and sex. But he had come to doubt this. Kareem Saman was not a simple man. Locked inside his shabby bunker, life was not reduced

41

to its elemental nature. That, ultimately, was Redding's job, the gift of the missile he fired, the absolute and irrevocable reduction it carried with it. To be incandescent for a moment, a shatter of snowy light, and then to be nothing at all.

The woman was no longer by the pool when Redding got back and he was irritated to admit he'd wondered all the way whether she would be waiting. He sat in the car outside his room and drank the second Bud Light. A few windows were squared in blue but beyond that there was only the soft hum of traffic on 275. He walked to his room and stared down at the pool. Two potted palms were lit with tiny up-lights staked in the dirt and the shimmers from beneath the surface waved up. He looked again for the woman, thought of her bony feet and spindly toes. He had never really gotten a good look at her face was the thing. Because of that, it felt difficult to put behind him, though he suspected he was simply lonely.

Finally, he found the ice bucket and several quarters, walked back downstairs and got two Cokes out of the machine, filled the bucket. There was another fifth left in the room and Redding intended to sit on his balcony until the rum was gone. He collected his ice—the little plastic liner meant for sanitation had slipped so that the ice rested atop it and not within it—and turned to find the woman behind him, one hand balanced against a rack of tourist brochures.

"You look bored," the woman said.

He was startled enough not to speak, the ice bucket hugged to his chest and a Coke beneath each arm, the aluminum cans cold through his shirt.

"I'm not going to bite you," the woman said. "Where you going with those?"

There was enough shadow to hide her face, but when she stepped forward he saw she was younger than him though not by a great deal, mid-thirties, he thought, her face stripped to a rawness usually reserved for late middle age. But she wasn't unattractive.

"I've got some rum up in my room," he said.

"Why don't you invite me up?"

He pointed up. "Just right up here."

"I know where you're staying," she said. "Why don't you invite me up?"

He said nothing and she looked at him as if waiting for a dumb child to speak. She was still barefooted and he saw her toes clearly, not as long as he had remembered though there was still something birdlike about her.

"Do you have any money on you?" she said.

"In my room," he said, "not here."

"Well, if you have any money on you we can have a good time. Why don't you invite me up?"

He shook his head but found himself asking simultaneously: "How much?"

"How much is it worth?" She pushed off the brochure rack and stepped toward him to finger the lapel of his bright shirt. A heat was coming off her body, a smell he associated with domestic animals, tangy but clean. "How," she said, "do you quantify lonely?"

He didn't know and staggered back until he felt the Coke machine behind him.

"But not in my room," he said. "Let's go for a drive."

"I'm not looking for a hassle."

"Just a drive. That's all."

She shrugged and looked out at the parking lot. "Bring the rum back down with you."

He bolted past her, shedding ice as he loped up the stairs and jammed the key card into the slot. It swung open and he stood in the center of his room and tried to think: the rum, his wallet. Then he put his wallet back on the nightstand and removed several bills, counted out one hundred dollars—*how do you quantify lonely?*—then one hundred more. He felt the manic lure of possibility in a way he hadn't in years—Lucy's birth, the summer on Prioleau Street—and wound up brushing his teeth with his finger. When he blundered down the stairs he realized he had forgotten everything but the money and his car keys. Then he heard her voice and stopped. She stood beneath a glare of light yelling at an Indian man Redding recognized as the night manager. He slowed to a walk.

"There he is," the woman was yelling, "there he is."

The Indian looked in the direction she was pointing, and there stood Redding at the base of the stairwell with his expensive shirt and sandy feet.

"Just ask him," the woman said.

The Indian—was he Indian? He could have been from Pakistan or Yemen or any number of countries that formed a single blurred mass in Redding's slow brain—wore khaki pants and a white-button down, a blue Maltese Cross tattooed just above the collar.

"I'm sorry, sir," the man said. "I am sorry but this woman says she knows you." He looked at Redding, a hard vole of a man, his features bunched in the middle of his face like a badly arranged centerpiece. "This woman says she is with you. You are staying here?"

Redding pointed vaguely up. "In 204."

"Room 204," the man repeated, "yes. And this woman, she is with you?"

Redding saw she had put on shoes, straw huaraches of some sort. An orange pocketbook hung over one shoulder.

"Sir?" the man said.

Redding looked in her eyes. He knew those eyes. They belonged to his spurned daughter, they belonged planted in his own head, the disappointment, the petty betrayals that should have been nothing but—in the end—were everything, as rowed and symmetrical as the cuts on Katie's arm, and all of it beneath the green eye of God, if God was watching.

"No," Redding said softly.

"Excuse me, sir?"

"I said no."

He watched the woman roll back her head and turn and he turned himself, crossed the parking lot as fast as he could and sat down in his car. They were still yelling at each other when he pulled out and he thought they would still be yelling when he returned. Then it occurred to him that he might not have shut his door and the woman would ransack his room, or the night manager would dump his belongings into the green Dumpster that sat behind a span of collapsing lattice. But none of it mattered. There was the illusion of safety in speed and he sought it, understood it, Kareem Saman barreling across the valley in a fit of laughter. If there wasn't simplicity let there at least be speed.

He jerked onto the ramp for 275 and weaved through the light traffic, bounced off again onto Hillsborough Avenue where he took the first right and was suddenly on a street crowded with pedestrians spilling out of clubs and bars. He jammed the brakes at an intersection where a pack of men and women shuffled across in skinny jeans and mod bubble dresses. His tires locked and a few of the women squealed, but most seemed not to have noticed him, laughing and gesturing, pawing at a man with a shaved head and a black loop expanding one earlobe until it appeared nothing more than a tongue of connected skin. Redding panted. He was soaked with sweat and for the first time he realized he smelled himself, not the alcohol and bad food but *himself*, the indelible heart of Redding, the cholesterol clotting his blood, the sadness in the gray folds of his brain. It was the one part of him that had been present for everything.

He was looking mournfully at his hands on the steering wheel when someone drummed on the hood, and he looked up and who should it be but Kris! Kris with his fiancée and boat! Kris with his calm request for permission to fire. What comfort it gave him, not his acolyte but his friend—for Redding saw him now as a friend, baptized and bloodied together. It was Kris!

Or was it?

The man looked at him with no recognition though Redding thought perhaps he saw only himself in the glare of the windshield. Redding watched after him until a horn honked and he realized the light was already going from green back to yellow and he gunned the engine on down the street. There was another traffic light up ahead but he already had the car up to sixty, seventy. The Acura's engine groaned to eighty and he realized it wasn't his car he was hearing but the drone. The world tinted green and suddenly he was looking down at his car as it careened down Highland Avenue and it took only a slight tip of the Reaper's eye to see closer, the man inside leaned forward and gripping the wheel, angrier and so much smaller than Redding felt he should have been. Then he looked ahead—and here was the great genius of the drone: to discern from the past what was to come, to read the pattern that had always been present if only someone had bothered—he looked ahead and saw the intersection, and saw it filling with cars, and saw too the Acura not stopping but plowing forward, faster and faster, until it disappeared in light.

PART TWO

THE CHILD DIED IN A SUNLIT MARKET. The child died in a Vegas ring. Still, the years came and went. Wars and rumors of war. A decade of erosion that ended with morning. Maybe half past four and a taste in Bobby's mouth like dryer lint. He heard the dogs outside, nails scratching the porchboards, and raised his head to see the beer cans that littered the room, little aluminum barrels in a pasture of gathering light. Somehow he had fallen asleep beside a Coors tallboy, the warm beer balanced perfectly in the mattress depression. The mattress otherwise empty. His wife and boy having not returned. His life having not been restored. Only the dogs to greet him.

He stood uncertainly, still a little drunk, and was halfway to the kitchen when he thought of his brother and remembered today was the day. *I'll be damned.* So that was what the party was about.

He dumped Purina into several Kool-Whip bowls and filled a pie tin with milk for the cat he sometimes saw. It was two, maybe two and a half hours down to the prison but it was early and there was no rush, time enough to sit on the porch and watch his dogs eat, two beagles and a big one-eyed collie-shepherd mix. He was glad. He loved this time of day best, how fragile it was, the light a clean presence, not unlike that morning in Baghdad, the way it laddered into heaven. He sat completely still and felt the world go steady and even, and if he could stay right there, just like that, he knew he could be happy. Or if not happy at least a little less sad. But soon—too soon—sun began to light the fields that fronted the house, broadened over the green grasses feathered yellow, and spread on down the gravel drive, past the shed to touch the swing set they had never come back for.

When it touched the wall of long leaf pines that marked the back of the property he knew it was over, and walked inside to undress in front of the mirror. Pulled off his shirt and stared at himself. He had gotten the tattoo in Colombia, a bald eagle with its white head and golden bill, talons ribboned with the slightest gleam of light, the most patriotic thing he could think of right there on his left pectoral, centered above the heart. It was meant to indicate some sort of gratitude, he thought, but he wore it now like a mark. He'd wanted that little shimmer he got when they played the National Anthem but wound up with a dead child—*murdered* child—and an air-brushed bird.

So now—goddamn it—he'd lost that stillness and was thinking of it again, unable to stop and when his breathing drew shallow and quick he walked naked into the bedroom and in a small notebook beside his bed read the last entry, made last night in the midst of his sad and private celebration:

FIREBOMBINGS:

HAMBURG, DRESDEN, KOBE, TOKYO . . .

He flipped back a few pages.

FORT PILLOW MASSACRE (APRIL 12, 1864)
DEAD: 297

That was enough, his shame contextualized, weighed and measured, and he showered and pulled his clothes from the dresser Nancy had left. Some boys told him he should show up in his Class As or at least his BDUs, get a little respect from the Corrections Officers running the joint, but Bobby knew what uniforms did—one motherfucker prodding another, comparing patches and campaigns— and didn't want his brother's release to turn into a pissing contest. He had the law on his side after all. For the last seven years Donny had been locked down at Lawtey Correctional in Raiford, a little nowhere town in the middle of a Florida pine range, nothing outside the prison but mobile homes and a skank-ass Mc-Donald's, all of it camped along the edge of a ten-thousand-acre National Guard artillery range. But today Donny was getting out. Didn't matter what Bobby wore. He dressed in jeans and a button-down almost on principle, good Tony Lama boots, then, just as he was headed out the bedroom door, grabbed a ball cap with SEVENTH SPECIAL FORCES GROUP twilled across the front because if there was one thing he had learned, it was that you don't ever know.

In the kitchen, he opened one of the Ripped Fuels stacked in the fridge, packed a thermos and cooler beside the box of Donny's CDs, the only thing his brother had asked for. His own mementos were as meager: a Swedish SIG 550 rifle and a single MRE (#4 Thai chicken), both in the closet along with a copy of *The Koran* in Persian Farsi. The rest was Nancy's. The kitchen full of knick-knacks and photos gone dusty and pale. His wife's stuff. The way she had left it, as if all she had wanted was excuse enough to run.

I'm not the one who killed that boy, Bobby.

Those two boys, he heard her say. *You and your brother both.* But she had not said this. She had just loaded the Civic, strapped little Bobby into his car seat, and drove away. He rinsed his coffee cup and put it back in the drying rack, told the dogs he'd see them that night, and left for town.

Hardees was off Main Street and he turned by the sanctuary of La Luz del Mundo to pull into the drive-thru. It was the only place open and he bounced up to the bright menu, the cooler secured with a bungee cord but the other junk rattling, post-hole diggers and scattered ten-penny nails, crushed empties he dropped through the slide window.

"Arlo Phillips," he said into the black box. "Quit snoozing on the job, boy."

"Bobby Rosen." The voice was scattered and loud. "You out early, sergeant."

"Headed down to pick up Donny."

"Is that right? Today's the day?"

"He'll be a free man by high noon."

"I thought I heard somebody say this was the big day but I never did know for sure. Well, good for Donny." the voice said. "Good for him. You know I've always thought the world of old Donny."

"I'll tell him I saw you. Let me get some breakfast here."

"Why don't you come inside and eat? We'll have us a pow-wow."

"I better get moving."

"Come on in, Bobby."

"I better not."

He took his food and pulled out. Plastic orange juice container. Steak biscuit. His jaw stiff and slow to comply, which was nothing new. There were mornings he felt himself growing old like a tree, long and gnarled, hands brittle from years of abuse. Everyone else was turning dumpy and pale, but not Bobby. He watched the housewives at the Dairy Queen, fifty pounds overweight and standing in line for biscuits and gravy, their fat kids hopping up and down. They would liquefy. But one day old Bobby would just up and burn. Not that he didn't deserve it.

He left Waycross and headed south through fields of cotton and soybean, big irrigation rigs trussed across the furrows like suspension bridges. Hit the St. Mary's River by seven and stopped just across the Florida state line to refill his thermos. He had the cooler in the bed of his truck, a few forties and a fifth of Jim Beam—a little something to welcome his brother home. It was for later, but he was nervous and took a nip off the Beam and a little more and before he knew it he was back on US-1 with a thermos half-full of liquor. Seven years was a long time. Donny had gotten eighteen months for a fight that went bad, not his fault really, an ugly night if ever there'd been one. Everything haywire and caustic.

Donny had almost served out his sentence when he'd gotten *involved* in an *incident*. Bobby sleeping in a metal shipping container in Baghdad when he heard.

Fucking Donny. Got caught playing lookout while two men took eight inches of galvanized pipe to the head of a thieving CO. He could have walked away, fingered the men, cut a deal with the State's Attorney, but wouldn't say a word. Instead he lost his gain time and had another five and a half years tacked on. Bobby had shown up hoping to talk sense into him. Staring through the plexiglass at the little jailhouse songbird tattooed on Donny's throat. The one thing his brother would never be.

"What the hell's my rush?" Donny had asked him. He leaned back and lit one of the Marlboros Bobby had brought him. "Besides, minute it even looks like I'm talking I slip in the shower, fall on a shiv that just happened to be there on the floor. Wind up with a four-pint transfusion and my name on a couple of organ donor lists." He shrugged. "Where's the hurry there?"

Donny's wife had already left him, his arrest not the reason really, just the *last* last thing. She had a kid with another man now, sick and shrunken headed, legs clattered down to almost nothing. Some sort of blood disease. Stephen, his name, a sweet kid, though Bobby wasn't even sure the boy could walk anymore. For a while people had come like pilgrims thinking the boy was some sort of conduit of grace. But he just kept getting sicker and after a while folks left him alone. And of course Bobby's wife had left him, too. He'd been at Bagram when he learned that, Skyping with his own boy when his wife walked in and told little Bobby to go in the other room for a minute, I need to talk to your daddy. She said some things about responsibility, about an absent father, but Bobby heard what was beneath it. In the end it was about her need, her want. And all of it stacked against the world. Which is why this is just so awful and hard. Yet she never shed a tear. Left it to Bobby to cry later that night on a cot while around him men snored and farted, dark for but the soft blue glow of men texting wives and girlfriends, in a fire-fight one minute and on Facebook the next.

After that, he'd come to the conclusion he didn't understand the world. So fuck it, fuck every last one of them. That had been his answer at one point. Except it only went so far. You could only say it so many times before you were alone and what you meant wasn't *fuck them* but *help me,* stay with me, be near to me. How we are all alone together—it had taken all four deployments for him to understand.

He stopped again at a rest area just north of St. Augustine. He'd veered too far east and knew it. Not unintentional if he was honest with himself. Which he wasn't sure he was up for this morning. He hit the head and gulped warm water from one of the automated faucets. It was morning now, late enough for the sun to burn the fog from the wide lawn of wet grass that separated the parking lot from I-95, and families were out, piling out of mini-vans and walking dogs. Sun visors. Mickey Mouse ears. A boy maybe six years old, same age as his own boy. He hadn't seen little Bobby more than once a month since his discharge, since the boys at CID had found *no grounds for further investigation* and he was quietly nudged out the door, his discharge honorable, his benefits intact. Today he was missing his son a little worse than usual.

He took a last drink of water and wiped his mouth on a paper towel.

He'd known what he was doing, then as surely as now.

When he got back on the interstate he almost immediately saw the mileage to Daytona Beach. Donny's night of reckoning. The trip was supposed to be a send-off: Donny was finally married and Bobby was on his way to shoot a few camel-jockeys. They'd be drinking beer and watching the Bulldogs play football by September. Good times were coming. Better days ahead. They'd driven down for the 500 and after Earnhardt hit the wall, they'd crossed the highway to the Hoot-ers where they proceeded to get fucked up twice over—once for Old Ironhead and once for themselves. Donny was standing in a booth, pitcher in each hand, howling like a wounded animal while the rest of the restaurant howled back. He dropped singles from between his teeth into the cleavage of passing waitresses, which wasn't really how it was done—it was a family place: Bobby could see sev-eral kids over near a bank of TVs playing ESPN—but no one seemed to mind, what with the pain, what with the unholy unfairness of their loss.

At least that was how it had appeared to Bobby. He'd sunk into the plastic banquette—drunk since noon—and knew he was beyond dislodging, crying and downing Bud. He was three weeks from Kuwait and then he would be down-range from those evil Iraqi fuckers and he sensed how tightly he scratched against the hard eyewall of the storm: there would be rage, and then quiet, and then his world would fly apart.

They were back in the motel parking lot when Donny got into it with a biker. Donny defending poor dead Earnhardt's honor when the man pulled a switch-blade from some hidden pocket and Donny hit the man so fast it seemed not to have happened. Then again and again, the man unconscious on the ground, a hairless side of beef with blood running through his nostrils and over the iron bolt fastened there.

Lawtey put him less in mind of the firebases in Afghanistan than of high school. Low cinder block buildings painted a piss-pale institutional yellow. A lot of un-happy people milling around the gate. Of course there had been no razor wire at his high school. Some mean-ass kids who probably could have used it, but no wire. Here there was roll after roll tangled along the chain-link that bowed inward as if shouldering an unbearable weight. It was the only soft shape to be found.

The land flatter than Georgia. The highway a plumb line of hot macadam. The slash-pines in ordered rows. He didn't see any gun-towers but knew somewhere men were watching.

The gate buzzed and he swung it open, walked to a folding table where a man in khakis and a Florida DOC hat sat with a clipboard and a Guardian hand wand. Early fifties, Bobby guessed. A patchy beard and eyes closing down in the corners. He gave the man his name and emptied his pockets, took off his belt buckle and walked through a metal detector. The man handed him what appeared to be a small pager with a large gray button in the center.

"Clip it to your waist," the man said. "There's a little clasp there on the back."

"Panic button?"

"Something happens hold it down for three seconds. Somebody'll come running."

"I'm just here to pick up my brother."

The man looked up from. "You Donny Rosen's brother?"

"That's me."

"I'll be dogged." The man almost laughed. "Good luck to you, buddy."

He left his driver's license at the control room and was escorted by a large black woman to a small sterile room. A metal table and chairs. An empty water cooler beneath a wire-grid ventilation fan. The bulletin board was tacked with fliers for worker's comp and third-hand camper shells.

"I'm gonna lock this behind me," she said, "but you need anything you just knock. He's been out-processing all week. It'll be a little while yet, but we'll bring him in here as soon as we can."

"Yes, ma'am."

She looked at him as if she didn't quite trust him. "There are some things you'll need to sign."

Sometime later the woman came back in carrying a cardboard box.

"His personal effects." She dropped the box in front of him. "You can sign for em good as him."

When she was gone Bobby removed the lid. Ragged Nike running shoes. A Braves ball cap. A t-shirt gone yellow with mildew. Donny's wallet—his license had expired. Donny's blue jeans—the Daytona International Speedway ticket stub was still in the pocket, folded around an illegible receipt from the Hooters. A time capsule on that night. And not a thing worth saving.

A little while later his brother came in wearing blue scrubs, his name and DOC number blanched off the front. He looked older, wizened, skin browned and smelling of sunblock. When he smiled—he was smacking bubblegum, smiling and smacking orange bubblegum—Bobby saw he was missing two incisors.

Finally looked like the pirate he'd always been. He signed three forms—his official release, his parole agreement, some bullshit waiver—and a half hour later they were in the parking lot, not speaking until Donny took two cold ones from the cooler and passed one to his brother.

"Happy birthday to me," Donny said. He popped the cap and sipped off the foam. Through the wire they could see the desk sergeant watching them, hands clawed through the links like a kid at a playground.

"Should we do this elsewhere?" Bobby asked.

Donny shook his head. "They ain't saying nothing. They're happy to see me go."

"He keeps looking over this way."

"They wouldn't have me back." He raised his beer. "This ain't even a misdemeanor in my book."

He downed it in one slow swallow and when it was gone gasped and wiped his mouth on the back of one hand. "I appreciate you coming down for me," he said, "but you know I can't go straight home."

"Mamma's looking for us."

"I hear you, but that don't change nothing."

"How do you mean?"

"I mean you just can't go from one to the other like that. You get edgy. You need a little in between."

Bobby looked back at the wire and off at the empty highway. "I think she's planning some sort of welcome home for you."

"She tell you that?"

"She kind of hinted around."

Donny nodded. "I just need one night," he said. "You could call her or something. You got any money on you?"

"A little."

Donny took another beer from the cooler. "Call her and ask her to wait one night." He opened the passenger side door. "Folks from church is all it'll be. I don't want to see them anyway."

They ate at a Taco Bell out near the interstate. His brother looking older and meaner by the minute.

"For the last six months I've just laid in my bunk and thought about today," Donny said. They were outside at a metal picnic table, cars stacked up by the on-ramp, a tour bus unloading in the parking lot. They were drinking forties but no one seemed to notice or care. "Then it gets here." He shrugged. "Shit turns out just like everything else." He pointed his burrito at the highway. "Let's head south for a little. What's the next town down?"

"Daytona, I guess."

"Scene of the crime. That'd be perfect, wouldn't it?"

When they were headed south Donny took his face from the window and looked at Bobby. He'd been snoozing since they pulled out, since Bobby had called their mother to tell her they wouldn't be in until tomorrow, nothing big, just a snag with the paperwork.

"So you're all the way out yourself now?" Donny said.

Bobby nodded.

"Mamma never said much in her letters." Donny with his eyes on the road, the forty clutched between his thighs. He had put on the old tennis shoes and jeans but left on the blue scrub top. Bobby was embarrassed he hadn't thought to bring him anything. "Talked about the church mostly. She went on about Marsha for a while till I told her to just forget it. But I never knew for sure if you were all the way out or not."

"I am."

"Honorable?"

"That's what the paper said."

A few miles later Donny spoke again: "Combat Tracker. That's the MOS, wasn't it?" He sipped the beer. I-95 a green wash. Billboards and fruit stands. Cut-rate tickets for theme parks. Neil Young's "After the Gold Rush" was on and Bobby remembered Donny playing it over and over growing up, maybe seventeen and the music vibrating through the walls. "I never understood how you could call a man that," Donny said, "and then he goes and *tracks* somebody in *combat* and they want to lock him up."

"It wasn't that simple."

"And to bring up all the Vegas shit. Like we had planned the thing from birth."

"It really wasn't simple at all."

"I never said it was simple. I just said I can't understand it." He turned in the seat and fumbled with the slide window. "Think I can reach that fifth? I meant to put it up here with us."

"We'll be in town in fifteen minutes."

He turned around in the seat. "You realize I haven't had liquor in almost eighteen hundred days. Had some nasty homebrew but nothing else. Liquor and women. I been dry on both counts."

They took the Ormond Beach exit and drove down A1-A, the highway clotted with traffic lights and families at crosswalks, arms full of babies and beach chairs. Late morning by the time they got a room at the Beachsider. Twenty-second floor. A balcony overlooking what you could see of the white sand though it was mostly just jeeps and pickups. Sun flashing off radio aerials. Folks plopped down with their coolers and umbrellas. Bobby took off his shoes and lay on one of the beds while Donny took a shower.

"I need to get some things," he said when he came out. He sat on the end of the bed and flipped on the TV. "Just maybe some jeans and a shirt. My underwear's all right."

"Get whatever you need."

"Look at this," Donny said. "The Spice Channel. I tell you some cat inside figured out how to rewire something or other and we had it going for maybe three days before they caught on? Every con in the joint packed into that sweaty little box." He shook his head and killed the power. "If you can float me I'll hit you back as soon as we get home."

Bobby pointed to the dresser. "My wallet's right there. Take what you need."

"I'll hit you back as soon as we get home. I got some money coming my way."

He watched his brother count several bills, twenty, maybe thirty dollars.

"Take—" Bobby said, and watched him leave the bills on the dresser and slide the entire wallet into his pocket. When the door shut Bobby closed his eyes. He had about four hundred dollars on him after paying for the room. Four hundred dollars and a Visa that may or may not be canceled by now. He didn't care. His only brother. Bobby had a job managing a giant pine plantation called the Farmton Tract. It didn't pay much but it paid in cash. He could withstand the loss.

He went into the bathroom, pissed and swallowed the vitamins he carried everywhere. A multi, Omega-3, B-complex. A plastic spoon of granulated creatine chased with tap water. Closed the bulk curtains and shut his eyes. Could feel the creatine between his teeth, the grit. He slid his tongue along his gums. His notebook was on the nightstand but he didn't bother opening it, just lay there, tongue working the warm space of his mouth. Atrocity, he remembered, is defined as 1. atrocious behavior or condition; brutality, cruelty, etc. 2. an atrocious act. And 3.—the one he thought of the most, the one he thought of right now—a very displeasing or tasteless thing.

When he woke it was almost one and Donny still wasn't back. Bobby was itchy and hot but lay there a moment longer, tried to sort the dream that was already fading. It was Nancy, he was sure of that much. Nancy that first time together, the way she looked at him, those liquid brown eyes rolling over his face, mouth twitching with the slightest hint of amusement.

Who is this man?

He was stationed at Camp Merrill in north Georgia and on their first date they took a canoe down the Chattooga in the middle of a drought—his idea, a terrible idea—and he remembered the way she looked at him after they dragged the sixteen-foot Old Town over the riverbed and were drifting in the warm waning light, the sun sinking slowly into the long evening, that languid sensuality as they floated past Russell Bridge. The day was hot and heady with the smell of laurel and jasmine and they kept having to stop to pull the canoe through broad shoals of egg-shell rock. But it was worth it to glide atop the deep pools, the surface a gauzy green and dusted with pollen. Bobby in the back and Nancy reclined into him, her head in his lap and bare feet on the gunwales. Her bathing suit was blue and clung to her stomach and when he took his face from her hair Bobby could see into the dark hollow between her breasts. They took out at Earl's Ford and wound up making love on a stack of life vests in the bed of his pickup, calves sandy, shoulders pink with the first blush of sunburn, alone in the graveled parking lot while above the sun slid west, slow as an hour hand.

The rest came quickly. They married and bought the house in Fayetteville between his deployments to Colombia and East Timor, their wedding reception at a white-columned inn, a colossal birthday cake screened from the highway by staggered rows of Eastern Hemlock. Bobby in his dress uniform. Nancy in her mother's A-line with its brocade corset and long train that spilled behind them as they hurried down the front steps beneath an arch of swords.

He put his hand beneath the sheets and slipped it into his boxers, held himself, thought of Nancy and waited. It scared him how monogamous he had been, all around him men and women hooking up in barracks or at resupply posts. Bagram one giant swingers club. The Green Zone even worse. Eating in a KBR cafeteria before screwing some leggy second lieutenant in a back room at the motor pool. Body armor and a box of Trojans—he knew men who wouldn't take two steps without both. But he hadn't even looked, let alone touched, and wondered now if that had been his undoing, his failure to adapt. He gave himself a few soft tugs. When he fantasized it had been some incarnation of Nancy, Nancy younger or Nancy older, Nancy that summer they spent a week on the Outer Banks. Nancy the weekend they got snowed under in Gatlinburg, just the two of them and a big jug of red wine. But to hell with it. He took his hand away and opened his eyes. He could lie here all day and didn't think it would happen.

He got dressed and drank down what was left of the Ripped Fuel, found a gym in the phone book and started walking up Beach Street past several surf shops. Farther along the street devolved into a wino seediness, better than half the stores shuttered, a shopping cart rusted on the curb beneath a sign marked NO PANHANDLING. Brown-bagged parking meters and trash that had blown against the boarded front of what had once been a beauty supply store. But it looked like a good gym, windowless and constructed from cinder blocks. The silhouette of a boxer crouched beside cursive script that read *Olunsky's Boxing and Fitness Emporium.*

Bobby hadn't been in a gym in years. He still hit the heavy bag in his shed at home or out at the Farmtown tract, but somehow the gym was different, something about standing there, hands taped and gloved—it felt like coming home. He and Donny had grown up boxing. Donny was the one with the talent but Bobby had stayed with it. He knew now he shouldn't have. He was a patient and skilled practitioner, but that didn't mean he could fight. He boxed his way through Golden Gloves mostly on guts, slipping through the lower rounds only to lose some bloody decision at another obscure regional championship in Jacksonville or Savannah. But he had never quit, and by twenty he and Donny were living in the Palm in Vegas, fighting Saturday night undercards for five large.

Bobby was lean and small-fisted but he was also a gym-rat, gorging on eighteen-mile runs and three-hour weightlifting sessions. Manny Almodovar had trained them before Manny's Parkinson got bad and Manny had a conditioning circuit he ran his boys through called 'The Gauntlet.' Most fighters made it through two, maybe three times if they were particularly badass. Bobby ran The Gauntlet eight times and was on his way to number nine when he simply keeled over. This fantastically muscled body lying on the rubberized floor, twitching. Manny told him later it was like watching a horse die.

But intangibles can only float a fighter so far, and eventually it turned, just as Bobby had known it would. By twenty-one he was getting routinely knocked out. By twenty-two he was sliding toward complete obscurity. He took a bad beating one night against a left-handed Mexican and finally had the good sense to walk away. Donny agreed but wanted one last hurrah. The fight against the Puerto Rican was supposed to be it, a sort of rear-guard action, a last payday before he followed his big brother back home to Georgia. But the Puerto Rican wasn't supposed to be seventeen, and he wasn't supposed to be as lithe as a fawn. And Donny most definitely wasn't supposed to kill him. But it happened because, as Manny told him, that kind of bad energy is always everywhere around us, lurking. Donny had just been unlucky. He didn't mention the kid. Then everybody went home to try and pretend like nothing had happened.

What had followed in Iraq—Bobby was always thinking of the similarity in age, the same dusty skin glossed with sweat—had proven that it wasn't so much bad luck as the mean edge of the universe, the certainty that violence would always and forever hang about him and his brother. An ugly avenging angel, but avenging what he guessed he would never know.

He hit the bags for maybe an hour, skipped rope and locked his feet into the sit-up board. It was almost three when he got back to the room. He showered and was back on the bed when Donny came in carrying a brown grocery sack and a shopping bag from TJ Max.

"I got some needed shit," Donny said, and took out a bottle of Wild Turkey and a Ziploc of pills. "Met a girl, too."

"You got something on you."

Donny looked at his shirt front. "Blood."

"Yours?"

"Hell, no."

He changed in the bathroom and went up the hall to fill the ice bucket, came back and topped two plastic cups with Wild Turkey and ice. He handed Bobby a cup.

"This is the official cheers right here."

"What are we toasting?"

"Everything," Donny said. "Me getting out. You moving on." He raised his cup. "This is to us getting over things." He drank and dumped the plastic baggie on the bed. Xanax and Oxy 30s, Percocet and Celebrex. A few others Bobby couldn't identify.

"Now," he said, "let me tell you about this girl."

The girl had dropped out of Flagler College and danced at a club called Soft Tails. Twenty-one, maybe twenty-two. Half Seminole. Her family wealthy horse people up near Ocala. They were meeting her that evening but Donny wanted some food first, some by God real food. They passed the Speedway and drove a few miles to a steakhouse he had heard about. An old mafia joint where Capone was said to have stopped on his way back and forth to Miami. The building a white stucco monolith with a wide picture window along the back wall overlooking the Tomoka River. But no sign out front, no tourists. Just grass-fed Wagyu beef and a six-page wine list. They sat at a table and drank Johnnie Walker on the rocks.

"I need to get a cell phone," Donny said. "I saw a Verizon place back up the highway."

"How much of that money's left?"

"Look here." Donny turned his arm over to reveal a number scrawled in Sharpie. "She remembered to include the area code, just in case, I guess."

"This the girl?"

"Kristen. You'll like her."

Their steaks came and they ate quietly, alone in the dark cavernous space, the restaurant seemingly abandoned but for a single elderly waiter and several ferns sprawling out of brass planters.

"Mamma wasn't upset when you called her?" Donny asked.

"She was all right. Worried but all right."

"What've people said about it? Me coming home."

"They're glad of it. They think you got railroaded."

"I'm sure there's plenty that aren't so pleased."

"The ones I talk to are glad of it."

"Except I heard you don't talk to anybody anymore."

Bobby didn't say anything.

"I'm not accusing," Donny said. "There ain't a soul I'd bother talking to either."

They drove to a strip mall where Donny bought a cell phone. Bobby paid while Donny took the phone into the bathroom. They were getting in the truck when a message came in.

"That's my girl," Donny said.

He held up the picture of blurred flesh and smiled.

"What'd you send her?"

"What do you think I sent her? These kids know how to reciprocate."

It was twilight by the time they arrived at the club, still early, the place empty and over-lit, the music quiet. A man kept walking onstage and gesturing for the lights to be raised or lowered. They sat at the bar and drank Jack and Cokes with several old men with comb-overs and boat-shoes, Donny's fingers jumping as the volume gradually increased. Bobby watched his brother's hands. His own hands throbbed and he clutched them in his lap as if they were warm animals, nearly-slain doves dying slowly, each in quiet possession of its own hurt. It was something he had come to accept, the pain, but tonight it was somehow worse. He realized all he wanted was to go back to the hotel.

"She ain't here," Bobby said.

"Give it time, brother."

"You all right?"

Donny switched his eyes from the door to the stage and back to the door, fished through a bowl of mixed nuts on the bar. "What's that?"

"Whose blood was that on your shirt?"

Donny smiled and shook his head, motioned for two more drinks. "How's little Bobby? I bet Nancy keeps him on a pretty short leash?" He laughed. "Both of you, I bet."

"He's doing all right. Seven years old. Will be on his birthday."

"Seven years old. Goddamn." He took a cashew from the bowl. "I heard Marsha's boy Stephen is dying. Some blood disease or something."

"He's pretty bad off. Some people claim he has these visions."

"Is he dying?"

"I haven't seen him in a long time. I don't think he's doing any good."

"Well, I tell you this, when we get back ain't neither of us going round there. Me and you, we got the death touch. Everything we lay hands on turns to shit."

A few minutes later the house lights went down. The place was filling up, dancers beginning to circulate. Young women in platform shoes and sheer dresses sat in laps or made the rounds with serving trays. One girl with a leg twined around a man's waist, a braceleted arm hooked around his head, finger stroking his hairy ear. A dancer came on stage. Smoke and lights and more noise. The room was cold—it suddenly occurred to Bobby how cold the room was.

"The fuck's wrong with you?" Donny asked.

"What?"

"Something wrong with your hands?"

"I'm all right. They just hurt."

Donny reached into his pocket and came out with a pill. "Take this."

"I'm all right."

"Didn't you just say your hands hurt?" Donny asked. "That's only a 30. Don't be so damn stubborn."

"I knew a fella at Bragg took a couple one night and never woke up."

"So because some asshole went and ODed you won't ease your own suffering?" Donny put the pill between his teeth, lifted his drink and swallowed. He looked for the bartender. "We both need us a Jager-bomb."

A little after ten Donny got another text.

"She's going to pick us up out front. Just leave your truck and we'll pick it up in the morning. We're going to Pound Town tonight."

She met them out front in a green Jeep, three girls, loud and drunk, and they piled in—Donny in the front, Bobby wedged in the back—and went wailing up the highway, drinking bottled Sangria and tossing the empties onto the shoulder, the stereo cranked.

"So what exactly were you two gentlemen doing in there?" the driver— Kristen, Bobby guessed—asked.

"Enjoying the sights," Donny said.

"That place is sketch."

"Like coochie city," said one of the girls beside Bobby.

They crossed the intra-coastal waterway, the bridge a span of humped concrete and decorative tiles fashioned in the shapes of leaping dolphins, the land ahead a scatter of light, beyond that the dark ocean, a few harbor buoys winking. Bobby couldn't get a good look at anyone until they pulled into the marina. They all three appeared in their late teens—better than a decade younger than Bobby. Kristen was tall and cinnamon in bikini bottoms and a yellow swim-shirt, the neoprene tight enough to flatten her breasts across her chest. Several piercings in her upper ear. The other girls were plainer through attractive, pale skin, bleached hair. Kristen introduced them: Jeanne and Destiny. They grabbed towels and Donny hefted a cooler. Kristen was already hanging all over him, kissing his neck, laughing.

Down near the dock they met two large Cuban men, older than the girls but younger than Bobby and Donny. One immediately began to wave his hands in front of him, palms down, as if signaling an incomplete pass.

"No way," he said. "No fucking way, girl. The boat won't hold that many."

"Oh, come on, Sami."

"Can't do it. What's the word I'm looking for? It won't—What's the word?"

"Displace," said the other Cuban.

"It won't displace that much weight."

"Then I guess we're leaving you two fat boys on the dock."

Donny pushed past the men and threw his shoes into the boat. "We balling now, baby." He cupped his hands around his mouth. "Fuck you, Daytona!"

"You in New Smyrna, dog," Sami said.

"Well, fuck New Smyrna and fuck you too."

Sami shook his head and stepped toward Bobby. "I'm cutting your boy some slack, but I don't mean to take his shit all night. He might want to cool out."

"I got you."

"I know Kristen say he just got cut loose and all, but he still might want to dial it down."

A few minutes later they pulled out, all seven of them and the Boston Whaler riding low and slow past signs reading NO WAKE. Across the water was a seafood restaurant with flashing neon lobster claws that opened and closed. Bobby could see people moving along the broad deck. A band was playing and the sound carried loud but unintelligible. Sami drove and the other man—they weren't Cuban, Bobby realized; he wasn't sure what they were—stood beside him pouting and smoking a joint.

Bobby was in the back, seated between Jeanne and Destiny, the warm flesh of their thighs pressed against his jeans. They sped up and slowed again in a narrow channel. Houses and dock lights. Lawns right down to the cochina seawall where boats waited, tarped and raised on hydraulic lifts. He listened: the voices of children, folks moving inside screened porches. Bug lights. The steady chug of a sprinkler. Families: entire lives that were not his. The joint made a round, another, Bobby holding the smoke like a mercy, longer than he thought possible while Kristen yelled at Sami to go faster and eventually he pointed a flashlight out over the water and onto the sleek back of the manatee that swam alongside.

Donny put something in Bobby's hand. The other Oxy.

"Don't fuck up our night together," he said. "Don't let it be like always."

Bobby swallowed it with his beer. He could smell the girl beside him, her strawberry shampoo, and it was something about realizing how long since he had sat this close to a woman, something about the glossy manatee traveling beside them as if in blessing.

Don't fuck up our night together.

Past the houses the channel opened into the backwater and the boat nosed up. The night air was warm and thick. Moonlight broke in the fold of their wake. They motored for another ten minutes and branched into a narrow channel where they idled toward a spit of sand. Sami cut the throttle and the second man jumped onto the beach and pulled the anchor line. The night suddenly quiet. The water like blood, warm and viscous, salt beading on the skin. Donny carried the cooler ashore and Sami dragged driftwood into a pile, lit a starter log beneath it. Long dancing shadows stretched over the water, the smell of woodsmoke, music from a tiny speaker. The three-quarters moon in and out of the high cirrus.

Bobby watched in merciful confusion. Inside the pill there was little sense. The gauze of Bobby's brain. It was not uncomfortable. More like familiar: the state he had occupied since his discharge. The trance of days. The job out at the Farmton tract. The absent family. The dry rot eating his heart.

He lay on the sand with his feet up and his head propped on his hands, the tide running in and out so that his heels sank deeper. He could hear them laughing and dancing, drinking and running around the fire that was now a small blaze. Visible from space, he thought. Not the glow but his own perdition. He wondered for a moment what his mother thought. Her two boys violent men. The ruined apples of her eye. It was always Donny who had excelled. Donny who got the girls. Donny with the genius IQ who could've made all As and gone to Harvard if only he would apply himself, Mrs. Rosen. If only he would listen. But he would never listen. That was Donny's undoing. Bobby's undoing was that he had listened too well. To his father and the men at the gym and later to Manny out in Vegas. To the drill sergeants and company commanders and finally to a puny PFC who, in the bright wonder of an RPG blast—a street in Sadr City strewn with plaster and destroyed fruit and, right there on the goddamn cobblestones, an entire human leg—had watched a boy flee from the chaos and screamed: *somebody kill that motherfucker.* It was Bobby who had chased him down and done it.

He raised himself onto his elbows and looked out at the dark water, something stirring there, the manatee, he thought. Then he saw the dorsal fin break. A dolphin maybe fifteen feet offshore. He climbed onto all fours and stood, staggered into the water. Toes into the warm muck. Jeans wet plaster. No matter. He wanted to touch it. He thought if he could only touch it there might be not revelation but light. He put his hands out and waded, thigh-deep, waist, chest. The dolphin appeared untroubled. Playful. Breaking the surface and diving, breaking and diving. He would go home and tell his boy about this, little Bobby, still small enough to marvel at the world.

He reached but it slipped past him, dove. He turned to follow it when something hit him from behind and he staggered forward, collapsed beneath the water. He twisted, but it clung to him. He rose up gasping. The girl. One of the girls laughing into his neck with her legs around his waist. She slid off and he stood near the rear of the boat, gagging. Around them a rainbow of spilled gasoline spiraled from the outboard. She moved against him and kissed him and he pulled back to spit seawater.

"Come here," she said, whispering, her hands on him, her mouth.

He moved again and she came forward and finally he pushed her back and she fell into the surf and was no longer laughing but screaming at him. *What's wrong with you? What the fuck is wrong with you?* He didn't know. He realized he was sweating. Standing waist deep and sweating and surely this was not right. She screamed again and he watched her go up the beach, wringing out her hair and twisting her hips. When she neared the fire he thought she was naked but couldn't be certain. All that shimmer. All that shine.

He settled back onto the sand. It was okay now. He knew he would see things through, though it scared him to think of how far he was from morning, how distant from daybreak. But that was the pill. Knew a fella at Bragg took a couple one night and never woke up. Which was true. Knew a lot of fellas at Bragg that never woke up. But don't fuck up our night together.

He slept then, or slipped inside the walls of sleep. When he woke Donny was on the sand beside him, a bottle of something in one hand. He waved a finger in front of Bobby. The finger sheathed with what appeared to be a used condom.

"That's kind of a dick move, ain't it?" Donny said. "Going after my girl's girl."

"She almost drowned me."

"Big boy like you?"

"Scared the shit out of me. Dynasty."

"Destiny."

Bobby sat up. "She all right?"

"She bitched for a while then passed out." He took a hit off the bottle and passed it to Bobby. Southern Comfort. "Get some of this."

Bobby took the bottle and drank. "What the hell are we doing here?"

"Having the night of our lives. Celebrating my getting out. At least when you're not assaulting the talent."

"I mean with them."

"Oh, you mean what are *they* doing with *us?* It's the novelty, man. On the beach with an ex-con. The sensitive dark-eyed beauty."

"Kristen's more like seventeen."

"She wants to look into my damaged soul. She wants to heal me. Listen to what she told me: Call this a bamboo cane, and you have entered my trap. Do not call it a bamboo cane, and you fall into error. What do you call it?"

"You always were lucky with the girls."

"Mamma always loved me more. That's my thinking right now."

"What about later?" Bobby asked.

"There is no later as far as I'm concerned. Later's just the next thing down the line."

"You didn't learn a thing inside, did you?"

"No, I most certainly did not. Pride myself on that." Donny pointed the bottle at the moon. "Actually one thing I learned inside—you'll appreciate this— it's that you can't learn a thing. You don't step in the shit twice. You know what I'm saying? It just rolls past. The first time I got the shit kicked out of me—wolf-packed outside the laundry room. I knew it was coming. Been looking over my shoulder for three straight days and all of a sudden they're on me and I'm right there with my face against the drain and I can feel a tooth come loose and all this blood in my mouth, you know. I kept thinking: it's happening; this is it right here." He shook his head. "But then later—I don't know—it was just gone, the whole thing. And what did I know? I couldn't even tell you what it felt like. So later I'm thinking about it and some guy, I hear him say to somebody else, this is real, this is fucking real. And I thought: no, it ain't. This ain't real. Ain't nothing real. You ever feel like that?"

"I don't know."

"I suspect it's a lot of the same shit over there. You get bored. Sitting around waiting for something bad to happen. But then when something good happens."

"It's like it's the sweetest thing in the whole world."

"It's like you didn't even know sweet before, like you couldn't even taste it. And then it's fucked up but you start to think: maybe it's worth it, all the shit for that one little taste." He flung the condom into the water. "You ever think it was worth it?"

"I don't know," Bobby said. "Maybe sometimes."

Donny seemed not to hear. "I want you to look up at the sky. You looking?"

"Fuck you."

"Man, I'm serious. Look up there. In a few days Mercury and Venus will line up with the moon. We won't ever see it like that again in our lives."

Bobby said nothing.

"You know what we should do, man?" Donny said. "We should plan something epic. I mean pack up, get a bottle of Jack and some good weed and just go cross-country with it. I'd like to see the desert. I want to see the desert again before I die."

"I don't know."

"Why not, man? Name me one thing that's tying you down?"

"Work."

"Work?" Donny shook his head. "I heard you were sitting out watching trees grow. Listen to me. Kristen said she'd go with us. She's going up to see her folks in Ocala. They've got some friends in Arizona. Supposedly got this house up on a mountain we could stay at. She said we could just pick her up."

"We got families."

"We got ex-fucking-wives is what we got. And let me tell you this: I don't want a family any more than I want a wife. It all came to me inside. Domesticity, man. It tethers you to this awful mediocrity. Without wives men would either be great or terrible but with them we're just all of us some kind of nothing. Just plain. It's no wonder you ran off to war. You get a wife and a house and a kid and pretty soon you're just drowning in that daily bullshit. No, sir. No, thank you."

He raised the bottle but it was empty now, passed it to Bobby as if for confirmation.

"I could see us out there on the open road," Donny said, "just pure velocity. A white streak down the highway. We could blow up the universe."

Bobby laughed. "You're gonna wind up in hell, Donny. We both are."

"Shit," his brother said. "We ain't going to hell. We're in hell."

PART THREE

AROUND THE TIME ALAN WAS TRUDGING through "Judgment Swamp" and embracing the *thisness* of his life, Lucy Redding's father caught her masturbating. Actually, not caught. Walked in on her. In truth, she doubted he'd seen a thing. He was like that these days. Zombie-dad, Lucy's sister Katie called him, stumbling glassy-eyed through the kitchen, brain mummified by the two hour commute to Tampa. I-4 to the Lee Roy Selmon Expressway on into MacDill Air Force Base where he did things she wasn't sure she wanted to think about.

That was her father, Luther Redding.

Alan was Alan Holman, and the more she thought about it, the more Lucy was able to convince herself that he was her boyfriend, and not just some random guy who was more or less ordered by the court to attend youth group. Alan had spent three months at the Canebrake Wilderness School for At-Risk Youth. This after Pre-Trial Intervention. Which came after the arraignment. Which came after the arrest. Which came, of course, after the fire. A green Dumpster loaded with cardboard that had somehow floated onto the roof of the Kissimmee Baptist Church. He had told her all about it that Wednesday night in June when he arrived at the "Soldiers for Christ" end of school cook-out in the company of a small Asian man who, it turned out, happened to be a Buddhist monk at the Dhammaram Temple just up Highway 11 in Deleon Springs. Alan's mother had—as his grandmother put it—lit out for parts unknown just before Alan was released. But apparently she had once been a fateful devotee of the Temple and it had fallen to Brother Vin to oversee Alan's transition back into the world. Which involved Brother Vin dropping Alan off at the nearest church he could find.

Lucy learned all of this sitting on the swings on the playground behind the church. It was after ten and the cook-out had broken up over an hour ago. The fellowship hall was clean and the parking lot empty, but Lucy had a reputation for sticking around the church after hours, doing whatever useful thing she could, and knew her mom wouldn't question her so long as she came home on the near side of midnight. So she and Alan sat in the swings and let their shoes drag in the sand.

It was a warm night, strangely dark, the moon having not yet risen. But she could see Alan's face if she leaned close enough, and there was something in the soft hum of his voice that had her leaning in a way she never really had before, not successfully, at least. Lucy had finished her first year at Jacksonville Bible Institute as chaste as expected. After that had been three weeks working as a counselor at an evangelical summer camp in Michigan where she had fallen for a boy from Taylor University. She must have been too obvious in her affections though, because one night as they circled the mirrored lake with its canoes and roped-and-buoyed swimming area—one night when Lucy was convinced he was going to kiss her— he had led her to an outcropping of rocks where he had bent toward her and gave her not his mouth but a copy of Thomas à Kempis' *The Imitation of Christ.*

When she started to cry he had hugged her, thinking her ashamed. But what poured through her was anger, anger not at the boy—she could see him now, stoop-shouldered and self-righteous and wholly unworthy—but at herself for having fallen for him. She'd kept her distance for the next three days and on the last day, when he reached again to hug her, felt herself go limp. The anger—and some shame, she had to admit it had become tinged with shame—lasted until a delay at the Detroit airport kept her at the gate for three hours and she actually started to read the à Kempis. She had barely finished the sentence *this is the highest wisdom: through contempt of the world to aspire to the kingdom of heaven* before she realized what a great favor the boy had done her, how her own barreling emotions had led her not to carnal pleasure but something far greater: the possibility of transcending a self she had come to loathe with great precision.

But all of that was absent the night she sat opposite Alan, both of them twist- ing the chains until they wound tight and let the swings spin wildly. They both giggled, Alan actually giggled, and she thought giggling at something as silly and sweet as winding a swing was the sign of a boy who might actually have the sen- sitivity not to attempt some form of public humiliation. They talked and talked, Alan about his friend Twitch—Alan considered him his spirit brother and stayed with him now and then, and later would write Twitch's number inside the back flap of Lucy's book—and his time at the Wilderness Camp, about his mother moving to Taos with one of her hippie boyfriends who sold bales of Haitian ganja so that Alan was left living with his grandmother, about those final thirty-six hours he had spent crawling and wading his way through the mosquitoes and muck of "Judgment Swamp," and how, when he had emerged, they had hosed him down, baptized him in a blue plastic kiddie pool shaped like a starfish, and declared him a new man, fit for the world.

Lucy talked about her family. For the last three years she had witnessed their collapse scarily mirror that of the nation. Her dad lost his job as an airline pilot right about the time his real estate investments collapsed. After that, her parents spent six months clawing at financial stability and, when that had been achieved, drifted into separate lives, her father going back to work for the Air Force, her mother turning herself into a middle-aged fitness queen. She watched them touch and not touch, and suspected her mother had never much cared to make love to her father. Not that her mother was particularly disinterested in her husband. It seemed to Lucy it was the act itself that summoned her distaste, as if the body should be held in reserve for more precise pursuits, as if Pamela was too much the *specimen* to engage in something so common. So, Lucy had told Alan, the woman she saw now—this cool, indifferent thing—wasn't a new person but the person her mother had always been. Of course, Lucy didn't want to think about such things. But she'd come late in life to so much it sometimes seemed she would be forever catching up, all her life the slow articulation of what should've been intuitive and never voiced. Which was perhaps why she had been so ill-prepared for her first year at JBI, largely incapable of functioning outside the Redding bell-jar. In high school they had called her Franny, as in *Franny and Zoey* which they read in tenth grade IB English. Franny the Jesus girl. A label for everyone, which was fine, really, honestly, it was, God was no respecter of persons. Yet she'd somehow carried it with her to college, the name, the reputation.

But at least that was over, though it did leave Lucy at home with her younger sister Katie the-great. Katie had a long history of turning the head of whatever boy might have taken shy interest in Lucy, but now Katie had decided she was going to Smith to become a lesbian anarchist or something equally ridiculous. Weekends when she told their mom she was sleeping over with friends, she was actually camping in downtown Orlando in a stinky nylon tent with a bunch of lazy hippies. If she wasn't physically there she was strategizing on an online discussion board. This was a constant source of tension between them, Katie insisting that if Lucy-the-good took seriously the Jesus she was always spouting off about then she would be out there camping too, trying to—in Katie's words—catalyze meaningful structural change. But the truth was that Lucy never spouted off about Jesus or anything else. She hardly even spoke. The reality of which seemed to goad her sister to ever greater heights of fury. And now they were home together for the next two months.

"I don't know how we get through it," Lucy had told Alan that night in the swings, and Alan leaned forward, nodding—listening, he had actually listened to her—touched her cheek, and kissed her.

In the weeks since they had seen each other almost every day, at youth group, or riding together to the mall, or ferrying Alan—his license was suspended until Christmas if you could possibly fathom how unfair that was—to the Dhammaram

73

Temple where he cut the grass and picked up trash along the highway, serving out his two hundred hours of court-ordered community service. Lucy had continued to read *The Imitation of Christ* but lately found she was less inclined to scorn her body than touch it.

Which was what had happened the day her father opened her door, stared for a moment at the shape beneath the covers otherwise known as Lucy, and then, just as abruptly, lumbered out. That had been an isolated incident but now, not so much. She and Alan had gone from kissing to touching—groping, the RAs at school had called it, heavy petting—and the strange thing was, the closer she had become to Alan, the more she had allowed him to run his hands over her clothes and, just once, beneath her t-shirt to cup her left breast, the closer she had drawn to God, as if admitting to the existence of her physical body had granted her greater access to Christ's mystical body. Or maybe that was just the à Kempis talking. Either way today, this beautiful day, this day the Lord hath made, she intended to allow Alan not just to touch her but to enter her. Her mother was going away for the weekend to a yoga retreat and Katie would be back at the Occupy camp in Orlando. So the house would be empty, no need to rush, no need to hide. Lucy would come to *know* him, Biblically speaking, and it would be very traditional and very beautiful and it would happen here in the very bed where she currently lay.

She would dress in the long nightgown her mother had given her on her seventeenth birthday—it was practically new, Lucy having been too embarrassed to carry something so delicately wrought to a college that offered its "outreach" classes in a strip mall—and take Alan by the hand, bring him up the stairs and undress him. A slow seduction offered in the sight of God, with none of the debasement she'd heard other girls talk about, the ripped anuses and hemorrhoids. Every student at JBI took a purity pledge that was remarkably anatomical, a pledge to keep inviolate their vaginal chambers. But—as so many girls were quick to point out—there were ways to adhere to the letter of the law while still having a good time. Except sometimes a good time wasn't so good and they wound up carrying a sister in Christ to the E.R. because she just couldn't quit bleeding out of her ass.

Lucy wanted none of that. She was a pillar in the Soldiers for Christ youth group and today the entire group was making its annual trip to the Holy Land Experience off Conroy Road and out near the Ikea. The Holy Land was a sort of biblical theme park—a little kitschy, maybe even a little exploitative—but Lucy had been going every summer since she was a girl and was excited to take Alan. That it mattered to Alan, that it made an impact on him, had become very important. One of the things drilled in the heads of the girls at JBI—but, funny, never in the heads of the boys—was that you should never date anyone you couldn't see yourself marrying. She knew she was getting ahead of herself—was dating what they were actually doing?—but she couldn't help peeking a little too far down that road, Lucy and Alan on their wedding day, Lucy and Alan with two babies (boys—she'd had her fill of sisters), Lucy and Alan in long and lovely decline.

But it couldn't happen if he wasn't a Christian. She might have abandoned quite a few of her standards in the last month but his faith was non-negotiable, and as of right now she didn't know where he stood.

She rolled onto her back and let her hands rest against her stomach.

One: he was always around the church. Maybe that was faith or maybe that was his desire to be around her. (Win-win, she thought.)

Two: he bowed his head during prayer and she had even caught him once moving his lips. (But think about peer pressure, Lucy—*everyone* bowed their heads. She couldn't even begin to count this one.)

Three: except there was no three. That was all she had, which, to be honest, was nothing. What she did know—and this might well be enough to cancel the rest right out—was that she had faith enough for both of them, and what she believed was that two things would happen today: Alan would answer the altar call at the four o'clock We Shall Behold Him! service that would crown their visit, and she would bring her reborn boyfriend home and make love to him.

She kicked the covers from her body: Lucy Redding on her back in t-shirt and underwear, the ceiling fan whipping above her, cool air falling from the vent. Be perfectly still, she told herself. Feel this, let it wash over you. She breathed in and breathed out. *I would rather feel profound sorrow for my sins than be able to define the theological term for it.* À Kempis again, heavily underlined, heavily annotated. But what she felt was the body, her body, thrumming. And she sprang to her feet.

Her mother was in the kitchen drinking yerba mate and something she'd made in the Vitamix, almond milk, hemp protein, flax and chia seeds. She wore Lululemon yoga wear from head to toe, maybe three hundred dollars of enlightened apparel. Lucy loved her, but couldn't help but feel a little sick at how good she looked. The same coat-hanger frame as Katie, long and lightly muscled, all of it visible beneath the tight fabric. The air smelled of the apple cider vinegar she drank to maintain body PH. The *Sentinel* was spread on the table.

"I thought I was going to have to wake you," her mom said.

"Yeah," she said, and moved to the refrigerator where she took out a cup of Greek yogurt and a pitcher of water. She poured a glass and sat down.

"Big day, isn't it?" her mom asked. "Field trip, right?"

"We leave at eight-thirty."

"Well, I'm out the door any minute so you and your sister will have to walk over to the church. Tell Katie I left fresh greens in the crisper."

Lucy looked up from her yogurt. "Katie's going?"

"I was kind of surprised too. But don't let it upset you, honey."

"It doesn't upset me. I just—" Lucy shrugged and took another bite. "I just didn't know."

"Didn't know what?" a voice called, and Lucy didn't need to look to know her sister stood in the threshold behind her.

"That you had taken an interest in the Lord," her mom said. "Come here."

"The sweet lard Jesus," Katie said.

"This is what I'm talking about," Lucy said.

"Come here, honey."

"In the sweet sweet by-and-by."

"This is exactly what I'm talking about."

"Katie," said their mom. "Come here, please."

Katie bent dutifully to their mother who kissed the top of her head. Her sister was in Athena leggings and a midriff shirt, a younger more elastic version of their mother.

"Good morning, Pamela," Katie said.

"Good morning, dear. I was just telling your sister how you two will need to walk to the church this morning."

"Where's daddy?" Katie asked. "I thought he was supposed to be home last night sometime."

"Your father's still at work."

"Daddy's always at work," Lucy said.

"Because daddy's a criminal," Katie said. She stood at the counter while the coffee dripped.

Their mom looked up. "Katherine—"

"Sorry," Katie said. "Because daddy is engaged in illegal activities."

"That's enough for one morning."

She had her coffee now. "I don't mean to step on your Zen, mommy dearest, but flying a Reaper drone or whatever it's called ends with daddy spending his retirement in an eight-by-ten cell in The Hague."

"That is seriously enough, young lady."

Katie held the coffee pot toward Lucy. "Do you want any of this or not?"

"You can't wear that on the trip."

"I know I can't. Do you want any, yes or no?"

"I'm fine," Lucy said. "Naturally caffeinated."

"Naturally horny," Katie said.

Lucy felt her mouth fall open. "Excuse me?"

Their mom flattened the paper on the table with a gesture of finality. "I don't know what's wrong with you this morning," she said. "All I'm asking is that you let me walk out that door with a shred of sanity. So what exactly is the problem?"

Katie shrugged. "Nothing."

"And yet you insist on acting like this."

"I'm sorry," Katie said. "I'm just not awake."

But she was by the time they started up North Arlington and made the right onto Pennsylvania. It was no more than a half mile to the church but Lucy resented the fact she was made to walk it. She moved with what felt a terrestrial heaviness—you absolutely *lumber*, dear, her mother had once told her—while her sister seemed to flounce. A long-legged gazelle in straw flats and a tennis skirt. Lucy wore her skinny jeans and a paisley top, lipstick, eyeshadow—eyeshadow was more or less a new experience—and enough foundation to cover not only her face but the slightly pocked skin just below her throat. Childhood acne is an absolute *plague*—her mother again, and please God why did she have to keep hearing everything in her mother's voice? She was halfway to the Atlantic Center for Holistic Integration in Palm Beach by now. So let her be in Palm Beach, Lucy thought, not here, not with me. It was something that happened too often to Lucy: letting the idea of someone colonize her mind. For years she'd fabricated memories until they bled into dreams, an entire catalog of events that she felt almost certain had taken place between her and the grandfather who had died a couple of months before Lucy was born. She didn't need it today.

She was already preoccupied with all the ways Katie might conspire to ruin her day, laughter, derision, maybe—please, Jesus, no—a sudden burst of affection that would convince her to stage a girls-night-in. Lucy couldn't bear the thought of spending the evening with Katie on her bed, legs in the full lotus and toes in foam spacers. Let's color our hair. Let's do our nails. Let's crawl under the covers and pretend like we're six. The bursts of affection weren't unwanted, Lucy loved her sister, truly, and she knew that Katie loved her, but please God, not tonight. Any night but tonight.

They crossed Garfield, the church just three blocks ahead.

"I haven't been to the Holy Land in like six years," Katie said. "This is going to be so fun."

"It's not really that different."

"Still, I can't believe how excited I am."

"This is a serious trip for some people," Lucy said, a little harsher than she intended.

"I know that," Katie said. "You think everything's a joke to me? You think nothing's sacred?"

No, Lucy started to say, I don't, I'm sorry, but the words stuck, and by the time she could speak Katie was skipping down the sidewalk where just ahead Lucy could see the parking lot full of mini-vans and station wagons, a few kids lingering by the church doors, the bus marked FIRST EVANGELICAL LUTHERAN already idling. Then she felt her eyes slide to the playground. That night with Alan. How dark it had been back under the canopy of laurel oaks. The summer smell of jasmine and honeysuckle. The sound of a squirrel in the garbage broken by the occasional car gliding past on the highway. The entire earth empty, it felt, but for the two of them. But where was he this morning? She felt a catch of panic before she spotted him beside his grandmother and the youth pastor, a man not much older than them.

Lucy licked her lips and thumbed back her hair. She was wearing one of her mother's expensive push-up bras, and okay, so that was embarrassing and she'd hardly been able to think about it as she walked over, but she was glad for it now. She wasn't dumpy-frumpy loose Lucy anymore. Besides Alan and the youth pastor, Pastor Jeff, in his Buddy Holly glasses and HE CARRIED OUR PAIN tattoo, she was older than anyone else on the trip. She was an adult. She looked like an adult. She licked her lips again just as Alan caught sight and gave her what had to be the sliest wink ever.

She loved the youth group kids and there had been moments at JBI where she had missed them more than her own family. Unassuming baseball-playing thirteen year old boys. Eighth grade girls in short-shorts and Justice tees. The people she had met at school had been more concerned with their image than anyone she had known in high school. Hipster evangelicals listening to praise music on iPod Nanos. Lots of piercings and dyed hair, which was all fine with Lucy, really, because it wasn't like she was judging so much as being judged. And she was used to that.

So it wasn't without some small bit of guilty pleasure that she noticed how nervous Pastor Jeff was as he merged the bus onto I-4. His right arm was sleeved with an elaborate Resurrection-Pentecost tattoo that looked like nothing so much as a pattern of brightly colored scales, and from where she sat in the front row with Alan, Lucy could almost swear his forearms were twitching.

"Can you check on my peeps?" he said.

She leaned forward. "What?"

He hazarded the briefest of looks. Despite the engine, she could hear him just fine and no doubt he realized as much. But Lucy wasn't above pushing him just a bit. In fact, it had come to define a good deal of their relationship—as much of youth group now seemed to be taken up with Lucy clarifying Pastor Jeff's theological points as with Pastor Jeff strumming his Martin acoustic.

"My peeps," he said louder, "the crew, can you check on them?"

Of course she could, it was what she was there for, wasn't it, to check on his peeps? She turned in her seat to face Alan.

"What did he say?" Alan asked. For the past twenty minutes she'd allowed his fingers to crawl from knee to mid-thigh.

"I need to do a quick make-out check," she said. "Don't go anywhere."

When he smiled she smacked a kiss on his lips so quickly he startled.

She turned forward and watched Pastor Jeff grimace in the rear-view mirror.

"Anything for you, Jeff," she said. "Right back," she told Alan, and started down the aisle. It wasn't a make-out check, of course. Most of the kids were buried in iPhones or Nintendo DS games, a few turned backwards in their seats to talk to the people behind them. It was Lucy's job to remind them *bottoms in your seat!* or, when they rocked their chairs back at youth group *four on the floor!* but now she could see that as Jeff's job—*Pastor* Jeff, as he insisted—and did nothing but smile all the way back to where Katie was holding court in the exit row, several tenth grade girls huddled around her.

It was one of the things that made her Katie-the-great, this well of generosity that Lucy constantly had to remind herself was mostly genuine and not simply another of her sister's techniques to be the most interesting person in the room. She talked to toddlers as readily and easily as she did to adults and everyone, without fail, seemed to hang on her every word. Be generous, Lucy. Be glad she came, she reminded herself. But the moment they caught sight of her they started stifling laughs and right then Lucy wasn't Lucy-in-charge but Lucy the shrill frump come back to stop them from talking about her. Her heart went wild and she felt blood race to her cheeks, Lucy-the-feral balancing in the bus aisle and trying to hold in check her reflex for flight.

"What's up, Luce?" Katie said.

"Just checking on things."

Katie moved her eyes over the surrounding girls who suppressed another wave of laughter. "We seem to be holding up. Want to sit with us?"

"I better get—" She trailed off, nodded back toward the front. "Pastor Jeff."

"Of course."

"We should be there in like thirty minutes," Lucy said.

"Yeah, absolutely."

She stumbled back to the front—Pastor Jeff had the bus swaying like an ark— and plopped down beside Alan. She smiled at him but when his hand went back to her thigh she brushed it away. The spell was broken, and what Lucy couldn't help but do was go into herself. Mope, her mother called it. Think, Lucy insisted, reflect. She got it from her father, and it was the primary reason she couldn't take lightly all Katie's jokes about The Hague or the International Criminal Court. Everything she'd heard at JBI, from her courses in Old Testament to Contemporary Theology to Pastoral Care, supported the war and would have considered her dad—had they known him—something of a hero. Maybe not a hero like the soldiers on the ground but a vital cog in a giant machine meant to root out the evil that was Islamofascism. But despite all that, or maybe because of it, Lucy couldn't reconcile the idea of killing someone with the Gospels, and she knew her father couldn't either. He wasn't particularly religious, but he was particularly moral, particularly scrupulous, and no doubt saw this as yet another necessity in what had become a long line of bad options. Losing a job and—Lucy had sneaked a look at the financial updates he kept on the computer—something like a million dollars in investments over the course of eleven months had a way of reducing everything to numbered columns. Moral complexity was for the rich. Except it wasn't, she reminded herself. It was just that he was her father, after all, her daddy, and how could she possibly judge the man?

That her daddy hadn't turned to his wife's parents for help—was that noble or stubborn? Her maternal grandparents were horse people in Ocala, though they had years ago sold the house and stables and everything with it to move to a gated community of ten acre manors. They still had three horses but spent most of their time traveling in Europe or California, their slate-tiled house, hemmed in with palms and water oaks, largely empty. When they visited it was to ride down to Winter Park for dinner where Lucy and her grandpa argued free will versus determinism or the joint-stock company versus the commune—such a game, dinner and debate, such an expensive game. But maybe they *had* helped her father, maybe her mother had insisted, because what did Lucy really know about it? They might have—then it hit her: Alan. She could take Alan there. It wouldn't be difficult: tell her parents she was going to visit friends in Jacksonville and sneak away for a romantic weekend. She thought of them sitting in the kitchen listening to birdsong, puffy-eyed from sleep, slightly rank from the love they had made. Lucy's hair—she would have it cut short, maybe she would drive down to that salon in Winter Haven, the expensive one, and have it cut short—her hair on end, as quietly electric as the moment.

She let her hand slide onto Alan's thigh and come to rest scandalously near his groin. She felt him look at her, felt him smile, but didn't dare look back, eyes straight ahead at the highway, Pastor Jeff sweating in the rear-view. The magic, she thought, all the magic was coming back.

At the last moment Pastor Jeff decided not to unload in the D lot but to actually swing through the Bethlehem Bus Loop where everyone could pile out beneath the Damascus Gate and wait while he trekked back across the parking lot beneath what was already a blistering Florida sun. Lucy and Alan were left to herd the thirty-two Soldiers for Christ beneath a speaker piping what sounded like easy listening adult contemporary but Lucy knew from her time at JBI was actually "praise sound," gospel pop a little heavy on Autotune and synthesizer. And already the kids were scattering, a few edging toward the Jerusalem Street Market and Gourmet Coffee Shop, a few more making for the Wilderness Tabernacle with its giant sacrificial stone upon which Abraham offered up his son Isaac every hour on the hour. And where was Katie? The youth group ranged from sixth grade tweeners to a few rising seniors but most were thirteen or fourteen which made Katie older and presumably wiser—wouldn't you get wiser spending your weekends in a smelly tent talking about Chomsky?—which meant Katie was supposed to help her. But of course Katie was nowhere to be found.

"You think you can go find my sister?" Lucy asked Alan.

They were back against the curb just inside the turnstiles, Lucy with her arms outstretched to huddle several wide-eyed twelve year olds who kept wanting to braid her hair or play with her phone.

"You don't want to wait for Pastor Jeff?" Alan asked. His eyes were pinched and he was scanning the asphalt like a man lost at sea. "You don't think we should stay together?"

"We're already not together," Lucy said, "and she's supposed to be helping."

"I think we should just wait right here."

"Please just go find her." She didn't like the whine in her voice, it was too much like her mother, but pressed him anyway. "Please," she said. "We'll wait here. Just get her, and get them," she pointed to several boys peering through the bars of a fiberglass coliseum marked LIONS VERSUS CHRISTIANS, "back over here too. Please."

"All right," he said, and she didn't like the whine in his voice either, but at least he was moving. What they had shared, what she *thought* they had shared, on the bus was so obviously over, but that was okay. A half hour of chaos—get the younger kids with Pastor Jeff, set a meeting time and place for lunch—and she and Alan would be alone together. She had carefully studied the event schedule and planned the day perfectly, every act, every moment—the Woman at the Well at 10:15, the Passion and Resurrection at noon, lunch at one in the Judean Village—all of it building toward the four o'clock altar call where he would kneel at the rail and cry for salvation. She would be right beside him, of course, and on the way out of the service would find some place, maybe some ornamental nook in the Christus Garden, lush with orchids and peace-lilies, and kiss him in a way that would let him know that she understood, that she was with him, that they were now a *they*. But first Alan had to find Katie.

Pastor Jeff came back before Alan did, sweaty and flustered. She'd never realized how skinny he was until she watched him hustle across the road holding his white jeans up with one knuckled hand, a buck-toothed rabbit with a whisper of soul patch.

"Where are the rest?" he wanted to know.

"They scattered," Lucy said.

"Scattered?" His head rolled back as if he'd been struck. "I thought I asked you to watch them, Lucy? Sweet candy confections, I can't keep track of like forty kids on my own."

"I'm sorry."

"You couldn't keep them here for like two minutes?"

"I'm sorry," she said again, and she genuinely was, though, in her defense, she couldn't help but notice it had taken Pastor Jeff more like half an hour to park the bus and walk back when any semi-competent person could do it in, say, ten. "Alan went looking for them. I think maybe Katie is with them."

"Well, thank the good Lord for Katie," he said, and took his phone from his pocket, looked at the screen, and dropped it back. "Can you text her or something?"

Of course she could, and why hadn't she thought of that already? Poor Alan didn't have a phone or she would've recalled him, apologized, took his hand and galloped away. But that was all right, everything was all right, or would be in another moment.

Lucy sent Katie a message and stood with the girls while Pastor Jeff moved around the plaza until he had wrangled the entire youth group with the exception of Katie and her three fourteen year old groupies. And Alan. Poor sweet Alan, Lucy thought, probably lost in the Qumran Caves by now, still tracking her sister, addled by glow-in-the-dark Dead Sea Scrolls but loyal to the end.

"All right," Pastor Jeff said. He mopped his forehead with a handkerchief and took a pocket watch from his jeans. Lucy could tell that he was already ready to go, already regretting the trip. "Nothing from your sister?"

"Not yet."

"Can you text her one more time?"

"I can, but she's just like this sometimes."

"Please, Lucy, for me. I need some organization here." He turned to the assembled group. "You all have your buddies. *Do not* leave your buddies. I repeat *do not* leave your buddies. Anyone gets separated you call me immediately. We meet in the Judean Village at one for lunch. Any questions?" He spread his arms as if in supplication. "If there are no questions you are all free to go. Have a blessed morning."

When they were gone Lucy was left with Pastor Jeff and maybe a dozen eighth graders, the hanger-ons, the ones who sang loudest when he played his guitar, the inner sanctified circle—though Lucy felt terrible thinking as much. He was laughing and strutting, soaking up the adolescent adoration, before he suddenly turned to Lucy as if she had bitten him.

"I'll find her," Lucy said before he could speak. "Relax. I'll find her and see you at one."

She checked her phone once more—no message—and set off.

The deeper Lucy went into the Holy Land, past the Theater of Life, past the Whipping Post where she wouldn't dare bring Alan—wouldn't it be way, way too much like the Canebrake Wilderness School?—the deeper she went, the angrier she got. This was so Katie, so Pamela, to be completely honest. The way her mother had manipulated her dad. And where was her mom now? Doing sun salutations on the white sand while her father sold his soul over the mountains of Afghanistan. When things were at their worst her parents had become suddenly tender in a way she had never seen, their lives verged on collapse and still lips would brush a hand, fingertips would graze the back of a neck. Except now they were never together, having drifted apart like polar ice, a blind drift, largely indifferent, that made Lucy question if the cosmic grace she had witnessed was anything more than desperation. In her worst moments it was her mother's fabrication, her ability to capture the moment and drag her husband along through it. It was, Lucy thought, as premeditated as what Katie was doing now, and it made her absolutely furious.

She walked around the Royal Portico where a crowd had gathered to watch two Roman Centurions sword fight, on toward the Crystal Living Waters, a rhombus of blue lake studded with fountains that fanned water into the air. She scanned the crowd and saw a few boys from the youth group but no sign of either Katie or Alan. Poor Alan. To manipulate someone like Alan—and how could Katie be doing anything but manipulating him?—seemed particularly loathsome. He had no family outside a grandmother he barely knew and a tiny Vietnamese monk who seemed to spend most of his time with Alan smiling and nodding vaguely. She didn't know how smart Alan was—was that awful to admit?— but knew too that it didn't matter. If she hadn't known it already, she'd learned that at JBI: a lot of very smart people were very terrible people, self-righteous and judgmental, *exclusive*. They were exclusive in that cliquey high school way that had reduced Lucy to solitude when all she had ever wanted was normality. Which—okay, Lucy, be honest with yourself—wasn't true. Normality wasn't *all* she had ever wanted. But if the radiance of Christ incarnate, the presence of a transcendent God was going to elude her, couldn't she at least have a date for the prom? Was it her fault? *We would willingly be at rest from all trouble, but because we have lost our innocence through sin, we have also lost our true happiness.* So was it her fault? Or was it Katie's?

And there was Pastor Jeff and his entourage coming out of the Temple Model, A.D. 66, and Lucy ducked rapidly to her left—*keep walking, keep walking*—and waited for them to pass. If she had to face that twitchy smirk there was no telling what she would say. Where's Katie? Where's Alan? Aww, does little Lucy not have anyone to play with? She waited until they were out of sight and stepped back onto the walk. It was nine-twenty, still plenty of time to find Alan and see the Woman at the Well but she had to find him now.

She decided to head back to the Damascus Gate thinking he was maybe waiting for her now but of course he wasn't. Nine-thirty-seven now and she was sweating, could feel it bead her upper lip. Decided to loop the park once more, so angry, so angry, passing lots of kids from the youth group, good kids—*hi Lucy! What's up, Lucy?*—kids she liked, but ignoring all of them. Almost jogging now, past the Smile of a Child Adventure Land, past the Shepherd's Field— nine-forty-two, nine-forty-three—Pilate's Hall of Judgment, the Whipping Post (again), almost ten o'clock now, until she stomped around a corner and there, at a table outside the Oasis Cafe, sat Alan and Katie and the three nameless brainless girls. And what was Alan doing but sipping on a Coke and laughing. And what was Katie doing but batting her eyes.

"Lucy," Alan said, looking up, "you found us."

"Found you?" She stood with her fists balled on her hips. She was splotchy and panting and she knew it, but she was also as angry as she could ever remember being. "Found you?" she said again. "What were you doing, hiding from me? Running around playing let's-all-dodge-Lucy?"

"No," Alan said.

"Luce," said Katie.

"And don't you," Lucy turned to her sister, "don't you dare say a word. You probably encouraged him."

"Encouraged him in what?"

"You know exactly what," Lucy said. "I know this is all a big game to you, Katie, make fun of the sincere believers and, hey, why not make Lucy miserable too? I know exactly how you think. You've always done this sort of thing to me."

"Please," said Katie and rolled her eyes down to her phone.

"Lucy?" Alan said in a voice so plaintive Lucy was ready to believe whatever he said, and in truth she did. But now that she had launched into things, now that, finally, she thought, I'm having it out with Katie, and poor Alan, dumb sweet loyal Alan is caught right in the center of things and too blind to realize it. "I found Katie and everybody and we were headed back and then I saw Pastor Jeff and he said you were looking for me so I figured, you know, sit down in one place and wait."

"Oh," said Katie brightly, "and here I just now see your text. Both of them."

"Come on," said Lucy, and she actually took him by the collar of his shirt. He stood abruptly. "Come on," she said, but softer, and Alan nodded, followed her, head down like a scolded puppy, while behind them the nameless brainless girls erupted into laughter and Lucy did not dare look back, did not dare look at Alan—she couldn't even let go of his collar—until they were safely away and somewhere deep in the Garden of Gethsemane. And it was there that Alan apologized, and she believed him, and forgave him.

"I wasn't doing anything but waiting," he said. "I'm sorry."

"It's okay."

"I swear I thought I was doing exactly what you wanted. Your sister—"

"It's okay," she told him. "But please don't talk about my sister."

They were sitting on a bench in a tunnel of greenhouse glass, around them dense tropical vegetation and, somewhere above, unseen birds singing in the iron rafters. They had missed the Woman at the Well but they could still salvage the day, the night.

"It's okay," she said again, "I'm sorry I blew up like that. It's just, things with my sister, my whole family really, they've always been—" But instead of speaking she put one finger on his chin and turned his head and kissed him just as she'd planned to kiss him after the service. And then she was in his lap and she felt his hand on her lower back and she felt her own hand—having no idea how it had gotten there—pressing against the stiff denim of his crotch. She heard the birds singing, louder, and she pulled away to find his eyes still closed and lips still pursed. She touched the tip of his nose *silly boy* and smiled, and he smiled, and she knew she loved him.

Lucy cried through the Passion. From the moment the child ran (nearly) naked from the Garden until the moment Christ's radiant translucent form ascended on guy lines into a bank of artificial clouds, she wept herself clean, heart and soul, of every nasty thing she had felt buried in her for the past three years. When she was finished she looked at Alan and for a moment didn't know him. Then recognized him and felt neither the love nor lust she had felt before but a gentle affection. The whole youth group was present now and when he tried to kiss her she shied away though it had nothing to do with the presence of the others and everything to do with this feeling she had, this purity she hadn't felt since she had first came to Christ as a lonely seventh grader reading the Sermon on the Mount in her bedroom floor, marveling that something as large as God might love her back.

My dear friend, à Kempis had written, *do not lose confidence in progressing in the spiritual life; you still have time and opportunity.* She seized both and walked straight to Pastor Jeff and hugged him, buried her wet eyes in his shoulder. He resisted, and then gave into the hug as if he had been waiting years for this embrace, and wasn't he lonely? she asked herself, straight out of college and so far from home. Wasn't he scared? She thought he might have wept a moment himself against her shoulder, or perhaps he only coughed, but when she pulled away his eyes were bright. *Thank you,* she mouthed, but did not say, only turned and found Katie who suddenly looked terrified but, just as Lucy reached for her, collapsed against her so that both sisters were crying, a wordless sniveling that said everything that three years of fear and frustration could not. When they let go they avoided each other's' eyes, just turned and sniffled, and it was off to lunch in the Judean Village.

Which, of course, was a delight of chaos. Here was Lucy: present yet slightly detached, as if new-Lucy sat viewing the old, beside Alan and Pastor Jeff and several preteens on a metal picnic table covered with baskets of fries and burgers and corndogs and, for Lucy, a badly burned nine-dollar Gardenburger. She was so happy was the thing, so content, for the first time in her life she felt outside herself, outside the worry that, she realized now, had always defined her: Lucy and a set of carefully articulated neuroses. All the social trauma and loneliness, she felt none of it. She felt drained, emotionally exhausted, that was true, but it wasn't a bad exhaustion, not tired so much as past things, past all the petty betrayals, the ills and hurts, her body wrung clean—wrung empty—so that what was left sat numbly smiling, half-conscious as she used a plastic knife to fleck blackened grit.

Around them kids were eating and jumping between tables, laughing, clowning. Pastor Jeff talked a little about the morning, about the service at four, pleasant talk, Lucy thought, silly and superficial, which was such a relief as she'd been scared he would try to say something about what had happened, the tears, the embrace. But she had to hand it to him: he appeared to have the sense not to ruin the moment with words. Instead he just smiled and glanced at his phone.

"Last Supper at quarter to two," he said, "who's with me?"

The table jumped up and he smiled at Lucy and Alan.

"You two are welcome to come along."

"Maybe not today," Lucy said, "thanks though."

When they were gone she looked at Alan. Now it was her boyfriend who seemed unable to recognize her, scrutinizing her face—is this the girl who grabbed my dick or the girl who cried when they nailed Him to the cross?—and she wanted to comfort him. I'm both, she wanted to say. I'm simple, I'm complex— just like you. It's why God loves us.

Instead she just said: "Hi."

"Hi," he said back.

"Hi," she said again. "How we doing over here?"

"We are doing fine," he said. "We seem to be doing just fine."

When they both started laughing she stood and took his hand.

Then they were walking back out of Damascus Gate, hands stamped so they could reenter, and then they were back on the otherwise empty church bus, and none of this, Lucy was thinking, none of this was planned. That you could move in and out of the park, that Pastor Jeff left the bus unlocked, that Alan would seem to know exactly where she was leading them—it was simply happening, everything seemed to just happen to this new Lucy, the world so deep and wide with possibility.

Lucy felt sweat track her ribs. Most of the sliding windows were open but the bus was stifling anyway. Not that the heat stopped them from moving down the aisle to the wide bench seat at the back where she pulled Alan against her and began to kiss him until his face shone with saliva, as bright as a polished stone. She reclined on the cracked plastic seat and pulled him on top of her, felt her shirt slide up so that they were belly to belly, flesh to flesh, sticky and sweating everywhere in the afternoon heat. When she moved her arm she realized her shirt now rung her neck and he was kissing her breasts through the cups of her mom's push-up bra. She slid her hand down the front of his jeans, wet, the scruff of pubic hair, touched him once, let her hand slide deeper.

It was only the sound of the door opening that pulled him up. Except it wasn't the door opening, only kids walking by outside, obliviously rapping their hands against the side of the bus. Alan looked around wildly, eye scanning like an animal that has just realized it was in a cage.

"It's all right," she whispered.

"Shh."

"Alan—"

"Be quiet for a second."

She reached up and touched his face, two fingertips, so gentle the motion, barely grazing his left cheek. "Alan," she said, but he was already tucking his shirt back in. She sat up, a little disappointed, surprised a second later to find that she was actually a lot disappointed. She wanted him despite the Pleather seat and the coiled spring against her upper back.

"We should get back inside," he said. "Someone's gonna find us out here."

"Nobody's gonna find us."

"Seriously, Lucy. This is kind of screwed up, don't you think?"

"Not really," she said, slightly hurt, though it was kind of screwed up. She sat up and worked her shirt back down. "But later, all right?"

It was after three by the time Lucy stood in front of the bathroom mirror and ladled water onto her face. Her makeup was everywhere but she managed to clean most of it off. What she couldn't help was the sweat. She was soaked—her shirt dark and clinging to her back—but she suspected everyone was soaked by now. It was ninety-six degrees with humidity thick as butter. Which was exactly how she felt: buttery, as if someone has spread her mother's five dollar tub of vegan substitute all over her body. *Slippery as an eel,* her father would say, were her father ever to return from his Tampa dungeon.

She mopped her face and neck with paper towels, pressed them against her armpits and stomach, tried to swab her back. It wasn't just physical though, the thing with Katie, the thing with Alan—the two things, she thought, though one was really just a continuation of the other. She needed time to process and right now there really wasn't time. She needed to be alone in her room. She needed to pray. But instead she was in the ladies room beside the Centurion Treats gift shop, Alan probably waiting just outside.

The thing with Katie—it came to with such sudden clarity: Lucy really was going to marry this boy, she really was going to marry Alan, and Katie would be her maid of honor. She saw it so clearly: her father easing her down the aisle where her sister and lover waited. Katie! She loved Katie and wanted to find her right then and tell her. I love you and I want you beside me on the day—soon, the day would be soon—when I marry my soul mate. And wasn't that exactly what she and Katie had shared? Wasn't that exactly what the weeping had been about? It had said: we might hate each other, but we love each other so much more. It had said: only the two of us will ever fully understand this. They spoke better in tears. They spoke better in touch. What were words between sisters?

It had deviled Lucy all through her first year at JBI, that sense that she was so separate from the other girls. It wasn't just that they didn't like her, or seemed to like her in the most obligatory good-Christian-showing-mercy fashion. It was that they felt so far from her and secretly—though she admitted it now, she stared into her own eyes and told herself she would admit everything now—she had wondered who here will be my friend? Who here will be present at my wedding? She had tried to argue for this girl or that, but saw how futile that had been, how silly. My sister will stand with me. My sister will be the one to understand me. And *that* was what they had cried about.

She toweled her face a last time.

Everything was perfect. Everything was beautiful. This really was the day that the Lord hath made.

They got seats maybe halfway between the foyer and the stage, right aisle so Alan wouldn't feel as conspicuous as he might walking down the center, a little distant but still close enough to read the WE SHALL BEHOLD HIM! banner that glittered above the altar. The spacious sanctuary, which held probably five hundred people, was maybe two-thirds full, but Lucy still managed to spot most of the Soldiers for Christ occupying an entire center pew a little farther down. Young men and women dressed in dark suits and long dresses—college interns, Lucy guessed—moved along the rail checking microphones and unfolding prayer clothes that could be anointed by the minister.

She studied the red-carpet that sloped to the front, and could see herself walking down this or any other church aisle. Organ swelling. Family standing. Alan waiting for her at the front. She imagined how Katie might appear through the softening gauze of the veil, a little easier to take, perhaps, her hard edges rounded to loveliness. Even their mother in tears, their mother thinking *Oh, to have thought this day would never come* which was really so uncharitable of Lucy even if she really did think it true. But Lucy let it go all the same. This wasn't the time to be stingy. This was the time to be thankful, and she reached over and gave Alan's hand a little squeeze.

"Here we go," she whispered.

There was a brief staticky soundcheck before a praise band took the stage, strapped on their guitars, called *this one right here's for the Bossman upstairs* and began to play. It wasn't until the minister, a tall smooth-jawed man, handsome in a plastic sort of way—Lucy thought he might have once played football for someone, the Dolphins? There was a team called the Dolphins, wasn't there?—it wasn't until he was fully into his message about the temptation of sin and the path to redemption by stepping forward right then, right this very minute and receiving Christ Jesus as your Savior, that Lucy noticed Katie and the three fourteen year olds stagger in.

They weren't drunk, they couldn't possibly be drunk, but they moved with a druggy hitch, as if their arms and legs had somehow fallen out of sync, all the way down the right aisle until they could practically look up the (utterly clean) nostrils of the minister. Then Lucy saw that they weren't stopping, and realized they hadn't just entered; they had been here all along. They weren't drunk; they were crying. And the last realization—the one that unloaded on her in a thrum of all sorts of feelings she didn't want to think about, feelings like *it's not fair, this isn't about you*—was that Katie-the-great and the girls weren't headed to a pew. They were headed for the altar rail. They were headed straight for Jesus.

Pastor Jeff was already moving. He high-stepped out of the center pew and fairly sprinted down the aisle, arms outstretched, white t-shirt untucked and waving behind him like a surrender flag. Lucy craned her neck. It was Katie at the center, the girls and now one of the interns huddled around her body that was fairly heaving with sobs. Other people, kids, women and men, were streaming to the altar, dropping on their knees to wail, but the minister had caught sight of Katie—of course he did, Lucy thought—and was headed that way, microphone in one hand as he kept up a steady patter of *yes, come, Lord Jesus, come.*

What to do? Should she take Alan's hand? Was this the moment? Lucy stole a glance and saw that he was intensely involved, eyes narrowed, bottom lip between his teeth. But how would he take it? That she was leading *him* to the Lord, or that Katie was pulling them both to *her*? Oh for Christ's sake, Katie, she wanted to scream—and she meant it: for the sake of Christ—a thousand nights at Soldiers for Christ, all those Sundays day-dreaming in the carpeted pews, and you choose now?

Then Alan took her hand and she felt every bad thought blow out of her mind like a candle flame, extinguished, gone. He looked at her with a word on his lips, something he couldn't quite form. *Yes,* she wanted to say. *Yes, I will go with you, walk with you, pray with you.* But what he said was: "You need to go to your sister."

"What?"

"Your sister." He gestured to the front. "I think you should go down there."

Lucy looked forward again. The minister—a tight end for the Miami Dolphins! it flashed in her head as unwanted as unbidden—kneeled above her. She could hear Katie now too, a gasping, a wailing.

"Lucy?" Alan said.

"What?"

"Listen to her. She's your sister."

"You don't know her, Alan."

He shook his head as if in disbelief. "She's crying."

"You don't know her," Lucy said again, "and she isn't crying. She's acting. I've watched her do this my entire life."

She hadn't meant to say that, didn't know where exactly it had come from, but she'd said it, and now she watched his jaw unhinge slightly, just enough to see the dark cavern of his mouth, the place she'd stuck her tongue not two hours ago.

I'm sorry, she started to say, but before she could speak he was pushing by her into the aisle where he stopped and leaned in. "She has problems just like everyone else," Alan said. "Did you know for a long time she was cutting herself? Did you even know that? Maybe it's sometimes an act, fine, but she's still your sister."

Lucy watched him walk alone down the aisle, the aisle they were supposed to traverse together, Alan going not to her, but away from her, an inversion of everything she had imagined, and then the bitter bitter taste of watching him kneel, arm outstretched not to touch Lucy, but her sister.

She was silent on the way back to the bus, but the by time they pulled through the bus loop and onto I-4 she had turned cheery and efficient, a smiling authoritarian walking up and down the center row addressing the teenagers like wayward toddlers. Katie was receiving all the attention, of course. Girls and boys hung over seatbacks to hear her speak in a strangled whisper. The tears had not stopped at the altar but spread and soon enough Lucy had realized she was the lone member of the Soldiers for Christ not kneeling at the rail. It was a mass revival, a come-to-Jesus the likes of which the First Evangelical Lutheran had never seen, and Pastor Jeff moved manically up and down the rail, shouting and encouraging like an officer on a firing line. Lucy watched until she realized she'd had enough and walked out to sit on a concrete bench and drink a four dollar bottle of apple juice.

She stood when the youth group came out of the service at five, a little chastened by their jubilation. Pastor Jeff was in the center, his arms above him, everyone smiling and singing *Hosanna, Hosanna* to the tune of the old Toto song "Rosanna." Katie appeared to be in aftershocks, still and serene and suddenly overwhelmed by another fit of tears, her supplicants rung about her like worker bees. Lucy tossed her apple juice away and forced a smile.

Now they were back on the bus. Lucy made a last pass up the aisle and sat down by Alan. He seemed distant but not unfriendly, and that was fine with Lucy because what had come to her sitting alone with her apple juice and anger was that she didn't want to marry this boy, but she did want to sleep with him.

Unloading was a festival of regret. The church parking lot was crowded with parents as kids stumbled off the bus, slightly sunburned and strung out on caffeine and tears. She stood with Pastor Jeff and Katie and Alan and watched the kids haul themselves into mini-vans.

"What a day," Pastor Jeff said. "What a miracle of a day."

He looked like a coach after a big win, standing on the sideline and wanting desperately to cling to a last shred of glory.

"What a day," he said again, and began to move dreamily toward his office. "You two take care of each other, and you take care of your sister, Lucy."

It was then Lucy realized no one but Alan had noticed her refusal. As far as anyone else was concerned she was still Lucy-the-good, and what welled in her was the same feeling she'd had that night on the shore of her Michigan lake: some shame, yes, but mostly anger. When Pastor Jeff was gone Lucy put one arm around Katie and the other around Alan and began leading them home, not out of love, she wanted to make clear, and not out of a desire to comfort. She put her arms around them and led them back out of fear they would otherwise spend the rest of their confused lives bumbling around the church parking lot, as lost to the greater world as they were to themselves.

The kitchen lights were on when they got back, the room overlit and blinding. Her mother deeply connected to the spirit of Gaia but unable to flip a light switch when she left a room (later she would remember that it was her, Lucy, who had left them on and that would be one more thing to regret, but at the moment her anger was a sort of voltage carried along the lines of her nerves). She cut the overhead and let the soft late-day sun yellow its way beneath the blinds. Katie sat at the table, slatted in shadow and slowly shaking her lowered head while Alan stood by the door, as awkward and skinny as a coat rack.

"I don't know where I go from here," Katie said. "I really don't."

"I thought you were going to Orlando," Lucy said.

Her sister looked up. "I mean in life. I mean where do I go in life."

"You should talk to Pastor Jeff," Alan said.

"Maybe," Katie said. She had let her hair string forward across her face giving her the look of a faddish waif, a punk-rock urchin lost in a Dickens novel. "What do you think?" she asked Lucy.

"About what? About Pastor Jeff?"

"Dude's got wisdom," Alan said.

"Pastor Jeff?" Lucy asked. "Are you serious?"

"Maybe I should just call him," Katie said.

Lucy pushed off the sink she leaned against and threw back her head. It was Katie's forlorn voice, the self-dramatization, the broken yearning. "Oh my God," Lucy screamed, "would you stop it? There's no one here to witness the act, Katie. There's no audience here."

Katie looked confused. "What?"

"Him," Lucy said, pointing. "Just him. He's the only audience you have. I wouldn't think that would be enough for you."

"Are you implying," Katie said, and rose up with a sort of wounded regal bearing, "are you implying that I'm faking this? That I'm doing this for attention?"

"I think I'll go," Alan said.

"You don't move," Lucy said. She turned to her sister. "And no, I'm not implying anything. I'm saying it, Katie. I'm saying it because I'm sick to death of not saying it."

"I'm just going to go," Alan said. "I can call Brother Vin."

Lucy stayed him with a hand. "You don't move."

"You don't tell him what to do," Katie said. "Or maybe you do, maybe you tell everyone what to do since you spend your entire life holier than thou. Maybe that's all you do. God," she said, and jerked up from the table, "I am so out of here."

"Off to your discussion board. Off to your tent in Orlando."

Katie was almost to the door. "Yes, off to my tent," she said, "and if you had the slightest tiniest most minute idea about all this Gospel stuff, all this Jesus stuff, you're always singing about you'd chain yourself to one of those tents and never come out."

She slammed the door hard enough to whip the blinds against the glass. Alan had sunk into the wall.

"I should go," he said.

"You come with me."

"I really should go. I didn't even tell my grandma where I'd be."

"You come with me," Lucy said, and took his hand. She pulled him through the empty house, through the living room and the soft pile of its carpet, past the plasma screen and the bookshelf full of Ram Dass and Deepak Chopra, past the faux-walnut newel post and up to the landing on the stairs where she pushed him against the wall and kissed him, her hands crawling over the sharp flares of his pelvic bones. It was a test, really, to see how far things had slid, to see what was still possible, and when she kissed him he felt pliable, he felt willing. But she needed to hurry before she talked herself out of everything.

She pulled him down the upstairs hall to her room where she set him on her bed.

"Wait," she said.

"I think—"

"Just wait, Alan," she said softer, "please."

He nodded and she turned for her closet, all perfect articulation now, as out of body, as new-Lucy, as she had been at lunch. She took the nightgown from her closet and whirled into the bathroom and began to pull off her clothes. In the mirror she could see herself red and splotchy and it certainly wasn't perfect, certainly wasn't just as she'd imagined it, but there it was, it was happening. She took her panties off last, uncertain if they should stay. The nightgown was sheer and looking down she could see the grainy shadow of pubic hair, but in the end it didn't matter. The nightgown was a formality; the nightgown was coming off.

But when she opened the bathroom door he was gone.

"Alan?" she said. She looked in the closet and out into the hall. "Alan?"

Then she saw the light beneath Katie's door, stepped forward and heard Katie laughing.

"Alan?" Lucy called. She banged on the door. "Katie, what are you doing here?" She banged again. "Katie?"

"*Voulez vous couchez avec moi?*" Katie called through the door.

"What are you doing here?" Lucy yelled. "Is Alan in there?"

"Alan?" Katie said. "Do you want to answer for yourself, Alan?"

"What are you doing here, Katie?"

"I came back for my jacket, dear sister," she fairly sang. "It gets so cold faking enlightenment, you know? All those pretend tears and I can barely maintain my core temp. And then I found loverboy here wandering the hall."

"Open this door."

"Hold on."

"Katie, open this door this minute."

"Hold on I want to read you something."

"Alan?" Lucy called.

"One second," Katie said. "Okay, I found it."

Lucy heard the box-springs begin to squeak and knew her sister was jumping on the bed.

"Please, Katie." Lucy let her forehead sink against the grain of the door. "Please."

"Hold on." She was bouncing, almost breathless. "Alan should hear this too."

"Katie—"

Downstairs the phone began to ring.

"*My friend,*" Katie read, "*I must be your supreme and final end if you wish to be truly blessed—*" and it took Lucy a moment to realize Katie was reading from her copy of *The Imitation of Christ*.

She banged the door. "Stop it, Katie. Open this door. Alan?"

"Alan wants to hear this. This gets so much better, Alan."

"Katie—"

"*If I am, your love will be purified and not be twisted back on yourself and on the things of this world, as it so often is.*"

She banged harder, crying now, the phone still ringing. "Katie—"

"Aww, Lucy," Katie called, "and right here you've got in the margin *Alan?* with this like big loopy question mark when I think maybe he's talking about God. But it's still so sweet. Don't you think, Alan?"

Lucy was kicking the door now, screaming *open this door, open this door* as insistent as the minister calling the sinners down to Jesus. *Open this door, open this door* and suddenly it was open and there stood Katie, the room otherwise empty.

"Where is he?"

"He's not even here," Katie said.

"Alan?"

"You must have scared him off." Katie pointed with the book. "I can actually see your vajajay in that."

"Give me that," Lucy screamed, and turned and threw the book down the stairs where the phone was again ringing, her father perhaps, having tired of whatever death he pedaled over the Hindu Kush, or her mother in Palm Beach, grown weary with her poses and AMEXed enlightenment. It could be any number of things, Lucy thought, but for the life of her she couldn't call anything else to mind, not Alan, not Pastor Jeff nor any of the girls from JBI, not even her Savior, and suddenly she realized she was alone here with her sister, just the two of them, Lucy standing on the threshold and Katie back on the bed, not quite smiling, but most definitely bouncing, higher and higher, as if at any moment she might disappear in a pillar of smoke.

The island was gated. It wasn't the most salient feature but it was the one that stuck. How did you gate an island? The car service had brought the two of them from the Atlantic Center for Holistic Integration in Palm Beach, south down I-95 to the MacArthur Causeway and there, across the bridge, past the stalled South Beach traffic and gleaming cruise ships, was the gate, a golf cart and two brown-clothed security guards waiting behind it.

"There's a gate," Pamela said.

Avi put his hand on her knee. "It's open."

"This is a public island, isn't it?"

"Relax. They're expecting us."

Still, she wondered things, things like: could you gate an island, a public island? She supposed you could, so long as the gate remained open. So it wasn't about the act of exclusion so much as the idea of it. Keeping people out. The barbarians, the hordes crowding the wings. They entered a round-about, a marina of some sort beyond, cluttered masts, the salt air that eats everything, then, as they made the turn, tennis courts, hard courts and clay and grass, neat as the squares on a quilt. When the road straightened she could see how narrow it was, Star Island, a spit of dredged sand as slender as a dancer's waist, as if even the geography felt the need to perform.

Avi squeezed her knee. At some point he had provided security for the man who was expecting them, counsel in the *dead of a November night,* Avi told her, because for a floundering financier it was always November and it was always night. Brussels maybe, Zurich, this man—this aspiring billionaire who at the time was a little old nothing, a hustler with an MBA betting huge sums of money charmed out of municipal pension funds—sitting in his expensive shoes and about to walk into a conference room with the CFO of Deutsche Bank when suddenly he opens up to his security man, to Avi, starts talking about some asshole bully back in Cleveland, a girl he knew at Williams, the one that got away. Years ago, but Avi had kept in touch and the man had never forgotten. It was something about the bonds you forge in a crisis of self, something about both of them being on the edge of life. Avi was only two years out of the IDF at the time, the specter of what had happened in Beirut his nightmare accompaniment, and they talked for what seemed hours though in reality had been only a few minutes, a catalog of frailty and ambition, at least until the man with Deutsche Bank beckoned.

The light softened.

Houses now, big Mediterranean mansions shrouded by palms and banana trees. Cobblestone drives. The road had a wide median planted with what she thought were kapok trees with their gray trunks and spiral roots and broad delicate shadows, as if their sole purpose was to lace the ground, the ornamentation of light and dark. Pamela had been raised with money but nothing like this. There were rumors Gloria Estefan owned a house on the island. Someone else said Dr. Phil. Lots of talk riding down of Mexican pop divas and retired Bulgarian arms dealers. Purely speculative, Avi said, and then insisted the house on the point belonged to the doctor who had invented the nicotine patch—*transdermal* in the fog of his Ashkenazi accent—but she found this ridiculous. Surely the man would have his own island? Imported trees with elephantine leaves. A discrete pad for helicopters.

"You're grasping," Avi said. "Stop grasping and relax."

And to some degree she was relaxed. To start with, Luther wasn't here. Which was probably the Alpha and Omega of *her* being here. But it didn't hurt, relaxation-wise, that she'd spent the entire day at the center, ninety minutes of Hatha followed by a hot stone massage and a half hour of meditating. Running and meditating came and went throughout her life, but she'd always had yoga. The ability to hold a certain pose, the alignment, the articulation of an otherwise empty space. She thought of posture as a form of moral rightness, a lesson she'd learned from her own mother, and now continually failed to not hold against her oldest daughter. The sight of Lucy slurping yogurt in the kitchen when all she lacked was form, the proper conjunction of spine, heart, and mind, when all she lacked was the ability to stand upright—sometimes it felt like the limit of what Pamela could bear.

The car slowed and she felt Avi's hand lift off her knee, noticed the intimacy of the gesture. His hands were familiar with her body but only in the strictest professional sense. They'd met when she started taking Krav Maga classes at his gym in Daytona Beach. It was Avi's idea she go on the retreat to the center. He was teaching all weekend and, as his favorite student—big smile here, toothy and uneven—she could tag along for free. She paid her tuition on principle but it still felt as if she was somehow indebted. Though she knew that was *the talk* talking, the months, years really, he'd listened patiently while she told him everything she couldn't tell her husband, her worries about Lucy and Katie, the financial mess of her and Luther's life, and, finally, the ossification of their marriage that seemed to come with it. That dry heap she felt blow by her, crumb by crumb, every night. The talking had felt like a form of cheating, an emotional undermining of the foundation of her marriage. She hadn't meant to betray Luther, but a life adrift is a spilly thing, and eventually, one way or another, it outs. It was only when Avi lifted his hand from her knee that she realized how deeply she regretted outing her life with this man

The house was smaller than she expected, though she knew the beauty rested in the exacting of detail, the travertine marble, a bas relief on the outer stuccoed wall. There was music from another room, Stravinsky, Lutowski—there had been a point in her life she would've known but that was so many years ago. A wet bar was set up in the foyer where two young Latinas in black pants and white button-downs poured prosecco and mixed Sidecars in stainless steel shakers. Pamela took a glass of Mionetto, a second, felt the wine splash cold in her empty stomach—she hadn't eaten since breakfast—only rise to the suddenly floating balloon that was her head. She almost missed the step and Avi hooked her arm, lifted her.

"Careful," he said.

And it wasn't just the wine that disoriented her. The foyer opened in a series of angular removes above what started as a small reflecting pool before splashing down into a series of infinity pools, each wider than the previous, each lit with a different shade of marine blue, until the third and final pool pressed flush against the dark mirror of the bay. Behind it the Miami skyline floated and glittered.

Pamela stopped, arrested on her three inch heels. She wanted to not appear some suburban rube and she wasn't—she'd been raised with money and horses and vacations in European capitals, she'd gone to Yale, for God's sake. Not that anyone would believe it. Too crude, too—what was the word? Pedestrian? Prosaic? There was another word: legacy. She was a "legacy" at Yale, which meant her father had enough money and old friends to make up for Pamela's lack of anything exceptional. She hadn't fit in, the other girls so tall and white or tiny and Asian. Like they came out of test-tubes or were grown from cuttings. When all Pamela was was real.

She thought of her husband. It was Luther who had been raised in genteel poverty, but Luther would have stomped in and owned the room. Or would have once. Not so much anymore, she suspected. Then wondered if it had ever been true. This had started when they'd almost lost the house, her distrust of memory, as if it all had been fabricated, as if in the present crisis there couldn't possibly have been better days. *You're dreaming it, Pamela,* Katie and her insistence on addressing everyone by their given name. *It was never like that. It was sort of fucked, you know?* Except she wouldn't say *fuck*. Though she had that one night in the kitchen. The cuts on her arm. Slivers of reddish brown scab. A rowed garden of hurt. How bad did it have to be not simply to cut yourself but to cut yourself again and again with the sort of geometric precision normally reserved for the space program?

A helium-filled shark floated past, remote-controlled tail-fin curled.

Avi put another drink in her hand. They were outside now, huddled on a sliver of grass that gave way to the dock. People around her. Smell of perfume and citronella. Paper lanterns sagged above the pool and up to the balcony where there were more people. Someone came around with a platter of ahi tuna and then Beef Wellington, but she somehow wound up with another drink, a little drunk, a little lost, looking for Avi but standing beside a blowzy woman who had pulled her fat feet up onto the yellow divan that Pamela had completely failed to notice. They were talking about *the man of the house* and she couldn't be certain if it was a joke or not. How had she lost that fine distinction between reverence and irony? The man of the house keeps his pleasure boat off Monaco. The man of the house raises grass-fed Kobe on his ranch just north of Bozeman. He comes down for Art Basel, he comes down to see Dasha, he loves Dasha. The man of the house with his Tod's loafers and his Rauschenberg combines. Have you heard his TED talk?

"Who is this guy?" Pamela said turning. "Is he even here?"

The woman was now fully reclined on the couch, skirt riding up her big thighs. "This guy?" she said, and laughed.

"He deals in financial instruments," the man said, "he manipulates them."

"Someone said he was a hotelier," Pamela said.

"He weighs and measures." The man was in, Pamela guessed, his late-forties, silver coif, defined jaw, an idealization of male beauty and, because of it, somehow hideous. "The tech sector," he said, "private equity, credit markets."

Pamela laughed. "Is he optimistic?"

"About what?"

"About life. About the world."

"He has a son in some sort of Mandarin immersion program," the woman said, still laughing, "eight years old and all the boy does is memorize ideograms."

Pamela turned contemplative. "You'd think the money might insulate you."

"No," the man said, "the money only opens you up. You begin to register keywords: decoupling in the Euro Zone, the contingencies in the bond market. At some point it acquires a holy nimbus. You look at credit reports and think you're seeing statuary, a garden of martyred saints."

"Sovereign Debt Crisis sounds like a band." She had just realized how drunk she was, though it was white wine-drunk, which was somehow more airy and fragile than any other form, the heart lifted, the mind held a delicate clear light. She thought she must appear absolutely happy and it occurred to her that, at least in that exact moment, she might actually be. The man put his hand on her elbow. "Maybe their second album," Pamela said, "commercially successful though critically panned."

"Come here, my dear." He looked close at her face and she imagined herself compressed in the sheen of his eyes, her entire life tucked around the glossy edges.

"Austerity measures," she said, louder than she intended. She'd gotten fucked over by a lot of this and she wasn't one to let things go. "I'm not one to let things go," she told the man, and leaned toward him. Her mouth felt wet and lush. Her mouth felt like a flower. "I got pretty fucked over a few years ago. There was something," she said, "a word for it, an expression—"

"Yes, well," the man said, "but I happen to think you're darling."

"A way to describe it."

"I happen to think you're lovely," he said, and she felt him guide her up the stairs and it came to her and she turned to tell everyone gathered on the lawn.

"Volatility in the stock market," she cried, and felt his hand, firmer now.

"I think you're darling all the same," he said.

They went up the steps, through the kitchen and past the woman—beautiful woman—at the piano and were headed for the stairs when Avi hooked her arm and led her back through the house and down to the dock, the whole motion dizzying enough that she stumbled back down the steps.

"He was talking about the man of the house," Pamela said.

"That was the man of the house. It's a game he plays."

"That guy? That was your friend?"

"It's a little game he plays, anonymity."

"Where the hell am I, Avi?"

"Outside," he said. "Breath deep. Sit down for a moment and breath deep."

She collapsed into a rattan chair and they sat quietly while a boat purred past, a yacht of some sort, a woman hula-hooping on the aft deck, her shadow a needle swinging wildly while techno music blared ridiculously loud. Pamela watched it churn the water. The ship was overlit, incandescent and billowy with a brightness that seemed to pour from every surface, a paper house, lit and cast adrift. When it was gone it left behind an unnatural darkness, as if a hole had been cut in the bay, absent the silvery black waves that rippled silently. She turned to find Avi sitting beside her, two drinks on the table between them.

"Let me ask you something," she said, "how do they gate an island?"

"Don't worry about the gate." He handed her a drink. "The gate is notional. The gate is ideation."

"A gate of the mind."

"The gate as a level of consciousness, a state to inhabit."

She put her head back and laughed. "That is both amazing and ridiculous at the exact same time. Because you know it's right there off the causeway."

"Pamela—"

"I'm saying this because I'm thinking: what's going to protect them? What's going to keep the world out? I have the sense the world needs to be kept out." She looked back at the paper lanterns strung around the pool. "That man up there said I had a winsome smile."

"That man was hoping you would follow him into the powder room."

"That was his word, *winsome.*"

"He was hoping you might follow him upstairs."

"I thought that was what you wanted."

He looked at her and laughed, almost laughed—what had she said?

"Is that what you want?" he asked.

"I don't know." It was an honest answer. "I'm still trying to figure that out."

Avi dreamed Beirut. The shells of imported Citroens, burned and stripped to blackened husks. Random graffiti that appeared overnight, illegible and confused, now an apple, now an angel. Conjured as much from the air as from memory. Rabid dogs and the twenty year old Avi taking an eleven meter RIB up the Litani River where they waited with Kalashnikovs and RPGs. Pamela dreamed collapse: numbers, home values, stock reports. A teetering column of paper, head-high, that all at once doesn't topple so much as swirl around her to mat against her face in a way that implies a desire for breath, for life. It was more abstract than Avi's—sometimes he dreamed specific license plates, fingered entry wounds—but no less violent.

"Should we be up here?" she asked.

They were on the second floor and the party felt impossibly distant, the sound muffled through the floor but drifting airily through the open balcony doors, graceful as birdsong.

"I want to look around a minute," Avi said. "I used to stay here for months at a time, teach at a little place off Twelfth Street."

"Yoga?"

"Combat arts. The open hands of the Muay Thai."

"Will they hear us?"

She stood near the balcony and felt her head swim over the bay. When she turned Avi was in an armchair, barefoot and nearly hidden in shadow.

"Hear us doing what?" he asked.

"I mean just walking around."

"I know what you mean. I'm joking." He stood. "Come see this."

The bedroom was cavernous and spare, the kind of controlled emptiness that came only with complete self-confidence, the Western affectation of presumed simplicity that, in the end, sniffed of money. She looked at the absence and knew she would never get there, never possess such contrived vacancy. Like Luther, she would always be grabbing. It was part of what bound them.

"Sit for a moment," he said.

"Where?"

"Wherever is comfortable."

Then they were on the bed, Avi beside her, propped on one elbow while she sat against the headboard, legs tucked beneath her. She felt a lazy pull draw her toward indulgence, the dragline of easy fatigue and its accompanying justification. You could do things after exertion you wouldn't otherwise do, you *earned* things. The logic seemed sound. She realized she was a little drunk but remembered it was just the right kind of drunk, the kind of numbed perception you could recline into. Oh, she thought, this is what possibility feels like, like sleep, like dreaming. What did her daughters dream? Her husband dreamed of tax shelters and fixed-wing aviation. His childhood, perhaps, which he'd never really told her about.

Hers was happy, though when Pamela considered it now it seemed more enameled than perhaps it had been. Her parents had attended Yale, from which she had also graduated—yes, yes, a legacy like the president, she could hear Luther think, but never say—her mother a social worker, her father earning a doctorate in Aeronautical Engineering from M.I.T. mere weeks before Pamela was born. They moved south, and he went to work for the space program, driving daily from their house three blocks off the beach in Cocoa, to a lab within Cape Canaveral where he helped craft the guidance system that allowed wobbly communication satellites to maintain orbit and would later help orient the Space Shuttle.

Her mother stayed home—all the mothers stayed home—and their neighborhood of shabby bungalows had about it an air of scientific bohemianism, five or six blocks of young moms teaching their kids yoga and French while their husbands worked to push science past the moribund strictures of the Cold War, their bosses suit-and-tie drones who'd flown bombers over Europe or, in a few cases, split atoms at Los Alamos, unable to understand this new generation with its hair over the collar, to say nothing of the sense of purpose that came not from fighting the Russians—couldn't they see already the Russians were finished?—but from immersing themselves in the future, no different than the deep ecologists, the friends from grad school who were beginning to live in biodomes or quitting jobs with Archer Daniel Midlands to open organic farms.

Which is to say, Pamela thought, times were hopeful. Which maybe accounted for the polished feel, as if her memories were handed to her, more inherited than experienced, the product of a collusion it had taken her years to realize she was party to. *Remember how nice it had been, Pam? Watching your father leave for work and knowing we had the entire morning together?* Driftwood, yoga on the beach, the weekend cookouts where some otherwise sedate physicist would strum the entirety of *Pet Sounds* on a ukulele. Had it been that happy?

"Cold War pastoral," Avi said. "It sounds idyllic."

Did it? And how much of this did she tell him? She didn't think she had been speaking but when she looked at Avi he appeared to have heard everything, though she wondered if perhaps even his appearance—like her own voice—was simply an echo in the dull chamber of her head. Perhaps she'd said nothing.

"Go on," he said.

But she was quiet now. Her shirt had glided up above her navel and she realized his hand rested lightly on her stomach. She had come to realize you lived your life there. Not in the heart or the mind but in the gut. Her abdominal wall was ridged with muscle and a small silver stud pinned her bellybutton—a moment of insanity with Luther—but it felt like it defined her existence, gave it contours. Her stomach, she meant—God, was she really this drunk?—brown and hard, the skin only slightly stretched by her two daughters.

What she loved, what she cherished about pregnancy was the closeness, the way she was never alone, the way she could protect completely the child within her. It was minutes after Lucy was born—the warm wetness of her daughter huddled against Pamela's chest—that she realized how open she would be from here forward, how vulnerable, how, so long as her daughter was alive, Pamela could be hurt, how even from the grave she would sense her child's pain, so sharp the edge of her love. But time wore even the blade of motherhood dull and soft, or at least masked its ability to cut. Was this scar tissue or moral confusion? It was the kind of question she would've liked to pose to her husband, but now did not seem the time (and hadn't she resolved *not* to think about the girls? For just once in her life to *let it go*). Avi was running two fingertips along the elastic band of her underwear and she was having difficulty figuring out if this was a positive turn or not.

"What are you thinking about?" he asked.

"The gate," she said.

"Don't let the gate concern you."

"The gate is notional, a gate of the mind."

But had it really been that happy?

Maybe, though she suspected it was never as good or as bad as she liked to think. Pamela the indulger, Pamela the vain, the loveliness of her childhood spoiled when they moved just south of Jacksonville. She was nine, and her father and a friend had decided to go into work for themselves as consultants to the aerospace industry. There was patriotism, certainly, there was the pleasure of science, there were all the things that had kept her father working for the government, but there was also money, and suddenly, once they had it, Pamela came to wonder how they ever survived without it. It was her mother who first suggested it was the money that had so isolated them once they moved; which sort of stunned Pamela: she'd always thought of money as their sole consolation. There were certainly no friends, not initially. They lived in a neighborhood of split-level ranches and Pamela began to attend the local Episcopal school (her mother deemed the local public school unacceptable; though why she was no longer homeschooled Pamela never quite understood). Pamela had no friends and believed, as a point of honor, this had to do with her parent's political and religious leanings.

"Doesn't he ever go to church?"

"Doesn't he ever pray?"

"He doesn't pray," she told the noisy brats in music class, "he meditates."

"My daddy said he probably works for Brezhnev."

She didn't know who Brezhnev was, no one at school knew who Brezhnev was, but the rumor that her father somehow worked for this man, that her father had been forced out of his job with NASA because he had sold certain things, important things, that were meant to be secret, became so commonplace that she finally asked her father. He was taken aback—*Oh, Pam. Oh, baby. People actually say this?*—and offered to show her everything. Thus the day she skipped school to ride with her father to a strip-mall near the airport, an aluminum building, unmarked, that, for a panicky second, looked exactly like the sort of a place a spy—the word *spy* had entered the playground lexicon—would hide. What her father showed her inside—a draftsman's table, two bulky desktop computers, a mainframe the size of a refrigerator, a desk hardened with mustard stains—was so ordinary, so uninspiring that she found herself wishing her father *was* a spy, that he *was* selling secrets to Brezhnev with his two-toned hair and thick eyebrows. The following spring, when her agnostic mother quit teaching yoga at a studio on Vilano Beach and, with her atheist father, joined the Episcopal church, Pamela felt the buttresses of her childhood strain and collapse, the sense that they were different, that they were somehow marked as special, the mythology that allowed her to exist as defiant and friendless was no more.

"Are you going to vote for Mondale, daddy?"

He was driving her to school on a Tuesday morning, one of the rare times she was alone with him anymore, what with the work, what with the pressure. *Think about the pressure your father's under*—her mother's words—*think of how much courage it takes to go out on your own.*

"Oh, I think old Mondale's all right, honey. A nuclear freeze. The ERA."

"Sadie's dad said if Mondale won we'd all be speaking Russian by the end of the year."

"Who is Sadie?" her father asked. "This is a girl in your class?"

She nodded as much to answer him as to force him to look at her.

"Well," he said, "I somehow doubt Sadie's father knows terribly much about it."

But when Pamela wrote to her friend Meredith back in Cocoa she learned that Meredith's parents were not only voting for Gus Hall and Angela Davis they had put up a giant—*completely and totally huge*—yard sign. When she told her father he clucked his tongue like he did when someone blew an easy answer on *Family Feud,* half sympathy, half condescension.

"Everyone has to grow up at some point, hon," he told her, "some are just later at it than others."

That summer she asked her parents if she could start the local high school. Ninth grade was approaching, she thought she might want to try cheerleading. When they responded enthusiastically she wasn't sure whether to thank them for their encouragement or curse them for their submission. Either way, she made the team, and suddenly everything changed.

She had friends now, she had so many friends she didn't know what to do with all of them, girlfriends, boyfriends, seniors who would circle by her locker between classes, *just to see how my favorite girl's managing,* coaches a year removed from college who *loved the way she moved.* And it was from these friends she first learned about sex. Sex as it really was, she thought, because it occurred to her within a few weeks that everything her mother had told her, everything about the union of souls or the seeking of individuated Platonic forms, had absolutely nothing to do with what was, at base, a sweaty physical act, not entirely unlike the distance running she took up in the spring. Pamela ran everything from the 400 up to the 3200 and it was one day on the track that her new friend—*best* friend, because you had to have these things—Sarah looked around at the boys running hurdles or throwing the javelin and said, pointing: "It was Rory I went down on. Eighth grade," she said, "I regret it but like don't either, if that makes any sense. And Thomas, he was so tender and I was like, Yes, I love him, but then he wouldn't do anything. People say Keith Howes has the biggest dick in the school."

Pamela felt herself blush. "People say this?"

"I think he's hot for you. He's looking over here right now."

It would be years later—junior year, when they were decorating the National Guard Armory for the prom—that Sarah would give her a slow kiss in the back stairwell, Pamela having asked to see the tongue stud Sarah had gotten. She leaned forward until the wet pearl of the stud was slipping along Pamela's lips, Sarah's eyes downturned, and that squeeze she offered Pamela's hand before pulling away, Pamela knowing her face was on fire, the moment embarrassing, and sudden, and too short.

By this time Pamela had cycled through the few boys she found appealing. She let three of them touch her and one enter her, but the sex was always unsatisfying and awkward, serving to damage the friendships she had so carefully constructed. By Christmas break in the eleventh grade she was done with boys and focused on everything else. She had finished third in the state at the AAAA cross-country meet and thought she had a reasonable shot at winning the two-mile in the spring. Her grades and skin were near-perfect. She was elected class and then student body president. When she realized she might be accepted to Yale as a legacy she took an SAT-prep course, an hour of analogies and logic games followed by an hour of sun salutations and sleep. She was socially involved but less social, abstaining from the casual contact—*above* the casual contact?—that defined the lives of everyone around her. The specialness she lost when they left Cocoa Beach returned, except now it wasn't borrowed, it wasn't the shared radiance of her parents, the solar run-off she collected as their daughter. It was wholly and completely hers.

It was around this time that Sarah kissed her, and to some extent Pamela considered it an invitation across the divide. *If you truly are different, let me show you different.* But it wasn't the kind of difference she was after. She was flattered, and only slightly surprised one day to find herself considering the implied offer, but in the end it was wrong for her, and she knew it. The world was beginning to spread out before her, wider than she'd ever imagined. Her dad was making money now, lots of money. He moved into a larger building and hired a staff of ten, flew to California every other week to consult with McDonnell-Douglas. They bought a horse they stabled in Elkton and took a vacation to France and then returned that Christmas to ski in Chamonix. Next came a winter retreat in Flagstaff, all glass and terracotta and perched on a ridge of red rock. Her mother was elected to the city and county councils where she forced through a school bond and a conservation easement on several hundred acres along the St. John's River. They moved into a bigger house, bought another horse, went in on a time-share in Vail. That her parents were becoming pillars of the community seemed to bother Pamela less and less.

The money helped.

There was always the money to cushion things. It *had* been a form of insulation for her, allowing her to assume certain postures, to offer judgments on subjects that would never touch her. You can behave wildly, you can make a mess of things, she realized, so long as you know your landing will be soft. She had no desire to wreck her life, but she did want to test the limit of things, to see not how far she *could* go—because, truthfully, she doubted she would ever touch the limits of self: was it wrong to admit as much?—but how far she *was willing* to go. It was the same thing she was after that summer in Charleston with Luther. That she had so thoroughly used him seemed to matter less, at least at the time, than the need to substantiate certain hypotheses.

So it was fitting that she first saw him at a track meet, Luther the Bear, Luther the Beast. He was a wrestler and defensive end by virtue of his side, but it was the hammer-throw that seemed to summon something more substantive, something inner. The quiet circling wind-up, the violent release.

Several years prior, their mothers had a brief and unsuccessful friendship that started when Luther's mom took a yoga class at the Vilano Beach studio and ended when she insisted Pamela's mom come see what proved to be her vaguely pedestrian paintings.

"Seascapes and landscapes," she remembered her mother telling her father, "pelicans on dunes. That sort of thing."

"Artistic mediocrity is no reason not to be friends," her father said.

"Oh, I know, John. But it wasn't just the paintings." Her mother flying out the door to another meeting of this committee or that organization. "It was everything about her. It was the frailty of it all, and how we could both see what an act it was. I couldn't get past how badly she wanted my approval."

(Luther's parents were dead now: did that make hers more alive?)

It was years later when Luther was in the Air Force and Pamela was back home after her junior year that she began to see the continuity between the high school track meet when she first saw him and the summer they listened to Stravinsky and slept together in the house on Prioleau Street. This continuity wasn't something she could articulate, not exactly, but she was still stunned that she hadn't discerned the pattern sooner. She'd needed time, she supposed, perspective, the nuances gained by trying on self after self which she had certainly done. So the summer after her junior year—this after her Jesus-freak stage, after her Zen stage, after her horn rims-and-study carrel stage, and, most especially, after the slow dissolution of guilt she had carried after the Charleston-and-Luther stage—that May she went back home and decided she would spend her last free summer getting a really killer tan.

What followed was the sort of soul-killing cliché that is simply too much fun to renounce. She had a fling with the assistant tennis pro at the yacht club—Wilhelm, the first boy she'd touched since Luther, and yes, her parents now belonged to a yacht club. She got incredibly fit and incredibly tan and at night drank Mai Tais on the club veranda, the bay spread like a dark fabric smoothed flat and occasionally pricked with light. It was all great fun, and she sort of loved her life and sort of hated herself at the same time. In a way, it was a lot like the summer she'd spent with Luther, except she had been younger then, and that summer bore a certain weight, a weight precious and overwrought, true, but a weight nonetheless, that was now noticeably absent. That what had ran once as tragedy was being replayed as farce made her feel grownup in a way that felt stagey and wrong, and she began to wonder to what extent she would ever be able to simply live her life rather than reflect on the living of her life while attempting to live it in the first place.

So when Luther came home for a week in late August, just days before Pamela was set to return to New Haven for her senior year, she felt more relief than excitement or fear, as if he might offer a way—a reminder, maybe—back to the person she had been. That they met only by chance—she was out running when he honked and pulled onto the shoulder—and that he had been home already for four days without bothering to contact her, old friend that she was, she wanted to chalk up to his being busy—he was moving from Pope Air Force Base in North

Carolina to Tinker in Oklahoma. But the possibility that he was snubbing her probably had quite a bit to do with the fact that she slept with him twice before he left three days later.

It was one of the few moments in her life she truly couldn't help herself. That weekend Luther seemed a different animal, all the indecisive brooding replaced by this lanky careless grace, so confident, so much—that word again—an animal. She wanted to be near him. It was important for people to know that they were together—though they weren't—that they knew he was hers—though he wasn't, not yet. At a party Friday night he sat in a deck chair, barefoot with a Maker's Mark in one hand, while Pamela curled at his feet and leaned back between his legs so that her hair was close enough for him to idly stroke her scalp. That affectionate scratch—*good girl, my girl*—and she would shiver and think of her hands going up under his shirt and across his chest. She felt she could hide in his vastness, get lost in him, big-hearted, big-handed.

When he was gone, she packed her own bags and returned to college, feeling that something, she couldn't say exactly what, but something, had been sealed. She started writing him that fall and when the Gulf War began in January the letters became feverish, long and florid and full of the passion the situation seemed to both summon and demand. When he was given leave in April—he'd spent five months flying cargo to Saudi Arabia and Kuwait—she cut her classes and drove out to surprise him.

The five days they spent together proved blissful enough to overlook a number of things that arose later, like the drab dusty heat of Oklahoma, the deep ratcheting whine of aircraft lifting off, or the way the peeling pressboard walls of base housing shook when they did. But none of that would register until months later, well after their June marriage and honeymoon through New England, after a summer and fall of champagne and road trips.

The newfound shabbiness of her life seemed clear only early the next year when Luther was deployed on temporary duty to Ramstein and Pamela, two months pregnant with Lucy and sick every day, was left alone for the winter. She had never really known winter—what they had in Connecticut no longer qualified—but she knew it now. It seemed to gather for a thousand miles, the wind leaning like a falling tree, pushing the snow ahead of it, so bright and sharp and wondrously predatory it seemed never to settle and pack, as she understood snow was supposed to do, but to attack, to fight its way through the old windows and warped doorjambs, and impossibly, she had to have imagined it, between the bedsheets and mattress.

She was still fighting the winter—heat, the absence of heat, seemed to consume her thoughts—when her mother visited. Pamela wasn't expecting her. After she had told her parents she was pregnant there had been a flurry of letters and phone calls begging her to come home, to visit, *Luther can't possibly expect you to stay alone out there with absolutely no people.*

He's not asking me to do anything I don't want to do, mother.

The nerve of him, probably playing golf in Ireland while you freeze to death, alone on Christmas Day. It went like that until it suddenly didn't. The letters stopped, the phone calls tapered to silence, as if her parents, in plotting their next overture, had simply run out of ideas. It had been fully a week since the last call when someone knocked at the door. Pamela looked out the window and for a moment didn't recognize her. (Later, when she told this to Luther he would laugh and explain how *his* mom and done the exact same thing, driven out to convince him to come home, and how he hadn't recognized her either. *It was just that she looked so old,* he told her.) Her mother wore jeans and a black sweater, terribly underdressed and visibly trembling beneath the yellow door light. When they hugged, Pamela felt how cold she was, and how small, her body sagging into itself while Pamela felt her own growing, thickening in her breasts and waist and hips. She made coffee and they sat facing each other, the living room so small their knees almost touched.

"You're going to freeze in here," her mother said, her voice sounding as if it had not been carried across the country but dragged. "Is there any heat at all?"

"I can't believe you drove."

"I came up through Tallahassee to Baton Rouge and then up through Little Rock." She was hugging her chest, and her mere posture suggested the possibility of a different life: come home, stay with us. We'll get help with the baby and you can go back to school. She shook her head. "I don't know," she said. "I imagine there's a better way."

"Does daddy know you're here?"

"I haven't called him yet, but yes. Your father knows I'm here."

"And he's okay with this?"

"He would rather I'd have flown, darling, but he knows exactly where I am."

She was surprised by how much her mother and father resembled each other. She'd never noticed. Then she realized it was something new. Her parents shared the stunned look they had worn for the better part of a year, ever since the wedding, and what she felt at that moment wasn't the defiance that had fueled her for so long—she realized that defiance had exhausted itself weeks ago—but sympathy, pity. They were older. They were vulnerable. And it was because of her. It came to her then: they loved her. They were on her side.

That night she lay in bed and listened to her mother whisper into the phone to her father back in Florida. The cord ran down the hall and under the door and in the thin, fragile silence she thought she could hear their words scratch along the line, quiet enough not the disturb the glass-like quiet that for two months had felt on the verge of shattering. The night swallowed her, the frozen scrape of branches against the vinyl siding, the dumb fuzz of sodium lamps, the pickups and muscle cars caped in snow.

I keep hearing the planes—her mother's voice, real or imagined?—*these damn jets that take off every time you just start to think your brain has settled.*

Outside someone was walking and Pamela heard the gravely squeak of footsteps, snow compacting, an engine groaning and catching. The wall lit, the slatted blinds, the shape of her desk and chest-of-drawers, and then the darkness, deeper than she had realized, and what followed was an accounting of her new life. What followed were the hairless patches along Luther's calves, worn bare by the shirt-tuck stays of his uniform. The weave his belt impressed in the soft flesh of his waist. She contrasted it against Luther-on-the-beach, Labor Day weekend Luther, whom she conjured once again, so light and happy in his madras shirt, moving like a dancer as he slipped around the edges of things, never seeming to care, never seeming to notice, gliding through the great big world like it was his to have and to hold.

What are we doing here? We don't belong here.

Oh, mother, please—

Later, much later, she thought she saw her mother standing in the bedroom door. It was possible her mother stood above her and touched her hair, though after Pamela could never be certain. The last year had been like that, she came to realize. She and Luther on the hot beach while fireworks went up in stars and spiders and bright lollipops that fizzed above the turning eye of the Ferris wheel. And now so cold, buried beneath two blankets and a quilt. Had any of it been real?

In the morning her mother made breakfast in the crowded kitchenette, Pamela safe in her knowledge that everything was aligned, dishes and glasses and plates, that everything had found its place. That he kept his uniforms in plastic bags in the office closet, there was comfort in that. That she had learned to iron the creases, it proved her commitment. *What are you going to do, Pam?* her mother not asking this. Her mother not saying *you read books, you can cook. You have good skin and this incredible future if you want it. Think of yourself just sitting here, waiting for him. Lighting the oil burner. Trimming the crepe myrtles along the walk.* Her mother saying none of this, but speaking lightly of Pamela's father, so that Pamela could tell that her mother was secretly proud of her daughter's loyalty, that she wanted badly to see her girl as brave and as worthy and now she had and she could go home satisfied.

She left that afternoon and Pamela walked upstairs and saw the bed was made. It took her a moment to notice that stacked on the nightstand were several Arnold Lobel books Pamela had loved as a child. *Frog and Toad Together, Frog and Toad All Year, Owl at Home.* She saw the books and froze, felt a rising panic, and quickly shook them out. There was no note and, more importantly, no check. If there had been a check Pamela would have hated her mother for it. She would have taken it, and cashed it, and never forgiven her. But there were only the books, left by her mother for, it struck Pamela, her grandchild. The subsiding panic gave way to shame and suddenly she wanted to do better, to be better, more patient and more kind. How unfair, she thought, that by the time you are old enough to love properly your parents you are on the verge of losing them, the ones who cherish you the most, with their stack of paperbacks, freezing in the Oklahoma cold. A thousand miles just to cook you breakfast.

What are we doing here? We don't belong here?

She had taken her parents for granted. It was natural, but no less right, and standing there she felt overwhelmed by the truth. How bitter, she thought, how bitter the truth.

Two days after her mother left Pamela found herself crouched and freezing in front of an antique oil heater that refused to light. She kicked it until she was certain her toe was broken, at which point she began to laugh. She laughed so hard she vomited and when she had cleaned herself up—which involved little more than exchanging one overcoat for another—she realized the worst was behind her and that everything, no matter how bad it got, would turn out fine. She wasn't arrogant, and she wasn't delusional. The clarity had just come to her, fully realized, and it wasn't debatable; it was cumulative. She put the dirty coat in the hamper and opened the door on a parking lot of dirty snow. It was shoveled and plowed and browning, but it was beautiful in its way, honest and smudged. The honesty moved her, the evident blemishes, unrefined, uncaring. She thought she might love it, felt certain she would, given time. That what little heat the house held had escaped seemed not to matter. What mattered was her awareness. After years of struggle, she knew exactly who she was and exactly what she could do.

She could stay. And she did.

But where was Avi's hand now, where was his mouth? And how much had she said? This was tricky because suddenly everything seemed off. He was on top of her, yes, his mouth in the soft bend of her throat, true, and here she hadn't even been aware they were touching. Which was comforting in its strange way, her general sense of disarray. Her whole life had been one confusion after another. What she had experienced that day in Oklahoma had been soothing but false,

111

though she often returned to it, forgetting for weeks at a time that she had eventually found herself out, forced herself to move past the lie of self-knowledge. The truth was, she knew nothing. She was forty-one years old and knew absolutely nothing.

Except that this man was touching her, her husband.

Luther moved his mouth over her bra—she was out of her shirt! another revelation—and down her stomach. He pushed his mouth against the fabric of her underwear and she felt his teeth pull at the waistband. He seemed to be pushing against her, nose and tongue, and she loved that about him, the way he had always known her. That was one of the best things about marriage, the way you came to know intimately the body of your other, the swales and gentle reefs, the places they had beached themselves for days at a time, hotel rooms, cheap and expensive, on the bed, on the floor, beside the oil heater in Oklahoma, beside the open window in Florida, the armchair in Charleston. Once, right after the wedding, they had driven to Chicago on a Friday night, spent Saturday in bed with their champagne, then driven all day Sunday to arrive home just before daylight, having stopped once to make love in an empty state park. But now they were back in the house on Prioleau Street. She was nineteen. She didn't care. She put her hand into his hair, scratched. *Oh,* she said, *oh, oh*—

Did she say his name? As easy as exhalation, as natural as breath.

He looked up at her and there was a brief moment of familiar confusion, a stutter of brainlight, the synapses misfiring before firing in wild correction, because here was the thing: this man wasn't her husband, and she wasn't in the house on Prioleau Street, and she certainly wasn't at home. She was she-didn't-know-where and he was she-didn't-know-who.

"Who—" she started to say but his mouth had dipped again to her groin. She raised her head and felt the room shift violently. He appeared to be drinking her.

"I can't—"

"Shh," he said.

"No, I can't—"

"Pamela." He said her name. He knew her name. "Relax, Pamela."

"No." She was thrashing now, beginning to thrash. "Let me up. Let me—"

He let her go and, again, the question arose: how much had she said? Enough, she suddenly realized, enough to conjure Luther because hanging there, past this man's bare shoulder and above the glow of the party lights, she saw her husband, green-eyed and floating above the balcony, simply hanging in the sky, watching her. She'd never been so certain of anything in her life.

"My husband," she said.

"It's all right."

"He sees us. He's right there."

It was enough to make the man look, a quick flash over his shoulder toward the balcony and the closed bedroom door. He smiled.

"No one sees us, Pamela."

"No, he's right there," she said.

"Pamela—"

"Oh, God, he's right there. Luther," she called. "Luther!"

"Pamela, stop—"

She was fighting her clothes back onto her body now, tripping off the bed.

"Luther!"

"Stop—"

His hand was over her mouth. She was pinned against the headboard and his face was close enough to see the trimmed hair that furred his nostrils. She didn't think he meant her any harm but she wanted his hands off her.

"Please don't yell, darling," he whispered

But she wanted his hands off her and before she knew what she was doing had struck his temple with her right elbow, exactly as he had taught her, and her arm was warm and slick and he looked staggered, as if his eyes might vibrate independently within the ocean of his face. And there, past him—she saw him!—Luther watched it all.

She was still pulling her clothes on when she ran down the stairs, her hair wild—she caught a glance of herself in a mirror, running, falling—and her arm lit with dark blood. Someone screamed—was it her? Talking stopped. Heads turned. A clownfish dipped from the ceiling in attack and she batted away the high whine of its engine. She heard the man—Avi, his name was Avi—heard Avi behind her calling *Pamela, Pamela, wait* but she was to the door now, down the steps and onto the street before she ever realized she hadn't put on her shoes. She ran as hard as she could. Warm night, wet night. The palms up-lit so that they shone like green stars. Down the cobbled street past the houses and the expensive cars and the people behind her that had flooded into the street and none of it mattering because Luther was above her, green-eyed and unmoving, and she saw him!

She saw him!

Oh, she did, she did, floating there above the skyline, above the causeway and the water, above the entire world, Pamela looked up and saw him!

PART FOUR

THE DOGS WERE ALL RIGHT. The beagles had dragged a small rabbit onto the porch and now the bones were clean and broken. A tiny thing with giant feet. Gray pelt. The shriveled heart intact, purple and dangling. Bobby fed them and shooed them into the yard and went inside and showered. He couldn't remember getting off the island. Couldn't remember getting back to his truck. He'd had to carry Donny at some point—he was certain of that—but when they stopped in their parents' yard Donny pulled himself upright, straightened his clothes and marched onto the porch. Mamma inside somewhere, Bobby lacking the courage to watch. He left, drove home and realized he must have forgotten some things in the motel in Daytona Beach. His shaving kit and toothbrush. His vitamins. Would have to stop at the Walgreens on his way home. He drank half a Ripped Fuel and found some B-complex in the bathroom, got in his truck and left.

Donny's ex, Marsha, lived on the west side of town, a neighborhood of dilapidated shotgun houses. Masonite siding and peeling chain-link. Furniture in the yards. It was mostly blacks and the Mexicans that huddled around the Catholic Church. Bodegas and liquor stores. Every corner littered with scratch-off lotto tickets and old diabetic men on electric scooters. Bobby needed to get to work but knew at some point he had to face Marsha, let her know Donny was home. As if she wouldn't have heard nothing but for the last week.

Marsha worked doing medical billing for a strip mall doctor out near the by-pass. Married to Donny for almost two years when he got in the fight. The engagement longer than the marriage. Donny always finding reasons to delay things. Moving in—twice, Bobby remembered—with another woman only to come whimpering back home. Marsha always taking him in. Donny simply taking.

Bobby parked on the street and put his keys in his pocket. Didn't bother much with that normally, but did it here. The porch was crowded with wicker chairs and ashtrays wiped clean. He rang the bell and when she came to the door he followed her in and sat on the couch. She went in the kitchen and came back with a cup of coffee.

"You've got just about the worse hangover on your face I've ever seen," she said. "The Donny look."

"Pretty much."

"Is this the official announcement?" she asked. "That what this is, the official warning?"

"I think Mamma's having some sort of welcome back for him tonight."

"Supposed to be last night, I heard. But then I guess Donny went and messed that up too." She pulled her legs up on the couch. Her hair was tied back in a paisley bandanna. Bobby noticed a can of Lemon Pledge and realized he must have interrupted her housecleaning. He couldn't imagine bothering to clean anymore, he couldn't imagine making that effort.

Marsha put one hand to her head. "He'd come home some nights just howling. And I mean literally and truly howling, and I would think: this man, I love this man. And then some nights. Some nights he just—" She made a little dismissive gesture with her hand. "How much does he know about Stephen?"

"He knows he isn't doing so well."

Marsha wiped something from the inside of one eye. "I haven't seen Stephen's daddy in over a year now."

"Out of the picture."

"Out of the world as far as I'm concerned." She shook her head. "When your mamma sent that invitation I thought for half a second she did it out of cruelty then I thought: that woman doesn't have a cruel bone in her body. Then I thought of Donny. It seemed like his sort of meanness, to invite me."

"He doesn't want to go himself."

"Oh, I know he doesn't want to go. But I can just see him getting your mamma to send that to me. Like even from prison he could still get to me just like he always could."

"I don't know," Bobby said. He motioned toward the hallway. "Is he back there?"

"Is that the reason you came by?"

"I just thought I might stick my head in, say hello."

She stared off into the middle distance, some space along the mantel among the ornamental plates, framed photographs, a crude drawing of a bird. Things collected and lost. Or if not lost, forgotten. Their significance neutered.

"He started going to that Catholic church behind the ball field," she said. "Did I tell you this? I think it's mostly just Mexicans anyway. The *Iglesias*. But he started going and then was going every morning. Walking until I had to start driving him. It's just like three blocks—I could stand here and watch him the whole way—but his legs were so bad at that point." She was shaking her head again. "Now the priest comes over and goes back there. Mass or whatever. Communion."

"That's probably normal."

"I haven't been to church since I was eight years old, Bobby. I'm not Catholic. I don't think I've ever set foot in a Catholic Church."

"I mean the other part."

"The God part. I know what you mean," she said. "How's your own boy?"

"He's okay. I don't see him that much."

She stood and put a hand out toward him, touched his arm. "You're a good man, Bobby."

"There seems to be a decent argument against that."

She tried to smile. There was nothing on her lips but he registered some effort, some attempt that refused to coalesce. "Let me see if he's up," she said.

She disappeared down the hall and came back shaking her head.

"He's asleep. But if you want to just peek in."

The boy was propped in bed, a small tract clutched in one fist. An animated Jesus ascending into the same clouds Bobby had peered into, the broken sky that first day in Baghdad, his private vision. What utter bullshit it seemed when placed against a dying child, his legs covered with a sheet though Bobby could see the stick-like outlines, his knees fists, bones frail as pipe-cleaners. He had no hair. Bald and barely breathing. Bobby stood for a moment and watched the shallow rise and fall of his chest. The occasional cough, sudden and fierce, a ragged wheeze. But his face appeared serene. The eyelids and delicate pink lips. He wasn't Donny's son, conceived and born while Donny was locked away, but Bobby could smell the Rosen in the boy's blood, a scent thick with suffering. A heavy Bible sat on the nightstand, an adult's Bible, worn and stuffed with bulletins. What could Bobby possibly know about him? He'd only heard things. The boy had once walked, with his mother at first, and then alone, feeling her eyes track him until Confederate Avenue turned into Lee Street and there was the church, the *Iglesias*, the russet brick and stone angels, the ivy that vined the gate.

He was four years old, and then he was five, and then he was sick and age no longer mattered. He clattered down, a brown-eyed insect unable to eat, and there were hospital visits and hospital stays and a feeding tube that protruded from his pale stomach and some mornings he lay on his back praying the rosary and feeling the milky glucerna dry on his warm skin. That, Bobby knew, was when the priest started coming, daily, at first, less often as the days progressed. The visitors were no different, faltering, late and vaguely apologetic. There were gifts and flowers and talk that he had assumed an ethereal glow, but that stopped soon enough as well, and he was left alone in his bedroom, his mother fluttering in and out, a rare bird, hollow-boned and nervous. Did Bobby dream this? Did he *know* it? That daily the child passed into light. Or felt the light pass into him so that he was reconstituted as something clean and clear and could no longer feel the way his legs ached or the way his thin back sank into the damp sheets or the way the ceiling fan spun coolly against his face. Transubstantiation. The body into bread. The body into nothingness.

This was the measure of his days: he prayed darkness into light, light into darkness. The taste of the broken bread and the bodega grape juice. Seventy-nine cents for twelve ounces. That he took the savior's blood by the teaspoon while his mother sat in the corner and did not speak.

You could name it.

The name for it was Aplastic Anemia.

The name for it was sorrow. And suddenly Bobby couldn't recall which child he was talking about: the boy in bed or the boy in Sadr City? His own boy? The boy Donny had killed in Vegas? When he shot the boy in Iraq great bubbles rose from the hole in his throat and that was life, he remembered thinking. But it was also just trapped air, and then, after a moment, it was nothing at all.

He took five twenties from his wallet and folded them inside the heavy Bible. They would find them eventually, the way the boy read.

He shut the door softly.

Marsha was on the couch. Her eyes crying. Nothing else.

"People say he sees things." Her eyes were shut. "Like angels and devils. This giant bird. For a while there were people coming over here like he was from another planet. They wanted to touch him."

"When's his next treatment?" Bobby asked.

She looked at him. "There is no next treatment," she said brightly. "We're done. He's done."

"Is that a doctor issue?"

"Versus what?"

"Versus a money issue?"

"Actually, it's an I-can't-watch-my-boy-suffer-needlessly-anymore-so-how-about-you-mind-your-own-damn-business issue."

"I'm sorry."

She nodded, eyes shut. "Everyone's sorry. I hear that all the time. How sorry everyone is."

He stood in the middle of the room uncertain of what came next. She had turned toward the front window, legs tucked back beneath her, face wet.

"It isn't getting better is the thing," she said.

"You don't know that."

"It isn't getting better. And I don't just mean Stephen." She waved a hand around her. "Everything. I mean all of it."

He continued to stand there. The clumsy bear. The regretful animal.

"I'm sorry," she said finally. "You come over and I fall apart like this."

"If there's anything I can do."

She smiled at him and sniffed twice. "Thank you for coming, Bobby."

"I'm sorry to have upset you."

"You didn't upset me. It was good of you to come." She stood and hugged him and he moved to the door. "Maybe I'll even go and see Donny tonight," she said. "I'd like to see your parents. You think he'll have a woman with him?"

"Donny? No."

"Then maybe I'll come. Maybe I'll just get out of this house for once in my life."

He headed to work from there. Fields of wire grass. Crows going up in dark clouds. South toward Folkston and the Okefenokee, the Farmtown tract perched along the swamp's edge. They told him he had gotten the job because he knew the community, but he knew it was because he had killed, and they figured that if it came down to it, he wouldn't hesitate to kill again. As for the shit with the locals, the ragged protests and screaming soccer moms dragged from Appleton County growth-board meetings, Bobby had dragged an ugly reputation home from Iraq and someone in corporate must have thought that might help. So he'd spent three weeks at a strip-mall outside Chicago shivering in a thin Carhartt jacket while being trained to do things like remove a bald eagle's nest or handle the blood-borne pathogens of some trespassing eco-terrorist he might have happened, however accidentally, to have shot. He figured most of it was illegal but didn't care.

Since his discharge he'd worked construction until the work all but disappeared. It was always catch-as-catch-can but then things worsened dramatically, bad enough to remind him of his days as a fighter—the feast or famine part— and he was too old to be reminded of his days as a fighter. The economy tanked around the time his marriage was breaking up and if Nancy wasn't on him the mashed face staring back from the mirror was. He told her he wanted to start over. She shook her head and spoke of reaching a certain point where it wasn't so much about your ability to go forward as your inability to go back.

"Fate," she told him one night in bed just before she left him to move in with a real estate developer, "is the only bastard who owns me."

So he became part game warden, part forest ranger, and for it got a pickup and a decent paycheck, a new .357 with a box of Jacketed Hollow Points, and out in the center of Farmtown's 39,000 acres, an aluminum shed with an AC in the window and an army-surplus cot on the floor.

It wasn't hard work, either, and when things like murder—he imagined no other word for it—got to him he would walk into the yard and fire rounds into the giant stump of an old live oak. In a few years the land would be plowed and tamed, the palm and scrub pine displaced by ten-thousand stucco homes with manicured lawns and cheerful yard ornaments. There would be elementary schools and office parks—at least that had been the plan before the bottom fell out. But for now he was three miles down a dirt road and God only knew how far from the nearest person. It should have made him reckless but instead had the opposite effect: he became keenly aware of his movements, tended to little things like keeping his socks dry or changing the timing-belt in the pickup, but ignored big things, avoided the fencelines, stayed out of the mangrove swamps and stands of cypress. Didn't call his ex. Forgot he had a son. Days he caught himself shadow boxing he was embarrassed and then furious, and then, as often as not, soaked in his own tears.

Today there was little to do and he drove the six-wheeled Kawasaki Mule down a series of rutted paths. Deer sign. Rattlesnakes and migrating Arctic tern. Now and then he would spot a small black bear loping through the brush but today he was mostly alone with the mosquitoes. He rode back to his shed and cranked the window unit. Took off his shirt and lay it over his eyes. The air conditioner whispered like a river and he thought of all those nights tied up below Quarter Mile Bridge, the power plant flashing above. Below, the Altamaha black velvet and fat with channel cats, whiskered and sinuous and sliding through the dark water. Donny on his back, line in the shallows. He knew every star, knew when planets aligned.

Bobby rolled onto his stomach and breathed deeply. He didn't want the memory. What he wanted was to enter that dreamless dark, that point where sleep is not so much rest as the mind's blessed refusal. A stay against the persistence of memory. He waited, and then he slept, finally, and deeply, not waking until after six.

Cars and pickups started lining the road a quarter mile from his parents' house, tucked onto the shoulder or canted in the shallow ditches. Men coming off the porch or from the backyard to walk back to the coolers in the beds of their trucks. His parents were old hard-shell Baptists, tee-totalers who wouldn't allow it inside but, he supposed, might allow it in the yard given the auspiciousness of the occasion. Bobby bumped over the abandoned terraces to park in the field across the street. His daddy's garden. Dormant for three or four years now. The emphysema too bad. There were still a few apple trees but without pruning they had gone feral, shaggy monsters dropping winey fruit, yellow jackets everywhere. He waved to several men who stood in knots, toeing the ground and brown-bagging evening into night.

Old Elzo Potts sat in the porch swing, a child sprawled across his lap. He raised one hand as Bobby came up the drive.

"Praise the Lord." They shook hands, the child asleep against Potts's shoulder. The motor of an ice cream churn whined so that Potts had to speak over it. "It's a good day for your mamma and daddy."

"Yes, sir, I hope it is," Bobby said. "This is your grandson, Mr. Potts?"

"Four years old. They just go at that age."

"Yes, sir, that they do."

"I get to moving and he'll wake. I'm just trying to keep still." He let his big hand fall. "Sit down with me if you got a minute. They said you went and picked up Donny up."

"Yes, sir." Bobby sat in a glider. "Got back this morning."

"Good," Potts said. "That was good of you. Your mamma's been fit to be tied all week. I hope it comes out all right."

Bobby nodded.

"I did thirty days in the county lockup once," Potts said. "This years ago, buck wild and full of piss and vinegar. Criminal mischief they called it but we wasn't nothing but boys being boys."

"Yes, sir."

"Lord, I hope it comes out all right."

Bobby looked out at the road. Music from inside. A piano and several voices singing *So I'll cherish the old rugged cross.* Someone laughing. Potts was an old church friend of his parents. Giant hands and cloudy, glaucous eyes. Same turquoise bolo tie he'd wore for the forty years he ran the tire place on Confederate Avenue. He closed the gauze of his eyelids and snapped them open.

"You better get in there, son. I know your mamma's looking for you."

The house was crowded with people and smells. Casseroles and cakes along the kitchen counter. People crowded around the piano. All the markers of childhood: the lace doilies and wood-paneled walls. Brown carpet curling like the lip of a wave. The bathroom sweat: cold water drawn from a well and beaded along the porcelain of the toilet. He pushed through the crowd—people were clapping him on the back, smiling. Marsha against the paneled wall looking clumsily beautiful in lipstick and a short skirt. She waved and he waved back, turned and made it to his and Donny's old room, both single beds covered with pocketbooks and a few light jackets. A gun rack on one wall holding a compound bow. A poster of Troy Aikman gussied up like a real-life cowboy. They'd shared a bed until Bobby was eight and came home one day to find a set of JC Penney bunks. Another memory: older then, Bobby seventeen and listening to fifteen-year-old Donny remove the window screen and hop down into the yard, jogging the mile down to Marsha's bed. Bobby had woken once, an hour from dawn and the morning fog glowing as if weeping light, to find Donny centered in the carpet, panting.

Daddy's gonna hear you one night. Donny pulling off his wet tennis shoes, pulling the covers up to his chin. *Daddy ain't gonna hear shit.* And he never had, or had never cared, which amounted to the same thing. Their father a slumping bear, apologetic and clumsy in his Member's Only jacket, the elbows glossed. Dickies uniform pants. OSHA-approved work boots. He'd spent thirty-four years operating a drill press and now, in retirement, appeared unable to come off the assembly line.

He was too gentle, that was Bobby's diagnosis. When he and Donny were nine and seven their mother had caught them fighting three older boys in the one of the weedy lots down near the Scotsman gas station. She sat them on the couch and forbid them to speak, promising their father would be home soon, never learning that the older boys had been throwing railroad cinders at them as they walked to the bus stop. When their father came home he marched them solemnly behind the shed, looked back once at the house, and dropped onto his haunches.

"I ain't gonna whoop neither of you," he'd said, "but you better not ever let your mamma see that again." He looked a second time back to the house. "Now put your left hand up by your chin, that's it. Spread your feet a little more, shoulder-width. This is called your boxing stance."

He had learned the rudiments of fighting in the Army but within two years the boys had outstripped his knowledge and were jogging the two and half miles to the gym in town. Their mother had never cared for it, the brutality. Her small rabbit-like self a cloud of iron-gray hair fixed and set above a big silver brooch. Beneath the perfume the metallic scent of the crawlspace under the house. She prayed constantly. Oh, how she prayed for them. Lips atremble. Her boys gone so wrong. Exactly as she must have known they eventually would.

Bobby stepped into the hallway and saw them both at the kitchen table, older than he had realized. With it came the knowledge that he was, at least in part, responsible for that aging, the ceaseless worry, the inability to do right. He couldn't bear to face them and slipped out the side door just as the ice cream was ready.

He found his brother in the porch swing hung beneath the oak, drunk and eating popcorn from a plastic punch bowl. Braves ball cap. Elaborately tooled boots in the dust. Fingers glistening with salt.

Bobby sat down beside him.

"They're looking for you inside," he said.

"Who is?"

"Mamma. Daddy. I saw Marsha all dolled up."

Donny shook his head. "They ain't looking for me. They might be looking for you but they ain't looking for me. We did our little song and dance this morning."

"How'd it go?"

He stuck his hand down in the popcorn and held it there. "I'm just about to break out of this place. There ain't a thing holding me here."

"Except mamma and daddy."

"Mamma was happier when I was in the joint. Three square a day. Always knew where to find me." He raised a golden kernel, tossed it into the yard. "Daddy walks around scared of his shadow." He took a bite. "I been sixty-three months clean and sober now I'm about to ready to light this candle."

Bobby said nothing. Looked back at the house. The gray shadow pitched from the roof. The cars holding the day's last light.

"I tell you what happened today?" Donny said. "I took mamma's car up to the Gate station. Gonna fill it up for her, be a good son. Well, I pull in and start pumping and this guy walks out and just starts goddamn berating me. I mean just laying into me that I'm pumping at the full-service pump. I didn't even know full-service still existed and here this guy is just laying into me. Well, I turned around ready to knock the shit out of him, right? But before I even took a step I started crying. I mean just bawling like a baby." He looked at his brother. "Then I realized it was on account of the meanness, just the pure-T hatefulness of it all. Seven years inside and me just crying my eyes out because some redneck yelled at me."

He ate some popcorn, mouth churning slow and meditative.

"I ain't sticking around a day longer than I have to," he said. "Call Kristen. Pick her up. We're dinosaurs, brother. There ain't no use sticking around when the world don't want us."

"Come on."

"Don't 'come on' me. I'm serious. You should go with us."

"She won't even remember your name, Donny."

"She's in love," he said. "You don't forget your beloved."

They sat for a while longer. Folks walked out of the house to start up their cars. Cones of headlight. Backing onto the road. The swing was in shadow now, almost invisible.

"I'm going," Donny said. "There ain't no grave," he began to sing, "can hold my body down."

Saturday night Bobby packed a thermos and two sleeping bags and drove out to see his boy. He crossed the Altamaha River and turned onto a secondary road. It was all country here, pastures and fields, and then the housing development that emerged out of the pine thickets and soybeans, as sudden as if it were made from air. Which, in the end, he supposed, it was. A ghost development: asphalt lane winding through a few stunted trees and on to little circular blobs meant to be cul-de-sacs but holding nothing more than lot numbers and markers for septic lines. Survey flags and a brackish retaining pond swaddled in Tyvek wrap. The faded hieroglyphs of orange spray paint. Wire grass everywhere. Occasionally you would see the cinder foundation for a two-story faux Mediterranean arrested and abandoned but even those were disappearing beneath the scrub. Plots for forty-five houses but there were only three complete; only one was occupied.

Nancy hadn't remarried but had taken little Bobby and moved in with a land developer. Vance something. Vance who now faced the abyss of bankruptcy. Her house—his house, Vance's house, at least for the moment—was two stories of vinyl siding and new brick. Even in the dark Bobby could see the driveway was washboarded, the yard all mud and scattered straw, matted and rotting up to a cape of dull yellow sod.

He had never understood her leaving, but did now. What happened in Sadr City had only given her an excuse, cover and commiseration from circles of sympathetic friends.

"I don't want the house," she'd told him over the phone when he was in Walter Reed. They were officially separated by then, Bobby under psychiatric evaluation and understanding that his life had narrowed to a single moment, the cold barrel centered on the Iraqi boy's throat.

"Take it and be happy. Don't contest anything, and I promise you can see little Bobby now and then." Bobby had stood there in the corridor, watched the one-legged men wheel by, gave little nods as they passed. "Are you there?"

"I'm here."

"Well?"

"I want to see my son, Nancy."

Her sigh like wind singing. "Just don't contest anything, all right? Jesus." It all seemed to amaze her. "Can you imagine if you actually did?"

A light was on in the downstairs bedroom but he knew it was late enough that little Bobby would be asleep upstairs. He parked along the highway and got out, careful to stay along the far side of the road as he looped the house. More graffiti had gone up since his last visit. A broken window in one of the facing unfinished villas. A peculiar silence in the rustle of ornamental trees.

He stayed along the driveway's edge, her beige Civic dwarfed by a black Navigator. The SUV belonged to Vance, he knew. And it struck him again how she had wasted no time moving out, finding a new job, a new body for the bed, a little heft to impress the mattress. He thought of the house they had bought in Fayetteville, remembered Nancy's preoccupation with bathroom fixtures. Hardware it was called, like it was something besides trinkets to impress the kind of people Bobby despised: the safe ones, moderately wealthy and healthily fat, the ones with model trains or ping-pong tables in their basements.

He moved along the windows, cupped his hands to the glass. No one in the living room. No one in the kitchen. He waited until the bedroom light went out and the house settled, silent as prayer. He knew he should leave, just get in his truck and drive away, but to hell with it: he missed his boy. He collected several wood chips from the flower bed and lobbed them toward little Bobby's screen. After the third strike he saw the sash go up and a small head appear.

"Dad?"

"Hey, son. Whisper for me, all right?"

"Does mom know you're here?"

"No," Bobby said, "but it's okay. Think you could get out without waking her?"

"Is it okay?"

"It's fine. Maybe just put your shoes on."

He met his son behind the house, his boy in dinosaur pajamas and Dingo cowboy boots. Hair matted and eyes puffy with sleep. Bobby hugged his slim frame, his body warm and tiny, all shoulder blade and rib.

"I thought we might want to camp out like we used to," Bobby whispered. "Maybe just down near the pond. The planets have lined up. Mercury and Venus. I want you to see it."

"Is this okay with mom?"

"It's fine." Bobby pulled him close again. "You're a good boy for worrying about your mamma, but I promise you it's fine."

"I asked her if Uncle Donny was home and she told me not to call him that."

"Call him what?"

"Uncle."

Bobby put his arms around him. "Let's walk down to the pond."

Bobby spread the ground sheet on the grassy slope that broke toward the water, unrolled their sleeping bags and gave Bobby the thermos of hot chocolate. The stars were out. The sky clear and banded. A waning moon three days past full, and there, beneath, as promised, the cold glow of planets. They lay on their backs, Bobby's right arm beneath his son's head, the warm thermos between them and the air heady with night smells. The honeysuckle that grew along the bank. Raw lumber.

"Look up there," Bobby said. "The first light, right there, that's Venus. You see it?"

He nodded.

"Above that's Mercury. See the way they're lined up?"

"This is really nice, dad. I wish mom was with us."

"Me too, son."

"I'd like for her to maybe just be beside us. We wouldn't even have to say anything."

They slept then, and sometime just before dawn Bobby woke, his son curled into Bobby's chest, the vinyl bag moist with dew and tight across his back. He sat up and gently pulled his son's head into his lap. The nape of the neck. The perfect funnel of ear. His son was beautiful. As fragile as the light just beginning to filter through the trees. Clean light. Washed in pine. He'd wished away so many days. Oh God. He'd wished away days when he was deployed, of course, but he'd wished away so many at home, too. Rainy afternoons with little Bobby constipated and defiant, nights his boy couldn't sleep. He wanted forgiveness for that, more so than for all the rest—the ceaseless violence, the pointless destruction—he wanted forgiveness for his irreverence, his failure to hold fast. He pulled his son onto his shoulder, rested one hand on his hair. Mercury and Venus were still bright, still visible, and he was overcome with the need to see it once more, to share it. Look up at the planets, son. It won't be like this again in our lives. It won't be like this ever again. He stroked his boy's hair but couldn't bring himself to wake him.

A while later they walked back through the grass and empty streets to the house. Slashes of dew across the leather cowboy boots. Birdsong. When they topped the hill Bobby saw Nancy on the front porch with her arms crossed. Pink housecoat and old tennis shoes, her mouth pulled into a straight line. They approached silently and she hugged little Bobby and told him to go inside. Bobby turned for his car.

"I need to talk to you," she said.

He nodded and walked on. A few minutes later she came out and sat in the passenger seat, handed him a cup of coffee and hugged her chest.

"You do anything like that again it won't be your brother locked up."

He looked out through the beaded glass. "He's my boy. I needed to see him."

"Vance thinks I should call the police."

"To hell with Vance. What do you think?"

"What do I think?" she said. "Jesus, Bobby. I think you shouldn't put me in these situations."

He sipped his coffee.

"Black," he said.

"You don't forget certain things."

She reached for him and he thought she might touch his face but instead she looked back at the house, retracted her hand.

"Is he coming out here?" Bobby asked.

"Vance? He's trying to stay out of this."

"Does he know about me coming over?"

"He knows you get little Bobby once a month."

"You know that's not what I mean." He watched the leaves tremble, their undersides translucent and veined. One floated free to drift down, swirling for a moment before coming to rest in the mud, a quiet rustle he imagined but could not hear. "I didn't mean to scare you," he said.

"I know you didn't. It's just." She stopped. Out in the yard the dead straw ticked with a ghost of breeze. "I thought for a minute you might have taken him and just ran."

"I'm sorry about that. I thought you'd see the car."

"I did see it." She waved away the concern. "It still scared me."

He touched her shoulder. "I'm sorry. Truly."

She pulled away from his hand and bit her lip.

"What's happening, Nancy? I mean look at us. Look at you." He touched the terry cloth of the robe. "You never dressed like this."

"You just never noticed."

"You're giving up."

She forced a laugh. "You have to make a deliberate effort to stay alive, Bobby. It's an everyday thing and even then you have to keep settling for less and less. I don't know what you might call it." She looked at him and back out at the street. "The law of diminishing returns. You taught me that."

"I'm sorry then."

"I'm not complaining. I'm just stating a fact."

Light came through the dewed glass, a rain-blown prism of sunrise breaking above the trees so that it seemed less a windshield than a panel of stained glass. Despite the lines around her eyes she was still young, lean and angular from swimming. It was the first thing they had together—that love for all things physical —and eventually it became the only thing. It wasn't enough.

"I went over and saw Marsha's boy," Bobby said after a moment.

"Donny ask you to do that?"

"Donny doesn't know, I don't guess."

"I doubt he cares."

"I don't know," Bobby said. "He's dying though."

"Poor Marsha."

"And then I thought of little Bobby."

She was nodding. "I'm glad, I guess, that he got to see you," she said. "I do still love you, Bobby. But I have to think about more than just me."

He tossed the last of his coffee out the open window. The wind gusted and a shudder of leaves showered across the dead grass, caught against the gutter and sailed free to cyclone into the street.

"Yard looks like shit," he said.

"Please."

"Just get him to sow some grass or something. He can't sell this place if it looks like this."

They watched Vance come out onto the porch and peer across at the pickup. Nancy gave a little wave and he nodded and walked back in.

"I should go," she said. She opened the door and put one leg out, stopped and looked at him for what felt like the first time all morning."

"Vance is going to Atlanta for a few days," she said. "Some angel investor who thinks maybe the market's about to turn and this place is a bargain."

"I thought you said last time was it."

"I never said that."

"So are you saying for me to come by?"

She put her hand on his leg, retracted it, stood up and leaned back in. "I'm not saying anything. I'm just saying he won't be around for a day or two."

"There's always that one last time, I guess."

"No," she said. "If Vance gets the money we're moving to Atlanta, Bobby. We'll be gone." She looked at the house, the sky, everything but him. "There won't be any more last times."

Sunday morning he turned on the TV and watched a televangelist stomp around the stage, drank coffee while the man whimpered and moaned. *There is healing if you wish it. There is mercy when you call on the name.* He went out on the porch where through the screen of trees cars moved along the highway, not even so much blurred shapes as ideas of color, red, gray, scampering past. Finally, he put his cup in the sink and went to the bathroom to swallow his vitamins. Taking care of the body was a holdover from the days when taking care of the body was everything. Attending to every bruised heel or strained ligament. Vitamins. Protein powders. His semi-precious diet of fruit and vegetables and lean meat. He would run eight miles down a dirt trail wearing a twenty pound weighted vest, count the variety of greens in a salad, start and finish the day with sets of push-ups and pull-ups. Its continuance was strange in that self-preservation no longer mattered except so far as it allowed him to pretend life hung not behind him but somewhere before him.

He ate lunch at the Bantam Chef in town. Folks staring at him. A couple of old farmboys pointing and talking over their coffee until he felt obliged to walk back and ask them if there was anything he could help them with? He felt like shit for it, standing outside in the mid-day heat, knowing the rumors were already starting up—*then that son of a bitch walked right back here and cussed me within an inch of my life, and me not doing a damn thing*—but didn't know how else to deal with it. For weeks there had been talk about Donny, Donny getting into shit, Donny setting up deals. A lot of folks believed he was going to be rewarded for his silence, his refusal to turn State's evidence, and Bobby figured that was likely true. He'd get a bag of money, or maybe cut in on a few deals running from Savannah along I-16, just enough to reward his loyalty before they forgot him.

Bobby would have to find his brother soon enough, make some calls, track him down, but didn't know if he was up for just yet. Instead of looking, he drove home to check on the dogs, hit the heavy bag for an hour and swallowed two Aleves. Sat on the porch and flexed his hands. The dogs at his feet. The fields thick with insects and butterflies. He'd spent the better part of his childhood outside but had never learned the names of things. Trees. Plants. Birds. He regretted it now. Like his past was lost to him. The mornings grouse-hunting. The languid summer days walking aimlessly through the pines. The sumac and staggerbush—he could only guess at it.

He showered and lay on the couch for a while. He was going back over to Nancy's, that much was of no concern. The concern was direction. The concern was damage. How much he might inflict. How much he might avoid. There had been a story going around Bagram about a Forward Air Controller who had called in a B-52 strike on what turned out to be a wedding. According to the story, when the guy had seen the mess of it all he attempted to pluck out his eyes with a Ka-Bar, Old Testament-style. It wasn't true, of course—he'd hear the same story in Iraq, except it was an artillery strike that hit not a wedding but either a nursery or a primary school, depending on the version—but it had about it the stink of truth. The deeper knowledge that Bobby carried like a lodestone: the initial fear that his actions would lead to his death giving way eventually to the fear that his actions would lead to his having to live with unlivable consequences. It was exactly what he should have learned in the ring and to a certain extent he had. He'd known it and known it. Until the day he hadn't.

Late afternoon he started making calls to all of Donny's old goodtime buddies, the sad-sack hangers-on who'd orbited him like mayflies. Donny was down at Randy's, probably shooting pool. Donny had gone down to the Okefenokee, poaching gators with Beardog and them boys. He was back with Marsha or he was drunk or in jail or drunk and sleeping one off in jail. Somebody said he'd already lit out for Miami. Haitians, they said. He met him a bunch of Haitians when he was inside. The Mara Salvatrucha, another said. And people just shook their heads and stared down at their boots.

It was all bullshit conjecture, fueled, Bobby had no doubt, by Donny himself. *Self-mythologizing* in the words of Bobby's eleventh grade civics teacher. Donny was always lit with a certain aura. He knew when to tell stories but more importantly he knew when to keep his mouth shut. In the ninth grade he had disappeared for three days. The police had been called, child protective services. When he showed back up he acted like nothing had happened, neither confirmed nor denied the rumors that swirled around him. Bobby asked him later and he'd said he just needed to think, things blowing through his head like a locomotive, what the hell was all the fuss about? That was Donny, his bullshit couched in layers of guile. A shelf of paperbacks given by an English teacher in love with him: Hemingway and Jack London, and when he'd outgrown that, Herman Hesse and Nietzsche and Schopenhauer. He'd never made better than a C in anything but gym and shop class but his IQ had tested 163.

Bobby found him on the top floor of a crack house behind the Flash Foods on Highway 17, a shuttered Victorian peeling stripes of yellow paint, garbage bags filling empty window frames and billowing like lungs, the dead house resuscitated and crowded with squatters camping on rolls of foam bedding. He climbed past the catatonic and howling, a couple of teenage boys shirtless and kissing on a second-story mattress, several people packed into a brightly lit bedroom where someone sung hymns in a child's voice. He climbed past them all up to the third floor where Donny reclined on a couch, a glass pipe balanced on the hairless center of his chest. By his feet was a small shrine, a candle lit on the floor.

"There's an actual widow's walk if you go up those stairs," Donny said. He was flicking a lighter, trying to get it to catch.

"You're gonna die in your filth."

"The fuck I am. This is my new kingdom. The bums downstairs, they were living in the Stone Age. No water, no power. It took me about four minutes to tap the water main. Electricity took a little more but not much. Still, I'm not long for the place." Behind them a toilet flushed and a woman walked out of the bathroom in panties and a Nirvana t-shirt. He patted his lap and the woman sat. "Am I, sweetheart?"

She took the pipe and lighter from him and it was only then Bobby recognized Marsha. She seemed not to recognize Bobby at all.

"Shit," Bobby said, and thought of the child singing hymns downstairs, "I thought I knew that voice."

He ran down the stairs and pushed his way into the bedroom where Marsha's son sat on a mattress, legs curled beneath him, a bright coin of light falling from the window to encircle him. Stephen's eyes were shut and he seemed to be bless-ing the men and women who sat cross-legged on the floor in front of him.

"Get away from him." Bobby pushed aside two men and a woman and picked up Stephen, the boy tiny and oblivious, his skeletal frame folding over Bobby's shoulder as he carried him out of the room and back up the stairs. Donny looked up when Bobby walked in. Bobby could hear Marsha in the bath-room crying.

"There's some money coming," Donny said. "Quite a bit, actually. And don't think I've forgotten about what I owe you either."

"Don't you ever bring him here again," Bobby said, "either of them."

"I didn't bring em." The crying became a wailing and Donny gestured to-ward it. "She brought him. He's something, ain't it? I think he's Christ incarnate. Wouldn't it be crazy to take him with us? He'd be like our little dashboard Bud-dha, a tiny little holy man."

"Tell Marsha we'll be out in the truck when she's ready."

"Don't think I've forgot what I owe you, Bobby."

"Just forget it and tell her to come on."

"Hell, no, I'm not forgetting it. You'll get what's yours. I'm still counting on you to be my wingman. The desert," Donny called when Bobby turned for the stairs, the child still in his arms. "We snag Kristen and head for Arizona. We're gonna do it, brother."

He drove Marsha and Stephen home, stopped in the street in front of their house.

"Don't lecture me," Marsha said. The crying seemed to have sobered her. "Don't you ever lecture me, Bobby Rosen. You have absolutely no right to lecture anyone, ever."

"Let me help you get Stephen in."

"I've come this far alone," she said. "I think I can manage myself."

He took his sixty-five hundred and thirteen dollars out of the bank, closed the account, and drove to his parents' house. They were out, as he knew they would be, and he sat in the kitchen and counted fifteen hundred dollar bills onto the Formica table. Five he put in the jar on the window sill above the sink. Five went into the drawer of the nightstand in their bedroom. And five he left in an enve-lope tucked behind the OJ. *Gone for a bit,* he printed. *Don't worry. Will call you as soon as I can. Love, Bobby.*

At home, he packed, cut off the water pump and unplugged the TV. He was going, *that last last time,* and wondered if he'd see this place again. He suspected that if he left that would be the end of it, that whatever tie bound him to his old life would finally be cut. But it was time, he supposed, Nancy and little Bobby living with Vance for over a year now. Moving to Atlanta, he had not the slightest doubt. They weren't coming back. Nothing was coming back.

He walked the fields, talked to the dogs and watched them lope ahead, on a scent and back again to nuzzle his legs. He was sweating. Mid-July and summer overripe, heavy and wet and collapsing under its own fat weight. He couldn't think clearly and wished for the clarity of fall, clean dry air, cider and deer hunting. But all around him summer fell apart without ever really dissipating. Heat and more heat.

He remembered his father talking of the three hundreds: one hundred days at one hundred degrees in one hundred percent humidity. Picking cotton in the lush shadow of thunder clouds on into the dry scorch of drought. It would have been a joke except it wasn't, and one day his father had caught him telling other boys about it and all of them laughing, Bobby miming his father hunched in the furrows doing the stoop work, and his father's face had tightened, blood flared into the keloid scars along one forearm as he leaned close and said *all them jokes and sayings are jokes and sayings because somebody lived em.* It was the only harsh thing he could remember his father ever saying and Bobby never laughed about it again. He'd survived though, his father. The cotton fields. The war. Joined the army and after Nam got a job at the mill. Took his discharge pay and bought a 1970 Dodge Coronet Super Bee. Got married and set about raising a family.

The remnants of Bobby's own family were in several Rubbermaid cartons in little Bobby's old room. Photograph albums, old letters and yearbooks and birthday cards. He washed his hands and fixed a drink in the kitchen, stood in the doorjamb and looked at the boxes. Nancy had refused them as if refusing their shared life, their past. All that was left him was copied out in his notebook, the place names, the numbers of the dead. He downed the whiskey and found himself shaking his head as if someone was watching. Still, it was their life, our goddamn shared existence, Nancy. She had always been stronger than him, that much had always been clear. He'd dragged her from Bragg to Campbell to Carson and then back to Bragg with deployments between every move, and every time she adapted. Or so he'd thought. Instead there'd been the steady and unseen accrual of resentment and frustration—the trashy base housing, the strip clubs and pawn shops—the steady dissolution of patience. Then one day it all collapsed. Or so it seemed, so it fucking seemed.

He loaded his dogs and drove out to the Farmtown acreage. His foreman was waiting for him by the corrugated shed. Mid-fifties, a heavy man in a silverbelly Stetson. Johnson, his name. Bobby didn't know if it was his first or last.

"I appreciate you watching them," Bobby said.

"I don't never mind having dogs around," the man said, "but I can't promise you your job back, you lighting out like this."

"I understand that." He gave the man two hundred dollar bills for dog food and the trouble. The man looked at the bills and folded them into a front pocket.

"I guess this has something to do with your brother getting back and all," the man said. "I guess I can understand that."

Bobby watched the dogs trot off into the pine scrub. "If I owe you more just keep track of it and I'll get square with you when I get back."

"This ought to be fine," he said. "It ain't the money concerns me."

Donny was on the same couch holding the same pipe when Bobby drove back to town to find him, except now his teeth were repaired.

"Marsha pay to get your mouth fixed?" Bobby asked.

"Go fuck yourself. You're too soon anyway, brother," Donny said. "The money ain't come in yet."

Bobby took the fat bank envelope from his pocket. "It just did. You call that girl?"

Donny sat up and the pipe clinked onto the floorboards. "Are you fucking with me?"

"You said she was in love with you."

"And you said you had a wife and kid but to hell with them too," Donny said. He stood, shirtless, barefoot in jeans, a little welt along one forearm. Against the wall was a stack of floor tiles and a rusted wet saw. "I need to make a few phone calls, get a shower."

"The water's off at my place. You'll have to go to mamma and daddy's. I don't want you going anywhere near Marsha."

"She don't want me over there no way." He slipped the pipe into his front pocket and smiled. "Take me to mamma and daddy's."

Bobby let Donny off by the front steps at their parents' house, their Pontiac back in the yard and parked beneath the awning.

"What are you gonna tell em?" Bobby asked.

"You ain't coming in?"

"I left em a note. If they say anything tell em we're going on a fishing trip or something. A big welcome home."

"Yeah right."

"Call that girl if you want." Bobby dropped the truck into drive and Donny took a step back. "I'll come get you in the morning. Early. Be ready."

He was happy on the drive out to Nancy's, gliding along the surface of his thoughts: he'd see his boy, spend the night with his ex. Tomorrow he and Donny would hit the road for a week or two. Drive out west and maybe raise a little hell. Atlanta wasn't that far. It wasn't like he couldn't keep seeing little Donny, drive up every other weekend, take his boy to Braves games. Or hell, why not just move to Atlanta too? Make a fresh start. All morning he had slunk around that other possibility—that he would not return—but it seemed distant now, submerged, and he rolled the window down and listened to the country station out of Valdosta.

He parked out front and found Nancy in the kitchen drinking almond milk and reading *Entertainment Weekly*. It was barely seven but little Bobby was already down for the night.

"This early?"

"I guess he didn't get much sleep last night." She sat sideways in a white ladder back chair, barefoot with her legs in sweat pants and crossed at the thighs. A little silver ring around her pinkie toe. "Besides, it's not that early."

"I'm just going to peek in on him."

"Don't wake him. He had a hard time going down."

He took a sip of her milk. "I'll just peek."

"Don't you dare wake him."

His boy was indeed asleep, his small head sweating, blonde hair matted and swirled. Bobby flipped the wall switch and looked at the fan. Nothing happened.

Nancy was still at the table.

"The fan's not working," he said.

"Nothing's working. The power's off."

"Why's the power off?"

"Why's the power off?" She finally looked up at him. "Jesus, Bobby. You are really something else."

He opened the basement door on cool darkness, found the switchbox, walked back to the kitchen.

"Fuses are fine. Did you call Vance?"

"Like Vance could do anything. Like he doesn't know." She took another drink of her milk, closed her magazine and leaned back. "Did you get paid?"

"Would it help?"

"Bobby—"

"I'm gonna stay tonight if that's all right. I can't bear the thought of driving back."

"Did you get paid or not?"

"I did." He took the bank envelope from his pocket and handed it to her. "I did indeed."

She licked the tip of one finger and counted the money, slid three hundreds out, passed back the envelope.

The bedroom was no cooler for its darkness and they lay atop the tangle of sheets, sweaty and panting and staring up at the motionless ceiling fan. That had become the thing about the occasional visit: the sex. The elusiveness. The way it felt—had become—forbidden. Coming to her bed now was a little like it had before they were married and he felt drugged by the tenderness.

"I'm sorry about the power," he said. "You should have said something this morning. I could have got it on."

"It's all right. It was only today. This afternoon really."

"You need power." He squeezed her hand. "It's hot."

"It's hot," she agreed. "But besides that it isn't so bad. At least for now. Little Bobby thinks it's like camping."

"Except it's cooler outside."

"He talked about you all morning." She touched his hair. "He said the planets lined up. Like it was some rare event, like it'll never happen again."

"It won't. Not in our lives it won't."

He showered with a flashlight and came out to find her sitting in floor in the lotus position, eyes shut, hands cradled, sweating again before he could get on a pair of clean boxers.

"I forgot to say," she said from whatever place she now occupied, "those kids are back. The ones throwing dairy products."

"The ones that came after little Bobby?"

"The ones with all the spray paint. I saw them again just before you got here."

"Shit, Nancy."

"They had all this rotten milk. I completely meant to say that the moment you walked in."

He took the flashlight, dressed, and walked barefoot into the still yard. Tree frogs and the hum of far-away traffic. All along the lane the street lamps were on, washes of umbrella light illuminating patches of nothing, and he couldn't figure that for a minute. Who was paying for it? The bank, he supposed. Some asshole in a Tampa high-rise. Cigars and a bi-weekly massage. Then he realized he was projecting. Me. The asshole in a Vegas high-rise. But that hadn't lasted, of course. He hadn't deserved for it to, if he got down to it. He'd deserved something much worse.

A moment later he caught the first egg. It came in at shoulder-height, grazed his arm and burst against the vinyl of the garage. Three kids on bikes. Maybe a fourth somewhere in the shadows. The fucking vandals. Spray painting giant penises and something Bobby thought was meant to be a three-eyed robot. Twice they'd terrorized his son. He slung a rock but they were already gone, hitting the safety of the highway, laughing all the way home.

He hosed the siding and walked back inside to find Nancy asleep. There was sticky yolk down his arm, warm as blood, but that was all right. He walked to the bathroom but didn't immediately wash it off, just stood there and felt it dry, hardening, thickening. He let it sit for a good minute before he turned on the faucet.

The truth was, he'd gotten off easy.

PART FIVE

KATIE WALKED FIRST ON THE SIDEWALK and, when she met Pennsylvania, down the center of the road. Without realizing it, or not exactly realizing it, she was retracing the path they'd walked twice that day, back and forth to the church. It was night now and rain fell softly through the trees except it wasn't rain but the lightest of breezes, a glance, a touch, but enough to turn the leaves, ticking them, so their gloss was hidden and their dull undersides shone with darkness.

After Lucy had locked herself back in her room and Katie knocked and pleaded for what seemed like days but was probably a few minutes, Katie's shame had morphed into a sort of indifference that suddenly flowered into a blind rage. She showered and pulled on cut-offs and a t-shirt, pounded a last time on Lucy's door, screamed that she was leaving, and walked out barefooted, halfway to the first streetlamp before it hit her that she was walking without shoes which, seriously, Katie, was really a stupid thing to do. That her feet hurt, that the flecks of rock and tar bit at her soles only ensured that she wouldn't go back for them. A little pain would do her good, she thought. It might ebb the heat, and maybe it had because she felt nothing now, no anger, no shame or sorrow. It was the same emptiness she had beheld at the altar if she wanted to open that shiny box right now which—be honest, Katie—no, she most certainly did not.

Just walk, girl.

Past the church, the power lines crossed the road to lay two narrow shadows over the asphalt, twin finish lines to which she walked parallel, meaning—*voila!*— that she would never cross them. Symbolic. Except don't be stupid. Scratching around for signs—pathetic, really, the gross neediness. Something in her wanting to hold the pillow of her sister's faith against the hollow cavern of her own heart, the way it echoed, held recesses and chambers she dared not enter. She wanted to self-examine, *introspect.* Except she didn't. Just keep walking. Walk this off. If possible she would walk all the way to the Occupy encampment in Orlando, but of course that wasn't possible. Or was it? Thirty miles along I-4. You'd be there by morning. But seriously, folks.

She kept walking, uber-fucking-bored, which was to say standard upper-middle class suburban ennui. Which itself was boring. She should have brought her iPod. She was learning French on her iPod, but then if you're going to be remembering things how about you start with your shoes, OK, thanks.

She turned off Pennsylvania onto Pine Tree Court, big houses here, decade old-two story ranchettes, forests of pine. Driveways with basketball hoops, trampolines in the backyards. The street was a horseshoe that intersected Rosedale, the road switching from asphalt to ocher paving stones, cobblestones, she guessed, that carried the night perfume of money. The trees got larger and the houses smaller, the McMansions giving way to the Arts and Crafts bungalows tucked beneath giant water oaks. It became harder to see. That was what it meant to have money, not the showy SUV-and-a-time-share-in-Cozumel money of big houses and heated pools, but real money, old money. What was visibility next to deferred stock options, or trust funds that kicked in at eighteen like reliable generators? Heat and light, darling. It was all around her. Every front yard a thicket of sculpted vegetation. Every sky a dome of Spanish moss.

A sound, a low whirring.

Look up: owls.

Two owls clung to the powerline above her, so perfectly arranged they appeared to be toys. Each about the size of her head. Gray owls. Great Horned Owls? Common Screech Owls? Thank you, daddy, for the trove of useless information, the trivia so much of the world confused with knowledge.

"Hello, owls," she said, and one of them rotated its head a half degree to follow her. "Goodnight, owls."

Up ahead was Rosedale Azalea Park, a sliver of good health that rivered through the neighborhood. Stone steps. Stands with doggie-bags. A few benches and a sign past them that read NO SLEEPING ON OR ASSUMING A HORIZONTAL POSITION BY ORDER OF CITY ORDINANCE 3.15.2. She walked along the cobbles past the bungalows tucked beneath live oaks and banana trees, big elephant-eared plants that shadowed the stone walkways and screened porches. Living rooms blued with television. Citrus rotting beneath mature trees. Oranges, limes, tangerines. She'd lived in Florida her entire life but could never get over the way people let wind-fall fruit gather and rot. A winey sort of decadence, as if there would always be too much of everything.

Beyond the street the park was intensely dark. She crossed the road and descended the steps into what felt an underground garden, the soil wet and giving. The park was a winding scratch, houses on both sides above the creek banks. She thought of trolls, the books she abhorred as a child. Having to sit silently while Lucy read them in her halting first-grade voice. Moss, ferns, little humpbacked bridges. Her eyes were starting to adjust, and she followed the thread of the creek. The sky obscured by a canopy of green shadow, above it the night moonless.

Someone was behind her, yes?

No. Of course not. Don't be ridiculous.

Still, she shivered. She wanted out of this place. It suddenly felt alien and she couldn't stand it a second longer. She started looking for stairs back up to the street but where were they now, behind her? She looked back and saw nothing, but she knew she had passed them so where the hell were they? This is how grisly fairy tales begin, Katie. No, this is how you get your throat slit, your dead body raped. She stopped to listen. Jesus, just walk up the bank, she told herself. This is ridiculous. You can actually see the house lights from here.

Except you're barefoot, dumbass, and that bank is covered with prickly pear. Except do it anyway.

She did, scrambled up the bank and walked down the center of the street, limping. Someone was following her and she stopped again to catch the man, the rapist, the sick-o. And, of course, sweet darling, no one is there. She hadn't expected there to be because it had just become clear to her: she wasn't sensing someone, she smelled someone. But was it a person she smelled?

She stood just beyond the reach of a streetlamp and tried to place it, this scent, this lightest and most pleasant of odors. There were childhood associations, some deeply shrouded part of her brain misfiring. She'd smelled it every day of her life but never noticed until now. Was it her? She didn't think it was. Yet it felt so near, *was* near. And if she named it, might it then belong to her, might she own it? But then the breeze picked up and it was gone.

She started walking again. What was Lucy doing now? Crying? Plotting?

No, don't go down that road. Metaphorically speaking. Steer clear. Other thoughts, better thoughts. But none would come. She searched the sky for more owls, the trees, the powerlines—could they have been toys, seriously?—but saw none. Then she heard laughter. Ahead the street bent and she had a partial view into someone's backyard. People were talking, laughing around the blue jewel of a pool. She thought she recognized one of the voices and moved off the street and onto the lawn, the grass soft and wet beneath her tender feet. The house was dark and beneath the chug of the front yard sprinklers she thought she could make it to the fence unnoticed.

A man and woman sat in lounge chairs, drinking beer. A guy in the pool. She didn't know the guy in the pool, but the man and woman looked familiar. Graduated with Lucy, she thought, or maybe the year ahead. Both students at Rollins, maybe? She'd seen them at parties but couldn't place a name and peeked through the lattice around the pergola. They seemed so gentle, bathed in blues, voices calm. Was that what money did to you, real money? Money as the absence of raised voices? Money as a deterrent to scenes? *I am thoroughly drama-retardant, my dear.* Behind them the house was a wall of dark glass, no lights, no movement. Just three twenty-year-olds laughing in the dark.

She felt the sprinkler hit the backs of her knees. She was seeping into the yard but it was a good sort of seep, pressure between the toes, the tickle of grass. Her feet hurt from the climb up the bank and how soothing this was, how pleasant. She shut her eyes and a second later the voice was behind her.

"There you are," the voice said. "Jesus Christ, we thought we had a bear in the yard. Did Niall text you?"

She looked at him. It was the guy from the pool chair, floppy blond hair and Sperry boat shoes. Mr. Rollins College. Jared. His name was Jared. She had no idea who Niall was.

"Jared," she said.

He smiled. "I know I know you but I just can't quite—"

"Katie," she said. "Katie Redding."

"Oh, yeah, of course. I know your sister. Well, Niall we'll be glad you're here. He's restless, I think, eternally." He motioned toward the gate. "Come on around. We're having an argument here. Come talk to us."

"We're not having an argument," called the woman's voice. "We're having a discussion."

"It's an argument at this point," Jared said, leading her through the gate. "It's devolved."

"Maybe you've devolved."

"And obviously Jacklyn doesn't want to shut up so I can proceed. Jackie, you know Katie Redding?"

"I think probably," she said.

"And that's Niall, of course."

"Hi," Katie said.

The boy in the pool looked at her and nodded.

"Sit down, Jared said. "We can drop this, really. We don't have to proceed. I mean if this is bothering you, Jackie."

"No, proceed, counselor," Jacklyn said, "by all means proceed."

Katie sat in one of the pool chairs. She knew Jacklyn from parties too, big-boned and sort of brassy, the kind of attitude that made you think of some take-no-shit waitress except she doubted Jacklyn had ever worked a day in her life. "So?" Katie said.

"So," Jared said, "the argument—"

"The issue."

"The issue—and I do beg your pardon—the *issue* is: what's the greatest gift you can give someone, and there's two possible answers."

"What if I don't like either answer?" Katie asked.

"They've already cut that possibility off," the boy in the pool said, Niall said, "this isn't so much a debate as an intellectual jack off session."

"Niall," Jacklyn said, "gross."

"Naill's just drunk," Jared said, "but listen. You can give someone the gift of basic human needs—food, water, shelter—"

"Salt," Niall said.

"Salt, sure. Or you can give the gift of enlightenment."

"Total consciousness of the universe," Jacklyn said. "Look here." She had taken out a small glass jar. Inside was what appeared to be a fat white board marker. "The judge gave me this."

"Ah!" said Niall, "the sacred one-hitter."

"Are we having this conversation or not?" Jared asked.

Jacklyn ignored him, took out the joint and placed it on a towel near the edge of the pool. "It's seriously potent."

"The judge and his homegrown," Niall said.

"Straight from I-95," Jared said.

"Who gets the gift?" Katie asked.

"Is this a trick question?" asked Jared.

"The word is seized," Niall said.

"Is this like the prize?"

"The word is impounded."

"Who gets the gift?" Katie asked again. She was already bored, but she wasn't ready to go home yet either. It was nice by the pool, the air fragrant. She could probably use a little of the one-hitter to help her sleep.

"Anyone can get it," Jacklyn said.

"It's irrelevant really," Jared said, "but for the sake of argument let's say some sad ass refugee in Darfur. The huddle masses. The wretched of the earth."

"Are we going to burn this or not?" Niall asked.

"In a second," Jacklyn said. "So it's set up like there's an obvious answer: food, shelter, et cetera. Which is fine, because it just totally nails home my point which is that it doesn't matter where you are, enlightenment is the ultimate gift."

"But what I'm telling her," Jared said, "is that she's speaking from a position of privilege. That she can only say as much because she has all of those things."

"When actually." Jacklyn whipped her hair back, a little dramatically, Katie thought. "When actually it's Jared that's speaking from the position of privilege. Like he's so the colonial overlord who himself is worthy of enlightenment but the poor natives just get the bags of grain."

"I thought they were refugees," Katie said.

Jacklyn drank her beer. "Natives, refugees, whatever."

"Let's suppose they are Senegalese," Niall said.

"Shut up and be serious," Jacklyn said.

"White Senegalese," said Jared.

"No," Niall said, "More like dusky. Dusky Senegalese Frenchmen. All of them tall. Six foot three-ish. They do phosphates and groundnuts." He drank his beer. "And tourism but I'm like whatever: who's going to Senegal?"

"Their currency got devalued in the nineties, I think," Jared said.

"Clearly neither of you are taking this seriously," Jacklyn said.

"No, no, we are," Jared said. "We've just arrived at something of a theoretical impasse. Speaking as I am," he said, "from my obvious position of privilege."

"There are yogis in like Nepal or Tibet," Jacklyn said, "who go their entire lives without food."

"That's bullshit."

"I swear to God it's not. Have you never heard of Paramahana Yogananda?"

Jared swung one foot at Niall's passing head. "What say you, waterboy? Sack of flour or the lotus position? A full belly and basic immunization or sheer enlightenment?"

His hair was slicked back and dripping. He wiped his mouth. "If by sheer enlightenment you mean a much-needed toke off the old one-hitter then my response is an unequivocal hell yes, bro, give me the transcendental oversoul, give me universal brotherhood."

"Consciousness," Jacklyn, "not brotherhood."

"Whatever," Niall said, "I still want my hit."

Jared shook his head and looked as at Katie as if to apologize for such triviality in the face of suffering. "You know what I wish?" he said.

"I wish you two would shut up and light that bastard," Niall said.

"No," Jared said, "I'm serious here." He turned to Katie. "I wish we could bring your sister into this discussion. You guys know Katie's sister, Lucy? We should call her."

"Please," Katie said.

"Seriously. You remember her, Jacklyn? We were in IB together," he told Katie, "Mrs. Flynn's class on culture and belief."

"Oh my God, you mean Franny?"

"You called her Franny?" Katie asked.

"We read like Emerson and Plato and the *Tao Te Ching*," Jared said.

"Who called her Franny?"

"The girl had some serious insight. You just don't want to admit as much, do you, Katie?"

She could tell he was joking, knew she should let it go, but this was oh so Lucy: her reputation as a saint prancing out ahead of a life that was nothing if not an exercise in complete hypocrisy.

"You have no idea," Katie said.

Niall had taken Jacklyn's beer from beneath her chair and was finishing it. "What's the deal with your sister?"

"They're sisters," Jared said. "What else? There doesn't have to be a deal."

"You honestly have no idea," Katie said again. She was keeping a level tone, almost whispering, not making eye contact. It was the kind of thing that pulled people's interest, made them lean toward you.

"Now I really want to know," Jacklyn said.

So she told them. Most of it, at least, the altar call and the kitchen tongue lashing, the direct accusation of making the whole fucking thing up. It spilled out of her, not Lucy in her sheer nightgown or the part with Alan after—what was the use in bringing that up since she could already sense how ashamed she would be at some future point?—but everything else. And even as it poured forth, even as she felt them pull closer, Niall at her feet, Jacklyn and Jared on each side of her, she regretted it. She was giving away something precious, she knew, putting her innermost on cheap display. Doing it for the thrill. For the attention. Her pearls before swine. She hated herself for it, but she didn't shut up.

"That is fucked," Jared said when she was finished. He stood by the side of the pool to light the joint.

Jacklyn let go of Katie's shoulder to brush back her hair. "That is fucked. Totally."

"I don't even know your sister," Niall said, "and I could say right out that is fucked. But mostly I just want to say: why are we sitting here not smoking this?"

"See that's when I believe parents step in," Jared said.

Niall rolled back his head. "Oh, Jesus."

"Yeah, yeah," Jared said. "I know you all think I'm this like conservative prick and all, but I honestly think that's the point where parents step in."

"My daddy's a banker," Niall squealed.

"I'm serious, man."

"My daddy's moves capital so that the little man can thrive."

"You can make fun of my dad, but I'm still serious," Jared said. He hit the joint and passed it to Jacklyn. "They have a role to play."

"So where was your daddy, then?" Niall said. He splashed water on Katie's bare foot. "Hey, wake up. Your dad's a pilot, right?"

"Dude, come on," Jared said.

"I'm just asking. I think it's badass. He flies like drones?"

"Dude."

"She doesn't have to answer me if she doesn't want to."

"He flies a Predator," she said, "or maybe a Reaper now." The joint was making her way toward her and she tracked its progress, the swelling glow, the thin cloud. "Out of MacDill."

"Yeah, Tampa." Jared was nodding his head. "That's what my dad said. I've got an uncle in the Navy so I'm like, yeah, I feel what you're feeling."

"No, you don't," Niall said. "Some uncle laid up with an Okinawan geisha. That ain't the same."

"Whatever, man. It's still the sharp end of the stick."

"Oh, Jesus," Niall said, "are you serious?"

Jared turned to Katie. "I'm just saying, I feel what you're feeling."

"Except I'm not feeling anything," Katie said.

Everyone laughed, a little stutter of laugh as if they simultaneously coughed.

"Nothing," she repeated. "Which is kind of fucked in and of itself."

She stood. She didn't want the joint. She didn't want to sit here a second longer.

"What's up?" Niall said. "You leaving?"

"Stay," Jared said. "Come on, stay."

"I should get back. I was just sort of passing by and—" She shrugged.

"Fucker shouldn't have said anything about your dad. That wasn't cool."

"Stay," Niall, the fucker, said.

"It's okay. I need to walk."

She started back across the spongy grass, feeling it give beneath her feet, beads of dew flung against the backs of her knees. They were calling *stay, stay and have a hit* and Jared was giving Niall shit about the drones and Katie's dad, but it had nothing to do with that. It had nothing to do with anything. That was what people never understood: that it wasn't about them. Everyone under the misapprehension that the world is paying attention. You snivel and beg forgiveness but, dude, I didn't hear you in the first place. She put her hand on the cold gate and swung it open. It's a private conversation. It has absolutely nothing to do with you, bro.

The path wound through the thick foliage, the up-lit palms and banana plants and ferns spilling out of mulched beds. She could feel the flagstones beneath her feet, cool and mossy and softly illuminated by the paper lanterns that hung in the trees. So much upkeep. Not just the grass to cut but the pruning and sculpting. A team of Salvadorans with lawn rakes and big electric shears. A spindly six year old hauling bails of pine straw.

She took another ten steps—stopped.

She had somehow taken a wrong turn and bent deeper into the garden. She suspected she might be back in the park that abutted the yard, but went a few more steps and hit the brick wall that marked the rear of the property. She would have to retrace her steps, walk back through that circle of assholes. She couldn't hear them anymore and the vegetation was thick enough that she couldn't see the glow of the pool either. It was like a fairy tale and she was waiting on some troll to put his wet hand on her calf, pull her down into the undergrowth. Maidenhair and Lilly of the Nile. Areca and date palms. A little gnome with fat thumbs and a speech impediment. How the hell do you walk out of the house without shoes? Pissed, she thought. To make a point. Which, of course, she hadn't.

Ahead the trail bent back on itself, so dark she shivered. Night flowers. Voodoo lily—a native perennial. And how the hell do you know this, Katie? Because she had a talent for detail. Like her father, hoarder of useless fact. When they locked him up he would know the relevant statutes, the international charters he had violated. Except they wouldn't lock him up. Killing peasants in Asia Minor, how was that a crime exactly? He'd probably wind up flying drones over greater Orlando, watching black kids boost souped-up Chevys. And, yes, she was lost, wasn't she? Lost in an acre of backyard, but swear to God it was more like Thailand than a suburban street. Any second now she expected an elephant to come crashing through. She had to go back.

She was halfway—maybe halfway, at least halfway—back along the trail when she heard someone moving ahead of her.

"Hello?" she called.

"Whisper."

"What?"

He chopped his way through the vines, Niall from the pool.

"I said whisper. I'd thought you'd left, but then I saw something moving back here and figured it had to be you. You're lost."

"No."

He smiled and put a hand on his hip. He was shirtless and wet in orange swim trunks, legs flecked with mulch. "Oh, I'm sorry, just hanging around for the hell of it. Of course, makes perfect sense."

"It's goes on for like a mile back there."

"Hey, you don't have to tell me."

"I couldn't even see the pool."

"Half my youth was wandering around back there." He had big white teeth, expensive orthodontics. "Hey, walk back with me and let's go for a swim. Jacklyn and Jared went inside."

"I don't even know you."

"But I know you," he said, "you're the occupy girl."

"What?"

"Look here." He took something from the cup of his hand: the joint, the sacred one-hitter. "You like?"

He re-lit it and passed it to her. She sucked deep and gave it back, waved away the smoke that seemed to hang beneath the canopy.

"Who's the judge?" she asked.

"Her father. And I know what you're thinking, but they're all right. Jared's kind of an asshole. Both of them actually. Spoiled, you know? But all right. Take another hit."

"I'm good."

"He says shit like 'sharp end of the stick' and thinks he's contributing to like the national discourse. They're inside making a sex tape."

She said nothing.

"I'm joking," he said. "That's a joke." He held up the joint. "You seriously good?"

She nodded and he shrugged and took one himself, smiled wider at her. When he took her hand it was so casual she barely noticed.

"So," he said.

She stood perfectly still. She was smelling it again, the same smell as before.

"You smell that?" she asked.

"It's cool. No one's home."

"Not that," she said. "It's like beneath it. I'm not sure what it is but it's so familiar. I've been smelling it all night."

"It's summer's long failing, Katie," he said. "The ripeness. The plants and flowers."

"I'm being serious."

"When you smell it you know they're dying, that old time is still a flying." He was running his thumb against her palm. She let him.

"Yeah, but that's not what I'm talking about."

"Come back with me. Let's swim."

"You really saw me at the encampment?"

"Eat the fucking rich."

"Seriously?"

"Like a million times. Come on."

It was harder to see walking back, the pot as much as the darkness, she thought, so she closed her eyes and let him pull her along. When he stopped she felt the heat of his chest against her neck and face a second before he kissed her, felt herself ease back until she was against the trunk of something scaly, his hands on her hips, her mouth opening to his, warm, the smoky luxuriance of the joint, eyes squeezed shut.

"Come on."

"What's the deal with Jacklyn?"

"Ohh," he said, "girl's got questions."

"Is her dad really a judge?"

"Girl's crafty." He kissed her again, softer. "Come on."

The pool was a rectangle of aquamarine light, wavy as the ripple of a flag. When she opened her eyes his trunks were around his dirty ankles, and she watched him ease off the side, dive, surface and wipe the water from his eyes.

"I didn't bring a bathing suit," she told him.

"No kidding. Come on."

She looked at the house, the windows dark.

"They're busy," he said, and splashed water at her. "It's cool."

It was cool, though she wasn't sure why exactly. She pulled her shirt off, unfastened her cut-offs and let them fall around her feet, stepped out of them just as she heard the sliding patio door slam shut.

Jacklyn stood with her hands on her big hips, topless in what Katie thought was probably her sheerest underwear.

"What the fuck is this?" she said.

Her hair looked blow-dried, poofy and brittle. The shadow of the roofline cut her with an ugly precision.

"Go back in the house, Jackie," Niall said.

"Why don't you tell me what this is first?"

"I said go in the house."

"You're out here with this slut when I'm barely gone for two minutes?"

"Jackie."

"I'm leaving," Katie said.

"This is the girl that was cutting herself, Niall? It came to me just now."

"Jackie."

"You remember all last year, the fucking drama?"

"I'm leaving."

"Stay," Jared said. "Go back in the house, Jackie. Katie, you stay."

But she was already past them, her shorts back around her waist, fastening them as she walked, her shirt pressed to her chest until she could fight her way into it. She made sure to find the right gate this time, crossed the front lawn where the sprinklers plumed their silvery tails. Her feet were thick with dirt and the broken cap of a single acorn. She stopped in the street to brush them clean. They were still fighting behind her until she heard the definitive thump of what must have been the door sliding shut. There was no privacy here. You paid for the old trees and the 1920s bungalows. Besides that you were on your own.

And she was on her own, beneath the dark sky and the hanging trees. The owls were gone and despite the lights from houses she felt herself to be alone. Somehow disoriented too. There was something vaporous about things. She looked at the houses and felt overwhelmed by the quantity of names. Dormers. Mullions. Soffit. Where had it come from, all this stuff? Where had it been all her life, this entire world of things? It was so real. This sudden density that made every branch appear an arabesque, brushstrokes where there should have been a simple lines, glassy voids instead of bay windows.

She walked back past the church, a car passed, light and then the way darkness rushed in, so greedily—hungry, hungry, hungry, the gnawing dark—and was back by the corner of Pennsylvania and North Arlington when she smelled it, so familiar, awareness on the tip of her tongue. Was it her? Was she smelling some essential odor? She didn't think so but went to smell her shirt anyway and right then, just as she dropped her eyes, something passed near her in a great uprush of air and she startled, jerked her head upright and turned once quickly and then a second time, slowly. But she already knew whatever it was was gone. She already knew she was absolutely alone.

For her part, Lucy had decided to weep for her life, past, present, and future. She'd examined her copy of *The Imitation of Christ*—it was still on the floor, left for dead at the foot of the stairs, though only slightly worn by her rage—but she had no way of contacting Alan, and it was Alan—not God—she wanted most to witness her suffering. She thought of taking a cab to his grandmother's trailer, maybe all the way to the Dhammaram Temple, but she knew she was finished crying, whatever reservoir the day had tapped now exhausted. What was left was a gnawing hunger.

Still, she needed to be certain, and twice walked outside, almost certain that Alan was somewhere along the yard's edge, waiting. She scanned the driveway that remained empty, followed the chain of light that pooled beneath the gas lamps the neighborhood association had bought five years ago. Along the street the houses were quiet and mostly dark and she heard nothing beyond the night sounds: a passing car, a cat. Whippoorwills somewhere in the wilted azaleas. The kitchen was overlit and when she looked back she realized anyone outside could have followed her every move, the pacing, the solitary crying. But who would watch? And what was to be seen? Alone and lonely on a Friday night, she thought it just another species of suffering, the expensive counter-tops and appliances uniquely suburban, the grief as common as rain.

She went inside and pawed through the cabinets and fridge, her mother's food, Katie's food, started taking out whatever she could find—a container of whole flax seeds, a baggie of chia, whey protein, apple cider vinegar, Bragg's Liquid Aminos, *fresh greens!*—started pouring things into the Vitamix. A banana. Frozen blueberries. She drowned it in almond milk and stared down at what appeared a gelatinous knot, something to be cut from the stomach of a dying man. Thirty seconds of LIQUIFY. The blender screaming like a jet engine, like the high-pitched wail of her father's drone. She could do this. She could drink this. She was hungry, after all. But the smell of the vinegar made her gag and she wound up standing by the open window, panting through the screen. How did Katie do this? Her daily shake taken bright-eyed and smiling. And for God's sake why? To spite her, Lucy realized. Of course: to spite the sister who could barely stomach cottage cheese and fresh fruit while Katie subsisted on air and grace and whatever pleasure she took in watching Lucy slowly molt into a lumpier and splotchier version of their father.

She pressed her face against the screen, felt the wire squares bulge on her forehead and nose, took a moment to savor the self-pity because what was coming next was self-recrimination, what was coming next was doubt. Doubt about Katie's intentions, doubt about Lucy's motives. What if the whole act at the We Shall Behold Him! service hadn't been an act at all? What if Katie had been—was, *is*—sincere? What if Lucy had frightened away Alan? What if she had frightened away all the well-intentioned girls at JBI? She felt her guilt stretch all the way back to the boy who had failed to kiss her by that Michigan lake, her life a string of failures as illuminated as the gas lamps along the street. How had she gone so wrong? She saw the pattern: she had grown content, she had failed to heed what à Kempis had made plain. She'd allowed herself to be happy. Her summer of contentment and here, at last, its inevitable arc, her arrogance always building to this: alone in the kitchen, gagging.

She had to find Katie, she had to find Alan. She wanted to retrace her life and unbend all that she'd made crooked and she knew she would. She could do it. The taste subsided and she was filled with clarity of purpose and hope. She could do it!

But she needed her phone, she needed her book. She thought of Alan's friend Twitch. Did Alan still have Twitch's phone? She would call him. She would text Katie until Katie responded and if she didn't, Lucy would go find her, wade into the sea of tents and posterboard, brave the drum circle.

She would—

The movement caught her eye, someone along the flagstones that ran to the garage. She pulled back from the window, leaned forward, cupped her hands around her face. Someone on the driveway, just beyond the reach of the street light. Alan? Katie? She put her face back to the screen and called *hello?* into the yard. *Is somebody out there?* And then—what was she thinking? Stupid, Lucy, calling out like that, letting them know you're here, all alone, because all at once she was scared, convinced someone was watching. She looked at the kitchen door, eyes fixed on the unlatched bolt, the door practically ajar. She turned the lock and slid the chain, two steps across the kitchen and panting with her back pressed against the wall. The light! She remembered how clearly she had seen into the kitchen and groped behind her for the switch. The room disappeared in darkness, reformed slowly, the edges of things—the plains of the counter-tops, the door of the refrigerator—as her vision adjusted. Slowly, so slowly, she slid shut the window and locked it. Someone was out there.

Or were they?

The fear washed out and she was embarrassed. Katie. Katie probably moving along the hedges, laughing and thinking of poor little Lucy holed up in her bunker. Or maybe—

She opened the door and took a tentative step onto the welcome mat, the night perfectly still, no signs of anyone. The yard was consumed by the weeping willow and its fringed shadowed, a lamp shade, an umbrella, its tendrils strung like tinsel into the mown lawn. But no sign of her sister.

"I know that's you, Katie," she called, and, after a moment, and much quieter: "Alan?" She moved along the walk toward the garage, started to worry that she had left the kitchen door open, reminded herself that this was her sister and not some wandering monster. She was crossing the cold concrete by the garage when she smelled him. Daddy! Her father! Colgate shaving cream and shoe polish. She always though them the loneliest smells. The car wasn't here but maybe he was in the garage and she'd just somehow missed him? Or maybe someone had dropped him off?

"Daddy? Daddy, are you out here?"

The smell was almost overwhelming, as if she were standing in his bathroom while he shaved, or sitting in the living room as he wrapped an old t-shirt around his index finger and rubbed polish onto his old Citadel leathers. The night should have smelled of dying flowers, of coming rain, of passing cars. It should have smelled of a thousand things but what she smelled was her father.

"I'm going in, daddy," she said, looked once more around the yard, and then did.

He was waiting for her in the kitchen and she startled at the sight of him, his dim figure in the bright guayabera she had bought for him from a street vendor in Kingston. He sat at the table, head lowered and hands clasped in front of him. A bracelet of blue light crossed his wrists like bindings.

"Daddy!" she said. "You scared me. I thought you were out in the yard and I walked out there and—"

He was slow to raise his head and when he did he looked at her as if he failed to recognize her, his eyes glossed in confusion or tears, she couldn't tell which in the failing halflight.

"Daddy?"

"Hey, darling."

"Daddy, what's wrong? Are you all right?"

"I didn't mean to scare you," he said.

She pulled the door shut behind her and moved toward the light switch.

"Let me just," she said.

"No," he said suddenly. "I mean just leave it off for another minute. Let my eyes adjust."

"Are you okay, daddy? What's going on?"

"Nothing, baby." He shook his head. It was impossible to tell if he was looking at her or not. "Or something. I don't know exactly. Your mother isn't here yet, is she?"

"She's at that retreat in Palm Beach."

"Of course." He nodded. "Of course."

"I don't know where Katie is."

"Your sister's fine."

"You saw her? Is she out there? We kind of had a fight." Lucy was inching forward. His eyes were hidden in valleys of shadow but she thought if she could only get close enough she could see them, if she could get close enough she could get past the ridiculous notion that his sockets were empty. She took another step. She wanted to touch the light that lay across his wrists, the hairs it illuminated.

"Katie's okay. Listen, baby. Don't come any closer to me, all right?"

She stopped. Tears were beginning to push into her eyes.

"Daddy, you're scaring me," she said.

"I'm sorry, baby."

"Daddy, what's wrong?"

"I'm so sorry. I'm sorry for everything."

"Please." She was just starting to cry, her tears in their infancy, and she held onto herself knowing that if she let go she would be submerged in whatever confusion gripped her. She watched him watching her, the blurry shadow of his face, and her fear became acute. "I can't smell you," she said.

"It's all right, Lucy. It's all right, baby."

"Outside I could smell you." She had lost it now, the tears, the grief. "It was like all I could smell and now I can't smell you at all."

He sat there impassive, a stuttering mantra of *It's all right, Lucy. It's all right, baby.*

She put out a hand.

"Let me touch you."

"No, baby."

"Let me just touch your hand."

"I'm sorry. I wish it was different. It scared me so much at first, but it's clearer to me now. You don't understand it, but it becomes clearer once you start to rise, once you gain perspective."

"Are you talking about work? Why are you talking like that?"

"I have to go soon. I have to go back up."

"Why are you talking like that?"

"It's all brightness at first, but then you begin to see."

"Why are you talking like that?"

"I have to go, baby."

"Wait," she said. She almost touched him but something held her in place, the sense that he had no shape—wasn't he wearing the guayabera before?—the sense that he was more dark absence, more emptiness, than her father. "Wait," she said, "please just wait."

She ran past him into the living room and to the foot of the stairs, dropped to her knees and began to flail wildly across the floor. Oh, please, Jesus. Please, God, I'm so sorry, let me find it, let me find it. Dust. A tassel of rug. Oh, please, Jesus. And then it was in her hand, *The Imitation of Christ,* splayed and open but exactly where it had landed earlier, and she scrambled onto her feet, the book tucked beneath one arm, because what she wanted was to pray with him, her father, what she wanted was not to touch him—already she sensed the impossibility of this—but to have him touch her book, the laying on of hands, they would each grip a corner, she would read to him—she knew just what—and they would pray. *But too late!* she feared, because it came to her, stupid Lucy! Why did you leave him? How could you ever leave him? She tucked the book and ran, oh Jesus she ran, all the way back into the kitchen—*too late!* she knew already—tore through the French doors and across the tile knowing, and then seeing *oh Jesus! too late!* that her father was already gone.

Light, again. She had every lamp and overhead burning, every closet and corner illuminated, the house bright as an ocean liner going down in the darkness of the sea. The kitchen was filled with the smell of vinegar and snot. She was back at the table, but refused to sit where her father had sat. *The Imitation of Christ* lay open to the back cover where, in his childish block letters, Alan had written out his number beneath the caveat

Lucy had spent the last half hour redialing SEND SEND SEND and the same re-corded voice *We're sorry. The customer has not set up a voice-mailbox. Please try your call, try your call, try your call again* on and on until it had become less about reaching Alan than conjuring a ghost.

It was after midnight when a voice answered.

"Who is this?"

"This is Lucy. Is Alan around?"

"Alan?" The voice that sounded sleepy suddenly seemed to wake. "Alan," it said, "what do you want with Alan?"

"Is he there or not?"

"You said this is Lucy?"

"Yes."

"Lucy Alan's always talking about?"

"I guess. Is he there?"

"He might be. But first tell me this, Lucy. What you want with Alan?"

"What?"

"Where you calling from, sister?"

"What? From home. Is Alan there or not? Who is this? Is this Twitch?"

"Lucy, darling," said the voice. "Calm down, baby."

"Is this Twitch?"

"Now you're right on the corner there of Orange and North Arlington, aren't you, baby? Don't be scared."

What was happening? She had lost control of things. What was he saying?

"What are you saying?"

"It's all right," he said. "Alan told me about you. I got you right here on Google maps."

"Put Alan on."

"Don't you worry about Alan. Alan's my brother and you know what brothers do? Brother's share."

"What are you talking about?"

"Are you listening?"

"Just put—"

"Just tell me first if you're there."

"I'm here."

"Oh, yes, you certainly are. I got you right here on my laptop. You sound scared and I tell you what I'm gonna do, baby. I'm gonna ride right over. That sound all right with you?"

And what was she saying? *Okay Okay* more whimper than words so that she couldn't be certain if it was her speaking or not.

"I'm gonna be right over, honey," Twitch said.

"Okay," she said, and apparently she'd been saying it all along, all her life, though even now, hearing it for the first time, it didn't sound like her voice.

I met a girl. That was the first thing Alan told Brother Vin the night Vin picked him up from the Soldiers for Christ picnic. *I met this amazing girl.* Brother Vin had spent the day at the Lawtey Correctional Institute, a Level II prison in Raiford, Level II meaning the place crawled with burglars and dealers but no murderers or rapists. For the past two years Vin had driven up five days a week to spend four hours speaking to whatever man sought him out, hearing what amounted to confessions and apologias, before he taught an hour long meditation class. It was a two hour drive each way and Vin was tired by the time he picked Alan up, but the boy kept talking and though Vin suspected he was supposed to deliver him to his grandmother's trailer he wound up taking him back to the Temple where Vin had a staked out a small room beneath the choir loft of the church.

This girl, he kept saying, *this amazing girl.*

Alan came and went, staying for several days with Vin before returning to his grandmother's or his friend Twitch. Twitch and Alan had been together the night of the church fire that sent Alan to Canebrake and Twitch to jail, and though Vin had never asked it was evident Alan carried a burden of guilt regarding Twitch, and had been overwhelmed with relief when he'd managed to track his friend to the motel in Deltona where he was delivering pizzas and renting a room by the week. Mostly though, Alan spent his days at the Lutheran church with Lucy. Which was fine with Vin. He came to miss certain moments—sitting zazen in the afternoons with Alan, or the day they raked the golden beech leaves and burned them in a barrel—but Vin was spending more and more time at the prison, drawn there, he thought, because he had always been simultaneously drawn to and repulsed by all forms of authority.

All of this floated lightly around Vin the night he picked Alan up from the Soldiers for Christ cookout and drove him back to the Temple.

"I met a girl," Alan said, "I met this amazing girl. Lucy."

One day Vin came in from Lawtey to find Alan and Lucy raking the walk down to the Temple. They worked conscientiously, head bowed, tines scraping the pea gravel. The girl seemed pleasant and vaguely innocent.

"She believes," Alan told him one evening when he stayed over, sleeping on a cot on the back stoop of the church. "I mean she really believes in a way that actually changes the way she sees the world. It kind of scares me sometimes."

Vin knew he needed to spend more time with the boy, knew he was derelict in his duty, but he was also distracted by his work at the prison. He led a meditation group five evenings a week but had started coming in the early afternoons to talk to whoever wanted to sit in the sterile block room with their coffee and cigarettes, metal table bolted to the floor, on the wall a poster that offered an animated guide to CPR. There was an old black man, Pappy, they called him, bewildered by his sixty-first year, shuffling into the room in blue scrubs and denim slippers.

"Tell me what you hear about the North Koreans."

"I don't hear anything."

"You ain't got no family there?"

"My parents were Vietnamese," Vin said. "Naturalized citizens. I grew up in Birmingham."

And the same thing the next time.

"Tell me what you hear about the North Koreans."

Vin smiled. "Not much."

"That's the point, ain't it, little brother?" His eyes appeared brittle, shot through with milky copper streaks. "They got artillery enough to level Seoul in fourteen minutes."

"But why would they do that?"

"Seven million lives obliterated in fourteen minutes. That's maximum time to total reduction."

Vin with his hand on his coffee, not raising it but slowly turning the cup. The poster read CLEAR AIRWAYS FIRST.

"I don't get it though."

Pappy nodded. "You saying a mouthful when you say that."

After three months he started taking Pappy things, legal pads and No. 2 pencils, soft packs of American Spirit.

"I was sent up to Bay Correctional in Panama City. They don't put the fears in you down here like they up to Bay."

"What kind of fears?"

"Don't matter what kind. Just matters do they come or not. I heard a boy call out last night to the Angel Gabriel. C Barracks, out past the incinerators." He leaned back and lit a cigarette. "I heard the Angel call back."

More men started coming, young and old, black, white, and Hispanic, the markings not the blue-green parabolas of jailhouse tattoos but elaborate spiders and crucifixes, almost decadent in their geometrical complexity. Great birds-of-prey. Animals-becoming-machines-becoming-angels.

"You shall know the wicked by their suffering," Pappy told him, "their death-in-life cries and calls."

"Their lamentations."

"You finally listening to me, dog."

Vin had been visiting the prison for almost a year when he heard that one of the COs had been beaten into a coma, his head a pulp of overripe fruit spread across the shower floor. All the men were talking about it. The fished-back eyes. The lobe of his ear plucked from the grate. Sanders. Vin thought he vaguely knew the man, stocky in his workboots and red handlebar mustache. The motherfucker was stealing, they told him. Extorting. Corrections Officer Sanders had it coming.

"But that don't mean some poor son of a bitch ain't going to fry for it," he was told, "and it ain't gonna be the two that did it."

The two who did it were somehow immune, above pursuit, protected by the charm of the names that floated past Vin like the leaves he burned in the barrel. The 2nd Street Fellows, the 6th Street Mob. Bigger names too: Zoe Pound, the Latin Kings, and—only whispered, never spoken aloud—Mara Salvatrucha. A week later they were talking about the man who was taking the rap, a smart motherfucker if ever there was one, keeping his mouth shut, knowing that's the only way to come out the other side.

Vin asked Pappy if the man would be willing to talk to him.

"He said no," Pappy told him. "Said he ain't interested."

Vin sent a note: *It is important that I see you.*

The man sent a reply: *What you seek cannot be found.*

Vin sent another: *All I seek is to share the contemplative stillness of this space.*

He recognized the reply as a line from *The Cloud of Unknowing: The Devil has his contemplatives, as God has His.*

The man finally came that spring. Five years had been added to his sentence but the weight of time seem strangely absent. He was skinny, haggard and sunburned and missing two teeth, but unquestionably good-looking. The cheekbones, the jaw. His eyes were gray. A small songbird swam at the base of his throat.

"I don't want your salvation," he said.

"I don't have any to offer."

"Work out your salvation with diligence," the man said. "Those are reputed to be the Buddha's dying words."

"Yes," said Vin, "buy dying into what?"

The second time he came the man appeared sullen. He asked Vin for a cigarette—Vin didn't smoke but had taken to carrying them with him—and leaned back in his aluminum chair.

"I'm not interested in prayer," he said. "I'm not interested in discovering that which I seek being the impetus of my search. I'm past that. I'm interested in systems of control, the institution as a teleological suspension of the ethical. They watch us. I know you've noticed the cameras, the towers. They watch us and think by seeing all they can control all. But the only way to see is the *via negativa*, to discard your misapprehensions. Which means the only way to control is to renounce the possibility of control." He studied the cigarette. "I stood there playing lookout while they took the pipe to his head. I could hear the way skull accepted the blows, and it did—" He leaned forward. "—it did accept the blows, as surely as Christ accepted the nails, the flogging, the crown of thorns."

When he looked up he appeared triumphant to Vin, smug, already assured of his canonization.

"You know the last thing he saw? His last temporal realization?" he asked. "The shadows, he saw the shadows flickering on the wall of the cave and thought, for that glimmer of a nanosecond before the brain shut down, those motherfuckers tricked me."

Pappy told Vin the man had been a boxer, supposedly a good one, out in Vegas, Pappy said. Vin asked him about it the next time they met.

"I wanted to know what it was like to hit someone in the face."

"What was it like?"

He shrugged. "Like everything else, except more so. What does it feel like to spend the day in the full lotus?"

Vin smiled. "Why don't you come to group meditation and find out?"

"That's an hour." He shook his head. "That's child play. I spent twenty-three days in solitary. I chased enlightenment like a rare bird."

"That's lovely, actually."

"Can you bring me some things?"

He wanted books, *The Snow Leopard*, Dostoevsky's *Memoirs of the House of the Dead*, *The Varieties of Religious Experience*.

"What landed me in here was actually taking a guy down," he said another day. "He was talking shit. I'd had a few. I hit him and thought of how many people I'd hit in my life. 'Simultaneously, I am myself, the child I was, the old man I will be.'"

"You're quoting now?"

"I learned Spanish when I first got sent up," he said. "Now, I'm learning Haitian Creole."

"Aren't you set to get out soon?"

"Thirty-one days so I'm cramming. I want fluency by the time I walk." He leaned back. He had the capacity to look superior and wounded at the same time which was perhaps what Vin had come to love about him. "I anticipate practical applications."

When the interview room was painted they had to sit with a Plexiglas partition between them, a ring of holes punched through the plastic.

"There was a discussion," he said, "I hesitate to call it a conversation, but we were down in the laundry room and this guy says to me 'if you wipe your ass, and the paper comes away clean, do you wipe it again?'"

"What did you say?"

"I said of course. I said naturally. One wants to be certain of such things. But there are schools of thought that would see such behavior as decadent. A failure of trust."

"Are you still studying Job?"

"I'm on to the minor prophets. I like Amos. All the rage is in Amos."

Vin gave the man his Braves ball cap and his phone number.

"I'm down near Orlando. I want you to call me the minute you get out."

A few nights later Vin was sitting on the back stoop when he heard someone on the crushed-shell drive. He rounded the building and met Alan in the parking lot. Even in the blue half-light Vin could see that Alan had soaked through his shirt. He was in shorts and his legs were nicked with scratches, the blood dried in blackish streaks.

"You all right?" Vin asked.

Alan stood with his hands on his knees, panting.

"I ran like the last three or four miles."

"Come inside and get some water."

"Just let me get my breath for a second."

When he had caught his breath they walked inside where Alan sat on the discarded pew that lined the wall and sipped powdered Gatorade mixed in a Nalgene bottle. Vin lit a candle while Alan told him about the evening, about the Holy Land and about Lucy leading him upstairs and how ashamed he had suddenly felt, for both of them, about how he slipped out while she was in the bathroom and how he both regretted it and did not. He'd finally found a pay phone two miles away on Grand Avenue but the receiver was torn from the base.

"So I just started walking up 11 thinking someone would stop but I guess, you know." He shrugged. "Then I figured if I was ever going to get here I'd better at least jog."

"What about the blood?"

"I tried to cut through some pasture, scare the cows or whatever. I caught a fence."

"That was stupid."

"Probably."

"Some random farmer with insomnia and a twelve-gauge."

Alan shrugged again. "Yeah, I guess. Big deal. I'm here."

Vin refilled his Gatorade.

"Anyway," Alan said, "it's probably over with her now."

"Why do you say that?"

"Seriously? Why do I say that?"

He fell asleep on the pew and Vin sat there until the candle sputtered and gasped and he blew it out and sat there a while longer. The windows were up and he could hear the tree frogs and cicadas down along the meadow all the way to the creek. That was the good thing about the Temple, about the grounds, the sense of isolation, the stars brighter, the night alive. He watched Alan sleep with a sense of regret, a sense of his own failure, but buoyed by resolve, by knowing that he would do better. Eventually he moved onto the back porch and sat cross-legged. The moon was down but he recognized the shape of things, the gray, almost silvered field, the darker trees beyond. It felt good to sit, a simple act, uncluttered. He sat and sat, sat until the sun rose over the pines and pinked the eyelids he hadn't realized were shut.

The same sun fell through the parted curtains to warm Lucy's sleeping face, filling her once again with the sense that it was late, what with the glow of heat, the brightness that felt more indictment than comfort. She raised her head from the pillow and felt her eyes throb. Too early, she thought, and self-corrected: no, too late.

She was naked in—no, on top of—her bed, a comforter pulled over her body. Her head felt splintered, broken and packed in ice. Her mouth was dry and tight and when she realized someone was beside her she felt panic rise in her throat like vomit. It tasted like acid, bile, whatever poisons she had ingested. Regret then, enough to make her bottom lip quiver. A little girl about to cry. Except she wasn't a little girl and she wasn't about to cry. She needed to think. She wiped the sleep from her eyes and tried to concentrate on the figure instead of the voice in her head that kept repeating *I hate you, Lucy.* The figure was skinny and sunburned, the comforter having slipped to his butt crack. *I hate you.* Batman wings covered his pink back.

Oh, please, Jesus, no.

He turned on his side and she was certain. *Oh, God forgive me.* Her room was littered with trash: a bottle of Stolichnaya vodka, glasses, a resinous baggie and an ashtray with the remains of what must have been a joint. Her childhood bedroom—besides the dorm room at JBI the only place she'd ever known, her sanctuary, her retreat. How many nights she had sat on the floor reading the Gospel of John and praying. She started to pray now but stopped herself: Just get up, Lucy. Get up and shut up. Just face the world for once in your pathetic life.

She pulled the comforter over his body so she wouldn't have to look at him and slipped into the bathroom. Another baggie sat on the counter beside a torn condom wrapper. *I hate you.* She washed her face and began to cry then, not because of the condom, not because of Twitch, but because—it had just occurred to her—that it hadn't been her father in the kitchen, it had been a dream, a hallucination. A product of the marijuana she now shook into the toilet and flushed, grains clinging to the damp seat so that she had to wipe it with tissue.

She brushed her teeth and palmed water from the tap, swallowed three ibuprofens, and took a hot shower. When she came out Twitch was awake and reclined on one elbow.

"Dag, girl," he said. "Now you just teasing me. Now you just being cruel." He dropped his head back onto the pillow and moaned. "Oh, man, that was some night."

She pulled underwear from her dresser, dropped her towel. What did she care?

"Damn, Lucy," he said. "Go, Lucy."

She was blow-drying her hair when someone knocked at the bathroom door.

"Go away," she said.

Another knock. Lucy in her bra and panties and pissed off at everyone, her sister, herself, mostly herself.

"Just give me a—" She opened the door on Katie, Katie dressed, sober and vigilant as a hawk.

"I thought," Lucy said.

"Come downstairs as soon as you're dressed. Everybody's waiting."

"What?"

"Everybody's waiting."

"Who's waiting?"

"Everybody." She turned and nodded at Twitch who was sitting against the headboard, smiling. "Maybe don't bring your boyfriend along."

"Does mom know—"

"Just hurry up. Grandpa wanted to come up here but so far I've managed to fend him off."

Katie pulled shut the door. Lucy dressed. Twitch kept smiling.

"Stop smiling," she told him.

"Damn, hate the game, not the player."

"At least don't look at me when you do it."

Twitch put his fingers in his hair. "Where's all that love you were showing last night?"

"Sit up here until I come back up. Try not to make a sound."

"Hey, I dig," Twitch said. "I'm Team Lucy."

She was on the threshold of the kitchen before she thought of what Katie had said: *grandpa*. What was grandpa doing here? She pushed open the door. What he was doing was standing behind his daughter, behind Pamela, his hands cupping her shoulders while she cried. Katie was at the table. So too was their grandma. Both puffy eyed, both exhausted, and Lucy realized the look on Katie's face wasn't vigilance but grief: she had been crying too.

Her grandpa saw her and came toward her, one hand on her back, one hand on her elbow, and Lucy let him lead her to the empty place at the table, the fourth chair, her father's chair—and she knew, her grandpa didn't need to speak.

"Where's—"

"Sit down, honey," her grandpa said. "Sit down for a moment."

"But where is—"

Her mother let go another sob. *No, No,* she was saying, but Lucy heard it as *go, go,* as in leave here before they can say it, leave here before the last real thing in this kitchen is not daddy's visit—she smelled the clot of vinegar and protein in the Vitamix, no one had cleaned it—but what she already knew her grandpa was preparing to say.

"Honey," he began.

Go, she thought, but made no move, *get out of here, go away, go back in time, back to before, just go, Lucy. Go.*

PART SIX

IT STARTED RAINING JUST SOUTH OF GAINESVILLE and it was the lashing that woke Bobby from a dream of his parents. He was maybe five and they were at the city park on a Sunday afternoon in early fall. Halfway up the sliding board ladder when a swarm of yellow jackets lifted out of the grass and attached to his thin shins and what he remembered now—Donny nudging him *Wake up and look at this map for me*—what he remembered was the way his father barreled up the rungs to tuck Bobby beneath his big right arm, both of his parents' faces floating above him as he lay on a picnic table, his mother cradling his head while his father sucked at the wounds.

Neil Young sang through the walls of sleep while Donny pushed something against his face, the map printed off the internet to the address Kristen had given them. They were lost in a gated community of broad streets and overhanging Laurel Oaks, massive Tudor style homes sitting on ten-acre horse pastures. Rain shivered from the trees.

"We're back in here somewhere." Donny tapped the paper. "Or at least we were. We might be back in all this mess by now."

Bobby turned the map to follow the blue line that wriggled from Georgia down to the outskirts of Ocala. *Horse people,* Donny had repeated when Bobby picked him up. *Lot of money down here. Lot of potential energy waiting to go kinetic.* Their parents standing on the porch. No way for Bobby not to get out and speak to them when he pulled into the yard. His mother clutching the neck of her ratty housecoat. His father with his big hands in his jeans pockets. *You were always such good boys, both of you.* It was like they were twelve and ten and headed to camp and not wastrels pushing their mid-thirties. Donny wore his Braves ball cap and carried a new Camelback and an old Camptown High athletic bag. Bobby threw both in the bed and hugged his parents. He loved them but he could no longer bear the weight of their sadness, already his mamma's lips moving in silent prayer. He'd seen it in the rear-view mirror and knew he would see it the rest of his life: a disappointed woman trying not to show it.

"This ain't even the right neighborhood," Donny said, and Bobby drifted back into sleep. When he woke again the truck sat on the road's muddy shoulder, rain thumping against the glass. Donny had his bag in his lap, stuffed between his chest and the steering wheel.

He stared out at the window at the green haze of vegetation. "You ever talk to old Manny anymore?"

"What?" Bobby said.

"You know why he never calls?"

"What did you pull over for?"

Donny ran one finger down the cool glass. "We're like bad reminders is why. It's like football players walking around a hospital. You get that taint on you and know you'll wind up in there if you don't stay away. It's not even like bad luck. More like voodoo." He looked at Bobby and Bobby could tell he had been crying. "You can't shed it," he said.

It was early afternoon when they finally found Kristen's parents' house. The parents themselves away somewhere in her father's De Havilland, Gulf Shores or Miami, maybe the Keys, she said, they're always flying down to the Keys. She led them through the house with its antique riding tack and expensive rugs. Five bedrooms, a viewing room with stadium seating and a sixty-five-inch plasma TV, a butler's pantry where Donny found a commercial-grade ice maker and started mixing drinks.

"So I'm throwing like a little soiree tonight," she said, leading them up the stairs. She did a little hop on the top step and laughed. "I so can't believe you two showed up. This is fantastic."

Bobby put his bag down in an upstairs bedroom, its decoration arrested seven or eight years ago. A collage of photographs were pinned on a cork boar. Kristen in high school, Bobby guessed. The tan bright-eyed center of a high school mosaic. Cheerleading. Prom. Lots of parties on boats or by tiled pools, tangles of girls in bikinis crowding the frame, smiling and holding red Solo cups of beer. Kristen with a somber girl who looked to be her sister. He walked to the windows. The room overlooked the dense front yard, the banana plants and a guava tree that shouldn't grow this far north, the beds of mulch overfilled with flowers.

He had no idea what he was doing here and walked into the hall. He could hear, or thought he could hear, Donny and Kristen downstairs, laughing, and he stood for a moment before he crossed to a back bedroom that overlooked the fan-shaped pool. The rain was less now, shafts of buttery sunlight beginning to break through the clouds, the gauzy-green surface of the pool near spilling. He could see back to the pastures and the red barn that sat in a field of timothy, the purple heads glistening with the sunlight that suddenly flowed over everything. Steam rose off the deck and Bobby went back to the bedroom and shut the door.

In his notebook, to remind himself, he wrote:

THE 504 SHOT IN A DITCH AT MY LAI.

And below that:

ALL DEAD. STILL DEAD.

He woke to music, the faint tremble of bass, voices beyond that, sat up and wiped his face. He was atop the sheets and still dressed. Shouldn't be sleeping like this. A sign of something, depression, most likely. Though he figured he had plenty of reasons for being depressed. Driving down, Donny had started counting Bobby's blessings—survived the war and made it out of the service intact, got a great boy that loves you, not tied down by a wife—and Bobby had felt it wasn't so much the cloud that was oppressing him as the goddamn silver lining. The day would come, he knew, when he would have to tell little Bobby everything. And not just about the two boys that had died, the one in the ring in Vegas by Donny's hand, the other in an alley in Sadr City by Bobby's; his son knew about that already. There was more, and it was worse, if you got right down to it. The day-to-day shit that had silted Bobby's heart, the moments even now he turned away from, never criminal, never evil, but the countless personal failings out of which he seemed constructed. He would have to answer for them someday, the bill would come due, and he felt that day was soon.

He found his watch—it was just after eleven and the party sounded in full swing—walked into the bathroom and drank water from the tap, washed his face. He wouldn't get back to sleep without a drink but couldn't bear the thought of facing whoever was downstairs playing their Emo and taking shots of Patron and for a moment he wished he had left Donny in the crackhouse where he found him, Marsha shit-faced and little Stephen suffering the homeless on a filthy mattress. He had his own boy to worry about, after all. His own life to fuck up. But he still needed that drink.

He stopped at the head of the stairs to let some kids pass through back toward the pool. They looked like fuzzy-faced models, all three of them in bathing suits, waifish and showing the dull edge of their pubic bones. Laughing, of course. He watched them and felt with clarity the extent to which he was antiquated. They were stripped down, androgynous and odorless, ironic and detached. Little virtual versions of selfhood who would find him quaint and vaguely threatening. Look at the bearded man. Look at the sweaty man. The soldier, the father, the failure. They would treat him with great respect but laugh the moment he turned his back, run outside and tell everyone about the dinosaur inside, *the authentic backwoods hero.* He understood, and though he resented them for it he didn't blame them. He had cared too much whereas they cared not all. That was their secret, the key to their immortality. Conviction aged badly, grew laughable. To hold any conviction was to risk ridicule, and there was no worse fate.

They disappeared onto the patio and he felt what a stupid move leaving his job was. The way the economy was—the jobs all gone to Mumbai or Beijing, the local kids run off to wait tables at vegan restaurants in Atlanta or Savannah—the Farmtown land would never be developed. He could've sat back there, alone, for the next forty years. Or until he grew balls enough to put a deer slug in his brain. Whichever God saw fit to bring about first.

The kitchen was blessedly empty and he filled a water glass with ice and Maker's Mark. There were bags of pita chips and popcorn on the counter, the kind of junk he usually avoided. But he took one bag, rolled the top, and scampered back up the stairs. The music seemed to have swelled by the time he crossed to the empty bedroom and pressed his forehead to the glass. Below him the pool. Bodies in motion. Diving toward the wall lights or gravitating in and out of shadow. Kids getting busy on a chaise longue. Couldn't tell the boy from the girl. He drank until ice clanked against his teeth.

"They'll stay at it all night."

He turned and was startled to see someone on the bed on the opposite wall, a woman sitting up on one elbow.

"I'm sorry," he began, but stopped when she sighed and fell back into the sheets.

"All fucking night," she said, and he realized the voice belonged to Kristen. "I was half-joking when I said it but your brother got all excited so I was like why not, you know?"

"Is he down there?"

She sat up in bed. "He does something to women, doesn't he?" she said. "Like has a way. I'm gonna turn on the light."

"I'm going back to bed. I didn't know you were in here."

"I know you didn't. Watch your eyes."

The room flared into shape and he saw her on the edge of the mattress in a white tank-top and shorts, one leg crossed beneath her. She pushed a stray hair behind her ear and he thought she appeared much younger than he remembered, physically smaller. Olive skinned and compact, her modest breasts pulling the ribbed fabric of the tank-top into horizontal lines. He watched her shoulders for a moment, where the neck joined the body, the smooth line of her clavicle that swept to the line of her jaw.

"I should go to bed," he said, but made no move other than to turn back to the window. "I don't see him out there."

172

"Oh, he's out there. He's most definitely out there."

"We'll get out of your hair in the morning." He took a drink, addressed his own reflection. "I'm not sure exactly what we're doing here."

"He said you two are headed out west."

Bobby shook his head and looked at her. Both of her legs were pulled beneath her now and she appeared not small but dangerous. "He's got that in his head. I figure we get maybe to New Orleans and turn it back. I don't know."

"I know a place in Flagstaff we could stay."

"Arizona?"

"It's not as far as you might think."

He put his drink down and wiped the condensation on his jeans. A photograph sat on the edge of the desk. "What about your parents?" he said.

"That's them you're looking at."

He picked up the photograph. The man a Florida cracker hiding in expensive clothes. He was manicured and coiffed, but it wasn't hard to see the hog butchering in his eyes, the sand from the creek bank clinging to his feet. He'd sang of the Pow'r in the Blood and cried out at tent revivals before he started spending weekends on South Beach. The woman was different. The woman looked exactly like Kristen.

"I'm of a certain age, you know?" she said. "They think I've gotten this snotty existential thing about me. They're telling me they love me but I can tell all they really want to do is smack the shit out of me. Early twenties."

"Or maybe just you."

"Likely just me. But likely early twenties, too."

He put the photograph down. "Do you really dance at that club?"

"Did your brother really get that tattoo in jail?"

"The one on his neck?" Bobby picked up his drink, swallowed ice and watery bourbon. She seemed to be enjoying this and he felt as clumsy and dull as an elephant. "Most likely. He said you were half Seminole."

"I'm half something." She cocked her head. "I'm an orphan."

Her parents had houses all over the place. Or maybe it wasn't her parents, maybe it was friends of her parents, or her grandparents. She was never clear on that and every time Bobby asked the story had altered. The place they were headed to was this side of Mobile but they were barely into the panhandle when Donny waved them off I-10 and south to a fishing village along the Gulf. What's the rush? he wanted to know. He knew this place. He'd been scalloping here once and what was the goddamn hurry? They were supposed to be enjoying themselves. Leaving Ocala, Bobby saw Donny had all the accoutrements: a pistol and a Ziploc of pills. The pipe was probably in there, too, and he suspected that was part of the reason Kristen was with them, that and playing at defiance, scaring the parents. Bobby had woken in a black mood, the bourbon packed in his skull like cotton. He showered and drank coffee until ten and by the time they were pulling out a team from Merry Maids was unpacking a rainbow of cleaning chemicals.

Kristen straddled the gearshift and curled into sleep, head against Donny's shoulder.

"How much does kidnapping get you these days?" Bobby asked, and his brother laughed and swallowed an Oxy 30.

All morning they passed billboards for alligator farms and orange groves. CROCODILE CREEK. SUNSHINE-CITRUS-FARMS: U-PICK. The land braided with dry creekbeds, tangles and thickets that doubled back on themselves. Bridge pilings and the legs of docks sank in the mud beside signs for family campgrounds. It was all motion, the flat black highway rolled out before them, the hum of the engine, the glide of the tires, and he thought of his past migrations, the retreats, the forays toward living that ended like a bird shattering itself against glass. What he'd wanted was to make it to the end of the road inflicting as little hurt as possible. He'd thought himself capable. He'd been wrong. There were many questions, but ultimately they were only sub-questions, qualifications, variations on a theme. *How much you could fuck up in one lifetime?* being the central issue.

South of the interstate the highway elevated above the cypress marsh and cantilevered over the Choctawhatchee Bay, ahead of them the Gulf like a black pearl, opalescent in the mid-day sun. The village was just that: a harbor of shrimp boats and their spidered riggings, a main street of diners and souvenir shops, a post office and bar. Donny knew a place here where he'd thrown darts with an aging ARVN frogman in the summer of '97 but couldn't find it.

"You know it might've been Texas I'm thinking of," he said finally. "Down near Corpus, maybe. But it's all good. Pull over and let me make a call."

They followed the coast to Grayton Beach, the shore swelled with dunes and the road lined with the occasional beach shack collapsing between monster summer homes, stopped for the afternoon at a motel converted into a beachside bar and grille where they sat in the center expanse around the small pool. Watched waitresses haul up buckets of Coronas to frat boys and bikers, plates of flounder and popcorn shrimp to the occasional family that wandered up off the sand. The salt breeze. Folks drinking Red Stripe and Landshark and nodding their heads to the reggae on the stereo. Donny ordered a pitcher of Early Death and wandered onto the beach. Bobby drank a glass of the punch and felt the rum slosh into his stomach, cold and light. Kristen had awoken as they crossed the Bay and was only a little less sullen with a drink in front of her, her straw going pink until her glass was empty.

"Friends stay late?" Bobby asked her.

"They aren't my friends."

When Donny came back he had them a place for the night, a cottage behind the dunes a mile or so from here.

"Now somebody give me a plan," he said. "Vegas?"

"L.A.," said Kristen.

Donny poured them all another glass. "What do you say, Bobby?"

"I thought maybe New Orleans."

"I've got a sorority sister in New Orleans," Kristen said, "down in the Quarter."

"I thought you dropped out of Flagler?" Bobby said.

She frowned. "I have a BA in Cultural Theory from Smith, asshole."

Donny's hands flew around the table. One moment he was downing his drink, the next moment he was pouring another. "Why not do it all? We hit the Big Easy on the way out. New Orleans, Vegas, L.A. Where did you say was the house in the desert?"

"Flagstaff."

"Flagstaff," Donny said. "We'll see the Grand Canyon. I've never seen the Grand Canyon."

It was a tangerine cottage, two blocks from the ocean, alone at the end of a cul-de-sac. Crackers dusting the linoleum. A Steve Miller Band flag shading the picture window. Everywhere empty Miller ponies.

"Somebody forgot to call housekeeping," Donny said.

"Who the hell did you rent this from?" Bobby asked.

Kristen had found garbage bags beneath the sink. "Just go outside," she said, "both of you."

The deck was stilted above a yard of patchy grass, another dune behind it, between them a dirty pool wrapped in busted chain-link. In the distance a Cessna pulled a banner that read: Gators Dockside! Ladies Night! They drank from go-cups and watched the plane glide along the horizon. Inside, they could hear Kristen shucking cans into the bag. A little while later they heard a vacuum drone to life.

"How long before she loses interest and calls mommy and daddy?" Bobby asked.

Donny shrugged. "We can drop her in New Orleans. She might be fun till them."

"She know you're carrying?"

"Carrying what?"

"That little pea-shooter in your bag," Bobby said. "What is that, a .22?"

"It's a .38." Donny tossed his ice into the yard. "Do I look like the type of man to carry a .22?"

When she came onto the deck in rubber gloves Bobby carried his duffel bag to the smallest bedroom and turned on the bulky air conditioner. The air spilled cold and he walked outside and called Nancy on Donny's cell.

"Stephen's back in the hospital," she said.

"He all right?"

"Perfect," she said, and he recognized the sunny falseness, an old trick of hers, the way she bent their suffering with an ugly brightness. "Absolutely perfect except that he's dying."

"Is little Bobby all right?"

"Relative to what?" she said, and he thought she might have been crying just before he called. It was that high pitch so near laughter, that trembly waver.

"I shouldn't have called." He paced from the mosaic tile walk out to the road and back. "I called at the wrong time."

"Implying there is a right time? Where are you, Bobby?"

"Somewhere on the panhandle. Florida."

"This is Donny's plan? The Florida panhandle escape."

"I don't guess you heard anything from Vance."

"And how exactly is that any of your business?"

"I'll call again in a day or so."

"The last man on the earth without a cell phone finally has a cell phone," she said. "I've got the number right here in my phone now."

"It's Donny's phone."

"Donny's phone. Donny's plan. Jesus, Bobby."

"I'll call back."

His room was cold now, the sink dusted with the same cigarette ash that grained a thin bedspread of pale tropical fish. The TV remote bolted to the nightstand. All of it honeycombed with sunlight. Outside, the air blazed. White-hot light jumped off the chain-link fence and the metal piping that supported the diving board. He walked out to find Kristen by the pool in a tiny chocolate bikini, rail-thin and wearing gold hoop earrings big as bracelets, earbuds planted in her head. In the cooler beside her was a liter of Bacardi rum and a six pack of Coke. She had an insulated glass filled with ice and Bobby stopped to watch her pour in the rum and splash Coke on top, watched her rub her body with baby oil.

"He's not out here," she called.

Bobby froze. He was in the deep porch shadow and had thought himself hidden.

"If you're looking for your brother." She raised onto an elbow. "I know you're back there."

"I have his phone." He walked out. "I just needed to give it back to him."

"Well, he's not out here." She threw an ice cube into the pool and looked up at him.

"What are you listening to?"

"I'm learning French if you must know."

"French."

"Yes, French. *Francais.* You have a problem with that?"

"No."

"You don't like me, do you? Why don't you like me?"

"I don't dislike you."

"You couldn't possibly." She turned back to the pool and tossed another cube. "You don't even know me."

Bobby looked out at the dune. When the wind was right you could hear voices from the beach. "It's more like your generation," he said.

She was throwing cube after cube now. "We make you feel old."

"You make me feel pointless."

"We're nihilists," she said. "And we all give head by middle school."

"I'm going inside." He put the phone down beside her and turned. "Make sure he gets that."

"Cybersex," she called. He knew she was mocking him. "Online bullying."

"Just give him his phone."

In the late afternoon a storm blew off the ocean and scraped at the window screens, Bobby propped on two pillows and feeling rain splash in. He'd showered but still tasted salt on his lips. He took a sip of bourbon and thought of Stephen dying, Stephen in that circle of light in the crackhouse, the room so bright he thought someone had set up a grow-room. Then he thought of his own son. It was only when you had children that dying became this secondary thing. Like it wasn't anywhere near the worse fate imaginable. It was an inconvenience, true, but the point was that your kids were okay. If they were okay you just got out of the way, made sure not to screw things up. Which was maybe what he was doing now. Maybe what he had been doing all along.

What had ruined him as a soldier wasn't so much shooting the boy in Sadr City—though that had certainly ended his career—it was having a child, the seditious thought that some toothless Pashtun man in a mountain hovel loves his boy just as much as you love yours, or that woman crying when you kick down her apartment door in Fallujah, she's crying for her girl. You can't go to war with someone who loves his children, not and expect to go home and love your own

177

properly. You give something up, arrogate some right to the Universe, and the Universe will fuck you over once and then again for good measure. He'd come to believe that, knowing simultaneously it was maudlin bullshit, just another ridiculous something you told yourself. In the end, you could kill anyone for anything, you just had to get down to the bottom. The only real issue is how far down the bottom lies.

He shut his eyes for just a moment, woke to heartburn and rain. He knew he'd been dreaming of his Baghdad vision but couldn't say what he saw exactly, heaven open above him, a ladder of daylight. Donny was knocking at his door, but when he said for him to come in it was Kristen who entered and sat on the wicker loveseat. She sank into the peach cushion, half-hidden in shadow, a big white three-ring binder across her knees.

"I can't seem to find your brother."

Bobby sat up in bed, his shirt was off and he pulled the sheet up. "I thought he was with you."

"I gave him his phone and he split. That was like two hours ago."

Bobby brushed the condensation from his glass. "I don't know what to tell you. He ain't hiding in the closet."

"You could at least offer me a drink."

"It's in the kitchen. I think there's still some ice in the cooler."

She came back carrying her insulated cup. She was barefoot and he figured her a little drunk, perched unsteadily on her toes and putting a hand against the wall for support.

"You ever hear of something called Dream Positive?" she asked. "It's like a hardcore MaryKay except they don't actually sell anything."

"You're talking about your parents?"

"I'm talking about a Ponzi scheme." She sat down and sucked at her drink. The binder was at her feet. "And here they were so thrilled when Madoff sank Palm Beach. Like the Jews finally got theirs and it was enough for all those years dad schlepped cut rate Lincoln Town Cars." She took another drink. "He hates Canadians, too."

"Everyone hates Canadians."

She snorted. "You're actually warming up to me, aren't you? But I'm serious. They go to this mega-church called Deep Springs. It has its own coffee shop."

"Yet they put you through school."

"A National Merit Scholarship and a Visa Platinum Rewards put me through school."

"You don't look old enough."

"I'm twenty-three."

"I would've said eighteen, nineteen tops."

"Well, you would've been wrong."

"Maybe. But I get the sense you're kind of bullshitting me," he said. "Like maybe you don't want to give your folks any credit."

"Like this is all just some construction? My entire life?"

"Parents usually aren't as bad as we like to think. Mine aren't."

"And so from your private, singular experience you've decided to extrapolate this entire universal law? The 'law of the decent parents.'"

"I don't know. I just think maybe you're bullshitting me, making this up as you go."

"For what?"

"For whatever. Kicks. Boredom. Maybe some kind of screwed up revenge."

The wind gusted and a fine mist blew through the screens. A ragged palm waving like a flag, beyond it the dune gone gray with rain.

"Is that what this is about," Bobby said, "getting back at them?"

"Partially. That's what Northampton was about. I used to Facebook pics of me kissing girls on my hall, knowing my mom would see, and I'm like as hetero as they come. When I was younger I did this cutting thing for a while, my arm, you know." She shrugged. "So, yeah. But partially I'm just a fuck-up, too. I look for the absurd, the ridiculous situation and see what unfolds."

Bobby lifted his drink, smeared the wet ring it left on the nightstand. "Well, this is certainly a ridiculous situation."

"Maybe." She shook her ice. "You know you're brother speaks Spanish and Creole. I heard him on the phone today. He said he learned it in prison. He also thinks FEMA is building concentration camps all along where Katrina hit."

"If he told you that he's just fucking with you."

"How would you know?" She stood up and he thought for a moment she was coming toward him. He hoped she wasn't. He was afraid of her. He had just realized that. "The other thing about Donny, not just the languages, I mean, but he can change the way he talks. Like that night we met: he was like this Georgia good ole boy. But then I catch him sometimes speaking like he has a doctorate in philosophy."

"He's not a dummy."

"You want to know who he's been calling?"

"No."

"I went through his call log. Somebody in Miami loves him. You know he's preparing for this mission," she said. "That's what he calls it: my mission."

"Mission to do what?"

"I told him he needed a juice fast. Ten days. You start with kale. You have to purge the toxins so that when they see inside you they don't see what's really there. I was joking but he took it all serious."

"When do they see inside you?"

"What?"

"When do they see inside you?"

"Oh, like airports, the TSA. That scanner they have. Except he comes back and says the scanner is just a metaphor. It's so you get used to that invasiveness. They normalize it. He comes back and says silence is the only real form of subversion left. No Facebook, no iPhone, no Twitter."

"No conversation."

"No nothing. And you fuck them that way because they can't own your thoughts."

"This is part of his mission?"

She looked at him. "I know this guy, this is strange but he sort of refused to let his cell phone die. Had it repaired even though it cost like a ridiculous amount and they would've replaced it for free. *It can't just die. It's a thing.* That's what he said." She looked away. "It was a point he was trying to make, I think."

He looked at his drink as if seeing it for the first time. "What are you reading?" he asked.

She touched the binder with one foot. "This? I'm training to be a Life Coach."

"Like a therapist?"

"Sort of but less formal," she said. "Mostly you give pep talks, try to help people think through their options in life. A lot of it's just building self-esteem." She looked at him. "This is the point where you tell me it sounds like so much bullshit."

"Helping someone sort through their life?" He shook his head. "I think there's probably worse things to do with your time."

"And you've done them, right?"

He took up his drink. "I wish there'd been someone to coach me."

He heard her for a while after that, pacing through the cottage, turning the radio on and off. A station playing beach music. The Chairmen of the Board. The Swingin' Medallions. When the rain stopped he put on shorts and his running shoes. She was sitting in the living room with her laptop open.

"Still not back," she said.

The parking lot was littered with palm fronds and beards of Spanish moss hung from the gutters or lay dying in shallow pools. Bobby jogged along the beach, the ocean flat, the tide out and the shore thick with kelp and seaweed. Along the horizon kids rode jet-skis in the gray surf. At the turnaround he saw dark blurs hovering beneath the surface and realized they were manta rays.

When he got back he walked to the Amoco they passed coming in and bought several protein bars. Donny still wasn't back when Bobby fell asleep but sometime later he woke to laughter and the rhythmic grinding of the headboard against the opposite wall. There was just enough light to see the meniscus of whiskey sway in its glass.

When he woke again Donny was shaking him.

"Get dressed," he was saying. "Hurry up."

"What time is it?"

"You are sleeping way too much."

"Leave me alone."

"Come on, get moving. I need you tonight, brother."

He stumbled into the bathroom, washed his face and pissed. So Donny had a plan. *The Florida panhandle escape.* On some level Bobby had known all along this was coming and took his time brushing his teeth, uncapped his vitamins and palmed water to his mouth. Donny beat on the door. *What the hell are you doing in there? Come on.* But Bobby made no move other than to splash his face again, stare for a moment into his own eyes, runny and beaten as they were. You knew this was coming, he told himself, you just wanted to fool yourself. He pulled on his jeans and walked out, sat on the bed and put on his good boots. When he stood Donny handed him a pistol.

"What the hell is this?" Bobby said.

"Just put it in your pants and shut up."

Bobby turned the gun over, a small Glock that fit neatly in his hand. He pulled the slide and ejected a round. "This is loaded," he said. "These things don't even have a safety and you hand it to me loaded?" He popped out the magazine and tossed it on the bed beside the single round. Donny had the .38 in the band of his jeans. "Where are we going?"

"Come on and let's get in the truck," Donny said.

"Tell me where it is we're going first."

"I'll tell you in the truck."

Donny drove, not turning on the lights until they were out of the cul-de-sac and near the main drag.

Donny lit a Marlboro and blew smoke out the open window. The .38 bulged against one hip. "You do your own time," he said. "Everybody in the joint's always says it. But the smart man's thinking more about quality than quantity. He's thinking about the other man's time, too."

The town was asleep, the houses beyond it dark monoliths, the traffic lights all flashing yellow. He turned onto a side road and slowed near an open cattle gate, turned again onto an oyster shell lane walled with vegetation and suddenly it was completely dark, only the phosphorescent glow of the instrument panel that lit his hands a ghostly green. Branches scrapped at the truck.

"We get there you let me do all the talking," Donny said. "You just stand there and look mean." He tossed his cigarette out the window. "You think you can do that? You're doing it right now."

The canopy thinned and they ground across a pasture, cows beyond the barbwire fence. Ahead was a dark structure, a barn light, beyond it what appeared to be marsh, beyond that open water. They pulled up and Donny cut the engine. "Everything's cool," he said as much to himself as to Bobby. They got out and were met by a big Haitian, dread-locked, arms crossed on the pile of his chest. He wore jumbo board shorts and a dingy wife-beater. Some sort of machine-pistol slung over one shoulder.

"Shit," Bobby said.

"Everything's cool," Donny repeated, "everything's copacetic."

He spoke to him in Creole and the man led them inside the barn where two men stood by the tailgate of a Land Rover, another Haitian and a smaller white man, khaki pants stuffed into rubber Wellingtons. He looked more like a surgeon than a bandit: short silver hair, fissures around his eyes, squinting in the dim barn. He shook Donny's hand and spoke with a British accent.

"I've heard good things," he said, "nothing but good things. This is your brother?"

"This is Bobby," Donny said. "He's the strong, silent type."

"I like that," the man said. "I like that very much. Where'd you get sent up, chief?"

"He never did," Donny said. "He's straight G.I. Joe. Did his time in the man's army. He got that look though, don't he?"

"He certainly does. He most certainly fecking does." The man waved them forward. "Out back, gentlemen."

Behind the barn an air-boat sat pulled onto the soft bank. One of the Haitians took a canvas rucksack from the Igloo cooler strapped to the bow and Bobby realized the second man wasn't Haitian but something else, West African maybe.

The man caught his eye. "Fuck you looking at, white man?"

"Gentlemen, gentlemen." The Brit looked up and smiled. "We have here," he said, "the United Nations of Narcotics. Let's do try to get along."

Donny and the man checked the bag, removed the shrink-wrapped kilos, touched each as they counted the eight bricks. They repacked and the man stood and dusted his hands on his pants. Donny hooked the ruck over one arm.

"Everything's been made clear, I suppose," the man said. "You have our number, of course."

Donny patted his pocket.

"So everything is good, everything is satisfactory?" the man asked.

"How could it not be?" Donny said.

They pulled up to the cottage around four, traces of light already gathering along the horizon. Donny cut the lights but let the engine idle and for a moment they sat with the windows down and listened to the low thump of the motor. Neither had spoken on the ride back.

"You gonna explain this to me?" Bobby asked.

"It's eight kilos there in the ruck."

"I fucking see that, Donny."

"Colombian Gold. It's supposed to be pure."

"What are you getting out of it?"

Donny touched the bag, the tarnished clasp, the worn stitching. "Fifty large on delivery in Vegas," he said. "They had some kinks in their distribution network and suddenly I'm on the scene."

"Fifty large is a pretty generous cut."

"Well I did a pretty generous thing."

"So this is your thank you for keeping your mouth shut?"

"Thank you and fuck you, both in the same breath. I take the money and I disappear—that's pretty standard fare. It's cool though. Eight kilos is enough to build a worldview around."

"Christ. These people are going to slice you from tongue to tail."

"No."

"I'm telling you, people like this."

"No," Donny said. "I'm just the runner. I'm not trying to step in anybody's game."

Bobby rubbed his face, left his hand over his mouth and looked across the street to the dark cottage. The safety light beamed over a patch of asphalt. "Tell me how it plays?"

"It plays beautifully, brother. We've got a week to get out West. Then we sell this piece of shit truck and I put ten Gs in your pocket, put you and her both on the first flight to Atlanta."

"So this is a one-way trip?"

"I got nothing keeping me. It's finished with Marsha and I wouldn't go back even if it wasn't. I need a clean start. I been thinking L.A."

Bobby nodded toward the cottage, toward Kristen. "She doesn't know?"

"And she fucking shan't. She's on a private kamikaze run. Ethical concerns prevent our intervening." Donny looked at him. "You all right with this?"

"I don't suppose I have a choice."

"I don't suppose you do." And then Donny did something Bobby couldn't remember him doing since they were boys: he put his hand on his brother's shoulder. "And I'm sorry about that, I am. I want you to know I'm not trying to drag you under. If there was any other way to do this I would. But I'm not going back to the joint and I sure as hell ain't going back to Georgia."

"All right," Bobby said quietly.

"You're cool with it?"

"No." Bobby opened the door and they were lit by the dim interior bulb. "I'm certainly not cool with it. But you're still my brother."

"For better or worse, right?" Donny said. "Till death do us part."

Bobby said nothing, just stepped out onto the warm street, the macadam stubbornly holding the day's heat.

"One more thing," Donny said, and pushed the rucksack across the bench seat. "Keep it with you, all right? Just for the night."

They pushed west all day along I-10. Kristen asleep in the back of the cab, Bobby driving. Donny in the passenger seat with the rucksack down behind his feet and tucked nearly out of sight. Kristen woke just past Mobile and wanted to know why they weren't stopping to see her friend.

"I thought your goddamn friend was in New Orleans?" Donny said.

He looked fried, sunburned and jangling with coke or meth, his skin just beginning to pucker. She frowned and went back to sleep, the exits clicking past, Pascagoula, Biloxi, Gulfport. They stopped for gas and to change seats and then it was Slidell and the oily sheen of Lake Pontchatrain. Donny hunched over the wheel, eyes a few inches from the windshield. "Doing time," he said. "You think about that a minute. Time all around you, this goddamn presence you face every morning, noon, and night." He looked at Bobby. "You are doing it, brother. You are doing nothing but."

Bobby could feel the ruck behind his heels, the bad energy radiating off it, the contamination.

"The hardest thing," Donny said, "is knowing your life is fluttering by. You hear what I'm saying? I mean you try to be useful but you know it's all bullshit."

Bobby looked at the sleeping girl. "You don't need to drag her into this."

"We can ditch her at her friends. She's got a roll of cash on her."

"She's young enough to still have a future. You get her involved in something like this."

"I goddamn just said we would ditch her, didn't I?" Donny slapped the wheel and Bobby noticed the ring that banded his brother's pinkie, a woman's gold band, studded with two birthstones. Donny turned it up to the light. "It's a joke," he said. "She gave it to me as a joke."

Bobby said nothing and Donny slapped the wheel again.

"It's a joke, Bobby."

"It's her mother's ring."

"Jesus, I should ditch you and take Kristen with me. Hand me something to listen to."

Bobby handed him a CD and Townes Van Zandt began to moan. *Sometimes I don't know where this dirty road is taking me. Sometimes I don't even know the reason why.* After Townes was Willie Nelson and Steve Earle—all the music they had grown up listening to. Kristen poked her head up and said this was good music to kill yourself to, this sad sack warbling, Neil Young singing *well, I dreamed I saw the knights in armor . . .*

"You don't even know who this is, do you?" Donny asked.

"I don't even want to. This is like music to play while sticking your head into an oven."

"Oh, my God," Donny said, laughing again, "I don't believe you, girl."

"I'm like five seconds from opening a vein."

They ate at what must have once been a biker joint just off Gentilly Boulevard—a diner facing abandoned railroad tracks with wood-paneled walls and a jukebox full of Glen Campbell and Don Williams—but was now filled with Tulane hipsters in flannel shirts and Buddy Holly glasses. Donny picked apart fried rabbit and ordered a second pitcher of Bud. He was coming down off something and he seemed calmer, his hands and voice slower.

"So who is this girl we're going to see?" he asked.

"Who, Chelsea?" Kristen was eating fried mushrooms and drinking a margarita. "She's just a friend. We used to go to parties some back at school."

"She know we're coming?" Bobby asked.

"I Facebooked her but I doubt she got it." She shrugged. "It doesn't matter really. This is maybe her dead grandmother's old place, somebody like that. We came down once for Mardi Gras. It's a sort of haunted feel. Ghosts and lots of cats and gold they hid from the Yankees or whatever. She'll be glad for the company."

Her friend's house was on Dumaine Street, not far from Burgundy and the park with its trussed white gate reading ARMSTONG, the dingy millponds rounded like organs, a grainy kidney here, a long fold of blue-green intestine there. They sweated up the back stairs onto the royal squalor of the sleeping porch. The black shutters and iron balcony. Stone angels and potted ferns. An occasional breeze turned a ceiling fan and it took Bobby a moment to notice the woman stretched on the divan, covered to her neck in a gauze of tulle. Two other men were on the porch, one a light-skinned black man, dangerously skinny and dressed in a white suit.

"How you making it, pilgrim?" he said.

"We're here," Donny said.

"And where might here be?" He began to giggle and Donny shifted the rucksack on his back. The other man wore bib overalls and green eyeshadow and was stretched on the floor in front of a bottle of vodka. The woman on the couch might have been dead but for her wet eyes.

"Chelsea," Kristen called from the stairs. "Wake up, honey. Pocahontas has arrived. Men in tow."

"Men?" called the black man. "Where?"

The women kissed and sat on the porch talking while the man in overalls—his name was Tulip—led Bobby and Donny inside.

He left the room and came back with three bottles of Abita. Besides the eyeshadow he looked like a backwoods Cajun, burly and red-bearded, barefoot above his rolled cuffs. "That's Prince out there," he said. "The guy's an asshole. You have to love Chelsea, though. Chelsea tolerates all."

"You live here?" Donny asked.

"Sometimes." He turned toward the hall. "Let me show you what's here."

Bobby wound up with a small room on the third floor, a garret really, the ceiling angling toward an octagon window that overlooked the garden. The walls were lime and cracked plaster lay in chunks. He dusted the pillows and his hand came away white. There was no air conditioning but a fan oscillated hot air across the room. He took off his pants and got beneath the sheets and listened to the voices from the porch, the laughter and occasional squeal. The thickness of the air reminded him of his shed out at the Farmtown tract and he wondered for a moment how his dogs were doing. Except they weren't really his dogs anymore. He'd lost them just as he'd lost any sense of order in his life. He had always thrived on that: order, routine. Mornings and evenings at home with the dogs, days out at the acreage, hitting the bags and jogging, seeing little Bobby every few weeks, the conjugal visits with Nancy. Everything was measured, everything had its place. It softened the edges but you could live with soft. It had taken him a long time to realize that. Most knew it from birth, those warm-blooded comfort-seekers, but not Bobby. He'd spent his life hurtling toward death and now all he wanted was that easy slide, to go in your sleep, eighty years old and a little drunk: you just don't wake up. What he wanted was fifty years of sameness, no more excitement, no more surprises. Like the shit in the rucksack. Eight kilos enough to blow any life apart.

He fell asleep and woke in the late afternoon. When he came down they were all in the living room drinking and listening to the *Grease* soundtrack, Donny holding forth on his guru, on Ganesh and the *via negativa,* a drink in each hand, everyone glassed and nodding as he whirled between the mismatched furniture. He'd read too much in the lock-up, spent too much time in solitary.

"What I'm talking about," he said, "is the complete absence of form. You lose the form and you get down to the broken tusk that wrote the *Mahabharata.* But the whole point of the institution is to preserve form. The shit I'm interested in is the apophatic moment, the reduction, the final erasure beneath which we find only the Ground of Being."

Bobby was halfway across the room when he saw the mirror on the coffee table, the lines cut on the glass, white furrows spaced evenly. He pulled Donny into the kitchen by his shirtfront.

"What is that in there?"

"A party," Donny said.

"You know what I'm talking about. You cut one of the blocks."

"I shaved the thing."

"You fucking cut it."

"I barely touched it. We're guests after all."

"You're going get yourself killed." Bobby let go of him. "You're going to get us all three killed."

Donny straightened his shirt. "I shaved it. The stuff's as fine as sugar. Relax."

The sink was full of dishes and beer bottles and Bobby stood over it for a moment and looked out at the rooftops, house after house and the steamy river bent somewhere beyond sight.

"You need a drink," Donny said.

"Let me borrow your phone."

"Let me fix you a drink."

Bobby turned and leaned against the counter. "I'm going out. Let me borrow your phone."

"I'll fix you a go-cup."

"Just give me the phone."

Donny clapped a hand against his pocket. "Can't do it, brother. Sorry, but it's business, not personal."

He found a phone at a garage a few streets over, pulled in across the air hose and dropped quarters into the slot. Big sign that read BRAKES-TIRES-MUFFLERS. Glossy 3x5 cards for escort services. Graffiti. The last public phone left in the city, left in the country for that matter. It smelled like piss.

Nancy didn't answer at home and he dialed her cell.

"I'm at the hospital."

"What's wrong?"

"The hospital," she said, her phone fuzzing in and out.

"Is little Bobby okay?"

"What?"

"Little Bobby?"

It was Stephen, of course. Nancy had never been close to Marsha until Donny was locked up. After that, she and Marsha seemed to bond over their shared suffering. She told Bobby to quit shouting, to let her walk outside and get better reception.

"It's all that hardware," she said. "CT scans and X-rays and everything else."

"What's wrong with Stephen?"

"We've been down here all evening. I didn't even realize it was still light out."

"What's wrong with Stephen, Nancy? Is little Bobby okay?"

"He's fine. You want to talk with him?"

"Is he there?" A truck bounced across the lot. "What the hell is he doing there?"

Little Bobby took the phone.

"Hey, dad."

"How are you, son?"

"I'm all right, dad, but Stephen's doing really bad." He voice was brittle. "I mean really bad."

"Put your mamma back on for me, son. I love you."

"I love you too, dad."

He heard the phone pass between them.

"Take him home," he told her. "Don't make him sit through this."

"He isn't going to live through the night, Bobby. That's what the doctor said."

"Take him home. Jesus, Nancy. He's on the edge of tears."

"We're all of us on the edge of tears here, honey." And he recognized that *honey*. "All of us that bothered to stick around."

He drove in circles back to Dumaine, not exactly lost but not exactly sure where he was either. Mid-City all the way down to the Marigny out to he didn't know where until he realized he had driven one giant loop and was back on Frenchman Street, then Esplanade. At a traffic light he paused by what appeared to be a butcher's shop, wide display windows open to the street. The light changed just as he saw it was a gym, and not just any gym but an old fight gym, boxers hitting heavy bags or skipping rope beneath the fluorescent lights, the kind of place that by and large no longer existed.

Those three weeks he'd spent on the edge of Chicago—Edison Park, the place was called—training for the Farmtown job, the gym reminded him of those days. They'd start at eight and break at noon, ninety minutes for lunch, and the other trainees, boys from Arkansas and Mississippi and Oklahoma, would pile into a company van and ride down the bypass to the Hooters or Wing House while Bobby drove his rented Kia to a gym in Oriole Park. He did ten sets up pushups and pull-ups and crunches, hit the bags for forty minutes. Nancy had bought him an iPod and loaded it up with Nirvana, Pearl Jam, the Stone Temple Pilots, a little Skynyrd or Marshall Tucker Band to mix things up, and he would pop in the earbuds and begin skipping rope, this busted up man in his early thirties shimmering with sweat, skipping and skipping as if there was nothing else in the world. He'd jump for twenty minutes, spinning and criss-crossing the rope, and eventually started attracting teens, kids in tank-tops and yoga pants who stood around and gawked, that old motherfucker, that motherfucker *just don't stop.* He'd shower and buy two cans of protein to drink on the way back to training, and easing now through the traffic light he felt a pang of longing for that gym, for those sixty minutes of anonymous sweat.

He drove on.

He drove until he passed a Catholic church out in Metairie, stopped even though he wasn't Catholic. It didn't matter. In fact, thinking of Stephen, dying or already dead back in Georgia, it felt somehow right. They'd both had their visions, hadn't they? He and Stephen.

The Church sat on a corner intersection, trim grass on three sides, the fourth given over to a playground and parking lot. He didn't know exactly why he was here. There were moments in the past when he'd felt overwhelmed by the need to pray. It would well in him and eventually spill and after that there was a place of calm. It never lasted. He believed in God, he supposed, but hadn't given the matter any real consideration. The Baptist strictures of his upbringing, that was God, the great cosmic prohibition. God was an incitement. He knew guys with cross-hairs tattooed over their hearts, as much a provocation to the good Lord as some hajji sniper.

He climbed the front steps into the nave. The church appeared empty, the walnut pews leading to the altar dull and unattended. Behind the rail was a mural of the transfiguration. Somewhere past that someone was playing a piano. Down front he spotted a man cradling his bald head in his hands, crying. Bobby sat on the pew behind him.

"I was wondering," Bobby began, and watched the man's head rise slightly from the frame of his hands, "I was wondering if you knew if the priest was around."

"The priest?"

"Or the father, or whatever he's called."

"You're looking for him?"

"Just anyone, really. I'm sorry. I don't exactly know how this works. I'm not even Catholic."

The man turned and Bobby saw his collar. "Well, if you're not Catholic I can't hear your confession. Did you come to take communion? You can't take communion either."

He was much younger than his voice, late-twenties, Bobby thought. Beneath his wireless eyeglasses his face was wet.

"I just wanted someone to talk to more than anything."

"To talk to?"

"I think I had some sort of vision once. I'm pretty sure I did."

The priest nodded and when he turned Bobby saw that his skin had a cold glossy shine. Whatever held him shimmered.

"All right," he said, "You can say whatever you want to say."

Bobby looked back across the pews. An old woman sat near the back, head bowed.

"Out here won't bother anyone?"

"Who might it bother?" the priest said. "If you have something to say then say it."

"Okay," Bobby said. "I killed a man once, in cold blood. Not even a man, more like a boy."

The priest's face showed nothing, a slight nod, a bead of sweat, or a tear perhaps, sliding down the jaw. "This was in your vision?"

"This was in the war," Bobby said. "In Iraq."

"And this happened over there?"

"Yes, sir."

"I see," he said, "I see. And does anyone else know about this?"

"Yes, sir."

"Then it was looked into?"

"There was an investigation."

The priest nodded and water fell from his chin. "I trust you were exonerated? That no charges were filed against you?"

Bobby looked up at Christ and back at the man. "They said it was just one of those things."

"Except to you it wasn't." He looked at Bobby for the first time and Bobby saw that he was crying again, his eyes full. "It wasn't just one of those things. It was a man's life."

"A boy's."

"I think you said that."

"Couldn't have been much older than my own."

"I see."

They sat for a moment, the priests head splotched and quivering almost imperceptibly.

"I'm sorry," Bobby said. "I guess we should have gone to your office or something."

"Sin is public."

"I mean just out of the church here."

"Sin is always and everywhere public," he said. "You don't hide sin by retreating to *my office*." He wiped his nose on his sleeve and looked up. "I'm sorry. I don't mean to be rude. If you were Catholic there would be certain rites. Prayers. Forms of penance."

"Do they work?"

"To the extent that anything works. Perhaps guilt is suffering enough."

"What's punishment enough?"

"I don't think—I don't think I could name such a thing. I don't think I'd be willing."

"What about never forgetting?"

The priest shook his head and stood. "I think that might be more punishment than one could bear."

"Maybe," Bobby said. "But I'm bearing it."

He got back to find the party had devolved, the porch and garden and rooms crowded with people. Music he didn't recognize. The smell of cannabis and night flowers. A girl in an Indian headdress. His life had become one sloppy party after the next, his life's work their avoidance. He looked for Donny or Kristen, couldn't find either of them, but ran into Tulip in the hotbox of the overlit kitchen. He had traded the overalls for a t-shirt of Santa Claus' face above the word BELIEVE in block letters.

"They left," he told Bobby.

"To where?"

"No clue, man. Just left."

Tulip followed him out of the kitchen and onto the porch. A blanket was spread in the grass and two men and a woman were in the tiny wading pool. People going in and out of the shadows drinking from champagne flutes. It was all very ironic, all very hip, and he thought of the party at Kristen's parents' house in Ocala, his fear of being seen, his fear of being found out.

"Where you headed?" Tulip asked him on the stairs.

"Just out."

"Walking?"

"Need to clear my head."

The stairs wound to a pad where a brick of ice cream melted on the concrete, a trail of ants crossing it.

"I'm headed down to a place," Tulip said. "You want to walk?"

They turned onto Bourbon toward Esplanade. Drunk girls with condoms pinned to bridal veils. Older couples, stone-faced and straight off the plane from Des Moines or Wichita. The occasional sailor laced in green beads and speaking German.

"Your brother said you were in the Army," Tulip said. "I guess you saw some shit."

"Something like that."

"Said you were a boxer."

"He say he was too?"

"He most certainly did not."

Bobby sidestepped a man vomiting into a storm grate. Up ahead were mounted policemen, their horses tipping from hoof to hoof like impatient children.

"Sounds like Donny said quite a bit."

"Ah, it's cool," Tulip said. "To be honest that's a little more my scene than all of this. Let's duck in here for a minute."

The bar was crowded and loud, club music over the speakers and a DJ calling out the names of girls that paraded down the center aisle. Drag Queens, Bobby realized. Heels and feathers and press-on lashes, every one of them over six feet tall. A tranny-granny in pearls and orthopedic shoes leaned over a table of middle-aged men in khakis and Lacoste. The place seemed equally divided between homosexuals and the staid couples who sat primly drinking their Hurricanes.

"They love a freak show," Tulip said. "Everybody loves a freak show. Follow me over here."

"I need to hit the head first."

"Back in the corner there. I'll be at the bar."

There were two exits coming out of the bathroom and Bobby walked out of one into an Italian restaurant, the place redolent with garlic and candlelight and the tinkling of silverware. He walked back into the bathroom and found the other door, slipped past a couple making out against the wood-paneled wall. Tulip was at the bar talking to a big-eyed Hispanic boy, his dark hair bristled, his jeans hanging off one pubic bone.

"You want a beer?" Tulip asked Bobby. "Jorge," he told the boy and handed him a twenty, "get us a couple more, how about it?"

The boy took the money and Tulip turned to watch him walk away.

"That's some sweet meat right there. I met one like that up in Baton Rouge. This was years ago and I was out with a buddy. Hey, you want to grab a seat?"

"I'm fine."

Tulip finished the last of his beer and put the bottle on the counter. "But this kid, he was a runaway or something, I guess, and by the time we got there some boys had already raped the hell out of him."

Bobby looked at him.

"I shit you not," Tulip said.

"I don't want to hear this."

"No, no, I'm serious, man. He was like twelve and right there on the river-bank wearing nothing but a My Little Pony t-shirt."

"I don't want to hear this." Bobby turned back toward what he thought was the door.

"Oh, come on, man, I'm just fucking with you. Sit a minute. I see my boy Jorge there coming with your beer." He stood. "If you like, how about we get out of here, just you and me? I think I might be your flavor."

"I don't think so."

He wandered off Bourbon away from the lights and noise, the side streets quieter, the occasional bar playing Dixieland jazz, folks sitting out on balconies drinking from giant plastic cups. He kept edging away from the light, finding a darker street and taking it. He'd been walking for twenty or so minutes when he realized he was back in front of the gym he'd seen that afternoon. The place hummed quietly, bright as a supermarket, the faint sound of men hitting bags almost audible through the door. An elderly black man in a bowling shirt manned the front desk. Bobby paid five dollars and signed a guest waiver.

"You got gloves and wraps?" the man asked.

"Not with me."

"They seven dollars for both. You get em by the hour."

"I'm all right," Bobby said.

"Good, then," the man said. "Go wreck your hands. They just your hands."

He took off his shirt and boots in the locker room, walked out barefoot in jeans and found a jump rope. When he had a good sweat going he found an empty heavy bag and started swinging, the jab first—dancing in, dancing out— the jab, the jab-cross, working up to the hook and uppercut. Two black teenagers sparred in the ring, but around him were mostly men in their thirties or forties.

Hitting bags at half past ten summoned a certain crowd. Men who'd found Jesus or kicked the bottle. No daddy, no title, no future. Everyone beating out their lives in four-punch combinations. Head-body, head-body until the arthritis got so bad they went home and rotted because what the bags gave them was a way to unspool the trauma of their lives.

When he felt loose Bobby began to swing a little harder. He knew he shouldn't—he could feel the fabric grate his hands—but couldn't help himself. He tried to keep his form solid. Hit with the big two knuckles. Twist. You swing with the body, not the arms. But his form was shit and he felt his knuckles began to tear, his already damaged hands ache. What are you doing, fool? Hammering back at nothing. Not his failures or shortcomings but vinyl and sawdust. He jabbed, swung harder. His knuckles were bleeding. He swung again, wildly, furiously. Jab, cross, another jab and something cracked in his left hand, a star of light and heat. He doubled over, panting and clenching his broken hand. When he looked up he saw several men had stopped to watch him cry into his puddle of sweat. Fucking pathetic.

The man at the counter pointed to the door. "You get the hell out of here," he said.

His truck was still out front of the house on Dumaine and he managed to work his key ring out of his front jeans pocket. He found Donny's Ziploc of pills in the Camelback along with a fifth of Jim Beam. He fished out what might have been a Celebrex and what he was almost certain was a Percocet, washed both down with the Beam and closed the glovebox, thought better of it and fished out another Perc he dropped in his shirt pocket. He hoped Donny'd had the sense to put the coke somewhere safe.

It was after one now and the house was mostly empty, a few stragglers on the couch or making out in the kitchen. The light-skinned black man, he said his real name was Nemo, dipped Bobby a plastic cup of punch and said that Pocahontas and Donny had left with everyone to go to a strip club in Algiers.

"Somebody said you ran out with Tulip."

"No." Bobby sipped the drink. "Just out."

"Well, somebody said it. Hey, what happened to your hands, doll?"

In the living room a girl kept trying to get into Bobby's lap and he finally gave up and let her sit there. She felt like a puppy, her warm breath against his neck. A Jeff Buckley album was playing softly and Bobby eased into the couch, the weight of the girl spread over his lap and onto his shoulders. On his first deployment to Kabul he'd had this sudden fear that when he got home little Bobby would be too big to hold, that while he was away his boy would cease to be a child. He told

Nancy and she laughed at him. Later she felt bad about it, tried to backpedal, but it was too late. It was always too late, which seemed to be the story of their marriage.

"Let's go to bed," the girl purred against his ear.

He'd thought she was asleep.

"No."

"Just to cuddle me up," she said. "Please."

"Better not."

But he liked the sensation of her sitting there, three fingers crawled into his sleeve. There had been a thing little Bobby would do when he was helping the boy get his pants up or down. Bobby would stand behind his two year old son to slide up his shorts and little Bobby would slip his small fingers up through Bobby's sleeves, let them rest just below his armpits. The intimacy of that, father and son. Nancy had laughed but Bobby had been right: when he got back from that deployment that had ended, the closeness evaporating like sidewalk rain.

The girl whimpered. "Please," she said.

"Better not."

His hands were tingling, slowly numbing out, and her limp weight was warm as afternoon sun. He thought he could sit there all night until she began to lick his ear and he lifted her off, put her down on the couch, and walked into the kitchen to refill his drink. Nemo was gone and he drank the punch standing up. He was trying to be very still. It was difficult to know if Stephen was still alive, but he believed he would feel something, some shift in the air, a breeze of tidal funk. But knew, too, that this was sentimental bullshit. He felt horrible for the boy, and horrible for Marsha, but the real guilt was in thinking of his son sitting in some antiseptic hospital waiting room, worn backcopies of *Time* and *Good Housekeeping*, sleeping with his head on Nancy's neck, waiting.

He left his cup in the sink and walked onto the porch. The wading pool was illuminated but otherwise the garden was dark, the sky deep and thick. He tried to flex his left hand and found he couldn't. The first metacarpal. He could almost feel it push out against the raw skin, the bone veering up into the soft palm, but painless, absolutely no pain. His knuckles were no better, still oozing blood and flecked with gray flesh, but he couldn't feel that either. Soon enough, though, it would come due. He'd feel it all soon enough.

He was still sitting there when he heard a woman giggling. She ran from the garden shed and stopped in the grass. She was wearing only her panties and appeared dripping wet, the pool light slick on her arms and breasts. A moment later a man swooped out and wrapped her in a bear hug. The woman dissolved in laughter. The man was completely naked but for a jester's hat.

Bobby waited until they were gone before he stood, swayed and righted himself against the banister. He felt his head swimming and staggered up the narrow stairs to his room where he drank water from the bathroom sink. Iron in his mouth, rust. He cleaned his hands, stripped to his boxers and lay atop the dusty covers. When he felt things rotating he put one foot on the floorboards for balance. Sometime later there was a soft knock and he saw the figure of a women enter. The girl from the couch. *Just to cuddle me up. Please.* She came toward him backlit by the garret window and he saw the easy lines of her body, felt her put her hands on his chest.

They undressed in the dark. He got on top of her and she began sucking at his throat, pulled away and came back with a pair of stockings she held before his face so that she appeared slick through the sheer fabric. She wrapped one leg of the pantyhose around her neck and made a sort of tourniquet.

"Wait," she said. "Get inside me first."

He did and she gave a little moan, handed him the ends of the hose.

"Now pull," she said.

"What?"

"Pull while you fuck me. Turn me blue."

He gave a little tug and the pantyhose slipped.

"Both hands," she said. "Turn me blue."

"This is crazy."

"Then fuck me crazy. Fuck me blue." She pushed her groin up against him, and he felt her nipples erect and hard against his chest, below them her soft stomach. "Come on," she said. "I'll do you next."

"I'm gonna throw up."

"Not yet."

"I'm gonna throw up." He stood. "Get out of here."

"I can wait." She put one end of the pantyhose in her mouth and grabbed the other end, pulled so that it constricted around her neck. With her free hand she began to masturbate.

"I'm gonna be sick," Bobby said. "Please get out of here."

She shook her head and smiled, blew him a kiss, teeth still clinched, just as he flipped her out of the bed onto the floor where she scattered like a puppet. He sat on the edge of the mattress. She was on her knees crawling away, trailing the pantyhose like a scarf, and he realized he had forgotten the way you could feel the pulse in the torn flesh of his knuckles. Which seemed like a cliché until you remembered how much it hurt. Which he had also forgotten.

"Just get out of here." His voice had gone soft and very quiet.

She was screaming *fuck you, fuck you.*

"Just go. Please."

"Fuck you, you fucking Neanderthal."

She grabbed her clothes, still yelling, and Bobby cradled his head in his hands as if it were some delicate object he was desperate to keep intact, not looking up until he heard the door shut. He listened to her bare feet pad down the steps before he walked into the bathroom and vomited.

PART SEVEN

TOMORROW WAS THE FUNERAL BUT NOW, today—this day that the Lord hath made—they were all in the kitchen. In the kitchen as if we never left, Lucy thought, or left only so that we might reassemble and take leave, for the truth was that for two days they had done nothing but come and go, entering seemingly for no greater purpose than walking out the glassed door that opened onto the walk and driveway, or disappearing back through the swinging door that funneled traffic toward the foyer and stairs (down which, she thought, flew my book, Christ forgive me). Entering and exiting as if motion alone might offer some semblance of order.

It should be enough, this motion.

But they wouldn't let it be enough, wouldn't pause, wouldn't wait. All of her father's food was out on the counter, the cereals, the small powdered doughnuts in a cellophane bag. Her grandma had them and what was it she was doing? Was she gathering them to throw away? Already? Wasn't there a window during which they were meant to act as if he might yet return? Or was it just the opposite: was now the time to scour the house of his presence?

But enough, Lucy.

They were in the kitchen but her father was not. They were together again, assembled. All but him. Her mother and sister and grandparents. The shock had dissipated but left behind its shadow, the radiance of surprise that gradually ebbed to grief and, slowly, as if by some alchemical design, resignation. As long as they kept moving they would survive, her mother especially. But the kitchen held a peculiar danger: to sit quietly was a form of abandonment she felt none of them were equipped to face.

She hadn't seen Alan—or Twitch, for that matter—since the night of her father's death. To be honest, she'd hardly thought of either. The day and night that began at the Holy Land Experience and ended waking in Twitch's scabbed arms hadn't fully registered, and she had the sense that if she kept going, attending to the little things, gliding over the wells of emotion, it might never surface. An experience never fully assimilated which meant, she hoped, never able to hurt her, at least not on that deep gut-level where pain seemed to linger. Even thinking about it now was a danger, as if considering not considering it brought her closer, these wary circles that inadvertently narrowed back to—back to what? Her father's translucent self, sitting at this very table? His ghost. His spirit. But she wouldn't allow herself to think of that, either.

Her mother stood at the sink. She was supposed to be rinsing dishes—why? the dishwasher was *right there*—but appeared to be doing nothing beyond staring at her reflection. Her grandparents, her mother's parents—her father's parents were, of course, dead like him—sat at the table with Lucy and Katie. None of them were doing anything. This couldn't last. *I can't continue in this fashion. I hate you so very much, dear Lucy, but I simply can't.* Some part of her knew that life would find a new rhythm given time, after the funeral, after the summer, after . . . what? When?

She needed out of the house.

She needed to get a job, something to make her dress nice, to bathe, to simply move. The original plan had been to save the money from her three weeks work in Michigan—which she had, little that it was—and spend the rest of the summer studying the Gospels. That was over. That was dead. *But which part, dear Lucy?* (She was doing this now, this sort of self-mocking thing, *dear Lucy, dearest sweet Lucy . . .*) All of it, she supposed, and didn't allow herself to consider it any further. The money was in her bank account, the nine hundred dollars she'd made as a sad-sack counselor *not* getting kissed, along with another seventeen hundred dollars left over from the school year, but she could blow through it pretty quickly if she put her mind to it, she could rid herself of it as easy as everything else.

There was money coming down the line, she knew. Knew it but didn't like to think about it. Hard to consider herself wedged in the eye of the needle, unable to go forward or back, fat with a yearly cashier's check, its string of zeroes and a wavy watermark. But it was known, if not openly discussed, that her grandparents had put aside a moderate trust for both she and Katie. For the past two days her grandpa had hinted that it was time to loose that money on the world, to soothe whatever financial hurt lay in wait. College, cars, a consoling gap year backpacking Europe. So maybe her father hadn't sought their help, Lucy's grandparents, his wife's parents, but they would have the final say. She would get thirty or thirty-two thousand a year for the next five or six years, she figured, and after that there would still be a relatively substantial sum awaiting her, something in the low six figures that would appear in her late twenties. A balloon payment on accrued suffering.

She hated life as reduced to columns of numbers, the spreadsheet as private spirit-guide, invisible hand, lover and confidant, but the more you hated it the more it became true. And the more you depended on it, quantified it, sat down and played out the scenarios, the X versus Y versus Z, which was—she could already see it—how she would come to live her life, the more it swallowed you, the more it became the sole measure of your days. It had a narcotic undertow no different from God. It would pull her if she let it, it would pull her under. She saw some future Lucy attending to her bank balance as meticulously as she attended to her prayers. *This is the highest wisdom: through contempt of the world to aspire to the kingdom of heaven.* Except what if it wasn't? What if her dear Thomas à Kempis—she was starting to think of him as some eccentric uncle, misguided but brave—was as wrong about this as he'd been about the body?

Her mother screamed.

Lucy looked up to see her buckle, knees catch, bang against the cabinet beneath the sink. Her grandparents sprang up as if they'd been too long coiled (they had, they all had), and Katie took a tentative half-step, undid it, as if first attempting to stand. Her mother was clutching her right index finger, had cut it apparently, though Lucy hadn't realized she had been cutting anything at all. She walked to the table with it bleeding through a paper towel, her parents at each shoulder, Katie in the wings. It was theater, a great production, and Lucy sensed how welcome the distraction was for all, the pain, the splatters of red slashed across the cutting board.

"It's all right," her grandma said. "It's all right. Sit down, honey. It scared you."

"I'm an idiot," her mother said.

"It's all right. Get another paper towel, Katie dear."

"I'm such an idiot."

The cut was deep. Her mother squeezed her finger and her mother's mother squeezed her grown daughter. This outward manifestation of inner wounds: we have been clumsy with our lives. We have not given due reverence. And somebody please for God's sake tell her what her father had been doing that night? Ninety miles per hour in a thirty-five? Why hadn't he come home if his shift was over? Why had he been carrying all that cash but hadn't had his wallet with him? And what was his blood alcohol level, for God's sake? Did anyone even bother to check? No one at the motel where he was staying claimed to have seen him though he'd stayed there like a million times. The Air Force offered a grief counselor but no answers.

"God, I'm stupid."

"It's all right now. Maybe one more towel, Katie dear." Her grandma's hand was bloody now, the faint discoloration that cross-hatched her skin. "Band-Aids."

"In the guest bath," her mother said. "Top left drawer."

"Katie?"

And there went Katie-the-dutiful to fetch the Band-Aids as her mother peeled back the disintegrated towels, plucked the wet fibers. The table was littered with them, a mosaic of shredded paper. She had been slicing strawberries and for a moment there seemed some confusion as to the flesh of the strawberries and the flesh of the hand.

"We may need to have this looked at," her grandpa said. "That looks deep."

"I'm fine," her mother said. "Just stupid."

Katie came in with a box of assorted Band-Aids, passed them to her grandma.

"Thank you, dear. Let's see." And she lifted the torn finger to the light. "I don't know. Maybe just run by the doctor and let him have a look-see."

"I'm really fine."

"A butterfly, Pam," her grandpa said, "maybe two stitches."

"It's in the bend of the finger," her grandma said. "We should get it closed, otherwise you'll just keep reopening it."

"I'd rather tear my hair out than go sit in a waiting room," her mother said, and suddenly Lucy was excited, suddenly Lucy was listening. Tear your hair out? Truly? Say it again, mother. No, don't say it, do it, tear it out, tear it from the bloody roots, and then, when you're finished, don't be. Keep tearing: your eyes, your tongue, your gray entrails. All of it. Tear it, rip it. This is what I came for, she thought. This is what I want to see.

But wait—what exactly did she want to see? What did she even mean? She didn't know. *What ever do you mean, dearest Lucy?* She had no idea, but the violence seemed as it should be, the violence seemed right. Appropriate. The exegesis class she'd taken first semester. Appropriate. To appropriate something, to capture, to seize, to assert sudden and everlasting ownership. An ugly word, an ugly act. She sent her mother brainwaves, urged her: Cut your finger off, mother. Cut off your hand. Wash us in your blood. You wouldn't cry any less. You wouldn't cry any louder. (*false, false,* this little devil-self that had arisen in her kept saying, *your mother's tear are false. She didn't love him. She could barely stand to touch him.*) The soggy paper towel folded in on itself, a collapsing tent gone so dark it appeared to purple. And why stop at the elbow, mother? Why stop at the shoulder? God, what was she saying, sitting here seething the way she'd always imagined summer sidewalks broiled, the concrete around the community center pool where they'd spent all those summer afternoons, the footsteps, the wet tracks almost birdlike from the ladder to the lounge chairs where they piled their towels and sunblock—the amplitude of SPF, the zinc oxide for their noses—but footsteps: the way they so suddenly erased, gone before you even realized they were going, faint traces. Jesus wrote only in the dust. Primitive and ephemeral. Everything fluid, everything capable of change. Was that why she couldn't stop listening?

But, really, honestly, what was she saying? *You are manic, treasured dearest combustibly sweet Lucy. You are absolutely losing your mind.* And she was, in a way, but was it in a bad way? Was it not to be desired? *It ends with daddy spending his retirement in an eight-by-ten cell in The Hague.* She should have hit Katie, slapped her, so disloyal, treating it as if it were a joke. But then Katie was right, wasn't she? It would've ended like that. How did it end now? In hell? Had he been on his way, a brief layover to visit the family, enroute to Gehenna? The light shines in the darkness, and the darkness cannot overcome it, until *BAM, motherfucker!* the light is snuffed out in a single-car collision.

Katie exploded into tears. It was almost violent the way her body shuddered and caved and suddenly her grandparents had moved from Pamela to Katie, hovering, cradling. *Darling, what is it? It's okay, honey. It's fine, it really is.* Their mother held up her bandaged finger as if it were something she had just found, a shard of glass, a prism picked up off the sidewalk.

"Katie," she said.

Katie was a hot mess of panting and tears. She was trying to talk, at least it seemed that way to Lucy—everything *seemed,* nothing *was*—but all that emerged was a sort of blubbering choke that sounded more like a seal barking than anything human. *Katie, Katie dear,* her grandma kept saying. Then Katie was emerging from it, a diver surfacing, finding air again, finding breath to her liking. I'm okay, I'm fine, I'm sorry, I'm okay. She sat beside her mother and Pamela put her left hand—her clean unbroken hand—against Katie's cheek.

"What was that about, baby?"

"Dad," she said, "I was thinking about dad."

"And I scared you. I'm sorry, honey."

"No, it's just—"

"I scared you. I am so sorry."

"No." Katie sniffled. "It's just—" A sense of wavering, as if she sat balanced on the lip of another deluge, a fit of grief that would suck her back under. "It's just—"

"I know," her mother said, "I know, baby."

"It's just that the other night," Katie finally managed to say, "I saw him."

"Who, baby?"

"Dad."

Lucy detected the exchanged glances, her mother looking at her own mother.

"When did you see your dad?" her mother asked, but her voice had changed. It was no longer soothing, it was testing, gentling its way across a mined landscape.

"That night," Katie said.

"What night?"

"*That* night. The night it happened. The night of the crash. Lucy and I had this fight, or an argument, or something, and I was walking home and—"

"She's crazy," Lucy said. It was so declarative, so righteous, it had the effect of a suicide bomb: traffic stopped, there was perfect silence and then that silence ripped with complaint. *Lucy! No! Let her finish!* and Katie herself erupted, Katie-the-well-hydrated it appeared, because a ceaseless river of snot and tears was again flowing down like a mighty stream. *No, listen, it's okay!*

"She's crazy," Lucy said. "She is absolutely out of her mind and I don't want to hear another second of it."

This time there was no complaint, only her red-faced sister, so chapped by her mourning, moving in front of Lucy, taking Lucy's hand so gently. She entered Lucy's vision like a wandering balloon, a little unsteadily, but holding her position.

"I saw him," Katie said.

Lucy looked at her. "No, you didn't."

"I felt him. I knew he was around me, his smell more than anything. I couldn't figure it out for the longest."

"No."

"It was after you wouldn't open your door. It was crazy, I kept knocking." She looked at her audience as if they were the jury here, turned back to Lucy. "Remember I kept knocking? I felt him that night. After I left I saw these two owls and—"

"No."

"Yes. I was walking home. I was near the church."

Lucy was shaking her head.

"But I did," Katie said plaintively. "I did, Lucy. It was this smell."

"No," Lucy said very calmly, "you didn't."

"If I can just—"

"You can't."

"If I may—"

"Oh, my God," Lucy said. "This isn't some question of grammar. You can't phrase the question so that you're correct and suddenly make him come back."

"Lucy," their grandma said.

"You can't frame things so that it didn't happen, Katie."

"I'm not trying to," Katie said. "if you would just let me finish."

"No." Lucy was standing now. "No, I will not let you finish. I'm sick to tears of letting you finish."

"Stop it," their grandma said, "both of you. Stop it."

Their mother was crying again, bandaged finger in her hair.

"I know he was watching me," Katie said quietly. "The night it happened. I know he was there."

"He wasn't," Lucy said. "Stop saying that."

"Lucy—"

"Stop saying that!"

"Both of you," their grandma said.

Lucy didn't hear her, or didn't care. "I don't care what you think you saw or felt or smelled or whatever," she said.

"Lucy."

"Walking around at the altar. You dreamed it, Katie. Look at me."

"Lucy!"

"You dreamed it. It isn't real. You're God is not an awesome God. This isn't some praise song. This is real."

"I know it's real," Katie said, quieter still.

"Enough," said their grandma. "Absolutely enough."

Their mother wept into her butchered hand.

"Enough." Their grandma whispered now. "We've all had enough, girls. For today at least. We've all had enough."

Lucy looked at their faces, the tight lines of their mouth. She looked like none of them. She looked like her father's side, her dead father's dead family, and she wanted them to speak because it had just occurred to her that only she could truly mourn him, and in order to mourn him he must be truly and unequivocally dead. There could be no tricks. Where had tricks gotten her? The resurrection. The bread of life gone moldy on her tongue. *Sick to tears.* That was her father's expression. Had been. Was hers now. She wanted them to speak because she held the power to silence them. Look at me, she could say. Look at me. Her grandma went to the sink, the dishes, the world beyond the panes and the tiny humming-bird feeder suction-cupped to the glass. Her mother's sobbing had diminished and in the coming seconds Lucy felt it expire like summer rain. Her grandpa, who had yet to speak, stared into the middle distance, some point that judging from his eyes must hang between the microwave and the refrigerator. Katie sat in inexorable beauty, her face bright and wounded, radiant with hurt. *Wherefore I say unto thee, her sins, which are many, are forgiven.* Luke what? Luke 7:47. She was almost certain. Such a whiz, Lucy, such a pathetic and useless whiz.

They began to move again, slowly at first, tentatively in the fragile silence. The dishes. Her mother raising her head. Katie walked over to the cupboard but didn't open the door, as if the act alone was justification, simply standing a measure of defiance. Their grandma went back to emptying the cabinets of junk. Their grandpa went back to the paper. Box scores. The American League. The

Marlins a joke if anyone bothered to notice. Lucy could see the columned batting averages, inverted and tiny, crawled down the page. Such quantification too easy, she felt. A form of reduction. Which was exactly what she wanted to avoid: letting anyone reduce this. No homily, no hugs, no grand cosmic scheme into which her father's death miraculously fit. She wanted them all to hurt, herself above others, an honest pain assuaged only by the everyday accrual of need: soap the skin; feed the body; shampoo, condition, rinse. She wanted waffles popping out of the toaster because that's what waffles were supposed to do. She wanted the syrup running down the plate in its fine amber sheen. She wanted it so badly she barely noticed when her mother spoke.

"He's here," Pamela said.

No one seemed to hear her.

"He's here," she said louder.

The paper crackled, that straightening sound that implies order.

"I can feel him right here in the house." Her mother stood so suddenly her chair crashed behind her: a gunshot. "He's here!" she announced, and suddenly Katie was beneath her arm and they were staggering through the kitchen and out of the kitchen, wailing *Luther! Dad!* and it was like a storm broke in Lucy's heart, it was like she would never stop crying and not because she believed he was there. But because she knew he wasn't.

Her grandpa was in the living room watching FoxNews on mute. Lucy stood behind the couch. Vaguely, she could hear her mom and sister still bumbling through the house, throwing open doors, calling and weeping, or thought she could. Maybe they were in a corner somewhere, huddled together on the edge of the bed, arms still thrown around each other. They'd been at it for the last twenty minutes and Lucy sensed an ebbing tide, the waning of cosmic energy. Oh, how ugly the crash that would follow such exhaustion.

"Hear them?" she said finally. "Grandpa?"

Her grandpa picked up the remote as if to silence the already quiet TV.

"They've been like that for I don't know how long," Lucy said. "It's insane."

He looked at her. His mouth moved, opened and closed as if he wanted only to speak, as if he wanted only to breathe correctly.

"It's madness," she said, and was immediately embarrassed by the word. It had only just occurred to her why she was so angry. Part of it—a very big part of it—was the certainly with which her mother had always shot down Lucy's imaginings. As a girl she had *fabricated* stories, utter lies, Lucy, this is madness, I don't know why you insist on such madness. Her mother always so quick to drag her back to the Real, to make certain she was ashamed of *misrepresenting everything,* where Lucy had simply understood it then as an extension of the Frog and Toad stories she loved as a girl. She understood it now as the beginning of her religious formation, that act of imagination, of empathy, necessary to approach the right hand of the Father. *Madness* embarrassed her because madness felt too much like that approach. Which meant her mother had been exactly right.

"Want to come sit with me?" her grandpa asked.

"What I want," she said, "is for the two of them to shut up."

"Well, I can't do anything about that, honey. But how about you sit with me."

She stood there, sighed theatrically, and was immediately embarrassed by that too.

"She has her ring," Lucy said, "her birthstones ring."

"What?"

"Mom must have given it to her. To keep, I guess."

"Lucy."

"What?"

"It's hard, honey, but what would you have me do?"

"I don't know. Maybe acknowledge the insanity of it all. Maybe call crazy, crazy."

He seemed exhausted too, when it was her, *me*, she thought, who should be tired.

"What would you have me do?" he said again. "It isn't particularly healthy, of course not. But then death isn't exactly healthy either. They'll shake it off. They're both resilient."

"They're crazy. They're overwrought."

"The body knows. The body self-corrects. It's a sort of evolutionary autopilot."

"The delusions."

"The delusions, the crying. They're processing."

"You don't say things like that. 'They're processing.'"

He looked at her with what felt like limitless patience. Indifference, too. It wasn't his fault. She was starting to learn that: how it wasn't anyone's fault. Everyone simply was who they were. "To some non-quantifiable degree it's about being wrung out," he said. "You have to give them space. This is what families do."

She had moved now to the edge of the couch, as if about to round it, as if about to enter the room. "What if I were to say that I saw him?"

"Your father?"

"After, I mean. Just before the Highway Patrol called but definitely after the wreck."

"Then I suppose I'd ask you about your methodology, honey. You're angle of approach. You don't seem like one to do crazy."

"Why not? I believe in an afterlife."

"For what?" he said. "The Atman? The transcendental over-soul? You're too smart for that, Lucy."

"It isn't a matter of smarts."

"Everything is a matter of smarts, young lady. Tell me this, do you believe in the continuity of memory? The ability to carry forward, say, that amazing day at the beach, or the way you absolutely love love love pickles?"

"It's ephemeral," she said, "this is my stance."

"Because if you don't believe in the continuity of memory, I'd like to know what this thing you call a soul is."

"It's something around the edges of self."

"Lucy, honey. What do you want me to say about your father? I feel like you're trying to provoke some sort of response out of me, like you want me to lash out or something. Make all this anger justified."

"I'm too busy trying to describe the ineffable to worry about that."

He laughed. "All right. You want me to say that he was a character actor? A technocrat, bored but efficient?"

"Some hazy phantasm, I think. You can't talk about it."

"That I felt a certain way about him, yes, this is true. This is not a secret." The discs of his glasses held light. "That he lacked focus? That they're grabbers—he and your mother both. Come on, Lucy. That he was a good man but messy in his dealings? I always seemed to be catching him with a corndog in his mouth. But that doesn't mean I loved him any less."

"It's beautiful," she said, "It glows like light."

"At the end of a tunnel. You don't have to try to convince me. Now get serious for a minute and tell me about this boy that we're supposed to pretend wasn't here."

"Everybody keeps saying *crash* instead of *wreck*. Have you noticed this? Like he was actually up in the air, up in his drone or whatever."

"Does he know how lucky he is?"

"If they come in I'm going to scream. Pamela-the-beautiful. Katie-the-great."

He put his hand out to her. It was somehow terribly tender. "I know, honey. Come sit."

"Katie wearing that ring like it belongs to her. I can't *not* is what I'm saying."

"Come sit."

She sat beside him on the couch, his arm around her shoulder just as somewhere her mother's arm hung over Katie, and she leaned against him, tucked herself beneath his wing. Onscreen crowds massed outside a stone building.

"What is this?" she said. "The debt crisis?"

"Grecian chaos," her grandpa said. "Throwing good euros after bad."

"A man attempted self-immolation but failed."

"It's embarrassing," he said. "The entire mess." He raised the volume. "But maybe their debt is our debt. Have you considered this?"

"What do you mean?"

"That it's metaphysical."

"What are you talking about?"

"Their debt. That it's essentially this metaphysical thing."

"No, essentially, it's not."

He squeezed her shoulder. "It's a way of being, honey, this approach."

"What are you doing here?"

"I'm testing a theorem on you. I thought you might like a little argument. Remember the way we used to debate?"

"And you're saying metaphysical?"

"It appears that's the position I have staked out."

"Well, you're wrong. It's not metaphysical. It's fiscal. And it's their debt. Which is why it's *their debt*."

"You are your mother's child. But let's suppose it's a test of our shared humanity."

"Wait, are these questions?" She straightened and looked at him. "Are you asking me?"

"Let's say I'm defining a position."

"Because it sounds like you're asking me and let me tell you: I think you're crazy."

"I'm maladjusted."

"Crazy and wrong."

He smiled at her. "I'm thinking about the moral arc of the universe."

"Long and bending toward justice." She sunk against him, grateful. "Yeah, somebody ran that by me already."

Later that evening she stood in her mother's door. Her mother piled in bed beneath the rumpled comforter. The ceiling fan spun wildly, irresponsibly, Lucy felt, above her. On the nightstand the tag of a washcloth fluttered. Her mother had spun equally out of control and in the end they'd had to grab her, settle her, force-feed how much Ambien or Xanax Lucy didn't know. Her wide mouth puckered, a baby, a kissing fish. She was somehow more beautiful for the violence done her.

"Mom?" Lucy said. "Mom? I just want to ask you something." She waited. "Mom? Are you awake?"

"What?"

"I want to ask you something. Are you awake?"

"Is that you, Lucy?"

"Yeah. Are you awake?"

"I don't quite know, baby."

"Well can you wake up for a second?"

"Okay."

"This is important."

"Okay, ask me, baby. I'm awake."

"Seriously, mom."

"Ask me, baby."

"What I want to know," Lucy said, "what I want to know is did he have wings?"

Her mother did not stir. Then a single hand went up to her face. Lucy could see the Band-Aid just below the fingernail. The air warm and humid, faintly medicinal. It held him, her father. It held her mother's sleep. It held everything that was and everything that would dissipate the moment she opened the window or left the door open too long. She breathed it a moment longer. The bitterness of Ambien dissolving yellow beneath the tongue.

"It's a yes or no question," Lucy said.

"Come here, darling." Her mother reached up for her. "I'm so sleepy."

"Just tell me."

"Tell you what, baby?"

"Did he have wings or not? Was he winged?"

"Who?"

"Daddy. When you saw him."

"What are you talking about, Lucy?"

"You said you saw him in Miami. He was flying, you said, and what I want to know is whether or not he had wings."

"I never said that."

"Yes, you did."

"I never." She touched her own forehead. "I don't know, I just." She looked confused, her face puffy and eyes wet. "I feel so dreamy. Come here, baby."

"Please just answer the question."

"It's like I'm fog."

"Just an answer is what I'm asking for."

"Not even that I'm *in* fog, but that I *am* fog."

"Mom, please."

"No," she said finally, "I don't suppose he did. No wings. He was more like a satellite."

"And not like an angel."

"No, honey, not like an angel at all."

When she looked out her mother's window it was like looking at the surface of the moon, that desolation, the lunar grief. How would it be different?

I hate you, Lucy.

Stop talking to me.

Hours later, her grandpa found her out in the yard, waiting for Alan. She didn't want to see him, Alan, but he kept calling and finally she gave in and answered, and gave in again when he insisted that Brother Vin drive him over. It was finally dark, the stars pale against the wash of streetlight, and it felt like a blessing. It stayed dark well past nine and what was that but a sentence of sorts, a punishment? But for what she had no idea. She was barefoot in the dewy grass. The spongy turf. Reclaimed water pumped through the sprinkler system. Every house in the neighborhood had them and when they came on it was a like the world became mist, an inconsequential haze, nothing real anymore. Not *in* fog, but *am* fog.

Her grandpa came up behind her. "What are you looking at?" he asked.

"Just the stars."

"But what in the stars? Everybody wants something from them. The root of *planet* is *planetes* if I remember correctly. Greek for 'wanderer.'"

"I think I knew that."

"So what is it you're after, then?"

"Solitude, I suppose," she told him.

"Good."

"That deep aloneness."

"Good, yes." He put his arm around her. "That's certainly up there."

She went back to her room. Where was he? Where was he? Oh, God. Except she wasn't talking about God. She looked into the gray space tunneled above her. The fan ticked. Where are you? She thought she saw some glimmer of light deep in the sky, looked for it, found it, fixed on it.

But then the light was gone.

And Pamela lay in total darkness.

Beneath the sheets but perfectly still, *feel how still, Pam, feel how utterly and completely still, it isn't passivity, sweetie*—was this her mother's voice, those early years in Cocoa Beach?—*but an active contemplation of what is, your stillness is alive, is active, ever-present if only you can summon the awareness. Dress yourself in quiet contemplation, honey.* But what she was dressed for was bed, someone had dressed her for bed. The blue silk of the pajamas she never wore. The smell of Lancombe around her eyes. The lotion on her feet, the ointments—she felt prepped for some service, some ceremony, but by whom? Her daughters? Her own mother?

She flicked the bedside light back on and off again, put her hands flat on her stomach and realized her shirt was mis-buttoned, remembered that she had dressed herself, stupidly, defiantly. Some screaming was involved. The sound of it emerged through the Ambien haze, a dense fog that rounded the edges of the previous three days, the little strung beads that began the moment she saw Luther floating above the bay and ended where, here? That she had fallen in Miami, that there had been a flying shark, a clownfish, a flurry of phone calls, that Avi—was it Avi? what had happened with Avi?—had driven her back to Orange City. (And why was her index finger bandaged?) It seemed both right and wrong, both realized and imagined. Which was to say that she couldn't think clearly, though she clearly recalled Lucy and Katie and her parents, clearly recalled the arrival of a small Vietnamese man who stood in the doorway and watched her. She felt certain she should be able to place him but could not. The crying, the gathering at the table—this was real. It had happened, or would happen. She still saw the star of light, the after image of blindness that hung on the retina like an ornament. And what difference did it make, understanding? The world, her world, came from something, or moved toward something, or—my God, is this the Ambien talking? Is this is the Xanax?—*was* something. It was only when she reached across the bed for Luther that she remembered the source of it all.

Did he have wings or not?

It pooled in her stomach, a small basin of cool grief, and realizing it, she knew she had sensed it all along, the worry of having forgotten something, the nagging concern that now took shape as the weight of absence: her husband, dead. There were petals of knowing, moments folded back to reveal the pistil—which was, of course, Luther-as-nothingness, Luther-as-gone. It started with the ride back from Miami. Avi had forsaken the car service and driven her home in someone's borrowed Lexus, stopped for drive-thru coffee, Pamela leaned against the door and sipping a latte, the silver stud in her navel cold and ridiculous. Katie was in the kitchen, Lucy asleep. Her youngest wept, confused, angry. There had been phone calls, the Highway Patrol, the Air Force grief counselor. There were questions, clarifications that needed to be made, and Pamela caught only the passing flight of things *an accident, a rental car, no identification on the body.* She wasn't sure how long it took for *the body* to register with her as that of her husband, to substantiate into dead flesh, but by then her own parents were there and it was morning and Lucy was hungover and staggering into the kitchen, some boy hidden in her room. By late morning the house was filled with neighbors who stood around and drank coffee. By lunch someone had the sense to feed Pamela several Xanax which was a good thing except she slept away the day only to wake at midnight, alone.

Her father handled the funeral arrangements, the visitation, the viewing, and what had struck Pamela that first night was that there were two more days of this to endure, two more days ordered around relative strangers bearing casseroles, around insomnia and prescription drugs. She showered and dressed and was in the kitchen by four AM, surprised to find her father there.

"Couldn't sleep?" he asked.

She saw that he had already made coffee.

"All I've done is sleep. Are the girls all right?"

"I keep looking in on them," he said, "I keep mixing things up, thinking Katie's you."

Her father had retired just as the Soviet Union dissolved and the Cold War warmed into memory. All the funding for NASA and aeronautics went with it, but it didn't matter: he had made his money, sold his firm and cashed out. As if the entire space program had been contrived for the benefit of dear old dad, and now that he was no longer involved it might be safely shuttered. Their life had always been like that, she thought: charmed. There had always been a certain resolve in their actions. But then their actions had always worked out, suffering had never intruded.

"What are you thinking about?" he asked her.

"Right now?"

"At this very nanosecond."

She smiled. "These languorous days in Miami. We used to go down there. The girls were I-don't-know-where and there was always this ever-present . . ." She shrugged.

"Heat?" her father asked.

"Heat, yeah. And everywhere these wicker chairs."

"Rattan."

"Plastic bamboo. The seat cushions won't stay put. They're always sliding."

"That's what you miss when you miss Luther?"

"What I will miss, I suppose. It's so early, you know? But already I miss certain things about those days. The hotels with same-day dry cleaning."

"You can still have that."

"Except it doesn't seem like I should."

"You don't want your clothes clean?"

"The steaming of business suits. The pressing of pants. All of it before the day is out." She shook her head. Everything she would ever do was behind her now. Whatever else came would be shadow play. Life would exist in her head, cataloged and classified. "It's so decadent. I want no part of it."

He laughed and touched her hand. "And this is the worry of your days?"

"This is it. My cross to bear."

The next day she became what is known as *strong,* which was, she thought, just another way of saying *indifferent.* Chores occupied her. The planning was done but why couldn't the grass be cut? the kitchen and bathrooms scrubbed? Half the day on her knees scouring grout, a bottle of Tilex and a sponge, Lucy cleaning the tub. They put the Carpenters on the stereo—*rainy days and Mondays always get me*—switched to Willie Nelson, pumped his cowboy songs through the house while they mopped and vacuumed to "The City of New Orleans." Katie was out, Pamela didn't know where, and her mother was at the funeral home choosing arrangements, her father in the yard edging along the sidewalk. It had all gone well, busy, so busy, until there was no busy left and Pamela felt something come loose. It was maybe the smell of Pine-Sol, maybe the way the bleach wipes dried the tips of her fingers, but she was overcome with the sense that it was all ridiculous, the absurdity of toilet bowl cleaner, of spraying the flagstones or raking the lawn clippings. It had been laughter this time, and tears, she supposed, and then, of course, the screaming, tearing through the house certain that Luther was somewhere present. *Overwrought.* Someone had declared her overwrought and this time the Xanax was coupled with Ambien, which brought her to here: the night, the darkness, the overwhelming dread of what the coming hours held.

Outside a storm was blowing up.

She had suspected it, wished for it, but only now did she hear the weeping willow begin to lash. She rose from bed and walked to the window. The stars were indistinct, lost in a mist of street lamps, but she saw, at least, the broad umbrella of the willow tree, its frayed edges shivering, a big dead jellyfish in a sea of air shiny with pollen. The sound of its rustling reminded her of the night in Oklahoma when her mother had visited, the phone cord beneath the door, the whispered words. She could see below her that the kitchen lights were on and she wondered, were she to slip downstairs, would she hear it again, her parents, one counseling the other, each in turn, growing old together, knotted at root and branch, the one essential thing that would be denied her?

She turned from it, crossed the room where the balcony looked out over the backyard and onto the neighborhood. She wouldn't go out there. It was a warm night but she wouldn't go out there. Too much like one of those evenings in Miami when she and Luther should have been home with the girls. But she was glad now they hadn't been. Warm, on the balcony while a storm broke, lightning falling into the ocean and the wind splashing the wine from their glasses so that they huddled over them as if they carried fire.

No, she wouldn't go out there. Instead she let her eyes drift up over the yard to the grid of streets. The house sat on just enough of a rise to give her some perspective and she could see from here who was awake and who was asleep, or see, at least, where lights burned. So much of the neighborhood remained empty. The big vacant houses dead teeth. The real estate company no longer bothering to have the grass cut so that occasionally Luther would randomly mow an empty lawn. Not for good neighborliness, he told her, they had no neighbors to be neighborly toward, but because it was measurable, a demonstrative good that offered something tangible in the way so little did. She felt sorry for him on those days. Sympathy wasn't a feeling she generally extended to her husband—there so seldom seemed the need—but on those blistering Saturdays he cut three or four lawns and came home with the green clippings pasted to his shins she sensed some intimation of dissatisfaction, a bone-level suffering that wasn't loneliness exactly, because it wasn't that he hurt for connection, but was something deeper—was it deeper?—that implied an abiding discontent.

Sometimes she saw it everywhere.

It had perched on her shoulder the summer after Prioleau Street. It was what ultimately drove her back to meditation. *Her Year of Zen.* Like it was a ninety minute Indie drama and not a cliché. Pamela, the legacy, cross-legged on her tatami mat. And when she began to feel like a fake: Pamela taking Mass. Pamela as seeker, aspirant, and, finally, that last unmarried summer: Pamela as tan.

The Zen Center here is just off Prospect and I guess for a while in the 70s it was hugely popular with all the Yale kids but just sort of faded after a while. I went there most of the fall and on into the spring of last year. I guess I'm a little embarrassed to say that, like the cause-and-effect of that summer on Prioleau is so plainly evident but I'm sitting here—it's way past midnight—and I can't seem to concentrate and I know I can't sleep so I might as well tell you about it, my dear Luther.

Later.

I'm praying now. I'm actually praying for you. Isn't that somehow embarrassing, as much for you as it is for me which doesn't at all seem fair. I think I was raised on 'Science & Industry' and the idea that something isn't Newtonian or doesn't adhere to String Theory or whatever is just too romantic for me not to embrace. And I'm blushing writing this, I am, thinking of you all the way out in Oklahoma reading gauges and getting clearance to land. I'm blushing but I won't take it back, Luther. I won't take anything back with you. I think you are the brightest star in all the starry sky.

Later still.

> *I can see now I have never been happy. Except I've become less skilled (willing?) to hide the discontent. Is that being selfish or is that being honest? Is there a difference? (too many questions, I know, I know . . . poor little rich girl while you're off flying in a war—the Patriot missiles are ours, right?)*

The discontent had ebbed, evaporated for years, but then came days she would sniff it out. For the past few years the streets had felt wounded, gouged by loss, but now they seemed to hiss, the raw voltage on the lines, the grass gone brittle. Were she to open the French doors—which she most certainly would not do— the air would blow hot, as if she were too close to some man's sleeping mouth, a stranger, his face split around red lips that steamed like an open wound.

She thought of her childhood streets, her home—the last home—the one they had moved to after her parents became rich. It sat on a gentle rise and over the roof of the facing house and through the tops of the winter trees you could see a small lake with its pale spillway and green fingers of land. She loved everything about that house. Her mother making pancakes in silk pajamas. Her father in his dove-gray fedora. He smelled of English Leather and in the summer they retracted the roof panels—the pool was indoors—to swim. Bright rhomboids of sunlight and the smell of Baquacil. Shamu rides: holding her father's thin shoulders as he dived to the bottom; spouting, a fine spray of water and breath and life. Her mother reclined in a deck chair, chasing the sun across the painted concrete that was hunter green one summer, fuchsia the next. The only fit Pamela remembered throwing was to go swimming on New Year's Day. It was warm enough, the pool heated. Why hadn't they let her? Because it seemed somehow decadent, she supposed. Too much a violation of decorum, a throwing of their good fortune in the face of the universe. That not even weather impeded them: to be careless with such freedom was one thing. To relish in it, to celebrate it, seemed an invitation to a disaster. A disaster that never came.

Until now, perhaps.

But was it? She made herself go back to *then.*

She had everything then. She had a tree house, a railed platform with a planked floor, old lace curtains hung along the two-by-fours for walls. They took it down the year she took the PSAT and made All-State in cross-country, but in her heart it still stood. The grass of the side yard skinned by her sledding a piece of cardboard through summer rain: in her heart it remained worn, the scab never healing because it was her scab, her life. She had neighborhood friends with their neighborhood basements where they would listen to records and sulk. Talk about boys. Sarah kissing her in the back stairwell of the National Guard Armory. That friendship had been a revelation: from the distance of years she wanted to pity herself but knew it was false. The disaster had never come. (Except now—but even that was a lie.) That nothing would ever be like before, that perhaps nothing ever *was* like before: it didn't matter. She carried it like a loadstone. She carried it in her heart. It would not erase.

She looked for the club house, the glossy rectangle of the communal pool. They no longer lighted it. The underwater pool lights had burned every night for years but one night they simply failed to appear. Of all the suffering, the money lost, the damage done, the very realness of families abandoning perfectly good homes to live out of U-Hauls or in motor courts off the interstate—there had been parties, actual goodbye parties to wish away the newly bankrupt!—of it all, it was the pool lights that possessed such unbearable grief. That certain point of orientation, the heated water, the tincture of chlorine. She remembered Lucy cracking her head once, the honey-thick blood on the textured concrete, the wailing.

How dare they suffer such darkness.

They could gate a goddamn island but they couldn't keep the pool lights burning? It was ridiculous. She knew it was ridiculous. Keep the lights off, she thought, I'm going to bed.

Luther waited for her.

She knew it before she lay down, before she felt the shift of the mattress, his impression filled. She smelled him though it wasn't exactly his smell but a collection of them, Luther's shoe polish, Luther's starched uniform, his shaving cream and the feral sweat he had begun to give off in the last few years. It was Luther spread across the spectrum of his days, stretched impossibly except it wasn't impossible: he was beside her.

"You came," she said.

She reached for him and they held hands, her forearm across the rise of his chest. He felt skinnier, younger, and she realized she was younger too, and how strange it felt to inhabit this body both familiar and foreign. She had known it so well, her old self, but it had been so long too. How old were they? Early twenties, she thought, the early days at Tinker, his body still shaped by his years wrestling at the Citadel. He pulled her to him, her face buried in his chest, and she began to cry.

"It's all right," he said. "It's all right, Pam."

"I missed you," she said.

"I know. But I'm here now."

She gasped for breath. "I didn't know if you were coming."

"I know." She was flat on his chest and he was stroking her head. "But I'm here now. There's time. They've given us time."

"Who has?"

"It's all right, Pam."

She looked up at him. "Who's given us time?"

He didn't answer but instead slid his hands down her lower back and beneath the waistband of her underwear, let his hands rest on her hips. That was his answer—his hands on her body—and she felt herself go limp because that was the only answer: to touch, to be near.

"How are the girls?" he asked.

"Awful," she said, "or not really. I want to say fine considering, but that isn't right either. Better than me, maybe." She waited a moment. "God, Luther, how could you? Do you know what they told us, the woman from the Highway Patrol?"

"It's all right, Pam."

"She told us—she said this but didn't really say it. She just sort of implied that you were going almost a hundred miles an hour. Luther, what happened?"

"I don't know, baby," he said. "I truly don't."

"But you can still see us?"

"I'm right here by you."

She slid off and tried to see him in the dark, his face a sketch of shadow against the white pillow. All the light she felt should have been pouring in through the windows, the gas lamps and car lights, the light that ruined the stars, was absent. She touched his face, his nose, his cheek. His face was real, but she couldn't see it.

"I spent I don't know," she said, "all evening, all night, looking back. Remembering things." They were on their sides, facing each other, his left hand on her right shoulder. "Who was the woman in the Bible that looked back, Luther? Salt. She turned into a pillar of salt."

"Pam—"

"Because it's a crime, isn't it? A crime against the day, a crime against the living."

He stroked her shoulder.

"It wasn't her life she was looking back at," he said.

"It's a crime against whatever this necessary moment is." She shirked his hand away and immediately wanted it back, burrowed her face into his throat. "You can't talk me out of it."

"It wasn't her life, Pam."

"It was her home." She yelled this, and then quieter. "Her home. Her everything." She almost choked, deep within the fold of his smells she almost choked. "I have the right to sound ridiculous."

"It's okay."

"I think right now I have the right to be overwrought."

His arms were around her again and he whispered *It's all right, It's all right* over and over as if it might yet be, the whole of it three days of illusion, Luther rising from the wreckage of the Camry, the tomb suddenly and miraculously empty. She would wake beside him and it would be a dream, nothing in its wake but a clean house with its scrubbed tile and trim yard. Her parents would be tired but pleased: *Luther! Oh, we thought for a moment there we had lost you.* But she knew it was more final than that. Even holding him she knew she was not. She ran her hands over him and realized they were older than they had been just minutes ago. How old? Late-thirties, she thought. The boom years, Miami, Luther and his 9/11 beach vision. He'd been wrong, of course, in the end he'd been wrong, she saw that now. But for so long he'd been so right, and it was that rightness they embodied now. One million twenty-six thousand five hundred sixty dollars. Their talisman. The number they had chased.

"I don't want you to go anywhere," she said.

"I'm right here."

"I don't want you to leave me."

"I'm right here, baby."

"Lot's wife," she said after a moment. "She didn't even get a name. Just 'Lot's wife,'"

"I'm right here beside you."

She kissed his neck, his ear, moved her hands across the shoulders and arms. The drawstring of his pajama pants, her own mis-buttoned shirt. A clownfish floated near the ceiling, a remote controlled shark. She heard the cargo planes lifting off the Tinker runway not a mile distant, knew it, remembered it. He shifted her on top of him and she remembered the bed in the house on Prioleau Street, the great headboard with its rods, the railings Luther would reach back for when she was on top of him, grabbing them as if he needed to be better anchored against the force of her hips, the steady motion of her presence. She had felt so strong in those moments, watching this man cling to the furniture. He reached back for them now and though she knew they were not in the bed on Prioleau Street, and knew that their headboard had no railings, she watched him grab them just the same.

Deep in the moment she began to strike his chest. First it was with the flat of her hand, and then the bottom of her fist, hard enough to sound a dull thud. She was fully upright, legs tucked beneath her, and found herself striking him in time with the movement of her body. He put his hand up to her face—she was sweating, crying—brushed a lock of hair from her face and she took his hand and bit it, softly, and then harder, hard enough that she felt him go rigid, hard enough that she felt her teeth sink, his flesh give. But she needed to know he was really there. She needed proof. When she dropped his hands she felt him grab her hips and thrust her forward and back, forward and back, and a little cry—surprise, pleasure, some pain—caught in her throat before it floated to the ceiling. She went back to striking him, panting. His chest was damp, the hair matted and swirled, and she began to pull it, put her face down to his throat and bit his shoulder. It ended there, chest flattened to chest, a syrupy stick of tears and perspiration. She had drooled down his clavicle and wiped her mouth on the pillow. They stayed like that for a while and when she rolled off she kept hold of his hand. They were older now, they were their own ages, forty-one and, it occurred to Pamela, dead, because the dead have no age.

"Stay with me," she said.

"I'm right here."

"Wrap me up. Please, Luther."

She started to say something about the girls but he shushed her and said, or perhaps implied, that he had seen them, that he could watch over them in a way he couldn't explain. She thought this later but could never be certain. For years to come she would try to reconstruct the night, what was voiced, what was not, and eventually she sorted the this from the that, the real from the imagined. It made a tidy narrative, their touching, their lovemaking. Lot's wife condemned by the sad nostalgia of that backward glance. But the one thing she could never arrive at was what, if anything, he had said about the girls, about protecting them.

He held her. She spooned into him, her back against his chest, and soon enough she heard his breath settle into sleep. She did not want to sleep. She had the sense that the moment she gave in she would lose this, day would push its way through, the needy light, the demands of morning, and in this she was right: she woke alone. There was no trace of Luther. She drank from a glass of water and saw that during the night she had swallowed another Xanax which made at least three in the last twelve hours. She had also seen the future, and though it dimmed now it was with her still. How this blade of a woman would sit in a restaurant and await the arrival of her grown daughters. Men would notice her, the olive skin, the string of glass beads. She would not care. It would be a lovely dismissal of worry not because she would no longer worry but because she would carry within her the cumulative weight of the past, the places she had been, the books she had read, the memories strung one to the next, no different than the necklace she would absently finger. There would be no more Avi, no more dreams of collapse, no more columns of paper, falling. In place of collapse she would grow old watching her daughters, venerating her husband, making an effigy of how damn hard she and Luther had *tried*. She felt like the water, hours after the sinking of a great stone, and she realized she must have slept well because she recalled all this and more, smaller things, little motes of the past that failed to alight. How it will be the accidents that save us, the oversights, the single thing to which we forgot to attend—that will be our salvation.

A gate of the mind. But how do you gate an island?

She would never ask that again: everything was gated, everything was closed, given enough time. It was all lost. $1,026,560—their number, which was also lost, and thus, like her memories, would never matter to anyone but her.

Yes, she must have slept well, she thought, because in the bathroom mirror she saw how puffy her face was, how healthy, how winsome. She looked like herself again, and she showered and dressed. She would be herself. But she had to hurry, there was so much to do. The morning for the girls, for breakfast in the kitchen, for assuring her parents and thanking her friends. The morning was for the living. And then, of course, came the afternoon, the funeral. The afternoon was for platitudes and murmurous regrets. The afternoon was for the dead.

PART EIGHT

THEY TOOK I-10 THROUGH HOUSTON and on toward San Antonio, nobody talking. The child was dead and for five hundred miles Bobby squinted down the white line and thought of the awful clatter, the code team, the pounding on his frail chest. He'd called Nancy that morning from New Orleans and she told him Stephen had died a little after ten. It was the ugliest thing she'd ever seen. The screaming. The way the crying spread down the hall like a spill. They'd gone home but she couldn't sleep, just lay on little Bobby's bed beside him and watched him breath.

"We were all alone," she said, "just me and little Bobby, and it struck me finally how we're always all of us alone. Like it took all this time to realize it."

"Where's Vance?"

"He saw birds as he died, Bobby. He saw some sort of crow."

"I said where's Vance?"

"That's not what I'm talking about."

"Where is he?"

"Back in Atlanta. Where are you?"

They stopped at a Dairy Queen outside Houston. Early afternoon. The day steaming beneath the weight of brown thunderheads. Sat at a concrete picnic table and sweated over their food, watched it go limp and heavy.

Donny took something from the baggie of pills he carried.

"This is all prescriptive," he said. "I got shit that ails me."

Bobby's knuckles were beginning to scab yellow and a long pencil of bruise traced his left palm. Donny touched his damaged hand.

"It's seeped into the groundwater," Donny said. "The cruelty. It's in our DNA now. You know what I heard yesterday?" he asked. "Are you listening to me?"

"No," Bobby said. But he was, listening and staring out at the parking lot, the heat and sadness that seemed to gather there in equal parts.

"Kristen?" Donny said, but Kristen appeared dead, open-eyed and corpselike. "They were talking about organ harvesting in China," Donny said. "They take them from death row inmates. Have these vans that drive around and they inject them in those. When they take the organs—this is exactly what they said—ninety percent of the people are dead. What does that say about the other ten percent?"

"Shut up, Donny," Bobby said.

"It says it's an awful world is what it says. The Hayflick limit. It's out there. But I think Stephen missed it." He slapped the table. "Of course he missed it. He was lifted bodily. He was pulled up into heaven. Our little dashboard saint."

"Please," Kristen's said.

"Escape velocity's seven miles per second."

"Please stop talking."

But Donny couldn't, talking on and on about physiological death, the shutting down of organs, the blind persistence of the heart. For a while people had come to Stephen as if he were a saint, a conduit of grace. He was said to see certain things, through the veil, across the divide. Through a glass, darkly, Bobby remembered. "You know it was a man he saw," Donny talking, always talking. "It was half-bird, a crow. Marsha told me all this while he was down ministering to the junkies, sitting on his little mattress and glowing like a candle. They went to see her mother up in Milledgeville and standing in the corner is this giant bird. They could all feel it, but Stephen, he actually sees the thing and they know, I mean they fucking *know* he isn't making it up. He said it carried him around in his beak. You believe that shit? She couldn't see it, but she swore up and down it was there." Eventually the people stopped coming, even the priest stopped coming and Stephen withered away, the frail houseplant into which his mother could not speak life. Donny went over and over it, the speculations, the rapid devolution. Bobby didn't have the energy to tell him to shut up again and then finally he did.

After that, they were two days crossing Texas and New Mexico, driving from dawn on into the night, no one speaking. They played Donny's CDs until all meaning was exhausted, the minor prophets unintelligible, and finally, just east of El Paso, cut the radio off and rode in silence. Donny wired on white crosses. Kristen sullen.

They cut northwest out of the desert toward the irrigated sprawl of Tucson and on to Phoenix where they spent one night at a run-down motor court in Tempe. At dusk Bobby walked the few blocks to the Arizona State campus. Things had become unbearable driving through New Mexico, Donny brittle with anger and the land dry as paper, liver spotted—if it could be such a thing. Bobby had been pissed at his brother for a long time—his entire life, maybe—but coming west from Las Cruces he began to feel sorry for him. The enormity of the world. The way it turns round you and finally over you. It was flat enough in New

Mexico to imagine you were seeing the curve of the earth, the road laid down like a plumb line and the far mountains blue and bending toward the poles, the distance between gas stations impossible. Everything was a trick of perception, even the kids Bobby saw now, walking in and out of bars and apartment complexes, laughing, horns honking. Happy, he thought, and their happiness weighed on him. Put fresh on this earth by the good Lord, his mother would have said. And what had Bobby done but fuck things up? His whole life culminating in, if not murder, abandonment. His whole life wound down to nothing.

He touched the tattoo above his heart and knew it had bled into him, not so much the ink as the badness, the exhaustion, the apathy. He'd gotten it in Colombia. They had been in the mountains south of Bogota, training teenagers to kill with the detached efficiency of a First World state. At night he lay awake while the jungle blew up into an angry hiss, the birds and screeching insects. It felt like another planet and maybe it had been, but maybe too it was the planet to which he belonged. The bald eagle a sort of brand, a mark by which he might know his place. It wouldn't wash away any more than the war would end. It wouldn't end because there wasn't really a war, not here, not even there really. Just the drones in the sky or the SEALs kicking down your door. Death is an incredibly private matter, he heard one night at Bagram. He would've cycled through forever if he hadn't killed the boy in Sadr City, deployment after deployment, back and forth across Asia Minor, a tiny presence in a war that would last forever not simply because they wanted it to—though, of course, they did—but because it wasn't real. At least not to enough people, or to the right people, or some such shit he couldn't quite get his mind around.

A seedier neighborhood abutted the east end of campus and he wandered into it. Kristen and Donny were back at the hotel, probably deep into the baggie of pills, or maybe whittling away one of the bricks. They seemed to have made some silent compromise and had both remained quiet through the previous days. He crossed the street and saw a woman, a prostitute, he realized, in fishnet and boots. Cornrows, plum lips. Further along he passed another, an Asian woman this time, and it comforted him to know they were out there. The edges had not yet been thoroughly rounded. The world had not yet been wholly dulled. They were still folks like him, a little broken, but big-hearted. Which, he thought, was pretty pathetic, pretty goddamn self-indulgent. But he also thought it was true.

Back at the motor court, he knocked on Donny's and Kristen's door. She was alone on the bed, her toes in foam spacers. She didn't know where Donny was.

"He's pissed at me, said he was headed out to Pound Town." She gave an exaggerated shrug. "I told him I could just sense the toxins that had built up inside him." One foot was her in lap, the nails a dull red, and he saw again how young she was, so sincere he almost wept for her. "He needs to cleanse," she said, "but it's so hard to find fresh greens."

When he realized she was serious he felt a dam of compassion fissure and break.

"I should've gone home days ago," she said.

"What kind of life did you have there?"

"Why didn't you leave me in New Orleans?" She was almost begging, the open country of her face plowed with sorrow. "I know you wanted him to leave him me."

"I don't know. He wouldn't, I guess. What kind of life did you have?"

"A toothbrush in a piece of pottery sort of life." She shrugged again. "I don't know. Meaningful, I guess. But also not so much. Like I'd brought it back from somewhere but couldn't remember when. We had birdhouses in the backyard. A quarter acre and maybe three birdhouses that had fallen or maybe we'd never bothered to hang them in the first place. Playdates with Mickey and Shamu." She went back to her polish, angry again, defiant. "They were plague years, really. There was a point with my parents—both, but my mom, especially—this thing with their email. They were making all this money then and I would watch them walk by the computer and just like tap the mouse. Just to see it, you know? Because it's there. Their account balance. But pretty soon you can see their eyes go straight to the computer. It's a form of addiction, minor, but real. This waiting. What were they waiting on?"

"The answer. The call."

"But the answer doesn't exist.

"I don't guess so."

"The call never comes."

"And now they're gone."

"Past tense," she said, "the call never came."

He was by the door when he felt her looking at him.

"Let me ask you something," she said, "about the dead."

"I doubt I'd have an answer," he told her.

In his room, he lay atop the covers and flipped through the channels, lingered on the snowy Pay-Per-View that would snap into focus, a body part, a mouth. The room smelled of dust and he found tiny particulates of sand bedded in his hair. He took a warm shower and crawled into bed, rested his broken hand on his chest, thought of his son and again of Stephen. They were linked in his mind: Donny and his god-awful speculations. The way the days fell out of him like stones. Stephen's father gone and his mother dragging her stunted frame from man to man, south Georgia a map of clubs and honky-tonks across which she bled like ink, slurring out only to slur back in, midnight, one two three in the morning and the key in the lock and her shushing whatever drunk had followed her home: laughter, footsteps, regret. But, again, was he thinking of Stephen or of his own son? Or was it the boy in Sadr City? What must have been the terrible din of the child's death, any child, any death: the same circus train of doctors and residents compressing the heart, the sway of the drip bags, the thump of the paddles. He fell asleep thinking of the paddles and when he woke in the morning his own heart felt mishandled but intact. He thought it some kind of holy spirit.

They drove north through the Painted Desert to Sedona where they bought sandwiches and ate at a picnic table at the foot of Teakettle Rock. Donny and Kristen sat together like a happy couple concerned for Bobby's wellbeing. They had it wrong, Bobby thought, but then they both looked clear-eyed and rested for the first time since Florida. Donny was wearing the birthstones ring again and wanted to make peace.

"We should do something together tonight," Donny said. "All of us. Get whiskey-bent and hell-bound." He looked at Bobby. "I been missing on you. We both have."

"I been right here."

"I know you have." He chewed for a moment and swallowed chicken salad. "But I'm talking about actual presence." He turned to Kristen. "How far are we from your family's place?"

"Not far," Kristen said. "Maybe an hour. We could go there tonight."

"I don't know if Bobby's got it in him," Donny said. "Bobby's gone all pissy on us, haven't you?"

"I'm fine to go whenever."

Donny smiled and looked at Kristen who had moved to the end of the table, her back to both of them. "You hear him? He sounds to me like a pussy."

"Leave him alone."

"And you too, little girl," he said. "Both of you, you've both gone and hung ole Donny out to dry, haven't you?"

"Leave him alone, Donny." The playfulness was gone from her voice. "Please."

"Please." His voice was a squeal. "Please, please, please."

Bobby stood up and threw what was left of his bread into a trashcan.

"And now big brother's walking away," Donny said. "Story of his life. Look at big brother off sulking."

"You're a bully," Kristen said.

"And now little sister's in on the act. Jesus Christ, I could do without you both."

He stood and pulled on the Camelback they had carried the food in. There was an extra water bottle and a road map and little else. The gun was jammed in his front jeans pocket.

"Where are you going?" Kristen asked.

"What do you care?"

"I thought we were driving to Flagstaff."

"I need to clear my head." He pulled on his Braves hat and adjusted the bill. "Just sit for a minute."

"Like two seconds ago you were happy," she said. "Could you be just a little more bipolar, please?"

"Just fucking sit."

"What if we decide to leave you?"

He looked at her and shook his head. Sadly, Bobby thought. "Neither of you have the balls to leave me."

They watched him stalk up the trail toward the first switchback, the ground chalky and studded with scaly vegetation. He disappeared in the swale and re-emerged further up, a small figure blurred by distance and ozone before he was gone completely. Kristen walked to the truck. Donny heard it start and after a few minutes noticed water dripping from the air conditioner onto the gravel road. He moved once down the bench to follow the angle of shadow, and then walked to the truck and sat in the passenger seat. She was reclined behind the wheel with her eyes shut and sweat beaded along her upper lip.

"Don't let it overheat," he said.

"I'm not an idiot." She spoke without opening her eyes.

"I never said you were."

He shut his own eyes and let the air wash over him but after a few seconds was freezing and had to close the vents.

"If you're about to tell me this is the point where I should wonder what I'm doing here," she said, "I'm light years past that point. I'm light years past everything."

"He'll come back before too long. He's just scared."

"I don't care what he is." She looked at him, leaned back again and recomposed herself. "I don't care at this point if he comes back or not. I miss my sister." A few minutes later she said: "You know it really does look like a teakettle. I was maybe eight or nine when I first saw it and I still can't get over it."

He looked up at the rock, the surrounding mountains, the swell of Sedona— streets and brightly painted houses—footed beneath.

"We'll drive to Flagstaff when he comes back." She seemed to be speaking to the Teakettle, head still back, eyes still shut. "He'll love it. And tomorrow we'll go down to the cliff dwellings at Montezuma. You can still see the thumbprints in the adobe. It's kind of restorative. Kind of humbling. Then we'll go to Los Angeles when this over."

"How much did he tell you?"

"Santa Monica. The Pacific."

"He told you what he's carrying?"

"Shut up, Bobby."

"We're not going to Los Angeles."

"Shut up, please," she said brightly. "Let's just sit here and think about the ocean."

The house was a castle of stucco and terracotta shingles, a burnt orange that seemed to melt into the surrounding hills and washes, the outer walls lined with palms and juniper and prickly pear and rock beds of catclaw. The inside was full of light, the tile floors blood-colored and cool, the bedrooms—Bobby counted five—opening onto a courtyard of banana plants and birds of paradise snugged around a rectangle of swimming pool. Beyond the back wall the desert sloped down before it rose toward the jagged ridgeline gone purple, the bright night sky behind it.

Bobby went to his room and fell asleep atop the bed, woke in the early evening sunburned and thirsty. He sensed the sun going down just past him, a red blister that paled beneath the eyelids he lacked the strength to open. Then it was dusk. He drank alkaline water from the tap, showered, and walked barefooted through the empty rooms. He looked for the rucksack in Donny's room but couldn't find it. Instead, he found Donny's old high school athletic bag zippered shut. CAMPTOWN WAR EAGLES fading from the vinyl. Inside was a Nevada driver's license in Donny's name along with a forged birth certificate and papers that read GEORGIA SOLUTIONS AND CONSULTING. There were several pages of small print and a final seal that certified the company as incorporated in the State of Nevada. There was also an officer's shield that read: Orlando Police Department. On a scrap of notebook paper Donny had printed:

Beyond a certain point there's no return.
That's the point that must be reached.

Bobby put everything back just as he'd found it and walked downstairs where Kristen and Donny sat on the patio, a bottle of bourbon on the wrought iron table between them. They were both giggling, Kristen's right hand inside Donny's sleeve, both dressed in Western wear, a pearl button shirt and Wranglers for Donny. Kristen in a high-waisted denim skirt and blouse thin as gauze. A watermelon floated in the pool, flush against the filter intake and surrounded by a drift of leaves.

"Get dressed, brother," he said, "It's time to celebrate."

"What are we celebrating?"

"Life," Kristen called, "the sun going down."

"You probably missed it, didn't you, you sleepyheaded son of a bitch?" Donny smiled. "Don't worry, it'll rise for you tomorrow. It'll rise for all of us."

When he came back down they were still laughing.

"Look at the right angles on the boy," Donny said. "The boy's shit is squared."

"He does look sharp."

"How bout a cold one, soldier?"

They drove to a roadhouse a few miles outside of town, a block building with an open air patio and a gravel parking lot that wrapped all sides so that pickups with giant aerials and a few dusty rental cars fanned outward like petals, ringing the building that shook with music. Around it nothing but rolling hills patched with scrub. The bright stars sprayed down to the horizon. Inside was a mix of locals and tourists. Hispanic men in jeans and boots. Ranchers in twirled shirts. Tourists in sundresses and golf shirts over from Palm Springs or the Grand Canyon. All of them drinking two dollar drafts while a band sang George Strait covers.

They got a booth and ordered a pitcher of Bud. The beer came with big plates of steak and baked potato and fried onions. Bobby was in a good mood, as happy as ever, and danced to the bar and returned with three shots of Jagermeister. *Jager-bombs for my people!* When karaoke started a woman staggered to the front and began to sing a song by the Eagles. She was drunk and the crowd applauded her and she took a great sweeping bow before staggering back to her table. Bobby stood a little unsteadily.

"Shit," Donny said, "I know you ain't getting up to sing."

"Gotta hit the head."

Kristen was laughing, Donny smiling.

"Well, hit it hard, brother," he said. "Hit it nice and hard."

Bobby found the bathroom and after wandered out to the patio. There was a thatch roof with an opening in the center, the woodsmoke from a fire pit rising in a slow pillar. Smell of mesquite. The music through the walls muffled and soft as he leaned against a rail and finished his Bud. Nostalgia. Camping that night with his boy down by the retaining pond. Venus and Mercury aligned. There had been good days, even in the bad times there had been good days.

He left his plastic cup on a picnic table and walked back up the road. The night was cooling but the asphalt still held the day's heat, a low thrum of promise ribboned up through the flat valley, the hills rippled like folds in a blanket, blue and now black. Just up the road was a gas station and he was almost certain he remembered a pay phone. He wanted to talk to his boy but wasn't about to ask Donny for his cell.

The walk took twenty minutes—long enough to sober up—but the phone was there, the glass box beneath an umbrella of light, maybe the last pay phone left in the country. Except it seemed he'd thought that before, he'd thought everything before. He dropped two quarters and when the operator asked for eight more hung up and dialed collect. Nancy took the call but wouldn't let him talk to little Bobby. All she wanted to know was one thing: are you coming back or not?

"You mean ever?"

"Jesus, Bobby, I assumed eventually. I meant for the funeral."

"I can't."

"Goddamn you."

"I'm sorry."

"Goddamn you and your no-good brother. If you had been here to see—"

"Nancy—"

"You both can go to hell," she said.

"Nancy—"

"You better know this, Bobby. You better know it good: we won't be here when you get back."

When he got back Kristen was up front on a stool quietly mumbling Patsy Cline. Donny sprawled in the booth, smiling.

"You believe her?"

"I didn't know she could sing like that."

"She can do anything." He drank from the pitcher. "I'm up next."

When she finished the room applauded and Kristen dipped her head demurely. Bobby leaned close to Donny.

"I talked to Nancy."

"What?"

"Just now on the phone."

"I can't hear you," Donny said. "Hold on."

Someone called his name and he skipped to the stage, grabbed Kristen and spun her once, dipped and kissed her as the music started. Hank Williams Jr. The words projected on the screen behind him:

If heaven ain't lot like Dixie, I don't want to go
If heaven ain't a lot like Dixie, I'd just as soon stay home

By the time Kristen got to the booth the catcalls had started. They were good-natured but Donny sang on, both middle fingers raised. That brought the boos.

Donny started thrusting his crotch and not singing but shouting: "Send me to hell or Air-ah-zona, it would about the same to me." The music stopped. "Yeah, send me to hell," Donny kept singing, "with your fat fucking women—" Men were standing and yelling as Donny moved along the platform, both middle fingers in salute. It seemed mean yet harmless until someone threw a bottle and the announcer pulled Donny offstage and took the microphone. "Now folks," he called over the noise, "now folks, please."

Donny made it to the booth, doubled over with laughter, and the three of them walked out while the crowd stood and booed. He was still laughing in the parking lot, balanced between Bobby and Kristen, a couple of big men in the doorway watching them go. Mohawked bikers in Westside Barbell t-shirts, arms sleeved in tattoos.

"Fuck them," Donny called and turned to the door. "Go fuck yourselves, gentlemen."

"Donny," Bobby said.

Kristen appeared sober. "Let's just go, baby."

Bobby got his brother's left leg in the truck before he staggered back onto the gravel and into Bobby's arms.

"You called Nancy you say."

"Get in the truck," Bobby said.

"I want to hear about it."

"Get in and I'll tell you."

The men were still watching from the door, five of them now. Kristen sat in the middle of the cab, seatbelt buckled and eyes forward. "Please, Donny," she said.

"Just answer my question," Donny said. "You talked to her?"

"I called her."

"What'd she say about the boy?"

"She didn't say anything." Bobby lifted Donny's right arm. "Get in the truck."

"Fuck getting in. What'd she say about Stephen?"

"Let's just go, Donny," Kristen said.

"You shut up," he told her. "You don't interrupt me when I'm talking to my brother. Don't you ever do that, girl. What we're doing is having a conversation."

"No, we're not." Bobby looked back at the men in the door. One held a pool cue. "What we're doing is leaving."

"I'll bet when he died it was like Christ on the cross. Lightning. Sack cloth. I'll bet it was loud. You know how loud dying can get?" Donny shook his head. "All the alarms, the code call."

Bobby pushed him. "Get in the truck."

"You think he screamed? I'll bet he was intubated," Donny said, and looked up, his face lit by the dim cab light. "But I'll bet he screamed right through that tube."

The punch came from Bobby's shoulder, the mass of his body shifting forward exactly as it should. He caught his brother on the left cheek and Donny fell against the door panel and onto the ground, came back up on his feet as if on springs. He held his face with one hand and waved the other around him. It took Bobby a moment to realize he was laughing.

"That's it?" Donny said. He looked at the blood on his fingers. "That's your right? That's all you have?" He sat down cross-legged in the dirt, rocked and laughed a sort of keening wail. The men in the door were still watching. "That's fucking it?" he kept saying. "Seriously? That's your legendary right? No wonder you washed out of Vegas." He got up and composed himself and sat in the passenger seat, tilted the rear view to study himself. "It's a joke, baby," he said to Kristen. Her face was buried in her hands and she was silent. "It's fine," he said. "It's just a joke. It's just brothers."

Donny fell asleep on the way back and they helped him upstairs to bed. The balcony doors were open and the sheer curtains billowed with the smell of chlorine. Donny pulled off his boots and crawled beneath the sheets.

"I'm not sleeping in here with you," Kristen said.

"Oh, honey chile. Oh, Baby—"

"Just please don't talk to me."

When she was gone, Donny motioned Bobby over. Donny's cheek had begun to swell and discolor, a half-inch scab of blood scratched onto the blue skin.

"What do you know about securing a perimeter?" Donny asked.

Bobby sat in the wicker chair beside the bed. His right fist had begun to throb, fingers swollen and curled inward like a burned spider, more painful than his left. "What do you mean?"

"Exactly what I'm saying, brother. About making sure nobody gets in."

"Who would want in?"

"I know you trained for all this."

"Shit." Bobby stood. "Don't try and scare me this late in the game."

He left his brother and walked downstairs. The patio doors were open and he saw the bottle of bourbon sweating on the table.

"He thinks too much of you," she called from somewhere beyond sight. "I think all he's really wanted this whole trip is to spend time with you."

Bobby stepped onto the patio. Kristen sat on a chaise longue in a corner of darkness, a bottle of wine on the tiles between her feet. The watermelon floated in the near corner.

"The truth is," she said, "he loves you."

"The truth is," Bobby said, "he hardly knows me."

"He knows you." She picked up the wine. "He knows you better than you think. Besides, that doesn't seem a very generous response." She refilled her glass. "What a lonely life he's had, you know? All those days and weeks and months in prison. How long was it?" She sipped. "I brought another glass if you want." She looked at him and then back at the pool. "I'm just sitting here thinking about maybe swimming, about how glassy the water looks. That sort of dark gloss it gets."

"Are you going to stay with him?"

"You're the one who wanted to dump me in New Orleans."

"Yes or no?"

Her eyes were fixed on the pool, shadows waved across her skin. "What kind of question is that?"

"I don't know how much he's told you about things."

She looked away from him. "I'm thinking of a swim," she said, and moved to the pool's edge where she slowly lowered herself into the water. "It's warm."

"You're shivering."

"Stop arguing with me, please. It really is warm." She was up to her chin and then floating on her back, her body veiled and half-realized, her face a pale island. "Warm," she said, and Bobby wanted badly for it to be so.

"Stop shivering."

"Stop arguing with me." She raised her face from the water. He could see her trying to calm herself. It had something to do with bravery and he knew enough to be silent in the face of it. How she was stronger than him, already. She eased her head back into the water. "He's told me some incredible stories about when you two were boys," she said.

"They're mostly true I guess."

"You guess. You were there, weren't you?"

He lifted her glass and finished what was left of the wine. "But just a kid."

"Donny too?"

"Both of us, but me more than Donny. Even if I am older."

"Fourteen, fifteen. Big-fisted and bumbling through adolescence. You made your mamma cry. Your daddy was secretly proud."

"But only up to a point."

She laughed and moved her arm beneath the surface. "Look at the way it shimmers. All this darkness and the pool like a star right in the center."

He said nothing and she came up the steps. Water seemed to spill from her limbs, more than he thought possible, and she wrung it from her hair before she sat beside him.

"The other glass," she said.

He poured both full. Everywhere he smelled sun, in his clothes and on her wet skin and even in the cool dry wind that prickled the darkness.

"We would come out here when I was a girl," she said, "and my mom and I would go shopping in Sedona. Turquoise jewelry. Amethyst or topaz or whatever. My sister never wanted to come."

"Where was your dad?"

She pointed with her glass. "It's funny because I remember spending half those trips wondering what the pool must look like from those hills up there. I could have hiked up—I hiked all over back then—but it was like it would ruin it, to see it and know." She crossed her slim ankles, her silver toenails and veined feet. "He's killing himself. You know that, don't you?"

He drank his wine and poured another glass.

"At first I had trouble imagining you in the army," she said, "but now I can see you there perfectly, quietly following orders, doing as you are told."

"I was a different person then."

"Twenty-two, twenty-three. Still bumbling through that extended adolescence."

"Except it wasn't me."

"Donny said a boy died." Bobby said nothing and she put one hand to her face. "We're out of wine," she said, and sounded as if this alone might break her heart.

He walked inside and came back with another bottle, filled both glasses.

"Things like this end badly, don't they?" she asked. "Or am I not supposed to ask those questions?"

"Two boys," Bobby said.

"Yeah," she said. "Donny said that too."

They drank the bottle. The night had cooled and she pulled a towel over her bathing suit, the smell of chlorine giving way to night flowers. Darkness softening, its plush exhalation, tomorrow low and irrevocable and hung above them like a cloud. The watermelon bobbed and lapped against the steps.

"He takes just about anything he can find," she said. "I've known people like that. They're just burning through, inside and out, sticking things in their body and figuring there won't be time for it to kill them." She picked up her glass. "One more?"

He was cold inside, barefoot in the bright kitchen, and thought of Nancy's kitchen with its expensive hardware and silver appliances. The kitchens they had shared were cramped and underlit, dingy closets that collected bad energy like smells. He came back with a bottle of Malbec. His head thudded but his hands no longer ached and for a moment he couldn't take his eyes off the oblong shape of water that had dripped beneath Kristen's chair. It appeared alive, warm. The stars appeared colder, if more distinct.

"You didn't hear him did you?" she asked.

"No."

"Sometimes he can't sleep. For days, I mean." She drank. "This is good. I like this." She finished her glass in a second swallow. "We would swim when I was a girl, just swim and swim and swim. My sister and me. Swim all day then eat and eat, so fantastically hungry. Strawberries my mother brought us. Then I'd sleep for what felt like days. These gigantic naps."

"What's your sister's name?"

"She's sort of a saint, I guess. I couldn't always see that. In fact, I hated her for a long time, but I can see now how good a person she is."

"It's hard like that, brothers and sisters."

"I always figured it was just me."

"It's hard for everybody."

"I guess it is."

He refilled her glasses.

"What was it you wanted to ask me the other night?" he said. "About the dead."

"Forget it."

"You can ask."

"No. It's nothing really."

He raised his glass, but she put her hand up.

"Wait," she said. "We should toast. What should we toast to?"

"To Donny. Getting out."

"All right. To Donny, then. Getting out."

They drank. She put her glass down on the dry tiles. "I didn't want to ask about this boy, Stephen. I didn't want to ask, but now that I'm drunk."

"Yeah."

"There's no undoing it, you know? All the stupid things I've done, or you've done, or whatever."

"But if you could."

"I don't know," she said. "If you could—I don't know. I'd love my sister more, my family."

"You can still do that."

"I would just love them. Maybe that's the only thing I'd do."

"You can still do that," Bobby said. "You can go home and do that."

"But do you think that's true?"

"I hope it is."

She nodded. "I wonder sometimes if maybe—I mean I know it doesn't undo the past, loving someone now, doing right by whoever is left. But do you think maybe it's enough? That it's that gesture, that *that's* what's asked of us?"

"What gesture?" Bobby asked.

"Loving someone. Properly, I mean. That that maybe satisfies what's required."

"What do you mean 'what's required?' What exactly are you saying?"

"God, I told you I don't know what I'm saying, just maybe that if you go home and love someone, truly, that you've done what you could. That it's enough. As a human, I mean. And you get it back."

"Get what back?"

"Your life, being human, maybe—" She stopped herself. She had risen and stood perched on a single foot, graceful as a marshbird. "Let's swim."

The water was skimmed with buttery pollen, warmer than the air, bugs everywhere. Moths the size of a child's fist lunged jaggedly at the submerged lights so that several floated on ruined wings, fine as torn lace. The leaves and watermelon had drifted back to the filter's mouth. Kristen leaned against the edge, her back pressed to the liner and arms spread on the tiles. Her hair was slicked backwards and her eyelashes glistened. She looked younger, almost childlike, and Bobby wondered if he appeared younger too, an earlier incarnation, less fragile perhaps. What he had been before the war. Then he realized he had always been old, damaged before damage could register. A dinosaur from birth.

"The wine," she said.

He grabbed the bottle from where it stood, took a long drink and passed it to her. She drank, sat the bottle on the tiles, and brought her face so close to his he felt the dry chap of her lips brush his own, her body pressed against him, the smell of sun, the stubble on her upper thighs. He closed his eyes and she touched his lips, lightly, delicately, murmuring something so soft and unintelligible he imagined it a prayer. When she pulled away he looked at her and something lingered in the vast and minute emptiness around her pupils, something born deep and nurtured by years of disappointment, but now climbing, as if pain had bubbled from that last locked place, the troubled rise of some final hope. They were still enough to hear the scrape of dried leaves flutter down and flatten against the surface. It was almost a shushing sound.

"I have to go to bed," she said, and turned for the stairs. "I have to go home."

He sat by the pool until he saw the light go out in her room, walked inside and checked the locks. The house was silent and he stood for a moment, let his ears attune to the quiet that soon enough was no longer empty but nuanced with sound. The ticking of the ceiling fan. The groan of the air handler just before the cold poured through a vent. There was a point where all silence was revealed as sound just as certainly as stillness was revealed as motion. You drove deeper into the difference until there was no difference, the thing was revealed as itself, only the scale had changed. Living was no different, he thought. There is a point where there is more behind you than in front of you. You pass it without any realization. And then there is the moment you realize it. You lost your life, any sense of control, but you gained it, too; you possessed it in a way you might never otherwise. That was part of what his notebook was about, the listing of massacres just another form of orientation.

He walked upstairs. The door to Donny's room was open and Bobby stood on the threshold, watching. His brother mounded in bed sheets. The balcony doors open and ceiling fan whipping. He counted to fifty and stepped into the room, counted to fifty again. His brother snored lightly. Bobby walked into the bathroom and eased shut the door. A nightlight glowed above the sink and he could see the athletic bag on the lowered toilet seat, the forged papers still inside, the driver's license and birth certificate and corporate documents, whatever they were. The Orlando P.D. badge.

He touched nothing and was three steps from the hall when his brother called to him.

"I can't sleep either," Donny said. "It is you, isn't it?"

"Yeah."

"Kristen all right?"

"She's asleep, I think."

"Good." Donny was sitting up in bed now, bare-chested, his lap an apron of white sheet. "I was a little worried about before, you know? Back at that bar. I got spooked for a minute is all. I didn't mean to mess things up like that."

"Don't worry about her," Bobby said. "Just get some sleep."

"Your hand all right?"

"No."

"You got a matching set. You're crippled."

"Semi-crippled. I'll see you in the morning."

"Bobby?"

He turned again, stood with one hand one each side of the jamb.

"You want to sit. Jesus, what time is it?" He motioned at the chair beside the bed. "Keep me company, just for a minute." Bobby sat and Donny eased back, hands crossed on his chest. "Sometimes I feel my heart winding down," he said. "You ever feel that? Just slower and slower like it's the heart of some old country woman mamma would know. Ninety years old and getting a little ragged. Like she spent her whole life tying up bean rows. You ever feel that?"

242

"Everybody does."

"No. Not everybody." He coughed and hocked something in his throat. "Hand me that water if you would." He drank and wiped his mouth with his finger and thumb, rested the water on his stomach. "What do you think of Kristen? I wouldn't mind getting away with her. The two of us out in California. We'd fly you out to visit, all of us drunk in some Marin County dive, Merle Haggard on the jukebox."

"I can't figure out how much I should tell her about things," Bobby said.

"Your looming moral obligation. I hear you."

"So I haven't said a word."

"I wouldn't have blamed you if you had."

"She asked me tonight if this ends badly."

Donny grunted. "Things like this have a way of playing out, I guess." He took another drink. "But we had a good night, didn't we? I mean I didn't fuck it up beyond all repair, I don't think. I've thought about a night like this, the two of us, you know, I've thought about that for a long time."

"You need to get her on a plane. You get her parents asking questions—"

"Her parents." Donny raised himself onto one elbow. He appeared blue against the sheets. "She's told me some un-fucking-believable things about her parents. I guess she told you she's adopted."

"I don't believe a word out of her mouth."

"Oh, I know. I don't either," Donny said. "But she's right when she says she's an orphan. Whether she knows it or not."

Bobby took the glass and put it back on the nightstand. "Put her on a plane, Donny."

"Yeah," Donny said, "I know."

When he started coughing Bobby passed him the water.

"Tell me a little bit about the war," Donny said. "You know how jealous I got sometimes, thinking about you over there fast-roping onto roofs, shooting hajjis."

"It wasn't like that."

Donny laughed. "I'm fucking with you now, brother. I'm just playing."

They were quiet for some time. Bobby's listened to his brother's breath settle, shallow and fast. Donny's coughing broke the silence.

"Bobby?" he said, "you still there?"

"I'm here."

"I think I dozed off for a minute. What time do you think it is?"

"Probably three or so."

"Morning soon," Donny said. "Morning soon."

He coughed again.

"There was one thing," Bobby said.

"What's that?"

"You asked about the war." He took a drink of his brother's water, fitted the glass back in its ring of condensation. "The thing that killed it with me and Nancy, it wasn't the money. It was all the deployments, getting sent over again and again."

"That was pretty obvious. Even mamma said as much."

"Except what no one knew is that after the first one they were all voluntary. I kept asking to go. I had a posting I could've taken in Dahlonega. Back at the Ranger School there. It would've been a good life too. But I just couldn't quit going back." He put one finger on the nightstand. The water had bled out in all directions. "I had all these ideas. I was going to stand tall, walk upright. You see men in the movies lean into a firefight like they're walking into the rain. It has something to do with dignity, I always thought. But mostly, when we got there, we were just rolling along, shooting the hell out of these technicals, these pickups with a fifty cal mounted in the back. Then we get to Baghdad and the first day we're caught in a street when two snipers open up. Maybe ten of us hunched behind a couple of Bradleys.

"So I'm down behind this brick wall and I can't get inside. I mean I could see straight inside it, the back door open, the ramp down. I can read the words on the first aid kit mounted by the door, that's how close I am. And all I'm thinking is that I'm going to die in this filthy street. First day in Baghdad. Meanwhile these two snipers are kicking up plaster dust, the sound ricocheting off the buildings. It's this terrible racket that sort of pinches the ear drums. There's this sonic thing. It isn't the same as just hearing a gun fired. The bullet goes by you and it's like it speaks. I'm being serious here. But then something happens to me." He looked at the dark shape that was his brother. "Before I can—are you awake?"

"I'm listening."

"I should let you sleep."

"No, I want to hear it. Before you can what?"

"Before I can even understand it, I realize I'm standing up, I'm standing up and walking out from behind that wall. Maybe I feel someone grab at my arm, hear someone yelling for me to get down. I don't know. They think I've panicked, I guess, and am trying to make the Bradley, but I'm not thinking about that at all. I'm just walking, upright down that street full of empty windows and the burnt-out frame of a car. A bag of spilled groceries—I see the bread right there on the concrete—a bag some woman has dropped. I'm walking and what I feel, man—I've left behind the self, the ego—you're the smart one, whatever you want to call it—but I'm walking up this street without any hope or fear. Man, I'm just walking. And when I look up."

Bobby touched the glass of water with one finger.

"When I look up," he said, "I see the sky has opened and it's all light, and I know beyond the shadow of a doubt that I'm staring up into heaven. And it's the most beautiful thing I've ever seen. More beautiful than the day little Bobby was born, more beautiful than the day me and Nancy went down the Chattooga. I feel like I'm floating and I start to shake because I know that in that moment I am witnessing everything that is. I am seeing it, brother. The sky has parted, the veil lifted, whatever you want to call it, but there it is. I am *seeing it.* I keep shaking but suddenly it's gone. I can hear again, I can feel. All around me is screaming and it hits me someone has been shot. I feel something hot on my face and it's my blood. My face is full of glass, thousands of tiny pinpricks. Cause this window has just exploded beside my head. Then I realize it's me that's screaming." He took the water. "I'm screaming and I'm hearing myself."

"Then what?"

"Then nothing. I kept going back trying to recapture that feeling. Walking down these streets with artillery dropping and sniper rounds whistling by. I'm doing this until they're talking about me like I'm either crazy or some sort of god. But it never happens. It never happens and it never happens and then one day there's an RPG and someone runs."

"The kid."

"The kid. My kid." Bobby stood. "I'm going to refill this."

He walked to the bathroom and waited for the water to run cold, set it back by Donny and stood at the curtain, listened as Donny rattled open a pill bottle.

"You shot him," Donny said.

"I did."

"In cold blood, as they say. The sights right on him."

"The back of his neck, this scrawny kid, running from me. I see it still."

"I'll bet you do."

"Except it's not him going down I see," Bobby said. "What I keep seeing, it's that moment before, when I hadn't shot him but somehow knew I would, even knew how wrong it was, how much I would regret it."

"Yeah."

"You can regret something you haven't even done yet. I hadn't realized it until that moment. But I had to shoot him, you know, absolutely had to. Except now I can't remember why."

"He was fucking up your movie."

"I don't know."

"It wasn't supposed to play that way. But you couldn't have done any different."

Bobby said nothing, but it was true. That day in the market, the day of the RPG and the way the even the fruit had smelled broken, that day there had been a moment when he turned to go after the boy, when Bobby had seen him fleeing, just a boy, a dark child barefoot and running. There had been a moment, though, his rifle braced against his shoulder and the blast sounding in his ears and the sights fixed on the base of the boy's brown neck, when Bobby knew what was to follow, and regretted it already, regretted everything. But knew just as surely that he was powerless to stop it. He would live in it forever, that awful before. Cradling his own boy's head while another boy's blew apart.

He stood at the window until Donny began to snore, snorted awake, slipped back into sleep, woke again.

"I left something for you on the counter," Donny said. "You still there?"

"Yeah."

"It's a gift but it's contingent. If you accept it you agree to go home."

"All right."

"That's your word you're giving me."

"That's my word."

"Look on the counter, then. And check on Kristen for me. I love her but that won't do either of us any good in the end."

Kristen was asleep. Downstairs on the counter was a padded mailer full of money. Maybe ten thousand dollars, Bobby thought, lacking the courage to count it.

In the morning Donny was gone. The truck was in the driveway but his bed was empty, the sheets tucked and arranged neatly. Bobby found Kristen out on the patio, drinking coffee. She said he had come into her room just before daylight and said he was going hiking and wouldn't be back until evening. The Camelback was missing and there was no sign of the pistol or the athletic bag. Bobby hadn't seen the coke since New Orleans and didn't know what had become of it.

He drove to a Waffle King on the edge of town and brought her back a plate of pancakes and eggs.

"You need to put something on your stomach besides just coffee."

She looked happy. "So you're looking out for me now?"

"Just eat it."

He doubted she would, and walked upstairs to swallow his vitamins and check the envelope of money he'd tucked in one boot. He thought of taking a few bills just for the taking, putting them in his wallet but didn't. There was something irrevocable in the act. He might carry the money for years but the moment he used it he knew he'd suffer, the wound self-inflicted, and he was already complicit enough.

He hadn't exercised since New Orleans and needed to sweat, maybe find a gym back in Flagstaff. His hands were stiff but the damage tolerable, localized, and he managed to open and close both fists three times before something scoured the nerve-endings. He thought better of it then, and tied on his running shoes, tucked his wallet in his waistband and rubbed Vasoline inside his thighs. In the kitchen he found a bottle of water.

Kristen was pushing scrambled eggs through amber syrup.

"I thought you might want to drive down to Montezuma," she called, "to see the cliff dwellings. He left the truck."

"I'm going running."

"I mean when you come back. You can't run forever."

But he wanted to try. He took the path that led from the back patio into the foothills, wound up the switchbacks to the high gap that opened onto a lunar field of rock and dust. Along the hill dry hunks had calved away to reveal fissures stripped horizontally as if by war paint. The striations of time and archeological period. The ground hot and dry and crumbling away to a fine red powder. Here and there were animal droppings baked to stone. He eased along the foot-trail. The air was dry and the sun barely floated over the eastern hills, more ghost than star, and this was a good thing, how small the sun appeared in the vast openness.

He broke an easy sweat and wound down toward the highway that ran as dark and straight as a line on a map. The heat thickened and by the time he reached the asphalt the sun was a bloody eye, all angle and glare. A precision of twisting shadows. The morning claustrophobic. When he left he had given up the possibility of space and realized now it was exactly what he needed most, the 39,000 acres of the Farmtown tract, the fields around the house, Autumn coming soon, the air going light and crisp. He could sit on the porch and listen to the dogs run, watch football with his boy, how much of that was lost? What had he left behind? A few bullshit artifacts: the SIG rifle, his token MRE (#4 Thai chicken), *The Koran* in Persian Farsi he'd felt compelled to take from a hovel in Kandahar. But more than that: open spaces. The world at large. The smell of grass pulled through the screens by the attic fan, his mother frying bacon in her housecoat, and—only once—sitting out on a hay bale with his son, watching a storm break. It was gone. It was gone because he had not treasured it. The only proper response to the world was wonder. And here he had gone and chosen indifference.

He took the highway in the direction of the roadhouse they'd been at the night before, running slow enough to breathe through his nose, his heart barely straining. Then he saw the gas station where he'd called Nancy and felt his throat constrict. Vance. Fucking Vance and his angel investor. Her new man. The man he was not. It was a lesson he realized he had failed to learn. Those days plowing with his daddy. Silage. Cutting the old corn stalks. The old plowed into the new. Another day, another harvest. How one thing followed the next—the world turned: there was never any standing still. But he'd stood still and now the world had turned around him and very soon it would turn over him.

He dialed her collect. He had no idea why she kept taking his calls.

"You've lost your job," she said. "Some guy called today, Johnson. He said he was sorry about it."

His hands had begun to throb. "I kind of figured."

"You kind of figured?" she said. "Good for you, Bobby."

"He say anything about the dogs?"

"I got the impression he'd be happy if you never came back for them."

"I'll get square with him when I get back." He looked up at the sun, not an eye but a staved-in head, gory and bright and hung just above the mountains. "Those kids ever come back?"

"What kids?"

"Those little vandals."

"I don't know, Bobby. I haven't thought about them to be honest. I haven't noticed."

"I guess not. How's Marsha holding up?"

"How is Marsha holding up?" she said. "Don't you dare, don't you dare ever ask about Marsha."

"I'm sorry for it all, Nancy."

"Don't you dare think you can apologize either," she said. "All I hope is that you understand how selfish you are."

"I'll come see little Bobby in Atlanta."

There was a long pause on the line before she said she didn't want him coming to see his son, she didn't want him calling back, either.

They drove I-17 to 260, stopped in the town of Camp Verde and parked in a gravel lot full of dusty tour buses marked SEE THE SOUTHWEST! in fat red letters. The streets were packed sand and barely wide enough for the buses to maneuver but most of the people were on foot anyway, walking between cafes and store fronts selling turquoise jewelry or horseback trips into the valley. You could sand-board down dunes or backpack along Beaver Creek. It was all very rustic but very high end at the same time. Iced coffee and three-hundred dollar hiking boots. Bobby and Kristen sat at a sidewalk table and watched the retired couples steer around the nomads, white kids with dreadlocks, mountain bikers with legs wiped red with road rash.

"You think he really went hiking?" Kristen said.

"He went on foot."

"Well, I know, but I thought maybe he might have—"

"What?"

She sipped her latte. "I don't know. Like maybe he met some people."

"What kind of people?"

"Just forget it," she said.

But she was still in a good mood when they walked down the gravel road that wound to the castle. Mini-buses and pickups ground past and they moved to the shoulder, the air full of dust.

"We've told each other a lot," she said. "This whole trip. I think that's why I'm worried about him. Your brother's—"

"I know."

"Yeah," she said.

Near the river the dust gave way to yucca and cattails and stunted walnut trees roped like vines, the expanse of sky closed to a lace of sunlight patterned through the canopy. Farther down, the air cooled and hushed and ahead they saw water ribboned through the yellow grasses, flat and dark as smoked glass. Cottonwoods overhung the broad shallows of the creek. Late morning fog. Rocks flat and smooth as gravestones. From the bank, Bobby saw the rise forms of whatever fish swam here. Not trout, he supposed, but had no idea why not. Something older, perhaps. Something less substantial. They crossed below a beaver dam where the water backed up and went green in the sun.

"Look here," she said, and tore the orange petals from a flower, "globemallow." She crushed it between her fingers and he smelled the bright tincture. "Give me your hand. The other one. The bad one. I learned this when I was a little girl." She rubbed the ground petals over his torn knuckles. He shut his eyes, the day pinking his eyelids, looked down at the neat part of her dark hair.

"Thank you," he said.

The castle itself was a cliff dwelling perhaps three hundred feet up from the creek. The walls piled stone, mud-plastered and trussed with sycamore beams, the doors shaped as Ts. Anasazi influenced, the marker read. The Navajo word for "enemy ancestors." Old and violent and gone. An entire race disappeared but for their empty houses, fingerprints still visible in the pocks of the cave walls. Out in the patches of brush he watched phantom families shoulder their lives into fiber baskets, strings of goats and mules, children webbed to the backs of women. Erasure of villages. Brown people lost in the sand. He'd seen it before, and moved out to the parapet, sipped his water bottle, watched as they moved toward the Great Spirit, watched until they were gone. Donny's *via negativa*. The what of what-is-not. The undoing of time.

He wished for his journal. It had begun as a way to reckon with his past, to situate his life in something larger, but it had devolved to nothing more than a compendium of holocausts. Srebrenica with its charred bodies, the boys curled fetally like burned leaves. The 2,800 dead civilians murdered by the VC at Hue, the countless French priests buried alive, mouths stuffed with old potatoes. 300,000 in Nanking in '37. All the villagers thrown from the door of Hueys. The Nazi death camps and Soviet Gulags. Rwanda. Darfur. The Belgian Congo. The Phoenix and Tiger programs. Haditha. The boy he chased. He would add the Anasazi, their own page, blank. He would number the dead, closet them.

Enemy ancestors.

An entire race of people, all gone.

Such comfort, he thought, a dead child face down in a market square paltry beside it.

Donny was sunburned and laughing, barefoot in the kitchen when they got back.

He waved a bottle of Sancerre and started pouring glasses. "The desert was exactly as advertised, friends. Dry, barren. Scrubby things everywhere. It was exactly what it's supposed to be which is such a magnificent fucking thing."

He had a bag of groceries and cooked country-fried steak and mashed potatoes, fried okra and squash, biscuits from scratch. It was a meal their mother would cook, Sunday dinner after church, daddy asleep in his chair, a race on the TV.

They ate out on the patio, listened to Van Morrison on Kristen's iPod, watched the day crawl toward night.

"What do you think mama and daddy are doing right now?" he asked Bobby. "I couldn't think like that inside. It would get to be too much, you know? You put your mind in a box, give it constraints, walls inside to match the walls outside. I still don't even know what day it is."

He had a bottle of Cotes du Rhone and waved it around him.

"I was just standing here before y'all came in thinking about all the good things that make it worth it. All the grandiose shit that makes it beautiful." He looked at Kristen. "There were four of us back before we fucked it all up, five counting Bobby's boy, and we'd sit on the porch?" He turned to Bobby. "You remember those days? Drinking beer on the porch, the girls with a blender of margaritas. We'd watch the dogs in the yard, listen to the radio. We thought we'd survived our youth but the fatal seeds were already planted, weren't they, brother? They had taken root. Bobby off taking the ASVAB and me with not enough sense to quit fighting. Bobby, too, really. The world full of knife-fighting Ju Jitsu Mixed Martial artists and here's the two of us, just swinging away like it's 1950 all over again." He was smiling with tears on his face. "There's no place for us out here, brother. They used us up."

Donny and Kristen were still drinking when Bobby went to bed. Windows open as the night cooled. The breeze rattling things, lamp shade, fan blades. He could hear them laughing and lay for a long time listening but not really. He started thinking of little Bobby, realized he was thinking of himself as a child. The damaged faces he and Donny had worn to school right after they started fighting. The woman from Child Services on the front porch, their daddy apologetic before their mother charged out and told her what was what. Years later: Nancy teaching third grade and reading *The Purpose Driven Life*. It was only his current incarnation that was damaged, she told him, only this certain attitude he wore like an undershirt, and she decided he could live with that until one day she said to hell with it, she'd been wrong. It wasn't just his current incarnation. It was past, present, and future: it was everything about him. And she put her books on the shelf and her crosses in a drawer and she was done with him, the Bobby Rosen Rehabilitation Project abandoned. That Skype chat in Kabul. Living in a shipping crate partitioned with the sort of walling meant for office cubicles, all pressboard and felt that stretched an inch from the floor to within a few inches of the ceiling. The sound of someone playing X-Box when Nancy's image appeared over little Bobby's shoulder. *Go in the other room for a minute, honey. I need to talk to your daddy.* The disconnection of voice and face when the satellite link wobbled. He'd spent the past three months teaching urban combat to the children of goatherders, day after day wearing earplugs and showing Afghan boys how to come in through windows quiet as the Holy Ghost. The disconnection was hard to take. But he'd taken it then and he took it now, the memory tucked into the nothingness of a dreamless sleep: the open space he'd spent the morning chasing, the only space he would ever find.

He woke to gunfire—two shots, another—rolled out of bed and lay flat on his stomach: the cool tiles, the sound of an engine starting. Waited. Listened. Made his way into the hall. Donny's door stood open, Kristen's was locked. Three more shots but they were farther away. Outside, he thought. Donny's Glock. It was his first actual thought—the rest all reaction. But now he was thinking, now he was processing. He stood at the top of the stairwell and smelled cordite, that old smell, that old feather of anticipation. He felt naked without a weapon and wished the Glock back into his own hand. What a dumbfuck he'd been to refuse it, as if by refusing it he might stave off what he knew was coming, what had come.

He knocked softly on Kristen's door, put his mouth to the wood panel.

"Stay in here until I come for you," he said. "Don't open the door."

He listened, heard nothing.

"Kristen?"

"Okay." Her voice a dry scratching.

"Stay in here. Don't open the door until I come back."

He eased down the dim stairs. A light was on in the living room and the angular shadow of a couch crossed the tiles. Across the room one of the sliding glass doors that led to the pool was shattered, crystals and larger shards that appeared aquamarine. Cold sweat streaked his back. Moved like fingers along his scalp. The empty bottle of bourbon still upright on the table. So sharp you think you've dreamed everything before it. That was what the shooting did: it made the rest of it less real.

"Donny?" he said quietly.

The body was in the kitchen, a large black man flat on his back. Bobby saw the wound, the point of entry a gummy mess that seemed to issue just right of his heart. It was the man he'd wrongly identified as Haitian, the West African they'd seen in Florida. *Fuck you looking at, white man?* So there it is, Bobby thought, and here we are. He had so long carried this sense of inevitability that it came as a relief. To know that now, finally, the game was in motion, that now, finally, would come the accounting, the weighing and gathering of all his personal failures. It was right there on the floor, this big bloody corpse nothing less than their collective future, and truthfully it was nice to finally know. Definitively, he meant, since in truth he had always known. But to touch it, catastrophe before them like a report of bad weather. *Yes, Jesus. I'm not going home. We're going to run.* The only question was how far.

Far enough, he supposed.

Donny came in wearing a white t-shirt and running shoes, an H&K machine-pistol slung over his back. Somehow the Glock hung in the waistband of his boxer shorts. Light was beginning to gather outside and Donny appeared to have been running, sweaty and panting.

"The fuckers," he said, and toed the shoulder of the dead man. "You all right?"

"This is the guy from Florida."

"I thought I saw the bastard back in Texas but figured I was just dreaming."

"What happened, Donny?"

He followed his brother's eyes to the body. The head was twisted showing the back of the man's neck, wrinkled and hard, the only hairs rising from a few stray moles. He was black and thick and everything about him bespoke violence, the surprise of it turning on him. Walking into the round like a summer shower.

"Donny?"

His eyes snapped up. "We should check on Kristen." He unslung the H&K and held it out by the strap. "Keep this. Don't refuse me twice."

Bobby took the strap. "Tell me what went wrong?"

"I want to check on Kristen first."

When Donny tried to walk past him Bobby grabbed his shoulder, harder than he intended. "What went wrong?"

Donny stood passively, shrugged away Bobby's hand. "I didn't make the drop."

"I thought the drop was in Vegas?"

"The drop was in Dallas. But I unloaded in New Orleans. Where do you think that envelope of money came from?"

"You son of a bitch. We're all three dead."

Donny took the Glock from his boxers and ejected the magazine. "Don't be dramatic. I did what I had to do. I didn't expect this."

"That they'd come looking for you?"

"That they'd find me."

"When did they spot you?"

"At the bar. I thought it was them. Then I thought I was crazy and said to hell with it."

"We've got to get out of here. Six shots."

He slid a new magazine into the Glock and chambered a round. "It's not ideal. I know that."

"Somebody'll have a SWAT team out here."

"You think I haven't considered that."

"We've gotta move. We gotta get rid of this body."

"Two bodies," Donny said. "But let me check on Kristen first."

The Ford pickup was three hundred or so meters up the dirt road, canted into a ditch so that the back left wheel was off the ground. The road began to wind out of the valley here, ascending toward the highway. It was a private drive but there was no reason to think someone wouldn't happen along. That they hadn't already seemed a miracle. Bobby stopped and glassed the truck. Virginia plates. A rental, he figured. Making a run for it when Donny opened up and got lucky.

He checked the safety on the H&K and approached from an angle. The back glass was shattered and he could see someone slumped in the driver's seat. Dead, he assumed, but couldn't be certain. A man bleeding out with a handgun was worse than a wounded bear. The desperation. You heard tales of men fighting with their guts in their hands. Jihadists backed into caves with nothing but Allah and a busted Kalashnikov. He crept closer. He didn't want to hurry but knew he had to be quick.

It was after seven now and full light. Donny was back at the house trying to talk Kristen out of her room. Bobby had wanted him to break it down, they needed to go, now. But Donny refused, just crouched and finally sat, whispering through the gap. They should be two hundred miles away. Instead it was fucking prom night, the morning after, the spurned King and Queen trying to kiss and make up.

Forty meters away Bobby stopped again: the truck was idling. He crouched by some brush and took Donny's binoculars back out. As best he could figure they were in a floodplain, six miles or so south of I-40 and just northwest of a National Forest. He felt calmer: the sound of any shots fired here would carry a long way but likely be confused with the stray shots of ranchers.

He put away the binoculars and stood in the shade of the brush, the wind rustling the branches and dying away so that he heard only the spinning of the engine. He looped in front and crept forward, gun raised. No movement. Just the slumped body he was almost certain was dead. When he opened the door the man fell out in a dust of blood and hair, the scalp and most of his brain separated from the cracked skull. Bobby propped him against the raised tire, his legs slack, his boots dusty. The flies were on him, lighting in the candy spill of his brain, flitting between his eyes and finding the blood that was already disappearing into the ground.

He managed to get the body in the truck bed and the truck out of the ditch. It was leaking radiator fluid but he made it back to the house which he found clean: the glass shards swept and every surface gleaming with disinfectant. Kristen's work: she was wiping the guest bathroom down with Clorox, erasing every trace of their presence, when Bobby walked into the hall. She looked at him and said nothing, just went on with her zombie cleaning. He could hear the washer running and assumed that was the bed sheets.

Donny had the body of the West African wrapped in a tarp out by the pool. "You got the truck running?"

"It won't make it far. We need to go."

"We need to be thorough is what we need to be. If anybody was coming they'd be here by now."

"Maybe." Bobby nodded toward the house. "What about her?"

"She'll be all right."

"She's in shock."

"She's keeping busy. She'll be okay. You found the other one? Perfect shot, wasn't it?"

"You got lucky," Bobby said. "We both did."

They loaded the West African into the truck bed beside the Brit and set off toward the mountains, Donny driving. Around the bodies was a plunder of gear and trash—flashlights and a hunting rifle, a coil of rope, wadded fast food bags and a Coleman lantern—that knocked and rattled as they bumped down into the low foothills. In the corner was what appeared to be an antique scythe, the sort of giant machete Bobby remembered from his deployment to Haiti.

Donny stopped in a jagged cut of valley, a narrow ravine that deepened as it threaded its way into the hills.

"I found it yesterday walking," Donny said, and opened his door. "A quebrada. We drag em from here."

It took Bobby the better part of an hour to lug the West African's body into the gorge. He tried to carry him over one shoulder like a slain calf but eventually took to pulling him feet first, the tarp swaddling his head catching on rocks and chaparral and just beginning to tear. Donny was somewhere ahead, the H&K slung over one shoulder, the Brit strung behind him. They would have to brush the drag marks on the way out.

Deeper in the walls began to tighten. The pass was perhaps four feet wide but better than a hundred feet high so that he looked up at a slim ribbon of sky. He could no longer hear Donny ahead of him. He was tiring, his hands cramping. He jerked the body over snags and one of the Adidas sneakers came off in his hand so that he stumbled backwards, catching himself on a foot sallow and fat with blood vessels. He held it by the heel, turned it, barely noticing the track marks between the toes. This was far enough. A small cave opened ahead and Bobby climbed inside and looked up. It was hollow, the entire mountain made of salt, and it was like looking into the universe, the sky at night, vast and carefully constructed. He could hear the creak of disintegration and crawled back out.

A few minutes later Donny bounded down the pass.

"How deep did you go?" he asked.

"Deep enough. Let's hope the truck is running."

"We leave the truck. Walk back. If anybody ever finds them they'll just look like drug dealers."

"They are drug dealers."

Donny smiled. "See how perfect it is?"

It was late morning by the time they got back to the house. Kristen had finished cleaning and but for the empty pane of the glass door there was no trace of their presence. They all three stood in the kitchen by a Hefty bag of trash, careful not to touch anything.

"What now?" Bobby said.

"Now we roll," Donny said. "Vegas."

Bobby carried the trash out and when he came back in found Donny whispering to Kristen who stood half-slumped against him. A few minutes later they were on the road, windows down, Donny at the wheel, Kristen crowded against him. When they hit the highway he put his arm around her.

"You did good, baby," he said. "You did really good."

She said nothing, and Bobby followed her eyes up to the rear view mirror, the rectangle of slanted past it carried there. Then he couldn't help himself and looked back, east across the broken terrain that stretched all the way home. A long damn way, he thought, and knew looking was a mistake, a luxury they were long past. He faced forward again, *all right, now we roll* squinted with the sun in his eyes and the wind singing through the high tension lines that paralleled I-40. *Now we fucking roll.*

They stopped at a gas station just shy of the Nevada line, eased around back and tossed the garbage into the Dumpster. Kristen had fallen asleep but stirred.

"You need to pee?" Donny asked her.

She batted her sleepy eyes. "Not really."

"Kristen, look at me. Do you need to pee?"

"I guess so," she said quietly.

It was the first thing Bobby had heard her say all day.

He let her out of the truck.

"Wait," Donny said. "Take your purse. Get us some water. Three of the big bottles."

"I might as well go too," Bobby said.

"Hang on a second," Donny told him.

Kristen was almost across the parking lot, Donny's eyes locked on her progress, her long bare legs carrying her away from them, going and then gone. When she disappeared around the building Donny told Bobby to get in.

"This is for her own good."

Bobby had barely pulled the door shut before Donny had the truck rolling. They bounced onto Highway 93 and accelerated up the asphalt.

Bobby looked back at the receding station.

"You should have done this a week ago."

"I know," Donny said.

"Think she'll be all right?"

"There's a thousand dollars in her purse if she has sense enough to look. She can at least get home."

"She's a tough thing."

"Yeah." Donny kept his eyes forward. "But sometimes even that isn't enough."

They made Vegas by lunch, the strip a crawl of traffic and glare. Donny had turned sullen and mean, his face bunched as they idled behind a Tahoe with California plates.

"Fucking Vegas," Donny said. "Did you think you'd ever come back?"

Bobby looked at him. "Nancy wanted to come once but I couldn't bring myself to do it."

They edged forward, stopped again. Someone hung from one of the Tahoe's windows to take a snap a shot of the Mirage. Rented Vespas kept scooting past.

"What did you say Nancy's boyfriend was looking for?" Donny said. "What's his name?"

"The boyfriend? Vance something."

"Vance something." Donny shook his head. "What was it he went to Atlanta for?"

"An angel investor."

"He ever find one?"

"I don't know. I guess he did. I think they're moving up there."

Donny kept shaking his head. "An angel investor," he said. "'Everything that seems empty is full of the angels of God.' So said Saint Hilary."

"I wouldn't know anything about it," Bobby said.

"No," Donny said, mean again, "I don't imagine you fucking would."

Donny's mood seemed to improve with lunch. They ate at a cafe in the Bellagio while outside people watched the fountains.

"She really an orphan?" Bobby asked.

"Fuck if I know. She tell you about being a life coach?" Donny had swallowed something in the bathroom and Bobby could see it had taken hold. he appeared lit from within. He filled his mouth with salmon, slid out the fork so that the tines shined with saliva. "That big white binder."

"Yeah."

"It was maybe the one thing she wasn't bullshitting us about." He folded greens into his mouth. The place was full of expensive hair dining on organic beets and grass-fed beef. "That and her sister. I hope her sister is waiting for her. May they *parle francais* in peace."

They got a massive corner suite on the thirty-second floor of the Taru. Donny walked through the rooms, opening French doors and spreading his arms. He sent the bellhop away with a handful of hundred-dollar bills.

"What do you think?" he said. "Just the fellas, a couple of high-rolling big wheels. The way it was always meant to be. What do you think mamma and daddy would say if they could see us?"

Bobby stood in the center of the room.

"I don't know," he said. "I need to rest."

"Well, shit. You got your own room. You got your own wing if you want it."

Bobby took a shower and changed clothes. When he came back out Donny was on the phone speaking a language Bobby didn't recognize. A laptop sat open on the glass table beside the Glock.

"Who was that?" Bobby asked.

"I thought you needed a rest?"

"What's up?"

"Nothing's up. Go rest. I'm going to head out for a minute."

"Tell me what's going on, Donny?"

"At this point, nothing. Go rest and we'll talk later."

Bobby sat on the side of the bed and rifled through the nightstand for a phone book. At least three gyms were within walking distance. He could get dressed, go lift. But he knew he wouldn't, and shut the phone book, took his journal from his bag and let the pages fall open randomly.

ARMENIAN GENOCIDE, 1915

1.5 MILLION

But it wasn't enough. A million and a half dead versus a lone child shot in a crowded marketplace. A world set against Stephen and a blood disease Bobby couldn't even think to name. Yet somehow it still wasn't enough.

He took a bottle of champagne from the mini-bar and sat on the end of the bed to slurp the foam that ran over his fingers. From his window he had an angled view of the Strip, a chain of cars down to the bronze facade of the Luxor. Such scurrying. The world such a lonely place. He tipped his head against the glass and realized he could see into another hotel. The unknown lives, the eventuality that had been made clear, that everything, given time, comes. Even death. It was small really, the world, but still too much to bear. He thought of home, of how it wasn't, not anymore and of how, perhaps, it had never been. He knew Nancy had cheated on him once. Years and years ago but watching the crawl of traffic he remembered it again. Bobby deployed to the Middle East. Operation Bright Star. Joint training with the Saudi and Egyptian forces and Nancy back home sleeping with one of his old teammates who had gotten out to work for a security contractor outside Fayetteville.

Bobby heard some things on his return and one day checked her phone. She hadn't bothered to erase the call log, and scrolling through 'sent' and 'received' he reckoned the affair short but intense. Three or four days meeting to have sex at his lonely apartment. Whispering Pines, it was called, squat and dingy and full of divorcees, enlisted men with families on food stamps, illegal immigrants with forged work papers. Fifty minutes of breathless pleasure stretched over half a week. Then the remorse set in. That's about what Bobby figured from the look in her eyes. He knew it the moment he stepped onto the tarmac at Pope, could see the regret stamped on her face, feel it in the way she babied him. There was always a sort of honeymoon after a deployment, a few days, maybe a week or two if he'd been gone long enough, when everything was right, food, sex, a cold beer waiting for him every time he turned around. But she had seemed especially attentive after that return, taking three days off work to tend to his needs.

Bobby never raised the subject. She was an Army wife, after all, and if she was content to let it go so was he. Besides, he understood guilt. He had lived for a long time with guilt, trying to make sense of this other self, so lonely it felt like even the stars had abandoned him. But what was it against the death of a child? Stephen. The Puerto Rican boy in Vegas. The Iraqi boy in Sadr City. He had never mentioned the affair. He never would.

He drew the bulk curtain and dreamed of garbage. Great mountains of trash left behind on countless deployments—Bel Air in Port-au-Prince, the Cazuca slum outside Bogota, Baghdad, Lagos, Kabul—and atop each sat the dead child Stephen, still as an idol, glowing. Bobby kept looking for his son but he was nowhere to be found, not picking through the mounds of plastic bottles or meticulously gathering soiled socks. His son had been erased.

There was no undoing it.

There was no undoing it, but then he remembered what she had said, what Kristen had said and it was the rightness that struck him, how if he could only love properly his own son it would undo nothing, but it might be enough. A small gesture, a way home: he could finally do right. He'd lost the boy in Iraq but he wouldn't lose his own son. He'd get back, find him, do right by him, do right by everyone. He knew it was in him. Look up at the planets, son. His boy's head against his arm. Look up with me. Because everything was there, above them, waiting. The whole world was waiting. He could do right. He could have it back, he might still. That was the wonder of it all: he might still have it back.

He woke in a fit of sweat. Donny wasn't back, and it came to him that this was his life: waking alone in hotel rooms, waiting for his brother to return. Waiting for that next bad thing. But instead of waiting he showered and left, crossed the casino floor past the ATMs and wall ads for escort services, the stickmen at the dice tables, the pit bosses. The noise was some universal tongue which was to say it was no tongue at all, every language as no language, and Bobby lifted above it until he saw it as a holy place, consecrated by its naked longing, and Bobby, Bobby as vaporous witness, adrift as another deck rose to the green felt. *There's no place for us out there, brother.*

Outside taxis nosed the sidewalk like animals at a trough. He started down the street, ahead of him the tower of the Luxor. He could hardly believe he'd ever lived here, field-less, with only the green crowns of the occasional palm for solace. It felt alien, the way the sidewalk radiated the late afternoon heat, and by the time he reached the Fun & Games Sportsbar he was sweating again. The place was tiered with stadium seating, an amphitheater of tables down to the bar, above it a bank of flat-screen TVs wide as doors. The waitresses dressed as referees, black and white stripes, short-shorts and silver whistles. Bobby ordered a seventeen-dollar burger and a draft Bud. Before him the room was full of the blithe though he knew it to be a lie: they weren't happy. It was a ritual they didn't know how to stop. It reminded him too much of that night in Daytona, the crowded Hooters, Old Ironhead fresh among the dead. A decade ago yet his life had gone nowhere. Or nowhere good. Ten years bookended by ESPN and overpriced beer.

He took a cab back.

Donny was on the couch in the center of the sunken living room with a man Bobby had never seen before. They both looked up from the television.

"Braves are on," Donny said. The ball cap sat beside him on a cushion. "You know their sorry asses are eleven games back."

Bobby walked into the room. "I haven't been following them. Who's this?"

"This is my colleague, Ratko."

Ratko. The man nodded. Russian or maybe a Serb, wiry in jeans and a white t-shirt, his skin mapped with liver spots. Late fifties with a dying cough. Still, you could see the tendons in his forearms tensed like bridge cable. He was a friend, Donny said. Ratko lit a Marlboro.

"We're celebrating," Donny said, "life."

Bobby went to his room. Later, he heard a woman laughing and went back out. Ratko was in the kitchen, smiling in his boxer shorts while a slender black woman stood behind him and ran her fingernails along his chest. The room was a mess, the sheets torn from the bed and dragged into the room, a mirror dusted with cocaine on the glass-topped table.

"Where's Donny?" Bobby asked.

"Who?" Ratko said.

The woman looked at him and growled, pawed the air. She had a frizz of reddish afro and wore a pair of men's underwear, her body blade thin but for the heavy breasts that sagged halfway down her stomach. Ratko walked over and opened the sliding balcony doors so that the curtains began to sway. Little particles of cocaine drifted like snowflakes.

"My brother," Bobby said.

Ratko smiled. "Why don't you help yourself?"

"No, thanks."

"You want company she can make a call," he said.

"You know where he's gone?"

"Your brother? Don't worry about your brother. Let her make a call."

"I don't know," said Bobby.

"I think you do."

He didn't. But he was also lonely and sometimes loneliness was harder to bear than regret.

"I think you do," Ratko repeated.

"Maybe," Bobby said.

Ratko turned to the woman and said something in French. She nodded and took a cell phone from her bag. She wore frighteningly high platform heels and stalked around the room like a giraffe, the tiny cell phone ridiculous by her mass of hair and breasts.

A few minutes later Bobby was dressed and in the lobby bar meeting the woman that had been called. She took his room card—a woman in perhaps her early thirties, supple and attractive despite a crust of mascara and a thickening middle—and led him to the bank of elevators. Before the bedroom door was shut she was sliding down the straps of her dress, pulling at Bobby's shirt and asking in bad English what is it you like? Tell me what you like, OK?

He kissed her mouth and she turned so that he licked the line of her jaw, tasted the tang of makeup there, powdery and faintly metallic. She was from Poland or Latvia or Estonia or somewhere. But where the hell was Donny?

"Get on the bed," she said. "Sit."

She stood before him to disrobe, the dress coming down and her breasts tumbling loose as if her pale body was melting, what was left held together by black panties and stockings, her nipples engorged and standing on end like wine dark stars.

"I'm a soldier," he said.

"I know lots of soldier. I know how to care for soldiers." She had his underwear halfway down and was pulling his penis through the fly like it was a fat fish. "I like this cock," she said.

"I have a family back home," Bobby said. "A son."

"I like this cock very much."

"Six years old."

"Shh."

She rolled a condom on him.

"Be quiet," she said, and pressed his face between her breasts. He breathed perfume and sweat, felt the tension in her thighs give way as she slid lower. Those good days with Nancy, he thought of them now, those days when he was home and everything would be right, those brief windows of good nature through which their child had been conceived. He thought of how gone they were, how lost.

"Choke me," he said.

"What?"

"Choke me. Put your hands on my throat."

261

"Like this? You like this?"

"Harder."

"Oh my," she said, "so we have a little gasper."

It was true, and it was terrible. So terrible Bobby hardly noticed he had started to cry.

He woke alone, half-dressed, damp and on top of his bed. It was dark but someone was moving. He heard a dull thud, solid-sounding, sat up and realized he was still wearing his boots. When he slipped them off water dripped out. Something about a pool, wading in. Bobby howling his pain while the woman laughed. Jesus, he thought, and heard the bump again. Lights were on in the living room, the same mess he vaguely remembered from before, the torn curtains and empty bottles, the couch cushions scattered like playing cards. Donny's crack pipe. An empty phial. He walked into the hall and stopped when he saw the blood. Against the bleary chaos it alone was distinct, smeared along the floor like Georgia clay, as if they had dragged their way across the better part of a continent, an ugly indefinite trail. But no question as to what it was. He felt naked before it, but not at all surprised. If he and his brother were capable of anything it was this.

The bathroom door opened and Donny walked out, pulled it shut behind him.

"Good," he said, "you're up."

"What the hell is going on?"

"You need to get dressed. There's been some complications."

"Who's in the bathroom, Donny?"

He stood with his back against the door. He was wearing the birthstone ring again. "Just get dressed so we can get out of here. Get all your stuff."

"You ain't going to tell me who that is?"

"I don't suppose it matters," Donny said, and Bobby supposed he was right.

They were in the desert by sunrise, directionless, looping north and then east and then west, back toward Vegas. We need a plan, we need a fucking plan, Donny kept saying. He'd slap the wheel. L.A., we get to L.A. But instead of L.A. they kept meandering through the sand, a ship with a damaged rudder, or no rudder at all. Donny stopped twice to puke. His Braves ball cap tipped back to keep it clear of his vomit. He refused to give up the cell. Bobby's head refused to clear. The idea that he could go home, that he might have back his life—how fucking ludicrous, Bobby. How goddamn simple can you be? He sat motionless and thought of the morning they left. Their father on the porch, eyes creased, still canted forward as

262

if shielding the drill press he spent the better part of his life operating: *You were always such good boys, both of you.* Donny shaking his head. *We weren't. We really weren't, daddy.*

The second time they stopped Bobby called Nancy. Donny was inside buying cigarettes and Gatorade and had left his phone out on the seat.

"Oh God, Bobby. He's all over the news."

"Who is?"

"Donny. You. I saw him this morning. His old mug shot." She seemed dreamy. He thought it might be the early hour but it wasn't that: she was hours ahead, it was mid-day back in Georgia. She already knew the future. "Funny how I had never seen it."

"What are they saying?"

"They think he beat some police officer into a coma in Orlando."

"Jesus." He looked at the gas station: Donny was checking out. "Did little Bobby see it?"

"But that's just barely it." She was crying now, an outright gasping. "Now they say he's shot a man."

"Donny?"

"It was yesterday, I guess. Last night. In a parking garage or something—you don't know this? Donny and another man I thought to God must be you."

"Oh, no."

"They've got a tape of it. Like a security camera or something."

"Oh, God."

"Why are you doing this, Bobby? I can't live through this again."

"Just don't let little Bobby see it."

"I can't live through this, not again."

He hung up. Donny crossed the parking lot and opened the door, dropped a plastic bag on the seat.

"What?" he said.

"You shot that guy," Bobby said. "Ratko."

Donny took out a bottle of Gatorade and twisted open the top.

"And?"

"And you beat a man in Orlando," Bobby said. "A cop."

But Donny was shaking his head now. "No, no, no," he said. "Not a cop. A goddamn abusive rent-a-cop."

"Nancy says he in a coma."

Donny finally nodded. "That's probably so."

PART NINE

LUCY'S DREAMS FELT MORE LIKE POSSIBILITIES than lives she had lived. It swallowed the funeral and everything that followed: the realness of her inner life outstripping reality, as if sleep—and she slept so well now, God, how deeply she could sink—had woken some long dormant section of her brain. She thought her father responsible. His kitchen table presence. What might he have told her if only she had sat still? That believing in God doesn't mean God will believe in you? That maybe the entire concept of belief was beside the point? She could no longer recall what it was that she needed so desperately to read to him. She could barely recall her mother and sister barreling through the house, throwing open the cabinets and closets. The dreams swallowed everything.

The morning of the funeral she dreamed of Katie's birth, which she could not possibly remember, but somehow did. To some extent it had always been this way: Lucy dreaming memories that did not exist yet feeling them—swearing them—real. Or at least she had at one point. But what was indulged smilingly at five and six was dismissed at eight and nine and never raised again beyond a single slip when Lucy was thirteen. Madness. Pure fabrications, her mother called them then, as if their very existence threatened her physical self. Utter lies. *Why do you want to sit there and lie, honey?* So could she call them dreams? It didn't matter. She learned to keep her mouth shut, and with her silence went the fabrications, *the utter lies* evaporated from the shallow pool of her imagination, atrophied into dust.

But now she was dreaming again.

The morning Katie was born, Lucy was alone with her Grandpa, her mother's father having bought Lucy a microscope as compensation for no longer being the only child. Her parents were at the hospital—Katie had come screaming into the world some hours earlier—and she supposed her Grandma was there too. Lucy and her Grandpa sat on the carpeted floor of the dining room they never used with its heavy-legged table and chairs and bay windows that overlooked the dead lawn and blistered street. Her Grandpa pricked his finger so that Lucy could examine the smear of blood left on a glass slide. This was a lesson. There was a way to touch the microscope, a way to see. There were parts: the stage with stage clips, the coarse and fine focus, the rack stop and arm and turret. Later, her Grandma came in and sat cross-legged in her mauve pants and baggy knit sweater—the sweater was the same tan as beach sand: if this wasn't real how on earth would I come up with such a detail, mother?—the jangly necklace that looped twice, twinned strands of amber glass, tinkling when she bent forward to touch the eyepiece. Red and white blood cells, platelets, plasma. Should she have been writing this down? Could she even write then?—no, of course, not, you were barely two, Lucy.

Later, her Papa, her father's father, came in from smoking Winstons on the concrete carport and she let him pull her up into his hard arms and onto his back where he horsied her around the house. But of course he didn't. Her Papa—how was it that he even had a name?—had died before her own birth. Nevertheless: she remembered moments with him, moments which were impossible but she felt certain had happened nonetheless. So it was a construction, she told herself, a backwards projection. All the stories she'd heard, the details of his Vitalis-rich hair and nicotine fingers. The winter chimney of his lungs. The slash pines row-cropped along the highway that led to his house. He took an interest in her dead pets. A.J., the blind husky that wandered into traffic. The kittens lost before they were weaned. That day they read the Frog and Toad stories she loved, and then walked through the cypress and black gum behind his house: it was early evening and the sun looked caught in the trees, orange and netted and slowly being drawn to earth. She even remembered his funeral, the somber days leading up to it, inclined in his bed, the sun washed gray in the clouds. The sharp rack of his emphysema: it seemed to saw through his lungs, the coughing, the hacking; she felt him break open like a stone, clean and thorough, while she sat at his bedside and held his hands.

"I'd do it all again, honey. If I could go back and have it start to finish, I'd do it all again, the good and the bad." He turned his head to cough, left some residue of self on the white pillow. "Except I'd be so lonely waiting for your grandma and your daddy and you and your sister."

"But how would you even know about us, Papa?"

He looked confused, his blue eyes clouded so that it was impossible to tell what exactly he was looking at.

"How could I not?" he asked.

This, she told herself, never happened.

She started reading about drone warfare online. It started the night after the funeral, her father's funeral. She couldn't sleep. Felt it gnawing at her. When the house was completely still she tapped her mouse and waited. There was something illicit in the act, like ogling pornography. She supposed it was a betrayal of sorts, but she keyed in the search anyway. Most of the new stuff was technical: wonder at the innovation, the bloodless long-distance intervention. It was the older stuff that was ethical, the articles dated and archived, as if the debate had long been settled, or at least forgotten. Targeted assassination. Collateral damage. A Presidential kill-list. There was the clarifying possibility that Katie was right: what her father had done was illegal, possibly a war crime. The Hague, Katie said. *It ends with daddy spending his retirement in an eight-by-ten cell in The Hague.* Her poor dad. Lucy thought of that morning they had driven north to Atlanta, just she and her father and the giant ranch with its rail fence. *They still die,* she told him. She still believed it, but she wished back the words. She wished him back too. Not to explain, but to be near her, because suddenly she was glad for what he had done, obliterating the bad guys. Was it possible that after a missile strike there was not an ounce of body left? She hoped there was not. She hoped for dust, for nothingness. *My father killed you so that I might live.*

The next day she and Alan drove to the Sanford Mall and wandered for hours. She had told him about sleeping with Twitch, how drunk she had been, how sorry she was, how humiliated—since it was like the moment at the lake with the boy from Taylor University only infinitely worse. She told him. He forgave her. And somehow they were closer for it: shared suffering, shared pain. *I would rather feel profound sorrow for my sins than be able to define the theological term for it.* She was reading Thomas à Kempis again and felt that she would always be reading him. They wanted her to believe that life was the slow accrual of nouns—tube and corpuscle; Unmanned Aerial Vehicle—while à Kempis offered another way: life as the shedding of nouns so that by shedding them she understood them in their base form—wood as wood, as she remembered from the Book of Jeremiah, stone as stone. She lost them in order to find them. She wasn't sure her reasoning would stand up to the harsh light of logic, but she wasn't sure she wanted it to, either. It was a way of mourning her father, and in mourning him, forgive him. She hoped he forgave her as well.

I hate you, Lucy, but now she meant it only half the time.

That night she dreamed herself into the woods behind her Papa's house, dreamed herself back to the wake that surely followed his funeral, the entire affair starting one summer morning. Her mother was there, stomach swelled with an unborn Lucy. Her father was there, too, of course, serving mimosas and Bloody Marys like it was a brunch, stoic and minimally sober with his orange juice and grenadine, little celery sticks spread on a towel like surgical instruments. He appeared to be in his mid-twenties, just as he had been when his father died, lean and crew-cut, but Lucy was nineteen, inhabiting the same body she possessed in waking. The ceremony was over and the gathering had drifted inside, paper lamp shades burning with copper light, a parchment map of St. Augustine sealed beneath glass.

Lucy—Dream Lucy—stood outside and through the windows studied the old men in wingback chairs, the middle-aged women in the kitchen carving melon balls, the distant cousins and vague relations she failed to recognize. She was still outside when Alan—Dream Alan—came around the building, hands in his pocket.

"I didn't even know your grandfather," he said. "I'm sorry. Can I get you another of those?"

She realized she carried in her hand a glass of white wine, and when she looked closer she saw reflected a face that both was and was not her own, a face pale and somewhat tragic, vaguely malnourished, as if strung out on cigarettes and diet pills. Her skin had a milky translucence so that even in the blush of early dark Lucy could see the webbing of veins spidered along her temples. She looked away from the wine and out into the night. It had just occurred to her that this was the self she would become.

Alan gestured around them. "This is kind of cool," he said. "Out in the woods like this."

They walked along a footpath and she told him about her Papa and about the land. How the marsh bled into the St. Johns River, the property bounded by a creek, beyond it all an old plantation turned into a tourist trap for busloads of Yankees. They walked for a few minutes before the trail bent, and when it began its slow decline Lucy knew they were near the plantation. They crossed the creek and a moment later the vegetation thinned and became sculpted: scrupulous mulched beds of banana plants and sego palms, yellow princess flower and dogwoods feathered in white blossoms. It had been dark but now, somehow, it was light.

She knew the house instantly from the black-and-white photographs she'd seen as a girl: a three-storied mausoleum with columns and a broad veranda, a green lawn dotted with outbuildings and live oaks that sloped down to the river. The place had been built in the nineteenth century by one of the original steamboat captains, a cathedral predicated on stolen wealth piloted north to Jacksonville. Abandoned during the Great Depression it had fallen into grave disrepair, a grandiloquent shell, a home for dry-rot and ghosts. Two decades ago some historical society had undertaken the task of restoration.

"Can we get in?" Alan asked.

"No. But let me show you something even better."

She took his hand and guided him back across the creek and into the dusky woods, the ground beneath them spongy loam, the trees around them a city of live oaks laced with Spanish moss. It was dark again, and the bare upper-works of the trees fingered the rising moon. They stopped outside a gray building of granite slabs. Bare of markings, lichen-crusted: it appeared a tomb. Inside, it was cool and damp. A little bench sat in the corner, dotted with several candle stubs and a glossy surface of spilled wax. She lit one candle with a lighter from her pocketbook.

"This was a stop on the Underground Railroad," she told him. "One of the very first ones, I guess. They hid slaves here."

"Like runaway slaves?"

"Sit down by me."

They sat on the bench and began to kiss, Dream Lucy feeling him put one hand on her breasts so that she undid the top buttons of her blouse, let the fabric gape. Her shoulder bones shone, the swales pocketing shadow. She reached for his groin and began to gently knead.

"Do you believe all that?" she asked. "All they were saying today?"

"All what they were saying?"

"About God and everything? Christ coming down off the cross and rising from the dead?"

"Don't you?"

She went back to kissing him. Her hand worked harder. "Not for a minute," Dream Lucy said.

"Which part not for a minute?"

"None of it." She looked up at him. From outside came the scrape of tiny feet, brittle and fleeting. He leaned back.

"What kind of place did you say this was?" Alan asked.

"A station on the Underground Railroad. They hid slaves here."

"Right behind the big house."

"I think we should talk about what happened with Twitch."

"I know what happened with Twitch," he said, and touched her face. "Which part did you not believe? That the preacher was saying, I mean?"

"I want to talk about that night."

"It was an awful night, Lucy, but it's done. There's nothing to talk about."

He kissed her, reached for her hand and put it back on his groin. His own hand slid up her thigh into the warm fold of her legs.

Now it was Lucy who pulled away, Dream Lucy, her lips gone numb. "God's Son on a tree." She said it with more force than she'd intended. "And that he'd just leave him there to die and not so much as raise his little finger. What kind of God would just abandon His own Son like that. It's ghastly."

"It isn't ghastly," he said. "How can you not believe in that?"

271

She said nothing and after a moment he stood, touched one wall with two fingertips.

"Was this some kind of church or something?"

"Sort of, I guess," she said. "I know they had services here, prayers for the slaves."

"It's so small."

"Yeah, I guess." She buttoned her blouse. She could taste the lipstick smudged on her teeth. "We should get back," Dream Lucy said (but all the while Lucy was screaming at her *no, stay, don't walk away, talk to him!* Or was it Lucy that wanted to go and Dream Lucy that wanted to stay?)

Alan looked at her. "You really don't believe?" he asked. "I mean I just can't believe that you don't—"

She cut him off. "Look: not a word of it, all right? I mean look around you. Look at where we're sitting. You think I'd touch you like that, in here, otherwise? Come on. Let's get out of here."

They walked back through a thrum of cicadas, the night warm and moist, and she took his hand in hers. "Look," she said. It was dark again and overhead the stars seemed to flex and strengthen, so heavy they threatened to fall. Then the stars were all around them, glinting through the trees and glimmering along the ground. The tree frogs were going. She had a flashlight—where did her flashlight come from?—and it made a mouth of weak light on the buttery leaves.

"Your father killed himself, didn't he?" Alan asked.

She didn't answer and they walked on, the ground giving beneath them.

"Think he's in heaven?" she asked

"Your dad? I thought you didn't believe in all that?"

"I don't. I'm asking you."

Now it was Alan—true Alan or Dream Alan?—that didn't speak.

"You think he's in hell then," Lucy said. "I don't even believe in hell."

"He's not in hell."

"The Bible says if you take your own life you go to hell."

Yet she felt a certain happiness ripple through her and walked ahead of him until they were almost back to the house. She heard Brahms on the record player and knew her pregnant mother had put it on and she knew too that her father was there, safe. But then it wasn't the loamy yard they were crossing but the shorn grass of the Newfound Cemetery, and it was blistering afternoon and everywhere light flashed and washed and she was sweating. Not night but day. Not Brahms but a lawnmower in a far section. Her father's plot behind her. She felt herself within the cotton of her dress, her mourning dress, the way it clung to her. Ahead were the cars, a string of them behind the black hearse. Alan came up and took her hand.

"Come on," he said. "Please, Lucy. Let's talk about this."

"There's nothing to talk about," she said, and she realized it was here they were having this conversation, now—or was it? "All I wanted to know was whether or not you believe in God. But I don't even care now."

"Is it because of what happened with Twitch?"

She shook her head. They were almost down to the cars now. Mourners climbing into vehicles, engines starting.

"Lucy? Stop. Is it because of things with Twitch? Is that where this is coming from?"

"Let's just—let's just go inside, all right?"

Because suddenly they were back in her Papa's yard. Brahms was playing. It was night again.

"I swear to you," he said, "I honestly don't care about that night."

"Truly?"

"Cross my heart and hope to die."

"Alone on a cross?"

He looked at her then. "There's something wrong with you, Lucy. I'm sorry about your dad, but there's something really wrong with you."

He pulled away and headed for the house and she thought that maybe there *was* something wrong with her, something beyond just the grief, beyond the shame. Was her faith dead? Could such a thing die? It was as much orientation as belief but standing outside her father's wake—for she was certain now that it was her father in the coffin, not the Papa she'd never met—Lucy felt alone and no longer happy, batting away the mosquitoes and watching Alan go around the hedges, lit for a moment in porchlight, before disappearing into the shadows. She could still hear Brahms, and she thought of her father while she stood there— who knew for how long—clicking the flashlight on and off and on again, waving the beam up into the still dark of limitless dust, watching it go forever and forever away.

The next day they drove to Lake Eola and walked around the playground and the amphitheater. Some sort of dog parade had just concluded and men and women stood in the grass with their leashed pets, muzzled Great Danes and cheery Labradors, tiny poodles carried like handbags. Several veterinarians and dog grooming services were packing up tables. Fliers drifted across the grass like sails—PAWS & CLAWS, POODLES AND DOODLES—matted on the lake, disintegrated and she thought of her father in the kitchen: for the life of her she couldn't remember what she had needed so desperately to show him. Paper, the connection was paper. Paper fluttered everywhere. She couldn't believe no one bothered to pick the sheets up.

"Let's keep walking," she told him.

Something strange had happened with Alan, something—Lucy believed—instructional: after she told him about Twitch, after she calmly asked for and received his forgiveness, Alan bought a cell phone of his own. The next day the phone inexplicably died. He took it back to the store where the salesman explained that it was a dud, it had simply died, he would replace it for free. But Alan refused to accept this: it couldn't simply die, he said. Somewhere there was a part to be replaced, a circuit or chip or something. He was insistent. The salesman took the phone and the next day Alan returned. The phone could indeed be repaired, but for far more than a new phone costs. The offer of a free phone stood. Alan refused it because *it can't just die. It's a thing.*

All of this surprised Lucy. She had thought him pragmatic and somewhat simple and realized she didn't know him, not really. She didn't love him, either. This was a quiet revelation that came almost as a relief. She saw her future self alone, wandering, their affair amiably withering in the August heat. Until then he was companionable, and he had allowed her to better know herself.

She was grateful for that, and all the way down she considered telling him her dream of the wake, though deep down knew she wouldn't. If it was a shedding of belief—and she thought it might be—it was a private affair, something only she could experience. *You can't fence it out.* And another thing she knew: she wasn't going back to JBI in the fall. Just before daybreak it had become clear how easily it could be avoided: a semester off, a year, let one bleed into the next, just let it go, act as if the school had never existed. People would understand, shake their heads, sympathize. There wouldn't be any need for a scene with her mother which was a relief as a scene was what she most dreaded.

They took a table at a lakeside restaurant, an open-air tent crowded with wrought-iron tables and dogs asleep beside the chairs. The waitress brought menus and water. Someone was pedaling a swan boat on the water and it turned in a tight fruitless circle, crossing and recrossing its own wake as if to remind her that she was back on the shore of another lake, with another boy.

"What if you could live your whole life over again," she asked Alan. "I mean your exact same life, from start to finish. Do you think you'd be lonely waiting for all the people you love?"

He wasn't really looking at her, shredding his straw wrapper and watching the boat. "What do you mean?"

"I mean like the person you marry, your kids."

"Would you know them already, in your new life?"

"I don't know," she said, and followed his eyes out to the water. "I actually have absolutely no idea."

They ate in silence, paid, waited for the change on the check. Several tables away a mastiff of some sort hiked its giant back leg and pissed a widening puddle of yellow. People were laughing, pointing. The urine pooled and ran, forked, forked again. Watching it, it occurred to Lucy that this was going to be her last real meal. You could live off what you could grind up in her mom's Vitamix, protein, flax seeds, and all that. You could live really healthily off it. She was going to wind up impossibly skinny. She was going to shed everything: God, Alan, her body. But she didn't have to be malnourished. Everything didn't have to be preordained. Then it occurred to her that she could simply stop eating, just stop, sit at the table and move the food without ever actually touching it. It was the ceremony, after all, the world demanded, the communal gesture. She would give them that.

"Do you think my dad's in heaven?" she said.

He looked at her. "Your dad?"

"Do you think he's in heaven?"

"Lucy—"

She tapped one nail on the iron table leg, already impatient. "I mean he killed himself after all."

"Of course he's in heaven."

"Why 'of course'?"

"Of course because where else would he be?"

She thought she saw the waitress coming with her change. "In hell."

"Don't say that."

"It's pretty clear in the Bible that if you take your own life you go to hell."

"But he didn't take his own life. He had a wreck. It was an accident."

"But I don't even—" She caught herself, not Dream Lucy, but Lucy: "I'm not even sure if I believe in hell because here's the thing about hell, all right? Assuming, of course, God could even contrive a place worse than certain places on earth. Why would God do that? What does that say about God?"

"I don't think you should be thinking like this."

"Think about Rwanda, think about the Congo."

"Lucy—"

"What I'm saying is that the people who probably most need God's mercy are the people least likely to get it. So what does that say about God? What does it say about us that we believe in that God? That we made Him up? And that he looks exactly like us?"

"We didn't make Him up."

She said nothing.

"Lucy."

"Just forget it."

"Lucy, I don't—"

"Could we please just forget it? All right?"

Past her a little boy stood at the edge of the urine and said: "Eww, mommy!" But it was mostly gone, the piss just a dark shape, an island in the packed earth. We Shall Behold Him! she thought, Praise Him! Praise the Father, praise the Son! but she wouldn't let the memory gather. At one point it had meant something to her and might yet again. If she killed it now she would always regret it. But the suppression made her impatient, she was ready for the end of the meal, the end of the summer. There was the money coming to her, her grandparents' trust. She could leave Florida come fall, leave Franny behind. Cut her hair down to nothing. Get some menial job, stop eating. Attend to the nuances, find light in the cracks, rush nothing, because otherwise you are only kidding yourself, Lucy, Franny. She thought of something the real Franny had said. People need the courage to be nobody. She thought she could do this, be nobody. It seemed an essential step. You had to learn to live before you could learn anything else. Why hadn't anyone told her that?

When her phone buzzed she knew it would be Katie. *where r u? r u in O?* Then another text: *fine. Dont answer. I dont care.*

Her chair scraped back. "Can we go now?" she said, because the change wasn't really that important after all.

It was only when they were leaving that she spotted the Occupy encampment, a collection of tents and an empty stage pushed back into a grove of trees. She sent a text back to Katie: *in O at park. r u here?* She paused with Alan for a moment at the edge of things, even thought to go look for her sister, but knew she wasn't there. Katie was at home, probably still in bed. Which was where Lucy suddenly wanted to be, safe beneath her own bedsheets, free from all these complications. Forever, or at least as long as she could hold out. She dropped Alan off, no kiss, just a little wave as she pulled away.

She went home. She went back to her dreams.

Katie went back to the discussion boards, 'protests do and don'ts,' 'Guerrilla marketing,' 'beware agent provocateurs,' 'beware trolls.' A lengthy thread on GetThe-FuckOutOfThePark.

Occupy_Joel: Be warned: GetTheFuckOutOfThePark is an agent provocateur. He is lurking on this site but he is actually physically present in the park. He calls himself "Jack" has short red hair and is well-groomed and polite and appears to know a lot about globalization/exploitation and gets very fired up BUT DO NOT BE FOOLED! He is there to incite violence and cause trouble.

Heathermeansbeliever: yes yes yes. He is carrying a radio and a tazer (sp?) in his kid's backpack (He likes trains!). DO NOT listen to him! He is hired by the police (or is police!). Stay strong! Stay peaceful!

The response was several posts down:

GetTheFuckOutOfThePark: LOL Occupy_Joel and Heather and everyone else. Glad to know I'm provocative but afraid I'm not getting paid (wish I was) mostly I just think you are a bunch of losers and should GET THE FUCK OUT OF THE PARK!!!! ;) to my haters.

She hadn't been back to the encampment since the funeral, a week ago tomorrow, the anniversary, his *new* anniversary, the only one that mattered now—but God, Katie, listen to you, how maudlin you're getting, how much like Lucy. Except Lucy wasn't Lucy anymore. And Katie wasn't Katie, not exactly. The point being the old Katie would be right there in the park, shaking off the grief and fighting, but this new girl—and it was most definitely a *girl*—was still at home, still sleeping too late and eating bad food. Hence the discussion boards, the hours of debate on how to combat pepper spray with olive oil or antacid or onion slices pegged in the nostrils. It seemed silly from a distance, a little self-important, a little delusional, which maybe was true or maybe was just her refracting the movement through the narrow window of her days. Which was why she needed to get back to Orlando, back to the park, back to the people—dammit, she couldn't even give herself a pep talk without sounding like a cliché, another online loser munching Dunkin Donuts and trolling the comments section of the local FOX affiliate's webpage.

The morning of her father's funeral she caught a ride with a guy she sort of knew but not really. They left a little after seven and were in the park by eight, people just up and out of their tents, brushing their teeth from water bottles while cars honked and the traffic began to back up along Ivanhoe Boulevard. It was a warm, overcast morning, a haze left from the rain that had fallen through the night, and Katie walked barefoot through the wet grass with her secret: my father is dead, in a few hours we will bury my father. She kept it tucked close, beneath her clothes, against her skin, this knowing, because it was precious and it wasn't something you gave away. Two loops around and through the park, three loops, because she wanted to know what it looked like, what alterations might present themselves. It was like the time she had taken a hit of Ecstasy in sixth period and, once the final bell rang, walked out to the baseball diamond to lie in the center field grass. She knew already that her world had changed, but wasn't yet sure how.

It had disappointed her, his death. She'd seen nothing that morning—no apparitions, no *gift of enlightenment,* not even Niall from the pool, not even his dusky Senegalese avatar—and it was only during the last few days that the change revealed itself as a diminishment of being. The world felt colorless, a little less alive. She wanted enlightenment, she wanted cloud shapes and spirit animals, but saw now she would have to settle for vapidity: soft foods taken in front of morning talk shows, too much sleep, too little passion. Turned out the world was composed of brightness, at least the part that mattered. You lose your father and a light goes out, just one, but it's enough to damage perception, all the edges rounded in the growing dimness. So this would be life, Katie thought later, grave-side, Lucy sobbing beside her, so this *is* life: a steady passage down a darkening corridor. It wasn't suffering exactly, it wasn't pain. In fact, it felt like the opposite of pain: it was a numbness that, given enough time, and given enough loss, would swallow her.

Lucy seemed not to have been informed. In fact, someone seemed to have told her the opposite. Which was why she wasn't Lucy, Katie thought. She was alive and thrashing, back with Alan, back at the church. Which was why Katie was so thoroughly avoiding her sister. When Katie had found her that morning in bed with Twitch it had been anger. Their father was dead and here was her sister hungover and naked with some methhead loser? Then there had been this flaring of pride, a little *frisson* (or was it *élan?* she was still learning French on her iPod) that would show them the way out of grief. You escape the abstraction of death through the particular, the concrete. And what was more concrete than this skinny boy with bat wings spread over his shoulder? She was almost back to the kitchen when she realized what was more concrete was death itself. Death was abstract, true. But it was also the most solid thing she had ever encountered. She could go *find* the hole left by her father, watch the bristles of his toothbrush go dry, his clothes go unfilled, his food—his nasty Little Debbies and slices of American cheese—go uneaten. He would not hold her. He would not touch her. He would not *anything* again. That was the measure of death, that was the Absolute.

So fuck the Absolute and fuck Lucy and her new boyfriend too.

Except he wasn't her new boyfriend—he wasn't her new anything—and it wasn't nearly so easy to simply wave away the rest. What her sister didn't understand, and what Katie was scared to death to tell her, was that something incredible had happened that day at the Holy Land. Except it wasn't at all what Katie had intended. When Lucy had embraced her, when they had both dissolved in tears, Katie had finally understood what Lucy was always telling her about belief. It wasn't belief as in a proposition. It was belief as in an affirmation of allegiance, as to the flag, or the family, or the whatever. It was saying that *I am with you, though I know you not.* You don't think yourself into new actions, Katie—she even remembered it in Lucy's voice—you act your way into new thoughts.

Which was exactly what Katie was trying to do when she started down the aisle toward the altar. The tears came because she had taken that first step. *I have taken the first step,* she'd thought, *I'm doing this! Finally, I am!* But what had been revealed to her, what settled over her when she settled at the altar rail, was the sheer emptiness of the moment. It was grand, cavernous, this sense of nothingness. She looked up at the vaulted ceiling with its flood lights and speakers and those around her had surely thought she was peering into heaven, up at the Father, but it wasn't that, not at all. She had looked up at the auditorium and thought: it's as empty as anything. Because what she felt right then with complete and total surety was that she was alone and there was no god or God. It was like opening a Christmas present to find a rattlesnake. There was the surprise, but more than that there was the malice, and she had wept bitterly.

That night in the kitchen when she'd said she didn't know where to go from here—had she ever uttered anything half as true?—it hadn't been artifice. What had started as theater ended in abandonment, and that sense, with the first tentative call from the Florida Highway Patrol, that her father's death was a response.

Two days after the funeral—the day before yesterday, actually, though it seemed impossible to imagine the awful compression of the last week, as if it had simultaneously been ten years and ten minutes—she had walked to the church to find Pastor Jeff. Stupid, she knew. But she'd done it anyway. There was always something corny about him, as if the tattoos and hair gel were all an elaborate disguise, deep cover to pass among the suburban masses. Somewhere beneath it, she suspected, was that Old Time Religion. Fire and brimstone. Angry Jehovah tramping out the vineyard where the grapes of wrath were stored, the thing that had sent her and her mother stomping wildly through the house, knowing *knowing* he was there. She wanted that. She wanted to hear something definitive. She didn't care if she immediately discarded it as complete and utter bullshit, she wanted to hear it anyway. He's in heaven, Katie. Or: I'm sorry but your father is burning in hell. She would burst into tears and walk out into the sanctuary and pick up a hymnal, not one of the new ones, no praise songs, no synthesizer or guitars, but one of the threadbare copies lost in the seatbacks. Songs copyrighted in the 1920s by companies in Cleveland and Chicago that had gone out of business before the second world war. My God A Mighty Fortress is Thee. That Old Rugged Cross.

She'd found Pastor Jeff in his office, updating his Facebook page with a passage from Joel Osteen. *Becoming your fullest, realest self* she read over his shoulder *is a matter of attitude as much as* and then he turned and saw her.

"Katie! You're here." He half rose and caught his legs on his desk, big wide-framed glasses on his nose. "You actually came!"

They sat in the matching armchairs in front of his desk and talked. He failed to comfort her. She simply refused the thought that her father's death was lynch-pin in some grand narrative. Soon enough it became more comedy routine than theology.

"So what does his dying mean?" she asked.

"It doesn't *mean* anything. It manifests itself. It's causal."

"Causing what?"

Pastor Jeff hunched forward, elbows on his knees, less solicitous than basic bad posture. "We can't know what it causes. We can only react."

"How do we react if we don't know what we're reacting to?"

"We do know," he said, "we react to his passing."

"Which is causal?"

"Yes."

"But we don't know what it causes?"

"Yes, yes," he said, "because it manifests itself."

"My father dying?"

"No, God's plan."

"You know my dad made his living blowing people up."

"Katie, sweetie."

She got the sense he wanted to go out with her. It wasn't arrogance. It was the clues he was constantly dropping like was she hungry and did she know that great coffee shop on Boston Avenue and maybe they should get together that evening and just like, you know, sort of relax into the subject and maybe see what they could uncover, because the truth was, processing an event like this, it was really all about process which takes time and maybe, I think, like a more inviting atmosphere, like a movie or dinner or something?

It made her mad. She sensed the loneliness he worked so hard to mask, she even felt sorry for him. But it didn't make her any less angry. Then something else did too.

"Why aren't there any crosses in here?"

He leaned back.

"What do you mean?"

"I mean on the walls or anything," she said. She'd noticed it several times but only now did it fully register. "I mean a crucifix or a picture of Jesus or whatever."

"There's a picture of the Boss right there."

It was a whitebread Jesus, suffering the lamb-eyed children. A Swiss beatnik surrounded by the expensively dressed kids of an IKEA nursery.

"I mean on the cross," she said. "You know, emaciated? Tortured?"

He looked like a man who had just come up from a deep sea dive and hadn't yet released his held breath. She thought he would cry. But then the look passed and he smiled. He looked dismissive. He even waved his hand in front of her.

"Katie," he said, "Katie, Katie, Katie. Sometimes I forget about the age difference and sometimes it totally comes back." He raised one hand like a docent. "Would I put a vampire on my wall?"

"What?"

"A vampire? Of course not. It would scare people away. It would make them uncomfortable."

"But this is a church."

It was a fatherly smile now, patient, if strained.

"That's my point. The whole crucifix stuff, the negativity of it. Did you forget He came down?"

"But isn't the whole point that Jesus died on a cross to forgive our sins? The tortured political prisoner—"

"Katie—"

"—in an occupied land?"

He leaned back, spread his arms, palms up.

"You're making my point for me, sweetie. Don't you see? *To forgive our sins.* Not to get us all mired up in negative thinking. That's a serious bring-down attitude you're talking about right there."

She went back home, back to the discussion boards, floated a sort of trial balloon.

Katie_in_Hell: Who here is willing to die for this cause? Who here is willing to truly suffer?

She ate Cheetos in the kitchen and when she went back to check for responses found her password and user name had been revoked. Someone had flagged her post as inappropriate. She created a new account. She painted her fingernails. She Googled The Book of Job. A girlfriend sent a text inviting her out on a friend's boat. New Smyrna. Tonight. She ignored it. What else might she do? She wouldn't cut herself. She knew that, not again. That had been a test, she thought, that proved pointless, pain without referent, which meant it wasn't really pain at all. She was debating prayer but found it too much trouble. You might be able to act yourself into new thoughts but you couldn't *fool* yourself into them. She was eating gross-ass Pop-Tarts when Twitch showed up looking for Lucy.

"I got a thing or two to say to her."

"Well, she's not here."

"Dag, girl, I know she's not," he said. "I already knew that."

Then what the hell are you doing here? Katie wanted to ask, but she just waved him in and watched him flop on the couch and pick up a Pop-Tart.

"I'll bet you don't even know where she's at, do you?"

Katie shut the front door and took the Pop-Tart from his hand.

"They're terrible for you. Nothing but corn syrup."

"Yeah, I only lived off em for like eight years." He put his feet up on the coffee table. "You don't have one clue where she's run off to, do you?"

"And you do? Yet you're here?"

In his lap was a white three-ring binder and he drummed his nails on the laminated surface.

"She's at that hippie encampment in Orlando," he said. "The one percenters. Fuck the one percenters and all."

"The Occupy encampment?"

"I don't guess you know who's with her, either?"

"I don't care who's with her. And get your nasty feet off the table."

But she did care. She cared deeply. Part of her thought this was the one good chance she might have to talk to her sister, to actually relate as something besides two miserable souls stuck in the same miserable house. Another part felt protective, jealous. If Lucy was at the camp she should be there with Katie, Katie as her guide, Katie explaining the common ground they had come to share. So you believe in God and I don't, she might tell her. Big deal, you know? Because we both believe in the *work* of God, in social justice, in God's Kingdom right here on Earth as it is in heaven. But then she was just pissed too: Lucy down there at the general assembly or drum circle while Katie sat at home and considered flossing.

"You don't have a car, do you?"

Twitch shrugged. "Let's just take a cab."

"You can't take a cab all the way to Orlando. Are you serious?"

"Let's take the train then."

"Now I know you're not."

That shrug again. "Amtrak," he said. "It runs like every twenty minutes right downtown."

It ran twice a day, and not downtown but out to the suburb of Winter Park, but they didn't know that until they were at the station and by that point Katie didn't care. She bought both tickets—*I tell you what, you get the tix and I'll get whatever else*—and they settled in the coach car. The giant binder was back on Twitch's lap.

"Life Coach," he said, "I'm in training."

"That's all bullshit."

"It's a forty hour core program. Half online, half on Skype. They got modules for pretty much everything. Positivity. Financial fulfillment. Sex."

"Complete and total bullshit."

Outside the trees whipped and blurred.

"People get like seventy-five bucks an hour," Twitch said. "I mean to start."

"Whatever. That doesn't make it legit."

"Listen, you need to loosen up. Tell me something: You ever think of running any bath salt, like maybe a little Ivory Snow?"

"No."

"Yeah," he said, "I don't even touch that shit."

The station in Winter Park was across a wide greenway from Park Avenue, seven or eight blocks of high-end boutiques and expensive restaurants that spilled onto the sidewalk.

"This is the dead fucking core of Central Florida," Katie said. "You tilt the state and all the rich pretentious shit that couldn't make the cut in South Beach slides right here."

"You got an awful mouth on you."

"I've got an awful everything."

Couples were having brunch beneath potted palms, shade-grown coffee, big malamutes and weimaraners asleep beneath the tables.

Katie took his hand and led him across the grass. She felt like he would get lost otherwise, abandoned.

"Stop staring."

"Me?" he asked.

They stopped between a chocolatier and a shop selling vintage bath and kitchen fixtures.

"I used to see a woman down here," Twitch said, looking up the street.

"Yeah? Who?"

"She owned a dress shop. Like really high-end stuff. I kept her satisfied, though."

"Oh my God, you are such a terrible liar."

He tabled his right hand above his eyes. "You want to see the place?"

"In fact, I do."

"I'm lying." He dropped his hand. "It wasn't a shop. It was like a whole chain of outlets, wholesale. This was just like the flagship."

"Cut rate stuff?"

"No." He shook his head. "Just shit they mis-sewed. But still classy."

Her laugh died in a sigh, suddenly overcome with sunlight and fatigue.

"We should eat," she said. "We might as well eat since we're here."

They sat down outside a cafe. It was a warm morning but the heat hadn't yet stiffened. A breeze came down the street. Around them the chatter of language. Not the Spanish you heard everywhere but something more glottal, German, Russian. There was a look about Europeans that identified them quicker than the footwear. Across the street in the park were a family of six or seven Brazilians. They appeared to be admiring the elaborate topiary around a fountain and Katie had to admit there was something civilized about the place, the trash and recycling bins, the doggie bags. Farther down the fairway-like expanse a black man in a jumpsuit cut grass and all of it made for a comforting scene, as if at least here order really did exist.

"The thing about being a Life Coach," Twitch said, "I know you're saying it's bullshit and all and I hear you, I do. But if people need it, it must not be bullshit, right? Like there's this sadness that takes over. Half that book right there is just telling people that they're all right, that they have the resources to achieve their potential."

"Are you quoting now?"

"I'm being serious."

"Is that like module five, or something? Finding the resources to achieve one's potential?"

"You can laugh at it all you like," he said. "It's a luxury to laugh."

The waiter came and Twitch ordered a waffle and a side of sweet potato fries. Katie asked for fruit and sprouted-grain bread. This was going to be the day she set right her life, the point from which she moved forward. She'd start exercising again, reading. All fruit and whole grains. Buy fresh greens and go on a ten-day juice fast, detox body and soul.

"You know about all this bullshit with his cell?" Twitch asked. "About him refusing a new one?"

"Who, Alan?"

"The sorry bastard."

"I thought it was sort of endearing," Katie said. "Sort of human, you know? A kind of grand statement is maybe what it was."

"Pathetic is what it was. The thing about your sister—"

"Were we talking about her?"

"The thing about your sister," Twitch said, "it hurts to even say it. The way she cheated on me with what I thought was my best friend."

Katie laughed. "Isn't that the complete opposite of what actually happened?"

He turned sullen. "It's an interpretation, Katie. It's a form of truth."

"It's a lie. It has nothing to do with the truth."

"Truth is constructed," he said. "Truth's a projection."

"So this is like module 8: 'How to win friends and bullshit people'?"

"Ask anybody."

"OK." She pointed to the waiter. "How about him?"

"Who?"

"The waiter there. How about I ask him if truth's a projection." Katie turned and raised one hand. "Excuse me? Pardon me, sir?"

He came over, mid-twenties, with long black hair and a diamond stud in his left ear.

"Everything OK?"

"Maybe," Katie said. She was smiling, flirting, she realized, and it was like the healthy food, like the fact that she would go home and read a book, something difficult and challenging—it was yet another thing that was going to bring her back. "My friend and I were just discussing the ontological nature of truth, like is there such a thing."

He smiled. She sensed he'd gotten away with a lot in life because of that smile.

"And you say?" he asked.

"I say yes, absolutely," Katie said. "I am pro-truth."

"I can't imagine how anyone could be against it." He raised the pitcher he carried. "Let me top off those waters."

"You see?" Katie said when he was gone.

Twitch smirked. "He was looking down your shirt."

"What?"

"That whole time he was just standing there looking down your shirt. He cares about truth about as much as that dog over there."

An Episcopalian church stood at the end of the shops and they walked to it, crossed the street and walked back. In the park a man sat cross-legged and worked two puppets, a dragon and what must have been a princess. A few kids sat in the grass tearing blades and looking bored.

"It's probably noon by now," Twitch said. "Let's take a cab over to the park."

"Let's take the city bus," she said.

"To hell with that. I used to ride the M-line everywhere. I hate buses."

"We're going to take the bus."

It had become like that. Mass transit. Cheap fares. The general inefficiency of living.

"It's the journey," she told him when they were on board and moving. "Didn't they teach you that? That it's all about the process."

"Whatever. I just want to find your sister."

They took the 436 back toward downtown. It was probably the least direct route imaginable. She didn't mind. It wasn't really about the journey but it certainly wasn't about the destination either. What she gradually realized, though she suspected she'd known it all along, was that she didn't care about the Occupy movement or the encampment or anything else. She could go or not go, it was the same ultimately. Except going filled in the space of days. She dreaded the hours more than anything, the inevitability of piling her life with distractions. Time was dangerous. That was the real message she'd received at the altar: that there was a pervading emptiness, and you better get busy trying to fill it up. Eventually, she would've arrived at that on her own, but the menace of time, that was the true revelation. You had to fill it, you had to duck it. You had to find a way not to let it swallow you because what was waiting on the other side was despair.

God, Katie, don't even think about. Just keep moving.

She sent a text to Lucy: *where r u? r u in O?*

Then, as soon as the text sent, sent another: *fine. Dont answer. I dont care.*

"You know you haven't even asked me about my father," she said to Twitch, "about how I'm doing or anything like that."

He was staring out the window, forehead against the cool glass and looked back at her, surprised. Guilty, too, she thought.

"Was I supposed to?

"I don't know. Forget it."

"You know sometimes I see that church roof going up in flames all over again. The way it spread. I don't even mean to."

"I said forget it."

They were downtown, ahead the concrete expanse of I-4 elevated above the streets, when her phone went off. It was Lucy: *in O at park. r u here?* She started to respond, but deleted the message instead. When Lucy texted again Katie cut her phone off.

They stopped by the Amway Center with its mural of Dwight Howard and electronic display flashing a Kenny Chesney concert, stopped again on Colonial Drive.

"Alan said he was in the Air Force."

She looked up to be certain he had spoken, Twitch, she meant. For a second she hadn't recognized his voice. He was holding a can of something. He popped the top and passed it to her.

"Was he a pilot or something?"

"What is this?" It was a Four Loko.

"Alan said he flew something or other."

"He flew drones." She took a sip and passed it back. "Like remote controlled."

"That kill people and shit?

"Sometimes," she said. "I guess."

"I have this fantasy where I swoop down on certain people in my life," he said. He held the can but did not drink. "It's like I come in and extract all sorts of justice, but mostly it's just me watching while someone hurts them. Except I don't really have the balls to actually watch. Other times I fantasize about my own funeral."

"Everybody does that."

"Yeah. Except I'm not watching everyone cry and shit," he said. "I think that's what most people do. I'm actually *in* the coffin, like scratching at the lid."

"That's kind of fucked up."

"Yeah, I guess." He turned back to the window. "It's just a fantasy."

They made it to the park seemingly by default, random transfers, a cab on Church Street, and finally, miraculously, a plane of green grass, the lake behind it, the skyline behind that. She'd remembered the tents as colorful and bright, almost circus-like with their air of cheery hope, but today they were all the color of mushrooms and basement mold. The air smelled like garbage. She no longer trusted her memory.

"Damn," Twitch said. "Finally."

They were just down the bus steps when she grabbed his elbow.

"What you said about that dog."

He wasn't looking at her, already scanning the park.

"What dog?"

"At lunch just now. You said the waiter cared about truth about as much as that dog. Look at me for a second." She pulled at his arm. "Well, that dog *is* truth. Just sitting there, panting. Eat when you're hungry. Sleep when you're tired."

"I never much liked dogs."

They crossed a field roped with orange-and-white traffic barrels. Most of the tents were pitched on the edge of the clearing in a copse of laurel oaks near an iron brazier and several picnic tables. The rest of the periphery was given over to stalls and tables selling crystals or turquoise jewelry, CDs peddled from the back of a conversion van, vegan meals from a woman with a portable kitchen. There were women constructing Native American headdresses and dreamcatchers, tattoo artists, banners for everything from the Rainbow Tribes of All People to the black flag of Anarchy. In the center people danced or splashed in the mud, the stage a distant platform barely realized.

"There's like a thousand assholes here, at least," Twitch said.

"We should split up," she said, because she was sick of him.

"You think?"

"See the big flag over there? The one with the unicorn? Let's meet there in exactly twenty minutes. Whether we find them or not."

He shook his head. "I'm not even wearing a watch."

"Well, just asked somebody. We're never going to find them just standing here."

"All right," he said. "Twenty minutes. Twenty minutes is cool."

She started walking and realized he was still beside her.

"Don't follow me."

"I was going this way already."

"Fine," she said. "I'll go the other way."

She didn't look back for fear that he was following her. Or worse yet: the fear that he was simply standing there, simple-minded and already lost. She had no intention of meeting him, not ever, she meant. He had bus fare and his return ticket for the train. There wasn't any need to feel guilty about it.

She spotted the Vietnamese man she recognized from the funeral about the same time that someone took to the stage and began to lead a chant. The crowd turned like sunflowers—the sheep—and the chant, something about saying *No! No! No!* lifted and sank like a failed prayer. Brother Vin, that was all she'd heard everyone refer to him as, stood smiling in an Alabama baseball cap, hands clasped peaceably in front of him. Beside him was a much taller man in cheap blue jeans and a Braves hat, wiry and good-looking until he opened his mouth and she saw that he was missing several teeth. But somehow that only added to the allure. His handsomeness not rugged so much as ragged.

"Hello," she said.

"Hi there."

"I'm Katie, Lucy's sister."

Vin smiled but said nothing.

"Lucy's Alan's friend. I wanted to thank you for coming to the funeral."

"Oh, yes, yes, of course," Vin said. He stepped forward and took her hand. "I'm so sorry not to have recognized you, Kristen."

"Katie."

"And I am very sorry for your father."

"I get that a lot."

She hadn't meant it to sound so harsh, more observation than complaint.

"They mean well," Vin said.

"I know."

"Words can only take us so far. And it's never far enough."

"I know," she said. "I'm sorry, it's just . . ." She hadn't intended to go glum on the tiny man and instead turned to his friend and stuck out her hand. "Hi," she said. "apparently I'm Kristen."

"Hello, Kristen." He had big hands, callused, rough-hewn. He seemed slightly amused by her but she didn't care. "Apparently I'm Donny," he said. "It's a pleasure."

"Donny and I were just catching up," Vin said. "He's an old friend from way back."

"Another time and place," Donny said.

"Another galaxy."

"I didn't mean to interrupt," she said.

"No, no," said Donny, and he was suddenly focused, eyes narrowed, hand on her forearm. "Stay and talk to us. Vin and I are likely to end in tears otherwise."

Vin gave a little laugh but she could tell he wanted her to leave.

"I was actually on the lookout for Lucy and Alan," she said. "You haven't seen them, have you?"

"Alan's here?" Vin asked.

"Supposed to be. If you see either of them tell them I'm looking for them. It was a pleasure, Donny."

"I've got a feeling I'll be seeing you again, Kristen," Donny said. "At least I hope so."

The wink was as much joke as rogue and she smiled and turned into the crowd. The chant was still going up though it seemed to have acquired a harder edge. Someone had a bullhorn and a few police officers were pointing. *Noise ordinance,* one said. A moment later three of them began to push their way into the crowd. Katie looped around the edge past the vendors with their soy ice-cream and PEOPLE OVER PROFITS t-shirts. By the time she reached the far side near the lake the crowd had begun to boo, a knot at the center around what she recognized as the police officers. Noise ordinance. She found herself for it. Anything to make them all shut up. Anything to make certain they understand how pointless and hypocritical they were. All she wanted was her sister. If she couldn't have that, she wanted silence.

The man on the stage was trying to quiet the crowd.

"People, people," he was saying, "let's stay focused. We are going to march on the Bank of America building. We are going to march to the withered heart of our collective suffering. People," he cried, "please!"

When she looked again she saw Lucy and Alan on the fringe near the swan boats. They had detached themselves from the crowd, as much with the passing dog walkers and joggers as the protesters, but Katie could tell they were listening, faces turned and pinched, stoic though clearly hurting, as if together they had channeled the world's collective suffering. Katie's instinct was to go to them, or to her sister, at least. Finding her sister, talking to her sister, was as much a reason for her being here than anything else. In a strange way she felt abused by the previous week, brutalized by the string of days that ran from the Holy Land Experience to this moment, everything stitched with cause and effect, which wasn't true, of course. It was random, it was chaotic.

She thought again of that moment at the altar, the vacuous church, the great space she had sensed, as if she saw right through the roof and on through the clouds and bands of ozone out into the nothingness of space. Katie-as-space probe. Katie-as-all-seeing. Which was what, maybe, she wanted to tell her sister. Or not so much tell her as intuit to her. There was always a shared understanding, an unspoken language accessible only to sisters. The shared survivorship of childhood. The broken toy of the past. She could walk right over to Lucy and just look at her and Lucy would *know.* They were from the same planet, Katie thought. They orbited the same sun—Lucy having traveled so far toward God, Katie so far away—how could it not be that they would inevitably meet? The graceful arcs of their knowing, fullness and emptiness converging in the single point of their locked eyes. It was all life afforded you, your family, the house in which you live, the ground on which it is built. It was all life afforded you if you were honest with yourself and that seemed to have become her project: Katie-as-honest.

She watched her sister push a lock of hair back from her face. She and Alan stood close to each other but not touching, a space between them. They were mutually oblivious and Katie thought of her parents after the salvaging of house and marriage: the cheery indifference, the parallel lines of their lives: always twinned, never intersecting.

Without meaning to Katie took two steps, caught herself, stopped. It was a symbolic act maybe, going to her sister, but that didn't make it any less important. Just crossing the grass, just approaching them, freighted with meaning. They'd cried manically at the funeral, held each other, wept, and then carefully avoided each other ever since. If they happened to meet in the kitchen or on the stairs their passing—and it was always a passing—felt staged, each attentive of the other, both ridiculously polite.

She was waiting too long.

She knew she was waiting too long and with every second felt the weight of their interaction grow. She already knew she was going to think herself out of this, *fool yourself into new thoughts, Katie,* but wasn't yet certain she could admit as much, as if the possibility of walking away lurked just beneath the surface of thought. She touched the bubble of leaving. It broke: She was going to walk, she was going to walk, she just knew it.

And then she did.

When she turned she saw Twitch. He stood at the edge of the stage near the steps, one finger raised in the air.

"Fuck those one-percenters!" he yelled. "Yeah. Fuck Davos!"

A few people had turned to watch him.

"We are going to march in five minutes," called the voice from the stage, "*peacefully*. We are going to march peacefully on the Bank of America building, people."

"We're going to levitate that motherfucker," said a man beside Twitch. He had buzzed red hair and a Thomas the Tank Engine backpack. She felt she should recognize him, but couldn't quite place him.

"Ho," said Twitch, "we gone levitate it."

"We gonna smash it," said Red Hair.

"We gonna smash shit left and right," sang Twitch. "We gonna smash shit all night."

The booing was louder, the voice from the stage calling desperately for quiet.

"We are peaceful," he said. "We are peaceful."

Twitch and Red Hair we're now chanting *let's smash shit, let's smash shit* and a few others had taken up the cry. When Twitch and Red Hair drifted behind the stage Katie followed them.

"Hey," she called. "Wait a second."

They were both bent over Red Hair's backpack, no one else around, just the placid lake with its distant swan boats and a few ducks in the reeds, downtown Orlando looming behind it all.

"Hey," she said again.

Twitch looked up, "Dag, girl," he said. "Shut up and come here for second. Check this out."

"Who is this?" Red Hair said.

"It's cool, bro. She's my girl."

She started to say something but then, right then, she recognized Red Hair: he was Jack! Jack the agent provocateur! He was GetTheFuckOutOfThePark with his mussed flat top and kid's backpack that, she saw now, was full of what looked like grenades of some sort.

"Flash-bang," said Twitch. "We're just about to go ape-shit on em."

"Get away from him, Twitch," Katie said.

"What?"

"Just get away from him, all right?"

"Say what?"

She had stopped approaching them. It was all she could do to keep from backing away. Jack's eyes all over her.

"Let's go back around front," she said.

"We will," Twitch said. "But we're making our plan right now."

"Let's go back around front."

"Jesus, chill, Katie. I said we would in a minute."

"You need to send the bitch elsewhere," Jack said.

Twitch patted his shoulder. "I told you it's cool, bro. Katie's just like, I don't know, like professional."

"Send the bitch away."

"Get away from him, Twitch," Katie said. "He's not who he says he is."

"You need to fucking skedaddle," Jack said.

He took a step toward her, more feint than anything else. She felt herself clinch. He looked like the kind of man who enjoyed small cruelties, the ones who spent ten years twisting their wives' arm before passing out drunk. The ones who pushed too hard and one nasty night bled out in a honky-tonk bathroom, heads against the urinals while their femoral arteries emptied.

"He's a spy." She kept her voice level. "He's trying to stir up trouble. He works for the police."

He took another step. Twitch looked from Katie to Jack.

"Dog?" Twitch asked.

Jack was between Twitch and Katie now.

"Just get her to fucking go," Jack said. "I thought you wanted to elevate your game."

"Don't listen to him."

When he took another step she screamed *Spy! Spy! Agent provoc*—but her face was already on the ground, teeth biting into the dirt and she was gasping, his weight on her back. Her ears rang—had he hit her? She thought he had. She could feel something binding one wrist, his hand on the other. Footsteps. More screaming though her ears rang too loud to make sense of it. His weight was all over her but no, suddenly it was gone and someone was pulling her up.

She saw his teeth first, the absence of his teeth—Donny! He pulled her up and turned and kicked the man on the ground in the temple, planted the toe of his boot just above the ear. Jack was flat on his stomach. The blow had turned his head but she could see blood in his mouth, black lines that clearly articulated his teeth. An awful sight she saw then, his left eye jellied and flat, glossy and unmoving. His hair was full of blood and she saw blood all over Donny's shirt. When she raised her hand to her own face she realized a plastic zip-cuff dangled from her wrist.

Donny pulled something from the man's backpack, a cell phone, a police badge he stuck in his pocket. A few people stood watching and Donny looked from them to Katie. There was blood all over his shirt.

"You need to get out of here," he said.

"What about—"

"Don't worry about him. Worry about yourself."

"Is he?"

"Don't look at him." Donny put his hand in her back and eased her away. "Just go. Right now."

Then she was looking at Vin, his copper face pinched, his hat pulled low. Had he been there the entire time? He took her elbow and led her quickly back from the copse of trees and through the tents. There were sirens now, several amplified voices made indistinct by the chaos and noise. Where was Twitch? And where were Lucy and Alan? She thought she saw Lucy once as they moved against the crowd—everyone was headed toward the stage while they headed toward the parking lot—but she couldn't be certain. Lucy's face rushing past. Lucy's face starlight in a sea of unrecognizable dark. But she wasn't really certain that she wanted to see Lucy. Wasn't it all somehow more trouble than it was worth? The fighting and yelling, the inevitable breakdown, the tearful rapprochement. Someone called her name—did they?—someone called her name and she wrenched around. Lucy? It was almost certainly Lucy calling *Katie! Katie, wait!* and she wanted to wait, she did, but she couldn't stop walking. She wanted to go back but couldn't go back for going forward. *Katie, stop!* Katie walked faster, Vin at her elbow. *Katie!* She was already forming her response: I have stopped. I am waiting on you, only I can't wait any longer. They had passed each other by. They had missed each other. She thought she might weep if only her feet would be still.

Vin led her through the parking lot to a green jeep. She realized he was trying to force the keys into her hand but she kept giving them back.

"Go," he said. "You have to go."

"But what about?"

She meant her sister but Vin said: "I'll get Donny. We'll get out. He'll be all right."

"I need to find—"

"Just go. Right now."

She started to say something else but found she was crying. Vin pushed the keys into her hand and folded her fingers over them.

"Go," he said. "You didn't do anything wrong."

"That man's a police officer."

"You didn't do anything."

"Is he dead? I know he's dead."

Vin put his small hands on her shoulders. "Call this a bamboo cane," he said, "and you have entered my trap. Do not call it a bamboo cane, and you fall into error. What do you call it?"

She looked as if she might cry.

"Go," Vin said, "please. I'll get the Jeep back later. And take this."

He pushed Twitch's white binder into her hands.

"This isn't mine."

"Just take it," he said. "And go. Please."

"Okay," she said. "I can do that. I can go."

"You weren't here."

"No."

"You were never here. This happened in a dream. Never ever here."

The sirens were louder now. The crowd had parted to let an ambulance cross the grass.

"No," she said. She climbed in, dropped the binder beside her. "I was never here."

"Exactly."

"Never ever here," she said.

But halfway home on I-4 it occurred to her that she had most definitely been there. How many people had seen here? How many cell phones had recorded her passage out? They would come looking for her. They would find her. Or was that paranoia? She dialed her grandparents in Ocala. She knew they weren't home but wanted to make certain. She could maybe go there for a couple of days, see what shook out. She remembered the text from earlier, the boat, New Smyrna. She called her mom. It went straight to voicemail, exactly as she knew it would. She was going to stay with friends in Orlando, she said. She didn't specify who or exactly where and knew that such precision wasn't necessary. At best her absence would only vaguely pierce her mother's pharmaceutical haze. Where is Katie? Oh, somewhere, I can't quite remember. Orlando, I think? She would pack some clothes. Maybe leave a note for Lucy and disappear for a few days. Disappearing felt right, felt prudent.

Her phone vibrated: her mom. Katie answered it immediately.

"Did you get my message?" It was like a challenge, a threat. "I just left you a message."

Her mother's voice seemed to quiver. "Honey, where are you? Are you with Lucy?"

"I don't know where Lucy is."

"I thought she went with you. I thought you both went down to Orlando." She seemed to stiffen then: the authority figure, the single mother that she suddenly was, severed finger be damned. "Baby, listen. Where are you? Are you close by?"

"Not really."

"Where are you?"

"I'm on I-4."

"I want you to come home, all right? I'm worried about you."

"There's nothing to worry about."

"I thought you were with your sister and then I got your message." She coughed—was it a cough? "I want you to come home, Katie. You don't sound like yourself."

"I'm fine."

"Katie, baby, please listen to me—"

She began to mentally compose her note to Lucy:

Dear Sister, dear Lucy, dear Franny,

I suppose sometimes it takes some catalyst, some awful thing to really put our lives in motion, to allow us to manifest who it is—but oh God, was this Pastor Jeff talking or Twitch's positivity training? It didn't matter if it was true—*manifest who it is we are meant to become. When I saw you today—I watched you and Alan, I should go ahead and admit that I watched you both.* But then the sight of the man, the sight of GetTheFuckOutOfThePark's dead white eye came to her again and she felt a hot contraction rise up her throat. Katie_in_Hell: Who here is willing to die for this cause? Who here is willing to vomit?

Then she heard her mother's voice.

Her mother had never stopped speaking: "Katie, are you there? I want you to pull over, honey. The next exit. Just pull over and I'm going to come get you."

I'm fine, she said, or tried to say, but couldn't speak, her throat full of breakfast, the taste of digested strawberries, the flecks of sprouted-grain toast. Her stoic sister. The dead man on the ground. Two days ago she'd caught her mother in Warrior Pose which meant Pamela would be just fine despite the fact her husband had been traveling at approximately ninety miles an hour when he entered the intersection. There was no evidence of any attempts to brake.

"Katie—"

She hit END, stopped at a CVS and puked in the toilet, washed her face and felt a little better, a little calmer. She was wearing the birthstone ring her mother had given her—she noticed it for the first time and that helped, just seeing it.

She found a pair of scissors in the school supplies aisle and cut off the zip-cuff, her skin stitched pink from the constriction. A little better still. A little calmer. She walked to the hair coloring aisle. Was this paranoia or wisdom? The boxes spread the length of the aisle, every shade. The women appeared either to be on the way to work at law firms or to just have just risen from bed, hair tousled by the hands of whatever man lurked just beyond the camera's reach. So, she thought, staid and managerial to promiscuous and slutty. Who did she want to be? Because it now presented itself to her as such: who did she want to be? Who did she want to become? How would time bully her, how would the emptiness of days chase Katie if Katie wasn't Katie? What had Vin called her, Kristen? It was another self, wasn't it? Because it came to her that was what her father had been doing flying drones: not merely finding a way to pay the bills, there were a thousand ways to pay the bills, but finding another self. The dislocation, the fragmentation. He was always half in Orange City and half in Afghanistan, always moving between the two. She chose a box called Auburn Rain—staid—and then a box of Beach Blush—promiscuous—because she was all things, and she was nothing.

She was halfway across the parking lot when she noticed the man leaned against Vin's Jeep, arms crossed, smiling, waiting for her. Donny, she thought, with as much excitement as panic because already—*already!*—she could see her future self, reckless and gliding away with him, headed toward her father, toward that gray center where the recognition of nothingness was not the exception but the rule.

PART TEN

NOT A COP. A GODDAMN ABUSIVE rent-a-cop, Donny told Bobby. A rabble-rousing woman-abusing narc son of a bitch. The real cop came that afternoon, a deputy that pulled beneath the island at a gas station in southern Utah. The whole thing unfolded in a series of regrettable missteps: their noticing him, his noticing their notice, the sudden awareness that these two grizzled men, the rumpled clothes, the eyes red-fused and tight, were the same two he'd seen that morning on television and again on the APB he had surely read. The gas station was an old country feed-and-seed. Beef jerky and red hots. Cash or check only. Donny shot the deputy through his gray duty shirt before he could put his hand to his holster. Only his eyes had lit. His eyes had killed him.

Donny started the truck and pulled onto the highway, the pistol on the seat between them.

And it wasn't that it happened so fast, Bobby thought. It was that it happened with such finality.

"I want you to listen," Donny said calmly. "I mean listen good, brother."

They rode another ten miles before he spoke again.

"You gotta carry this back with you," Donny said.

"We're not going back."

"You gotta explain things to the world."

But there was no more explaining than there was going back. There was only this final act, the trail of bodies in their wake that would terminate with their own.

I can't live through this again.

They started on the pills as soon as they hit the state line. They were headed for the Grand Canyon. Donny hadn't said it but it was clear enough—the only landscape big enough to encompass the act—and they wound slowly down Highway 89 past the Kaibab Indian Reservation toward the North Rim, Point Imperial, Point Sublime. The road was newly topped and cut through hills scratched with green scrub. The San Francisco peaks wavering on the horizon like dredged ghosts.

Donny eased off the gas.

"Put Neil Young on," Donny said. "Track seven."

Young began to sing *Well I dreamed I saw the knights in armor* . . . and Donny mumbled along. When it played through he skipped it back and played the song a second time, a third. There was nothing hurried now. It had played out. It was done. Bobby regretted the inevitable ending but he welcomed it too, so long in the offing, but now drawn near. Every second brings it a little closer, he thought, death. But that was always true, true for everyone. So why suffer it? Why complain? He already knew what pain felt like. The only thing left was its management. He took whatever Donny gave him, washed it down with Gatorade. They were both flush with the day's violence but cooling out too, awash on a pharmaceutical tide. It was all slowing down. It was all starting to make sense.

"Just on our terms," Donny said. "You hear what I'm saying? Every-fucking-thing has been on their terms. Our whole lives. This has to be on ours."

"I just don't want any cameras," Bobby said. "I don't want him to see."

He meant his son. Donny nodded and started the song over.

"That's your terms then. That's your last demand." He took another pill. "We'll have lights here in a minute."

But they didn't, not yet. Just the big RVs and tour buses they would settle behind before slinging past, a brace of Harley Davidsons strung out over a quarter mile. Donny was chewing pills now, manic, his mouth a pale blue froth of Oxycontin and Tropical Mist Gatorade. He couldn't stop talking.

"You know what they did," he said, "You know what they fucking did? They used you, you ever thought about that?"

Bobby said nothing. They were nearing the Park gates. Ahead he could see traffic backed up, red taillights wavering.

"They used you."

"No, they didn't."

"They needed somebody to go in those caves. They needed somebody to smoke those turbaned motherfuckers out and you went, you did it."

"Slow down up here."

"Except you weren't supposed to come back home. You were supposed to die a holy death so we could just settle it all with a parade. But then you came back—"

They were near the stalled traffic now.

"Slow down," Bobby said, but they didn't.

"You came back. All you motherfuckers did and what you make em do is look at the wreckage. You can't compartmentalize that shit when the man next to you is missing an eye. All those dead babies. The car bombs. The IEDs. Some sorry son of a bitch dying in a stress position. They used you."

"No."

"Listen to me. We are dinosaurs. They raised us up in their image, built us to do their violence, but they don't need us now and we are going to disappear. We are going to be exterminated. The *via negativa,* brother."

"Stop the truck," Bobby yelled.

"Stop bleeding," Donny screamed. He pulled off his Braves cap and slapped it against his thighs. "You're bleeding out your eyes, man." He was crying. "It's all over you."

"Donny—"

"Just fucking stop."

They were near enough to read the tag off the Arctic Fox RV in front of them. Bobby put both hands on the dash and realized they didn't hurt anymore. He realized they would never hurt again.

"Stop!"

But instead of stopping Donny whipped the pickup into the other lane, running a car off the road into the dirt. The park gate was ahead. Bobby felt his crown cold with sweat but gradually leaned back. Ahead of them traffic was veering onto the shoulder. They would plow the gate, launch themselves into what? The canyon? It wasn't possible.

"There it is! There it is!" Donny pointed up. "The silver spaceship! Thousands of them!"

Bobby looked up through the glass. The sky was full, but not of spaceships. It was full of manta rays. No, he thought, kites, big diamond-shaped kites.

"Shoot those motherfuckers," Donny said.

But when Bobby looked back up there was only a single kite in the sky, black and orbiting. He'd last seen one in the sky over Afghanistan, a Reaper drone keeping watch. He left the pistol on the seat between them.

"We're going to disappear in a series of erasures," Donny said quietly. "First will be the body." They tore through the Park entrance. More horns honking. A Park Service police car behind them now, light flashing. "Next comes memory. You accomplish this by destroying physical reminders. Burn the artifact. Bury the ashes. Without the tangible the rest turns to dust," he said, and jerked the car onto an access road toward the Cape Royal Overlook.

The Park Service car had cut its siren but the light was still behind them, not gaining, but not falling away either. Bobby realized the CD player was still on. Neil Young. That hurtful wailing. How long had he heard it? All his life, he supposed. He looked back: there were two Park Service cars now.

"I didn't think it would happen this fast," Bobby said.

"I know." Donny checked the mirrors. "It creeps and it creeps until it just sort of swoops down and gobbles you up. You never think it will really happen."

"I've known all my life it would happen. Every waking second."

Donny looked at him, suddenly becalmed.

"You're a better man than I am," he said, and Bobby heard sincerity in his voice. "You always have been. Just don't lose it at the end."

A moment later the Park Service cars stopped and they watched them recede in the mirrors.

Donny started laughing. "Call this a bamboo cane," he said, "and you have entered my trap. Do not call it a bamboo cane, and you fall into error. What do you call it?"

"Let's pull over."

"At certain moments you discover the arc to your life," Donny said. "You hear what I'm saying? Like you see that causal chain—Vegas to the joint to here—you see just exactly how one moment fits to the next. You think he can see us?"

"Who?"

"God. Stephen. That sorry-ass Puerto Rican kid," Donny said. "Your own boy."

"I wish I could see him one more time."

"We'll find somewhere we can just be still." Donny started crying again. "Your eyes are still bleeding. I'm so sorry about your eyes."

"Just pull over."

They cut onto a gravel service road and turned again through an open gate. Past an empty paved lot was a wall of chain-link, beyond that the road ended in a wash of gravel and sand. They pulled in and Donny cut the engine. The windows were down and they could feel the warm air that curled down the ravine's open mouth. Heat and exhaust. The high mica-rich berms that hid all the world but a panel of blue sky.

Bobby took another pill and shut his eyes.

Sand ticked against the glass. Wind. Heat. The heat would grow and grow and suddenly flatten in a rush of breeze. He felt time pass. He had no idea how much, but when he opened his eyes he saw that Donny was unconscious, a beard of foamy vomit and a shaft of late afternoon sun, gold as the band of the birth-stones ring. The Braves hat by his feet. His eyelids twitching as steadily as his hands. Breath shallow and slow.

His brother. His only brother.

Bobby took the baggie from his hand. The pills were almost gone, the impossible heft of what Donny had carried the morning they left Georgia nothing more than a few strays in the bottom. Bobby fished them out, swallowed what was left without prejudice. When the wind picked up he thought he heard sirens and shut his eyes, let Neil Young exhaust himself and here, finally, felt himself slipping away, as if he were translucent and here, finally, there was a clarity to things, a serene stillness, like a pool just after first light.

"Donny," he tried to say, but there were sirens, and it was unclear if his brother was breathing. This was significant. Bobby knew he needed to mark this and focused on the face of his watch, but a shadow swept over the cab, crossed, returned as smaller: no larger than his hand. Then Nancy's voice: *I'm not the one who killed that boy, Bobby.* No, it was him, it was Bobby. It always had been. Manny had felt it, that bad energy. Donny was right from the start: they were dinosaurs from birth, predestined, condemned before the act.

Still, he had to make note. Carry home word.

Or just shut your eyes.

And he did, he shut his eyes and what he heard wasn't the wail of police lights but his son, breathing. They were back by the retaining pond. It was night—he could hear the low thrum of tree frogs and cicadas encircling them—and again Bobby touched his son's hair, watching Venus and Mercury in alignment, his son asleep on his shoulder like wet laundry, something abandoned in the machine, warm and limp and barely comprehending while above a crow went up into the sky, a wide-winged bird, black against the black night, as if it had already taken everything from him, which of course it had, and still Bobby smoothed his boy's hair and said, over and over, look up at the planets, son, it won't be like this again in our lives. It won't ever be like this again

ABOUT THE AUTHOR

MARK POWELL is the author of three previous novels, *Prodigals* (nominated for the Cabell First Novelist Award), *Blood Kin* (winner of the Peter Taylor Prize for the Novel), and *The Dark Corner*. Powell has received fellowships from the National Endowment for the Arts and the Breadloaf Writers' Conference. In 2009 he received the Chaffin Award for contributions to Appalachian literature. Powell holds degrees from Yale Divinity School, the University of South Carolina, and the Citadel. He is an associate professor of English at Stetson University in DeLand, Florida, and for three years taught a fiction workshop at Lawtey Correctional Institute, a level II prison in Raiford, Florida